**A COMPELLING SAGA SET IN THE
HEART OF THE WESTCOUNTRY**

Tansy

A COMPELLING SAGA SET IN THE
HEART OF THE WESTCOUNTRY

Tansy

Nan Dalton

HALSGROVE

𝔚estern 𝔐orning 𝔑ews

First published in Great Britain in 2002

Copyright © 2002 Nan Dalton

British Library Cataloguing-in-Publication Data
A CIP record for this title is available from the British Library

ISBN 1 84114 227 1

HALSGROVE

Halsgrove House
Lower Moor Way
Tiverton, Devon EX16 6SS
Tel: 01884 243242
Fax: 01884 243325
email: sales@halsgrove.com
website: www.halsgrove.com

Printed and bound in Great Britain by MPG Ltd, Bodmin

❖ Contents ❖

For Robert, Elizabeth and Josephine
with love

Acknowledgements

I acknowledge help and encouragement in writing this book from Esther Sanders, Christina Green, Anne Rolls and other members of the then Estuary Writers Workshop; Margaret Stonell who never stopped encouraging me; Newton Abbot Ramblers with whom I walked Dartmoor and South Devon and Anne Barclay of Anne Barclay Enterprises for her enthusiasm in transferring my typed manuscript on to disc.

Biography

NAN DALTON was born in Essex, worked in London as a Secretary until marriage brought her to Newton Abbot where she discovered the language, culture and history of South Devon and Dartmoor. These experiences produced music based articles for *The Lady*, poetry prizes, readings on the B.B.C. and publication of two collections *Beachcombing* and *Gleaning the Seasons* (N.P.F). Nan lead local poets in readings at public libraries and the *Ways with Words* literary festival culminating in the production of an audio tape (supported by the Arts Council) titles *Quintessential*.

Bibliography

Mrs Beeton's *Household Management*, First edition.

Chase, Beatrice, *The Heart of the Moor*.

Crossing's Dartmoor Worker, Peninsular Press, Newton Abbot.

Downes, John, *A Dictionary of Devon Dialect*, Tabb House, 11 Church Street, Padstow, Cornwall.

Hart, Edward, *The Golden Guinea Book of Heavy Horses Past and Present*, David & Charles, Newton Abbot.

Hart, Edward, *The Hill Shepherd*, David & Charles, Newton Abbot, Devon.

Hemery, Eric, *High Dartmoor*, Robert Hale Ltd, Clerkenwell House, Clerkenwell Green, London, EC1R 0HT.

Hemery, Eric, *Walking Dartmoor's Ancient Tracks* – a guide to 28 routes.

Jones, Roger, *A Book of Newton Abbot*, Penwell Ltd, Parkwood, Callington, Cornwall.

Longton, Tim and Hart, Edward, *The Sheep Dog*.

Newton Abbot Town Official Guide.

Perham, Molly (compiler), *Devon Country Recipes*, Ravette Ltd, 3 Glenside Estate, Star Road, Partridge Green, Horsham, Sussex.

Rhodes, A.J., *Newton Abbot: its History and Development*, 1904.

Smith, Vian, *Portrait of Dartmoor*, Robert Hale & Company.

Stirling, Revd D.M., *A History of Newton Abbot and Newton-Bushel*, 1830.

Chapter One

May Day

It was the first day of May and Eva Drewe had risen early to bake pasties, slicing potatoes and turnips thin as wafers, scraping beef skirt. Now the pasties lay warm from the oven, wrapped in a cloth in her deepest basket.

'Eighteen and not yet spoken for!' Tansy moaned as she broke off a piece of pasty from the last batch.

'Leave that pasty alone!' Eva exclaimed, slapping her daughter's hand away. 'You don't want to worry about marrying yet. Why, you're hardly out of the nest. Go and see if Bessie's coming while I find my hat or we'll miss the train.' Tansy sighed and slipped out through the hall door, into the Post Office where Edward Drewe worked behind the grille.

'Are you off then, Tansy?' he asked and she nodded, slipped round behind him and wrapped her arms about his neck, a cascade of red curly hair tumbling down his face.

'If I find a young man today at Lustleigh, Father, will you let me marry him?'

Edward laughed, put up one hand to hers. 'I would have to see him first!' he exclaimed.

'And what would he have to do to win your approval?' she demanded, straightening up and struggling to control the strands which had already escaped her morning's coiffure. 'Must he be rich?' And now Edward looked up into her face, his smile faded, his face became serious.

'Must he be clever?' she persisted.

'He would have to be capable of keeping you in a manner no less comfortable than we enjoy here. And if he were clever that would be an advantage, as long as he used his cleverness to benefit his fellow man.'

'Father, don't be so solemn. It'll be hard for me to find such a paragon in Lustleigh!' She picked up her best straw and placing it on her head pierced it through with coloured glass pins which matched the wide green ribbons falling from the crown. Then she smoothed the muslin gown over her hips and Edward, watching her, felt a sudden pang of impending loss as he said, 'Don't be in such a hurry to marry. Marriage lasts a long time.'

Now Eva's voice came floating along the hall from the kitchen, urgently, 'Haven't you gone yet, Tansy? Don't dawdle there or we'll be late!' Tansy ran lightly across the wooden floor of the office where the sun made a pattern of bars from the shadow of the heavy door. She hesitated, her hand on the knob.

'If he had to have just one quality only... what would that be?'

Edward replied immediately and without hesitation as if he'd been waiting for her to ask this question all her life. 'That's easy. The only virtue on which I would insist would be that he love you enough.'

Tansy, disappointed at such a simple condition, passed out through the door into Southernhay and a warm spring day. The sky was the colour of her mother's blue bag with which she turned soiled sheets to a sparkling white on washday. Clouds piled in soft turrets like castles where Haldon met the horizon in the distant hills across town.

She hesitated when she reached the bottom of 148 steps, deep in thought. Whatever did her Father mean, she wondered. To marry one had to have love. Of course she would be in love with the man she chose to spend the rest of her life with. And of course the man she chose would love her. But the way her Father had spoken seemed to indicate that it couldn't be taken for granted. It seemed from what he'd said that there were degrees of love.

Thoughtfully, she climbed the steps till she reached halfway. Reached the place where Rosemary and she had spent their childhood, exchanged secrets, wondered about boys, talked of what they would do when they grew up. And into her mind came a memory of last year's chapel outing when she and Rosemary pushed coins into the machines at the arcade on the end of Teignmouth Pier. She had run out of money by the time they reached the brass-bound machine, decorated with curling irises and the words 'Love Meter' over the glass front. Perhaps there would be a love meter at the Penny Arcade which was due open the following Market Day. She must make sure she saved enough pennies and did not spend them all on fairings today at Lustleigh. She turned through the Brimmacombe's gate, pushing past hens which ran at her, cackling and squawking across bare soil.

'I thought I heard the gate!' Rosemary appeared, her neat figure sober in dark blue gown and matching straw. 'I'm trying to persuade Ma that the world won't come to an end if she leaves Newton for just one day.'

And they embraced, faces a stark contrast, one so different from the other. Rosemary's eyes grey, her brows and smooth hair dark, her complexion slightly sallow. Wrinkles etched the corners of her full mouth, witness to years of pain when as a child she had suffered from poliomyelitis. Now her wasted leg was supported by an iron and she moved into the house with a slight limp.

'You know you want to see Thirza crowned, Mrs Brimmacombe. Besides, Mother will be disappointed if you don't come. She's sent me to get you. Just putting on her hat she is. Robert and James are so excited they can't keep still and the train leaves in fifteen minutes.'

Still Bessie hesitated. 'I shouldn't go. Saving up for my Johnnie's work suit,' she protested, 'just look at his trousiz, Tansy. Almost up to his knees' – she turned her son this way and that. 'Look at his sleeves,' Johnnie pulled hard at the frayed sleeve ends and tried to make them bridge the gap between jacket and wrist. ''Tis no good, Johnnie, you'm growing so fast, soon be a man, won't 'ee my son?' She pulled him towards her plump bosom.

'Don't, Ma. I'm too old for all that,' Johnnie protested. He pulled away from her and took a piece of kindling from the pile by the fire, getting out a knife from his pocket he began to whittle away until a rough shape began to emerge.

'A day out of town will do you good, Ma,' Rosemary exclaimed, and took an egg crock from the mantelpiece. She handed it to Bessie with a smile. 'You can spare enough for the train. I'll pay for Johnnie.' With that Bessie gave in, took off her apron, knotted her best lace shawl across her bosom and, pinning on her black straw market hat, closed the door behind her.

'Now you behave yerselves, chucks,' she commanded her flock, which closed round her skirts in expectation of feed, then she set off down the steps into Southernhay to meet Eva and the twins, who waited outside the Post Office, impatient to be off. Edward had volunteered to stay behind and Norah, taller than Tansy by a foot, waved them off.

'Just look at her' she remarked to her Father. 'The day only just begun and her hair falling down already! I can't think how she manages up at Courtenay House!' But Edward just smiled as they turned back into the Post Office.

'Don't be so hard on your sister,' he said. 'Seth tells me she's highly thought of by the Vallances. Apparently she's the apple of Cook's eye, so don't begrudge her her day of freedom!' He paused before going inside to call after the departing figures of Eva, Tansy and the twins. 'Be good. Help your Mother.' Robert turned and waved to him as he and James proudly carried the basket of pasties between them. Halfway across Courtenay Park the excitement of the trip became too much for them and they broke into a run. The basket tipped and the pasties fell out.

'Here, give it to me,' Tansy shouted, seizing it from them. 'Can't be trusted with anything, can you?' she scolded gently, at the same time wishing she could join in their wild dash to the station. The unused freedom of a day away from Courtenay House lent an air of adventure to the outing and she urged the party on. 'Hurry up or we'll miss the train,' she said and quickened her pace to fall in beside Johnnie, who walked ahead of the women. 'Don't you feel excited?' she demanded, and Johnnie, fair and pale, flushed and stammered.

'I'm too old to get excited,' he said, adding proudly, 'Going to work at Bradley Mill in the summer, I am.'

'Should be going to Art School, not work!' Rosemary interjected. 'Show Tansy your carving,' she urged and Johnnie produced a wooden cockerel from his pocket. Body, tail feathers and cockscomb were correct in every detail. Impressed, Tansy handed the bird back to him.

'That's wonderful. Will you carve something for me one day?' Then, not waiting for a reply, added, 'Come on before the best seats are gone,' and ran across the road to join the queue for tickets. Once they were all seated, back to the engine so as to avoid soot smuts, Tansy felt sorry for her enemy, Janet Luscombe, lady's maid at the Vallances. She and Cook were left to look after the family while Tansy and Hetty Westcott, the parlour-maid, had the day off.

'I'm going to make the most of today, Rose.' She turned to her friend, 'Next year it'll be me and Hetty who'll have to stay behind,' and she took Rosemary's arm in a display of affection, adding, 'I wonder who'll be at Lustleigh?'

'You mean will we meet any boys we know!' Rosemary laughed and Tansy squeezed her arm and responded, 'I mean will we meet any boys we don't know.' Robert and James ran from side to side of the carriage as it wound its way through fields to Heathfield, then on to Bovey Tracey, where a herd of cows ran in terror from the steaming smoking monster.

'You'm just in time my beauties!' the ticket collector told them as they got off the train at Lustleigh. 'They went a-maying early this morning. 'Ave enough blossom to deck out ten bowers!'

The party fell in behind the May Queen's procession as it began its long perambulation round the village, stopping here and there for the schoolchildren to sing songs and give a welcome rest to the perspiring youths whose job it was to carry the Queen and her bower. They stopped yet again, halfway up the hill to the church, and Tansy fell in beside the nearest bearer, a handsome boy of 19 or so, dressed in dark suit and neatly darned shirt, rough brown hair sticking out from under a Sunday cap, a blue and white 'kerchief at his neck.

'Where's Thirza Hill?' Tansy asked him, saying the first thing that came into her head in an attempt to capture his attention.

'Inside the bower, of course,' he replied, making a face at the fronds of heavily scented blossom which concealed Rosemary's cousin Thirza completely. Blue eyes met green and, for a second, one eyelid closed over blue iris. Thus encouraged Tansy went on, 'We've come all the way from Newton to see Thirza crowned. Rosemary here – 'tis her cousin, you see.' She pulled Rosemary closer, as once more the young men picked up their burden, and enquired, 'Live in Lustleigh, do you?'

He blushed and stammered his answer. 'Just outside the village, on the Moretonhampstead road.'

Rosemary squeezed Tansy's arm in alarm and whispered, 'Don't be so forward, Tansy,' while Tansy shrugged her arm away and, determined not to let this opportunity of meeting a possible marriage candidate slip through her fingers, persisted, 'You'm a farmer then?' as she noticed the square, work-roughened hands holding the wooden frame of the bower, the deeply tanned face and the sweet smell of hay which hung about the young man.

'That I be,' he agreed, turning sideways to bestow yet another wink from the deep blue eyes. 'Staddens is the name of our place, you would 'a passed it on your way here.'

Now they arrived outside the church where the Reverend Septimus Crocker-Wallace waited at the lych-gate to bless the procession. After the blessing the children sang another May Day song and the hymn 'Joy because the circling year brings our day of blessings here.'

The procession moved off across the village green where house martins flew about thatched eaves. Reaching Wreyland Manor, thirst brought the walkers to a halt and Tansy's new friend set about the pump handle to bring a flow of cold, clear water from below the ground. Then, thirsts slaked, they struggled uphill to where the crowning stone lay, waiting the arrival of the May Queen. At last and with sighs of relief the young men set down the bower – it parted and out stepped the Queen herself, Thirza Hill.

Tansy began to giggle and was promptly shushed by her mother as Rosemary moved forward to greet her cousin. Thirza stood blushing under her crown of early roses, her plump figure straining at the seams of the white muslin dress which had fitted so perfectly when it had first been announced she was to be May Queen. Now, six months later, Thirza had put on such a spurt of growth that the dress had become a constant source of worry to both Thirza and her mother. The more both had worried the more Thirza had eaten and the more weight she had put on. However, Rosemary, kind-hearted as ever, ignored such considerations and clasping her firmly in her arms placed kisses on Thirza's perspiring cheeks.

'Don't you look pretty,' she said, making way for Mrs Crocker-Wallace who now stepped forward in a black bustled dress to declare Thirza 'Queen of the May'.

She replaced the garland of roses for one of gold (seemingly made from a cake doily) and held out her hand with a view to helping Thirza mount the stone, but the girl's weight pulled the small woman over and together they rolled down the slope, locked together and gathering speed as their bodies gained impetus. Their progress was finally arrested by Jack Avery, the market auctioneer from Newton, sticking out a booted foot just as Mrs Crocker-Wallace's bustle came uppermost for the sixth time while Tansy, always quick to take action, charged after Thirza's rolling figure, grabbing her hair and bringing her to a stop just as she was about to disappear underneath the cider stand.

After Jack Avery had helped the vicar's wife to her feet and brushed off mud and grass, both she and Thirza climbed the hill once more and the crowning was accomplished to the immense relief of all present. Mrs Crocker-Wallace moved to a safe distance and Thirza was hauled up onto her granite seat, where she blushed and blushed at being the centre of so much attention.

'I never knew a crownin' to be so entertaining,' Bessie exclaimed, as concertina and fiddle struck up for the maypole dancing which about to begin. Girls in grey dresses with starched white pinafores, and boys in cut-down trousers and jackets, each held a coloured ribbon which was attached to the top of the pole – Miss Thomas, the schoolmistress, blew her whistle and they began. With six children facing clockwise and six anti-clockwise, weaving in and out and as they skipped, the ribbons of red, white and blue, wove a tight pattern at the top of the pole. All went well until Thirza Hill's little brother Billie went out when he should have gone in and chaos ensued. Miss Thomas, red-faced with embarrassment at this contretemps, brought the proceedings to a halt by blowing great blasts on her whistle.

'Think, Billie Hill! Think what you're supposed to be doing!' And she walked him back to his place until the tangle of ribbons was sorted out. The dancing recommenced and at last the children reached the centre pole, the pattern was completed and a round of applause broke out among the audience. Before the unwinding was accomplished Robert and James became bored. Hot in their thick Sunday suits, they took off ties and stuffed them into pockets, ran between legs and teased terriers who yelped and fought.

Tansy looked round for her farmer but he was nowhere to be seen. She thought he was perhaps at the stalls, and she seized Rose's arm and dragged her off towards the fairings. Robert and James, faces flushed, ginger hair a mass of tight curls, came running up.

'Father's given us a penny each,' Robert exclaimed and circled stalls trying to decide between gingerbread and sweetmeats, while Tansy and Rosemary fingered lace bobbins and ribbons.

'Look at that,' Tansy giggled, pointing to a china piece showing a couple dressed in night-shirts in a four-poster bed, chamber pot and candlestick to hand. Rosemary read the motto aloud 'Last one in bed to put out the light.' Both girls giggled and blushed until Eva came to tell them the picnic was set out and waiting. They sat high above the village, Eva and Bessie surrounded by their children, watching the house martins skim low across the field while they devoured Eva's pasties and ripe tomatoes.

''Tis going' t'rain avore day's out I do reckon,' Bessie said, as she passed round hard-boiled eggs. Tansy searched the field for the tall solid figure and felt a glow of warmth settle on her as she remembered the way he'd winked at her. Winked at her twice in fact, but where was he now? They drank home-made lemonade from stone jars till a sudden commotion arose in the beer tent and the village constable took out his truncheon and hauled out the culprits. Not wanting to miss the excitement, Tansy's party hurried across the field in time to hear the constable chide them.

'If you'm wanting a fight then 'ee can entertain rest of us,' he said, and pushed the men, protesting and struggling, towards the wrestling ring, but both were too drunk to stand and were dragged off and dumped in a granite trough at the side of the field.

'Look,' Eva nodded toward Jack Avery as he climbed up on to a wagon in front of the beer tent, 'What's happening now?'

He raised a megaphone to his mouth and began: 'Ladies, gen'lmen and visitors, we're going to have the first stage of this year's step-dancing competition. Winner goes through to the next round which'll be held at Kingsteignton Ram Roast on Whit Monday. Final at Whiddon Down in September.'

A crowd of men emerged from the beer tent, pots in hand, and listened while Jack Avery spoke to the children clustering about the wagon, eager to see what was going to happen.

'You little tackers, you kin sit down at the front here,' and as soon as they were settled he asked, 'Who'll take on our own Martin Webber from Staddens?' Tansy's grip tightened on Rosemary's arm as her young man pushed his way to the front of the crowd, then took his place beside Jack Avery, who went on, 'Prize is a side of good red Devon beef. Best of three rounds. Can't say fairer nor that!'

'A handsome prize that, I must say,' Bessie commented to Eva while Tansy started forward towards the two men, ever ready for a lark.

But Rosemary grabbed her and pulled her back. ''Tis only for the men,' she hissed and Tansy, abashed, remarked, 'Tidd'n fair. Men have all the fun!'

A movement in the crowd produced a short slight figure who pushed his way to the front. 'If I can borrow your board I'll have a go.' His voice had an alien ring to it, a strange lilting quality issued from the full lips, his grey eyes sunk in a pale, pitted face beneath a wide forehead and thatch of thick black hair, streaked with white at the parting. Martin Webber looked at him for a long moment then nodded acceptance of the challenge by extending a hand. Hands met against a stir of interest which brought the crowd pressing round the wagon.

'Not from these parts!' 'A furriner!' 'Baint one of us!' Jack Avery addressed the challenger, 'Am I right in thinking you'm from away?'

The man straightened and spoke proudly. 'Indeed I am, man. Evan Williams is my name – from the Welsh Valleys, I am, but no stranger to the step dance.'

Jack Avery, impressed with his confident look and clear speech, shook him by the hand. 'Our rules may be different here, 'tis like this,' and while he set them out to Evan, Tansy compared the two opponents. Martin Webber, broad shouldered, strong, smart in good jacket and trousers, shiny black boots, clean white shirt and blue spotted 'kerchief at his throat; Evan Williams, clothes hanging loose on his slight frame, the jacket patched at the elbows, trousers darned at the knees, striped shirt open at the neck as he stood coughing into a khaki handkerchief.

'He don't look fit enough to last three rounds, do he?' Tansy turned to Rosemary, who shook her head dubiously. 'How old do 'ee think he be?'

But before Rosemary could hazard a guess Eva and Bessie came to join them. 'Has the look of my Sam avore he died,' Bessie said, and Eva put an arm around her for comfort. 'How long has he been gone, my dear?' she asked and Bessie wiped a tear from the corner of her eye with her shawl. 'Six years 'tis. My Johnnie was but a little tacker.' Eva said, 'He would have been so proud of Johnnie now, your Sam. He'll be a credit to you, Bessie, you'll see.'

Now Jack Avery lifted a megaphone to his lips to announce, 'Quiet please. We'm about to begin. Three rounds. First – setting, second – stepping back, front and off the sides, third – a medley of your own choice. Best performance wins, judge's decision final.'

Martin climbed the wagon and laid down his board which held his feet with hardly an inch to spare.

'Hope he doesn't fall,' Tansy muttered. 'Can't believe anyone can dance on such a small surface. 'Tis no bigger than a dinner plate!' Forgetting herself, she shouted, 'Good luck, Martin Webber,' then giggled and covered her face with her hands in embarrassment. Martin blushed but ignored her as he waited, listening intently for the music to begin.

'Uncle George's hornpipe,' the man with the concertina announced, struck three chords and began. Martin's feet rattled on the mahogany as he set, then sent his feet flying off the edges of the board. His face shone with effort as he carried out the steps and Tansy's heart beat in time to the rhythm of the dance. Her thoughts went back to the conversation with her father early that morning; she'd only meant her question as a joke, not expecting such a serious response from him. Yet, here she was, already half in love with a handsome stranger. She watched as his feet hammered out a medley of staccato clicks and jumps to a burst of clapping and cheering. She put her hands together in delight and positioned herself at the exact spot where Martin would step down from the wagon.

'Well done, Martin Webber,' she exclaimed. He blushed again and took off the 'kerchief to wipe sweat from his face and neck.

'Now Evan Williams will take up the challenge after that excellent performance from our own Martin Webber. Evan, step forward, if you please.'

The mahogany board changed hands and the slight figure climbed up, this effort alone producing a paroxysm of coughing. Tansy experienced a moment of concern as Evan wiped his mouth once more.

'Look,' she said to Rosemary, 'there's blood coming from his mouth.' Closer to him now, she noticed the lines of pain etched round the grey eyes as he turned to the concertina player. 'Can you play a little faster, if you please?' Then he took up his position, placing dusty work-booted feet on the board. He tucked small hands close to his sides and began. Tansy held her breath. Please God, she prayed, let him get through this without collapsing. He looked as if he could do with a plate of beef now, she thought, finding herself wishing that he, not Martin, would be the winner. The compulsory sixteen sets he executed faster than Martin, the second round sent his feet crossing in front, behind and off the edges with a lightness and neatness that was quite breathtaking. All resemblance to Martin's performance was at an end as Evan won the attention of the toughest of the hill farmers present. There was no sound but the lilt of the concertina and the tapping of Evan's old cracked boots. Two bright red spots bloomed in Evan's cheeks, his grey eyes shone with pleasure as with a final high leap his dance came to an end. A spontaneous burst of cheering erupted from the crowd and Jack Avery's announcement, 'I declare Evan Williams the winner,' came as a mere formality. Martin shook him warmly by the hand as he received back the board. Jack spoke to Evan then held up his hand for attention. 'He is a worthy winner and will go on to the next round at Kingsteignton in a few weeks' time. Will the Reverend Crocker-Wallace kindly present the prize.'

But now at the sight of the huge piece of meat which was brought to the fore by two of Jack Avery's assistants, a muttering grew among the crowd. 'Should 'a gone to a Devon man.' 'Tidd'n right, good beef going to a furriner.'

Suddenly the mood of the crowd became threatening, they pressed in on Evan, some shaking fists until he gave way from stress and exhaustion, his legs bent under him and he slid to the ground, blood spurting from his mouth. At once Tansy rushed to his side, knelt on the grass beside him and began to unfasten his jacket and loosen the shirt at his throat.

Martin took up a defensive position between the prone man and the crowd. 'Give him air. Can't 'ee see the man's exhausted?'

Jack Avery spoke up in an effort to disperse the ugly crowd. 'Evan Williams walked here from Newton to take part in our competition. Now how's he going to get his prize home?' As the murmuring continued Jack tried another tack. 'Tells me he used to walk four miles underground to work his shift at the coal face. Coal to burn in our hearths.' He paused, then when no-one was forthcoming he pleaded, 'Come now, someone?' Martin sprang to his feet.

'I'll take 'un.' Tansy got to her feet and touched Martin's hand in a gesture of appreciation at his generous offer. Eva, who had fetched water from the pump, held a soaked 'kerchief to Evan's forehead and afer some time he recovered enough to rise slowly to his feet. Together he and Martin carried the beef to Martin's pony and trap. Tansy and Rosemary trailed along after them, still concerned at the state of Evan's health. He sat in the trap to recover and Jack Avery's new announcement came to them across the field.

'Now 'tis turn of the ladies. Take your partners, boys for Strip the Willow.' They listened as the musicians struck up the familiar tune; the crowd broke up as young men sought partners and the older men retired to hide in the beer tent lest their wives and sweethearts caught them. Later perhaps they would be cajoled into joining in.

Tansy, putting on her most winsome smile, stood in front of Martin and Evan. 'You're such wonderful dancers. You can't refuse to dance a reel with us!' She turned and dragged a reluctant Rosemary forward, looking longingly to where longways sets were already taking shape. Martin blushed and smiled and offered an arm to each of the girls, only to be stopped by Evan.

'It would indeed be a pleasure to dance with such lovely young ladies,' he responded, giving each girl a slight bow, 'but I must get back to Gwynneth. She's been on her own with the children all day,' he hesitated, 'her not being well and all. You must forgive me on this occasion.' His face was still flushed from the result of his efforts in the dance, but his eyes shone with excitement. 'Want to show her the beef, d'you see. 'Tis a long time since we ate meat.'

He turned to Martin. 'Of course if you wish to stay, I'll walk.' But Martin shook his head vehemently and dropped the girls' arms. 'I'll have to go back for milking so 'tis no trouble to leave now,' then, seeing the look of disappointment on Tansy's face he added, 'Perhaps the young ladies would like a ride home to Newton with us?' And when Rosemary objected, 'But we've got tickets for the train...' Tansy stamped on her friend's good foot and accepted at once.

'That's kind of you, Martin Webber,' she said, liking the feel of his name on her tongue for the second time. If she couldn't dance with him, then a ride beside him through the lanes would be the next best thing. 'I'll not be a minute,' she said and ran across the field to beg Eva to let her go. Reluctantly Eva agreed.

'Yes, you may go but only if Rosemary goes with you,' she said, then turned to pacify Robert and James, who declared, 'We want a ride back to Newton in a trap.'

Rosemary, amazed at the ease with which Tansy had abandoned her favourite pastime, dancing, for a ride with a stranger, was hauled up into the trap. It was a tight squeeze, Evan on one side clutching the side of beef, Tansy and Rosemary giggling on the other and Martin in the middle, encouraging a reluctant pony to pull this extra load. As they rode back along the lane from Wreyland the twins ran past them, followed a moment or two later by Eva and a struggling and panting Bessie.

'We're going to catch the train. Race you back to Newton!' Robert, always the spokesman, shouted as they disappeared across the village green, heading for the station. There they were rewarded by finding an engine with a head of steam up, ready to leave.

'Come on, my beauties,' the guard called, and, while Tansy and Rosemary hung onto their hats and clung to the side of the trap as Tom broke into a brisk trot, Eva and Johnnie held tight to the twins for fear they would fall from the carriage window in their excitement.

❧ Chapter Two ❧

Furriners

The next day Tansy stood watching Seth skin game in the kitchen of Courtenay House. She put out her hand to touch the soft fur of the rabbit where it lay lifeless on the bench, its colour a mirror of beech woods and ploughed fields.

'Why, 'tis still warm,' she exclaimed, 'When did you catch it, Seth?'

Seth paused, straightening his back wiping blood from his hands. 'Early this morning avore the mist rose. Feeding by the edge of Decoy Wood 'twas.' He slit the animal's underbelly and with one deft movement separated the skin from the body. Tansy's hands moved on to the long body of a hare which lay on the wooden table while Seth explained.

'Patch flushed out the hare at the top of Cull's field. Set off the moment it saw Patch – fast they are, hares. Only a dog as good as Patch could 'a caught 'un.'

The dog, banned from the kitchen, whimpered by the back door at the sound of his name.

'Come on Seth. Don't stand there jawin', us wants to get patè and brawn started avore lunch,' Cook interrupted.

'Hare needs hanging, Cook, but 'ee knows that, don't 'ee.'

'There's not time.' Cook bustled up to the bench, seized the rabbit carcass, and took it back to her table where she began to joint and chop, talking all the while. 'Holy Terror's coming and Missus wants us to get ahead. In a proper state of panic she is, as usual.'

Tansy and Seth looked at one another, appalled.

'On no!' exclaimed Tansy, 'That'll mean scrubbing the house from top to bottom.'

Seth felt the edge of his knife. 'That means taking the old girl out every afternoon, calling. Well, Maister'll have to make his own way home this time.' He looked grim as he swabbed down the bench, then crossed the kitchen to throw out lights for Patch, who whined with pleasure. 'Keeps us out too late, her do. 'Tis the same every visit. There's never time to chop wood or shoot for the pot when she'm here!' Seth wiped his knife and replaced it in the knife rack.

'Best to look on the bright side,' Cook interjected. 'Just think she could be living here all the time. Think of that, Seth!'

Each went about their tasks dwelling on the way their lives changed whenever Charles Vallance's mother Beatrice came to stay. Sundays were particularly hard for Tansy when, after chapel then lunch, Beatrice Vallance joined the staff in the Servants' Hall and bombarded them with questions on the Bible. This was followed by making them look at the huge copy of John Bunyan's *Pilgrim's Progress*. Tansy loved books but not this one with its illustrations of Christian in the slough of despond, writhing snakes threatening to drag him down. She shivered and turned her mind to more comfortable thoughts.

'Rabbits are such pretty creatures,' she said, 'It's terrible to kill them.'

Cook only laughed at the look of distress on Tansy's face. 'And do 'ee say No when your Ma makes a tasty rabbit pie at home?'

Now Tansy had the grace to look ashamed, remembering the steaming dish her mother made whenever Rosemary's brother Johnnie caught a rabbit on the hill.

'You haven't told us about May Day, Tansy. Who was there? And who crowned Rosemary's cousin Thirza Hill then?' Cook firmly closed the subject of rabbits and when Tansy told them how Mrs Crocker-Wallace and Thirza rolled downhill at Wreyland she and Seth laughed until the tears ran.

'Was the Vicar sober? If so, then 'twould 'a been the first time he took a blessing without the aid of a bottle!'

'You should have seen Evan Williams doing the step dance – wonderful he was.' Tansy paused, her hands deep in a huge pile of vegetables she was peeling for the Vallances' lunch.

Cook interrupted, 'Who be 'ee then? This Evan Williams and where be he from? Not a Devon name that for sure!'

Tansy told Cook how, when they got back to town in Martin Webber's trap she had discovered that Evan and his family had just moved into a house on Bowden Hill quite near the Post Office.

'Well, that's strange – how was it your Ma and Pa didn't know they was there?' Cook demanded as she began to mince rabbit and hare livers, placing them in a dish with slices of bacon while Seth cleaned knives in the new Kent machine.

'They only arrived Sunday, all the way from Merthyr in Wales they are. He's sick, can't work down the mines anymore. Says he's heard the climate was warm in Devon and that there was work to be found.'

Cook stopped her mincing and began to grate bread. She sighed. 'My dear soul, us've heard that avore, but saying it don't make it true do it?' She and Seth shook their heads, both knowing from experience that work was never easy to come by.

'Well the Williams will be all right this winter,' Tansy went on. 'Evan won the step-dance competition, a huge side of beef. Ma and Pa have gone up the Hill to help them cut it into joints. Going to salt it down they are.'

Cook nodded at this piece of information, then, fixing Tansy with a long look, asked, 'And what about this Martin Webber? Where do he come into it?'

Tansy blushed and turned away to fetch a large pot while Janet Luscombe came into the kitchen. A tall, fair girl with bold blue eyes, she wore a dress of soft pink rose, covered by a lace-edged apron, her uniform as lady's maid to Caroline Vallance and her daughter Emma.

'Where do 'ee live then?' Cook pressed Tansy for more information. Spending most of her time in the kitchen, Cook relied on her fellow servants to keep her in touch with the outside world. At mention of Staddens Farm it was now Janet Luscombe's turn to pry. She advanced on Tansy, only stopping when her face was merely a foot away.

'If you'm talking about Martin Webber, then you can forget all about him. He's already spoken for.' Tansy stared back in surprise and Janet Luscombe added, 'He's walking out with my sister, Fanny.'

Surprise released Tansy's grip on the saucepan, sending it crashing to the kitchen floor, a cascade of carrots and onions pouring onto the stone flags, soaking Janet's feet. She let out a wail. 'Now see what you've done,' she exclaimed, but Tansy stood her ground.

'That can't be true! Why he wouldn't have brought me home to Newton if he were spoken for,' and when Janet didn't reply she demanded, 'Why wasn't your sister Fanny with him yesterday at the May Fair then?'

She had the pleasure of watching Janet's face flush red with anger. 'Had to work, didn't she. Same as me.'

Tansy looked triumphant. 'I don't believe you, Janet Luscombe,' she said, 'He's too shy to be asking out one maid while sparking with another.' She bent down and began to gather up spilled vegetables, replacing them in the heavy iron pot. 'How does Martin Webber know your sister Fanny anyway?' she wanted to know.

Now it was Janet's turn to look triumphant. 'Dairy maid at Staddens Farm is our Fanny. Sees him every day does Fanny. About to propose he is.' She tossed her head. 'About to propose is Martin Webber – any day now!' Then she stooped down to mop at her soaking shoes. Tansy hesitated, not wanting to believe Janet, who had shown nothing but animosity to Tansy ever since she'd come to work at Courtenay House a year ago. How could Martin have led her on if he was going out with Fanny Luscombe? How could she be so sure Janet was telling the truth? Should she trust her instincts and Martin, for whom she felt a strong attraction? As she struggled to place the heavy pan onto the hot range she felt again the touch of his strong hands as he'd lifted her down from the trap the day before. She saw again the sun-bleached hair and clear blue gaze, his open face had seemed guileless as a summer's day. She turned back to Janet, head up chin out, defiant.

'Well, we'll see who he meets at the Ram Roast, won't us?'

'You'm wasting your time if you thinks Martin Webber will be looking for you. You can ask his Ma if you don't believe me.' With that Janet picked up a pile of bed linen and stalked out. Tansy and Cook exchanged glances, the older woman shrugged.

'Take no notice, Tansy. Jealous she is that's all. Like a bear with a sore head all day yesterday she was – all because she wanted the day off same as you. Furious she was when Miss Emma came down to ask for you.'

Cook placed weights on top of the dish of patè and changed the subject. 'Did you know Hetty's mother's very sick?' When Tansy shook her head she added, 'They sent for her yesterday, put straw down outside the house.' Both Cook and Tansy knew what that meant, Kezia Westcott must be very ill indeed; putting straw down to deaden the sound of passing carts was a sure sign that someone was at death's door. Hetty Westcott was parlour-maid to the Vallances; a tall slim creature, her serious face framed by dark brown hair worn severely combed back in a bun. Hetty was kindness itself and had taken Tansy's part on more than one occasion when Janet Luscombe made life difficult for her.

Cook continued, 'She's a lot to worry about, what with her Jack being out there in South Africa. Seth seen a photo of they Devons in the Gazette, it said they was singing Old Uncle Tom Cobley as they marched into battle.'

Cook paused to wipe bloody hands on a cloth and Tansy asked, 'Has she heard from her Jack?'

Their conversation was interrupted by a jangling of the morning-room bell. Tansy dried her hands and hurried upstairs. She was soon back.

'Miss Emma's playing tennis at Forde Park this afternoon. Going to bring back College friends for tea – Missus says can you make some fancies?'

Now Cook grew red in the face and shook her fist towards the service stairs. 'Thinks I've got ten pairs of hands she do. Well, I'll see if there's time after lunch. If not they'll have to make do with my fruit cake else.' She banged down a large plate and began to carve ham for lunch with such venom as to put lives at risk.

The back door opened with a sudden thrust as Seth brought logs into the kitchen. 'Where does this chap from Merthyr think he's going to get work?' he wanted to know. 'I suppose he could try clay pits or Hexter's brick works at Kingsteignton.' He straightened and stood scratching his head through the thick greying hair. 'Can't say as how I'd want to have to start all over again somewheres strange.' This was a new thought for Tansy. She began to wonder how she would feel if Eva and Edward had to leave the Post Office and set off across country to find work; she shivered at the thought of it.

'Perhaps I'll go up the Hill and visit them,' she said, 'although it'll have to wait till Wednesday week now,' she added ruefully, knowing her May Day off automatically cancelled any free time till the following week.

⁘

The following Wednesday brought a reprieve from Caroline Vallance, who was astute enough to know that Tansy would work twice as hard after a day off.

'I'll need you to help Hetty wash glass and clean silver on Thursday.' Tansy bobbed and thanked her, then set off without a moment's hesitation for the Post Office.

'Where's Norah?' she demanded as she rushed in, giving her mother a hug. Eva sighed and looked up from the counter at her youngest daughter who hovered, out of breath, face flushed and, as usual, in a hurry. She laughed and returned the kiss Tansy planted on her cheek.

'She's studying – you should know that; getting near the entrance exam. I doubt she'll leave her books, even for you.' But Tansy was determined to involve Norah with the new people up on the Hill and, giving Eva another kiss, she ran lightly upstairs to the room she and Norah had shared all their lives until a year ago, when the decision had been made which was to change both their lives forever. Norah, the absolute opposite to Tansy – quiet, dark and serious – was working as a pupil teacher at Bell's school whilst studying for the entrance exam in the hope of gaining a place at Goldsmith's College, the first training college for women in the country. Tansy, it was decided, would go into service, thus contributing to the family income while Norah went through college. After that, Eva and Edward had promised that she, Tansy, would have her chance to become whatever she'd set her heart on. This decision still caused Tansy moments of extreme anguish and, as she pushed open the bedroom door and saw Norah sitting working steadily in the window, jealousy surfaced once more.

'How long have you had that table?' she wanted to know, at the sight of a polished oak piece piled high with books and papers. 'I've not seen that before.' But Norah, deeply engrossed in writing an essay, didn't hear and kept on with her writing. Tansy went close to her sister and shouted in her ear.

'Where did you get that table, I asked?'

Norah jumped visibly and swung round, a frown between her brows. 'Tansy! I didn't hear you come in. You could have knocked!' she added reproachfully.

'Knock to come into my old room!' Tansy stormed, then, at a warning glance from Norah, she stopped, bit her lip and said more quietly, 'You haven't told me why you're working up here'.

Norah laughed, used to her young sister's ways. 'I suppose I won't get any peace until I tell you. I couldn't work downstairs because of the twins so Father bought this table at Cross's sale.' She picked up her pen and turned back towards the half-finished essay, but now Tansy grabbed her hand.

'Leave all that, Norah. Just for me. Just for an hour. I want you to come up the Hill and meet the new family that's moved in. You know, the ones Mother and Father have been helping with the beef.' Then, as Norah still looked uncertain, 'I met Evan Williams at Lustleigh on May Day when we went to see Thirza crowned. He's a wonderful step dancer.' She broke into a series of dance steps, making such a racket that Eva banged on the ceiling, her signal that there were customers at the counter and that they were to be quiet. At last Norah gave in, unable to resist her sister who stood, hot and flushed, every part of her body alive and anxious to be off.

'I can see you won't leave me alone until I've met your precious Williams'.' She crossed the room to fetch a black straw hat and wool jacket from a corner wardrobe. 'Perhaps you'll come for a walk on the Hill afterwards like we used to when you were living at home. But after supper, mind, I must get back to work.'

Tansy was satisfied with that. She danced ahead up the steep pavement, cross-hatched against the winter snows, so steep that both girls used the handrail to haul themselves uphill between redbrick terraces. Each house had a brass knocker that shone, a doorstep that gleamed white from years of scrubbing; all that is except the last house at the end of the terrace. Here, the door knocker was green with neglect, the step grey and a crowd of children formed a human chain outside, passing a bucket to the tallest girl, who filled it from a spring flowing from the bank where terrace met field. Then, she in turn passed it back along the line of children until the one at the door carried it inside. The water made a swishing sound as it slopped onto the pairs of feet as it passed from hand to hand. By the door at the opposite side of the step sat a tiny child cuddling a doll and busily sucking her thumb. The next but smallest emerged from the house and, bucket empty, the procedure began all over again. None of the children wore shoes or boots and Tansy and Norah stopped, shocked and embarrassed at this evidence of such poverty right here almost on their own doorstep.

'I've seen children in the Courts playing barefoot...' Tansy left the sentence unfinished as they approached the group. The chain stopped and it was Norah who recovered first.

'Best let me speak,' she said, laying a restraining arm on her impulsive sister. 'Good morning,' she addressed the eldest, a girl, with her warmest smile. 'I believe you've just moved in. I'm Norah Drewe and this is my sister Tansy.'

The chain stopped moving. The bucket, full of water, was set down and the line of children stood, open-mouthed, staring at the well-dressed girls.

At last the girl spoke in a soft, lilting voice. 'Drewe? Then you must belong to Mr and Mrs Drewe who came up from the Post Office to help Mam and Dadda with the beef last week.' She smiled and held out a grubby but slim hand. 'I'm Blodwen Williams. This is Owen, Ifor, Emrys, Myfanwy and this,' she said, lifting the toddler from beside the front door, 'is Poppy.'

As she announced their names each boy bowed, a sharp bow from the waist, and each girl bobbed, hands to skirts, in the direction of Norah and Tansy. Their beautiful manners touched the girls, who noticed that their bodies were so thin, just skin and bone. Now the children stood back from the door waiting for Blodwen to speak for them again.

'Will you please to come inside.' Her musical voice gave the invitation a welcoming sound as she shushed the children away. 'Go and play in the field till I tell you it's all right to come in,' she commanded, then stood aside for Norah and Tansy to enter the house. The hall was so dark inside that at first Tansy could see nothing, but when Blodwen invited them through into the living-room a small fire sent a bright glow into the room, which was almost bare of furniture. When Blodwen invited them to sit Tansy looked round for a chair, knocked her legs against a sofa behind her and hastily sat down on it. A movement by her side drew her attention to a small woman lying full length and taking up most of the sofa. The oval face, framed with soft brown hair, was lined and stamped with suffering, but the grey eyes held a welcoming warmth.

'I'm so sorry,' exclaimed Tansy, 'I didn't see you there.' She made to get up but was stayed by a gentle hand on her arm.

'No, no, don't go – it's so nice to have someone come in to visit,' and her voice rose and fell as had Blodwen's, enveloping Tansy and Norah with its alien but warm sound.

'Put the kettle on, our Blodwen – make our visitors a cup, there's a love,' and Blodwen removed a saucepan from a trivet over the fire, a pan from which an appetising smell of meat and vegetables rose. She stirred up the fire, filled a heavy black kettle with water from a bath in an alcove near the window and set it on the trivet to heat.

'Your Ma and Pa were very kind to us,' Gwynneth Williams said. 'Everyone has been so kind – the young man who brought Evan home with his prize, the doctor too. This,' she pointed to the saucepan cooling on the floor, 'is the first meat meal we've had for a very long time.' And here she broke into a fit of coughing which brought Blodwen hurrying to her side with a cup of water.

'Don't talk, Mam. Remember what the doctor said – you must rest.'

'It's hard not even to be allowed to speak,' her mother said between gasps which produced a rattling sound from her chest. 'Blodwen must speak for me then,' she said, settling back under her shawl, content to watch the three girls.

'It is lovely here in Newton – so open, so fresh, so clean. No slag-heaps behind the house.' Blodwen produced two cups and saucers from a cupboard beside the fire. 'If only Dadda can find work.'

'What lovely china!' Norah exclaimed, admiring the cups with their bouquets of pansies. Blodwen smiled. 'They belonged to our Grandmother Williams. Hand painted they are,' she said and polished them on her skirt until the china shone, translucent in the fire's flame.

'I love your names, they've such a musical sound,' Tansy volunteered, trying to ignore the bare walls and stone floor covered with just one small rag rug. 'The midwife called me Tansy after a wild flower. What do yours stand for?'

'Owen means youth, Ifor is the Welsh for Ivor, Emrys is Ambrose and I'm not sure about Poppy.' She paused, wrinkling her brow, then rushed on, 'Oh yes, I remember now, Poppy was named for a flower that grew out of the coal dust at the back of the house one summer. Do you remember, Mam?'

Gwynneth smiled, then her smile faded and she sat up, her eyes full of alarm. 'Where is she, my Poppy? Go and see, Blodwen, see she's not come to harm.' She sat tense until Blodwen returned with the little girl in her arms. Poppy snuggled up to Gwynneth and, bright-eyed, watched Tansy and Norah from the shelter of her mother's arms.

'It's lovely to have the field so near,' Blodwen said. 'At Merthyr it was a long walk out of the valley – nearly an hour it took to reach the fields,' she added wistfully.

Norah responded. 'It's wonderful up there in the summer – brambles covered in berries in August and mushrooms in June and September. You can take a path across the fields down to Bradley Woods,' and here she paused, 'Tansy will show you.' Tansy smiled and nodded, eager to share her favourite haunts with this family who seemingly had so little.

Now, one by one, the children crept into the tiny room and, as each settled by the fire, Tansy tried to match name to figure. Myfanwy came first with her cloud of black curly hair, then came Ifor in patched trousers, Emrys who she judged to be the same age as the twins came next, then last of all Owen, much taller than Blodwen. He had an air of confidence about him and kept apart, lounging against the wall close to the door.

'Dadda says we can keep a pig,' Emrys told Norah, who advised him, 'Best make sure Farmer Cull is agreeable – the field is part of his land.' She then asked Owen if he still attended school.

'Naw, schooldays are done for me, it's work I'm to do now.'

'Have you found anything in Newton?' Tansy wanted to know. Owen blushed and looked down at his bare feet.

'Dadda's bringing home leather to mend our boots, then I'll get something.' He sounded so sure. 'I've worked down the mine,' he added, fiercely proud, 'Are there any mines here?'

Impressed by his keenness to work, Norah tried her best to help. 'There's tin mining on Dartmoor but it's a long way and you would have to stay in the huts every night. I'll ask Father if you like, he might know the captain of one of the mines.'

Introductions over, tea drunk and friendship firmly established, it was time for the girls to leave, doubtful that Evan and Owen Williams would find work so easily. But both girls underestimated the resourcefulness of Evan Williams, who had that very day secured work at Watts & Blakes clay works, and the following Sunday led his family into the gallery of the chapel, the boys thin and pale in chopped-down trousers and much-mended jackets, their faces scrubbed till they shone, and the girls in neat grey serge frocks with starched white pinafores, thick black wavy hair tied with white ribbons where it hung down their backs. Astonishing to Norah and Tansy, all wore boots, boots which shone with a shine so bright that the toe caps reflected the carvings on the ends of the pews. Their Welsh voices swelled the sound from the gallery and Evan's tenor soared high above the choir, as pure as the song of the lark on Dartmoor. Only Gwynneth Evans was absent.

✣ Chapter Three ✣

The Holy Terror

Beatrice Vallance stepped down from the station cab and stood, ram-rod straight, waiting for her daughter-in-law to greet her. Caroline Vallance hurried forward, touched the austere cheek with cool lips through her mother-in-law's veil, tightly pinned at the back of brown hair which Caroline suspected to be a wig.

Emma came next. She took a deep breath, gave her grandmother a slight bob, then, blushing, stepped straight back on to Cook's toes. Cook gritted her teeth and smiled at Beatrice Vallance through the pain. Ignoring Emma, Beatrice Vallance nodded with approval at Cook, who had been brought up from the kitchen which she never left, whatever happened upstairs. It was a rule she stuck to throughout the length of her working years, using successive kitchen maids to act as go-between. The one exception for whom she would leave her domain was Beatrice Vallance.

'Have you made some of your excellent patè, Cook?' she enquired and Cook immediately spoke up.

'Yes, M'am, made your favourite game patè and some nice brawn.'

Beatrice smiled a small, wintry smile, full approval being kept in reserve for Charles Vallance, her only son. She moved along the row of servants who waited at the bottom of the steps. Her black gimlet eyes missed nothing and when she stopped in front of Tansy, the kitchen maid felt as if those eyes could see into her very soul.

'Drewe, isn't it?' she asked, and when Tansy bobbed, added, 'I remember you from my last visit.' She paused. 'Fancy a trip out onto the Moor, young woman?' And when Tansy, surprised, nodded and mumbled 'Yes, M'am,' the old woman added, 'Speak up girl! Need someone to come on our trips, don't we Howell?' Here she moved toward the tall awkward figure of the man who stood, turning his cap nervously in his hands. 'Start on Monday while the weather holds. Nine o'clock sharp, Howell.'

Then she stalked majestically up the steps, followed at a respectful distance by Charles, Caroline and Emma, while the servants scuttled back round the house and into the Servants' Hall in order not to miss the first jiggling notes of the bell setting off a flurry of demands now that Beatrice Vallance was once more ensconced at Courtenay House for her annual spring visit.

❦

'Come on, Blodwen,' urged Tansy, as Evan Williams' eldest child tried to keep up. At sixteen, Blodwen had been taken on by Caroline Vallance to help Tansy in the preparations for Beatrice's visit.

'Not going to find any dust in my house!' Caroline had exclaimed and the girls had scrubbed and polished till their knees ached and their hands became raw. They were only allowed to stop when every surface in the house shone like a hundred mirrors. A smell of lavender and beeswax permeated stairs and hall and filtered into every room of the large house.

'She looks a real dragon, Tansy,' Blodwen exclaimed as they entered the kitchen to the sharp jangling of the drawing-room bell.

'Didn't waste much time, did she?' Hetty Westcott remarked as she set off upstairs in answer.

'My mother would like a glass of Madeira, Westcott,' Charles announced, 'and some ratafia biscuits.' Hetty crossed the room to the sideboard where a Cranberry glass decanter and glass sat waiting.

'I see you've taken on another girl,' Beatrice observed as she accepted her glass, then turned to Caroline impatiently. 'For goodness sake, Caroline, do sit down instead of standing there fidgeting!' Caroline Vallance, all her normal poise gone from the moment she heard her mother-in-law's cab scrunching up the drive, sat immediately as if she had no will of her own.

'Yes,' she agreed, fanning her face which had heated at Beatrice's rebuke, 'She's from a Welsh family who've just moved in above the Post Office on Bowden Hill. Good chapel-going people they are I believe.'

Charles left the fireplace, where he'd stood since his mother's arrival, and took a seat beside her.

'The man's started at the clay works and I'm told he's an excellent worker. Has a good tenor voice too, could be an asset to the choir.'

Here Charles took a silver half-hunter watch from his pocket and began to polish it with a large white hanky.

'And how is 'The Messiah' coming along?' Beatrice wanted to know. Now Charles smiled; this was something he'd been saving to tell his mother over lunch, but he might have known she wouldn't wait to be told.

'Next Thursday evening it's to be performed at the chapel. Specially timed for your visit, Mama! We'll see how many people come. Then, if it is a success, we'll arrange for it to be performed at the Alexandra Hall in the autumn.' Satisfied with his announcement and its reception by his mother, he replaced the watch in his pocket.

'I should like to meet the choir afterwards,' Beatrice announced, and Caroline's heart sank as the ten-day visit stretched ahead in a welter of unwanted activity. She sighed and put aside the party she had planned for Emma when she left Lawn College in June. Bitterly, she watched Charles bending over his mother, trying to anticipate her every wish. She thought of the new bathroom she wanted to install in the following weeks and had been on the point of asking Charles for. Now she must put this off until his mother had gone. Yes, she thought, that would be best. Then he would be in a good mood. She must put herself out to please her mother-in-law. Perhaps, she thought wistfully, she would win her over this time, make her see how times were changing, how wives were becoming more important in society. She turned to smile at Beatrice resolutely and, as soon as Charles left to return to the Mill, she spoke up, 'Did I hear you ask for Drewe to accompany you to Dartmoor, Mama?' she enquired as Beatrice took pins from her bonnet and removed her veil, merely lifted during lunch.

'You did indeed, Caroline. Emma can come with me to visit some of the Moor folk. She and Drewe can be my legs. Take a picnic with us.' A look of pleased anticipation spread over her wrinkled face. 'Yes, that's what we'll do. I have a fancy to visit Lustleigh, call on Biddy Pidsley and ask her to make me some new lace pieces.'

Emma grimaced behind her grandmother's back at Caroline who, determined to placate Beatrice at all costs, shook a reproving head in her daughter's direction. She must have a word with Emma, explain her plan.

Meanwhile, downstairs Janet Luscombe was grumbling in a loud voice to Cook. 'Tidd'n fair, always Tansy Drewe as gets the treats. Why can't it be me as goes out with the Holy

Terror on her trips? I'm Miss Emma's maid, ain't I? I'll get even with Miss Tansy Drewe one day, that I will.' And she slowly and deliberately wiped her dirty hands on Tansy's afternoon apron where it hung, crisp and white, in the hall.

Meal times were changed, Beatrice preferring to eat dinner midday.

'Suits my digestion better at my time of life,' she declared, although her age was a closely guarded secret. She pronounced Cook's patè excellent, as were her mutton cutlets, artichoke with white sauce and cabinet pudding.

'Tell Cook I'll be down first thing tomorrow to discuss the week's menus,' she said, and Caroline's face became suffused with rage at this total abrogation of her authority. She stifled the angry words that rose in her throat, holding on to a vision of the ivy-decorated bathroom suite she would demand from Charles the moment Beatrice's visit came to an end. It was the very least he could do in recompense.

'Charles,' Beatrice said at dinner that evening, 'last time I visited the Moor the gig wasn't entirely to my satisfaction.'

'Why was that Mother? We always enjoy the sensation of being out in the fresh air when we get up to Combestone.' Charles produced his watch and began to polish the case vigorously, a sign of a battle ahead.

'I want you to get out your father's carriage. I take it you've kept it?'

Charles breathed a sigh of relief, glad he hadn't accepted the offer made by the London Mews the previous autumn.

'We let the horses go years ago, Mama, but then you must be aware of that. It would take a pair to pull it and we've only got Tinker. A pony couldn't pull a heavy carriage, Mama.' He shut the half-hunter and replaced it in his pocket with a smile of satisfaction but, even after all these years, he had still underestimated her determination. She pursed her lips and tapped her teeth with a black lace fan. She rose, deep in thought, to pace about the room.

'I'll see Seth Howell first thing in the morning. Always found him a resourceful man. I'm sure he'll know where you could hire a pair of carriage horses.' Now she gathered her black skirt into her hand and moved towards the door, where she turned to face her son and his wife.

'I wish you both goodnight.' Charles and Caroline rose in deference to her age and position. 'I have a plan for Emma I wish to discuss with you,' she hesitated for a moment then added, 'but that will keep till another time.'

She waited for Charles to open the door then swept through, walking erect and proud along the gleaming hall and upstairs to her room, high in the gable where she liked to look out over Decoy Woods.

Downstairs, Cook sat mulling over the message Hetty had delivered from the dining-room after lunch. She and Caroline Vallance had already planned the week's meals. Did Beatrice's proposed visit to her kitchen in the morning mean all her preparations were to be swept aside? Her varicose veins began to burn and throb and her chest heaved as she mustered her defences. She reached for the bottle of Silver's Pills and a glass of water and looked at the clock. It was ten o'clock and time she was off to bed. Tansy had gone long since, worn out with all the extra scrubbing and polishing that had gone on for the last two weeks. Even so, she must get her to polish the dresser first thing and wash over the kitchen flags before Beatrice Vallance came down. She lowered the oil lamp and stepped into the pantry where she checked the cooked gammon and brace of pheasants hanging from the ceiling. She admired the hand-raised pigeon pie and hard-boiled eggs set out for Monday's picnic, the bottles of home-made elderflower cordial and milk shapes standing on the marble shelf. If Beatrice Vallance was going to change the menu completely then the Missus would have to send out to Balster's for replacements.

Cook sighed heavily, shut the pantry door, turned and almost tripped over Minnie, the cat, hovering in the doorway in the hope of slipping unseen into the pantry. Cook aimed a well-directed foot and the cat howled and scuttled into a corner by the range to lick her wounds.

All day Sunday Seth worked hard on the Vallance's family carriage. As he polished he thought of Absolam Vallance who had died in the Mill fire when he, Seth Howell, first came to work at Courtenay House. How proud the old man had been of the ebony coachwork decorated with gold leaf. He set to with soap and water and the leaves and curlicues emerged from behind years of dirt and neglect. The smell of leather brought him pleasure as he dusted and applied beeswax to the leather interior. Tansy came out to the coach-house after chapel and polished the mirrors above the seats, excited at the prospect of tomorrow's picnic.

'Don't it look grand!' she exclaimed when they both stood back to admire their combined efforts. Seth nodded his head slowly in complete accord.

'Proper job,' he said.

'Wonder where she'll take us to tomorrow?' Tansy asked and Seth laughed ruefully.

'The last place one would expect, I'll wager. If 'er behaves true to form, think of the most likely, like Fingle Bridge, then you kin reckon she'll go opposite direction.'

Seth straightened from his polishing and asked, 'Where would 'ee like to go then, my beauty?' The unexpected question had Tansy blushing and pulling at the frill of her apron.

'Lustleigh Village would be nice,' she said, adding hastily, 'Rosemary Brimmacombe's cousin, Thirza, lives there.'

But Seth wasn't fooled and his eyes twinkled as he replied, 'I'm told there might be another reason you be wanting to go Lustleigh, something to do wi' a young man called Martin Webber?'

However, Tansy wouldn't be drawn and merely tossed her head and hurried back to the kitchen to help Cook get ready for supper, which had now replaced dinner which had now replaced luncheon. She looked forward to a slice of the delicious-looking beef and horse-radish Cook was arranging on a large platter.

'Fetch out the chutney, Tansy,' Cook commanded, and Tansy climbed the stool in the pantry to select Beatrice Vallance's favourite runner bean, adding a jar of pickled walnuts for good measure.

'She hasn't asked for the Wedgwood yet, Cook,' she commented, knowing it wouldn't be long before Beatrice Vallance sent out invitations to 'The Dinner'. Invitations to members of the oldest families in and around Newton. Then there would definitely be work to do, thought Tansy.

Sounds of Miss Emma practising her piece for the evening carried down the service stairs whenever one of the servants answered a summoning bell. Emma Vallance shared the same music teacher as Rosemary Brimmacombe, Tansy's best friend, but Emma didn't share Rosemary's talent. As the door into the hall opened yet again and stumbling sounds of

Chopin's 'Fantasie Impromptu' floated towards Tansy, she felt sorry for Miss Emma and glad that she herself hadn't to face the ordeal of performing for Beatrice Vallance.

※

Monday morning arrived in a blaze of spring sunshine which made Absolam Vallance's carriage flash and gleam. Seth spoke softly to the pair of greys hired from the London Mews in town.

'Come up, Bonny, come up, Major,' he called and they whickered with pleasure, ears pricked, sensing an outing. They allowed Seth to fasten buckles to the pole while Tansy emerged from the kitchen carrying rugs and a picnic hamper. She was excited and hoped their destination was to be the Moor which beckoned across the fields and villages to the north. She'd been to Dartmoor only a few times in all her seventeen years, once in the minister's trap with her father and once in a Sunday School brake one Bank Holiday, but never in a carriage and never on a work day.

'What shall I do with these, Seth?' she asked, and he took the hamper and stowed it in the boot.

'The rugs can go inside,' he said, opening the door with a bow for Tansy and she, pretending to be a lady of rank, stepped in. After arranging the rugs she admired her reflection in the mirror above the seat.

''Tis gonna be better than polishing brass and washing crocks, ain't it, Seth? Do you know where we'm going yet?' she begged to know, but Seth couldn't or wouldn't say.

'Just have to wait and see won't 'ee, my lover,' he teased, and with a click of his tongue encouraged the horses to walk round to the front steps where Beatrice Vallance and Miss Emma stood waiting.

'This is excellent, Howell. Well done indeed. Very well done!' Coming from Beatrice, this was praise of the highest order.

'Come along, Emma. Let's go while the sun's out. You can ride outside, Drewe.'

Tansy climbed up beside Seth who seized whip and reins, slapping Bonny and Major lightly on their glossy rumps and the carriage moved off down the drive. Tansy waved to the other servants gathered near the house to see them off. She caught a glimpse of Janet Luscombe standing at the Mistress's bedroom window, a look of malevolence on her face.

Charles Vallance had left early for the Mill where, in the absence of Seth to bring him home in the gig, Harold Yeo had been ordered to leave his bench and tether Tinker to a small patch of grass close to the Mill in Bradley Lane.

Caroline Vallance waved Beatrice's party off from the front steps, relieved to be free of the Holy Terror for the day. She rang for Hetty.

'Tell Cook I shall be out to lunch – I'm going to town with Maude Westaway. I shall be back in time for tea. I should think my mother-in-law will be home by then.' She smiled and looked into her dressing-table mirror, then re-arranged a curl which was escaping her upswept coiffure. 'Send Luscombe up, will you Westcott, please.' She then opened up her wardrobe and selected two gowns from the rail.

'I want you to begin shortening hems, Janet. *The Times* says Paris is showing shorter skirts this spring. Ankle-length please, Luscombe. Begin on the grey and magenta but just pin them until I can try them on. Four inches to start with, then we'll see.'

'Are the shorter skirts just for daytime, M'am?' Janet wanted to know and Caroline nodded.

'It seems necklines are changing too, getting lower I believe, but let's try the hems first. I'll see how they look when I get back.' She put on a silver grey coat, adjusted the fur collar and added a flower-trimmed cloche. Collecting gloves and bag she went to sit downstairs in the drawing-room window to watch for Maude Westaway. It was unthinkable that she had no means of travelling about during the day. Whenever she mentioned a brougham to Charles he put her off.

'Automobiles are the coming thing now, Caroline. Just be patient. Next year we'll see about getting something. Then we'll know which way the war's going. If orders for serge keep up we could afford a Pannard or,' and here his normally business-like face became dreamy with longing, 'or perhaps a Daimler. Then you can have the gig all the time,' he added.

Yet, thought Caroline, here was his mother demanding and getting whatever she wanted. 'Tidd'n right, tidd'n fair,' she muttered to herself, lapsing into the language of her youth.

❧

Seth had held in the horses as they descended the steep curves of Courtenay Road into town, keeping them to a slow walk until they went over St Mary's bridge and out on to the Ashburton Road. Now, as they entered the world of rutted lanes bordered with the fresh green of early spring, he clicked his tongue and the pair broke into a brisk trot. The scent of honeysuckle hung on the air as Tansy held on to the handrail and let her body move with the motion of the carriage.

She felt sorry for Miss Emma, stuck inside with her grandmother. When they reached Ashburton, Beatrice Vallance tapped with her stick on the roof of the carriage and, as soon as Seth found some space in North Street, she descended to walk about the town and Miss Emma emerged looking pale and shaky and was promptly sick outside the baker's shop.

'You'd better sit outside from now on, Emma,' Beatrice announced in disgust. 'Fetch some water, Drewe.' Tansy hurried inside the shop where the woman behind the counter suggested, 'Best to have a cup o-tay my lover.' As soon as Emma drank the tea she recovered. They swapped places and Tansy found herself scrutinised by the steely gaze of Beatrice Vallance as she sat opposite and began to enjoy this new experience. She was surprised at the difference between riding outside in the fresh air and riding inside. Inside it was hot and stuffy and the rolling motion of the vehicle more pronounced. Beatrice seemed oblivious to both but Tansy thought she should speak up before it became too late for her.

'Could we open the window, M'am?' she plucked up the courage to ask as nausea began to creep over her. Beatrice herself bent forward and lowered the window. 'Don't want another sickly girl or we won't enjoy our picnic, will we?' She laughed and leaning forward, pointed out the Dart as it bubbled towards them below the road. When they reached Poundsgate, Seth stopped and politely but firmly asked the young women to walk the steeply winding road, leaving Beatrice sole passenger.

'You must think of the horses,' he said.

'I don't think much of this for a treat!' Emma exclaimed as she picked her way over the stony surface in her best shoes. I hope she doesn't want me to come again. I'd rather have gone into town with Mama. The new spring fashions are in at Badcock's and I've been promised a new dress for my birthday.' She pouted and moaned as Tansy took her hand and pulled her up the steep incline.

They stopped at Dartmeet and Seth spread rugs by the river, unharnessing Bonny and Major to graze free in the meadow. Tansy leapt agilely from rock to rock, balancing sure-footed as a goat, but when Emma tried to follow her example she slipped and fell in, soaking shoes and dress. Beatrice laughed at her but, when the time came to set off, wrapped Emma in rugs and settled her in the corner of the carriage where, exhausted, she fell asleep.

'We may as well complete the circle,' Beatrice said to Seth. 'Go back by the Forest Inn at Hexworthy, then past Combestone Tor. The evenings are light so there's no need to worry on that score,' she added when he looked doubtful.

''Twill be nigh on fifty mile time we gets back to Newton,' he expostulated, but Beatrice had made up her mind.

'Nonsense Howell!' she retorted, climbing back into the carriage and inviting Tansy to ride inside. She rapped smartly on the roof and Seth, sighing in resignation, gathered up the reins and they set off again towards Two Bridges, turning off through Huccaby. They paused opposite Jolly Lane Cott so Beatrice could tell Tansy and Emma the story of Sally and Tom Satterley, who built the cottage in just one day.

'How was that possible?' Tansy wanted to know, gazing at the substantial building across the river. Beatrice smiled and explained, 'It was the custom, you see, that if a man could build a house in a single day on common land and have a fire burning in the hearth by nightfall it was his with enough land around to support him and his family. That's what Tom and Sally did with the help of their families just sixty years ago.' Tansy's eyes shone at the sheer audacity of the scheme.

'How did they get away with it? Where was the farmer who owned the land?'

Beatrice laughed and went on to explain, 'They chose Midsummer's Day when he was off enjoying himself at Holne Village Ram Roast. Tom's dead now but Sally still lives there.'

Now Tansy wanted to see this sterling character who had not only helped build her own house but managed to live there ever since.

'Can't we go and call on her, M'am?' she wanted to know. 'I'd love to meet her.' Beatrice shook her head in deference to Seth's reminder of the distance they still had to cover to reach Newton.

'Perhaps another day – now we have just one more stop to make and that's Combestone Tor.'

Tansy and Emma were to alight again to climb the steep and winding road past the old miners' inn at Hexworthy, but this time Emma refused to leave the carriage and it was the old woman who walked with Tansy. As they approached the towering granite rocks ahead Tansy sensed a growing excitement emanating from her.

'Give me your hand, Drewe,' she commanded and she and Tansy set off across the heather and gorse to the Tor, which towered high above the valley of the Dart. Together they stood looking down at the river, sparkling invitingly below. Neither spoke for several minutes until their attention was caught by a soft mewing and Beatrice pointed to a pair of large birds circling high above them in ever-descending spirals.

'Buzzards,' she exclaimed, and Tansy laughed and clapped her hands with the sheer joy of being at one with the Moor.

'Look, the hawthorn's out,' she said, looking at the hillside where the warm spring sun had brought firm buds out in white blossom.

'Charles' father brought me here when we first married.' Beatrice was speaking in a slow soft voice, her normal brusqueness gone. 'He loved every tor and combe of Dartmoor.' Her eyes became dreamy. 'His father farmed down there,' she pointed, 'over there d'you see?' Tansy's gaze followed her pointing finger to a cluster of soft granite buildings nestling tight into the lee of the boulder-strewn hillside.

'Yes, that's it. Look's as if it had grown from the hillside, don't it? Not at all as if it had been built by man!' Beatrice turned to face Tansy, eyes moist behind the veil. 'I had an instinct about you, Drewe,' she said, 'had a feeling you would love the Moor as much as I. What's your given name?' And when Tansy told her she laughed and nodded.

'Well I must say Tansy suits you very well.' She turned to look once more across the valley and Tansy thought of Martin Webber working somewhere out there. She thought too of Janet Luscombe's words and asked herself if she believed her account of Martin's supposed interest in her sister Fanny. Most of all she felt intoxicated by the space all around, the stretch of moor to the distant hills whose names she was learning for the first time, feeling a sudden longing to fly, fly free as the buzzards circling overhead. If she could take off and circle the Moor she would find Martin and, if she did, would he be waiting for her? She would soon know, she thought – next Monday was the Kingsteignton Ram Roast and step-dance competition and she had persuaded Hetty to change days off with her. For this favour she would take Hetty's place, wait at table on Wednesday, and Wednesday next was to be the day of Beatrice Vallance's dinner party. Up till today she had been filled with apprehension at the thought of it. Now, coming so close to the old woman, her fears had evaporated and she felt a confidence growing inside her that had not been there before.

Suddenly she became aware of Seth's approaching figure.

'If we'm to get back to Newton in time for supper, Ma'm, we should start now.' Beatrice sighed as she turned away from this place of past memory, past happiness.

'Very well, Howell,' she agreed, 'better hurry, hadn't we? Don't want to do anything to upset your Mistress, do we?' adding in a soft voice, 'You shall come out again with me, Tansy Drewe.'

It was gone seven o'clock before Bonny and Major plodded wearily up the hill to Courtenay House, the carriage covered in dust, wheels caked in mud. Supper had been kept waiting over an hour and Cook was furious, a fury she took out on Tansy.

'My sweetbread casserole is all dried up, and the rice pudden burnt. I'm not putting up with this caper every day I can tell 'ee.' Tansy, with stars in her eyes and the warmth of the day rosy in her cheeks, did her best to pacify Cook, who merely grunted.

'Don't 'ee go traipsin' about wi' Holy Terror next Wednesday,' she roared, 'or I'll have 'ee's guts for garters, make no mistake!'

✣ Chapter Four ✣

Lustleigh

The next two days passed in a whirl of preparation for the coming Whitsuntide. Bells jangled constantly in the kitchen as plans were made and remade at the whim of the Holy Terror. All the families on Bowden were involved as Thursday, the night of 'The Messiah', approached.

Rosemary Brimmacombe, Tansy's friend, on account of her musical ability was to turn pages for the deputy organist from Exeter Cathedral. Evan Williams had been given a place in the choir at the last minute.

'He should be singing the tenor part with that voice,' Beatrice Williams declared, but was restrained by Charles.

'The principals have all been engaged, Mama,' he protested, 'there will be plenty of opportunity in the future for Evan to perform. There's the Gilbert and Sullivan in the winter,' Charles added, concluding, 'Besides I hardly think he's recovered enough to sing a large solo part.'

Then Beatrice asked, 'Are there to be refreshments after the concert?' and when Caroline replied that she thought not, she exploded with indignation.

'No refreshments – why that's unthinkable!' she bristled. 'At home 'tis expected,' and when Caroline pointed out, 'Exeter is a city, Mama, not a small working town like Newton Abbot,' Beatrice snorted, 'What has that to do with it, pray?! The principal singers will expect it, besides, it's such a splendid opportunity to raise funds for the chapel.' She turned to Charles and demanded, 'You, Charles, must arrange refreshments now before it's too late.'

A hurried meeting of the Chapel Elders was held that evening and Charles, embarrassed and infuriated by Beatrice's interference, promptly offered Cook to do the baking. Edward Drewe, aware through Tansy of the extra work caused for the staff at Courtenay House whenever the Holy Terror visited, insisted that the chapel women be asked to bake a small batch of cakes or scones.

Eva Drewe sighed, sensing a precedent, but reached for a bowl anyway and began to sift flour, salt and cinnamon. She rubbed in butter, adding sugar they could ill afford and wondered how much longer Beatrice Vallance was staying in Newton. The only one who seemed to be enjoying her visit was Tansy.

'What are you making, Mother?' Robert and James, the twins, pressed round the table. 'Is it pudding?' When Eva said that she was making teacakes for the chapel, they asked, 'Can we have some when they're ready?' They hung round watching as Eva warmed milk and added yeast, making a well in the centre of the flour and pouring them in. 'After school,' she laughed, 'if you're good.'

'Can we have one for Emrys?' Robert asked and Eva nodded, laughing ruefully as she watched her batch reducing by the minute.

'How's Emrys getting on at school?' Eva enquired. Emrys was the same age as the twins.

'He's ever so clever, Mother – can do all the sums in a minute and knows the name of every country in the whole world, but the others laugh at him. Why does he wear such funny clothes?' Robert asked as, although hand-me-downs were common among the working-class families of the town, mothers took care to disguise the fact as much as was humanly possible.

'His Mam's sick,' Eva replied as she kneaded sultanas into the bun dough and, covering the bowl, set it to rise in front of the fire. 'Now off you go or you'll be late,' she chided, and the twins scuttled out of the living-room and set off downhill for school.

✱

At Courtenay House Caroline and Beatrice were locked in battle over the use of the carriage. Caroline was looking forward to arriving at the concert that evening in the newly refurbished vehicle, but Beatrice wanted to use it during the day to visit Lustleigh.

'Time is running out for me,' she announced dramatically at breakfast as she lifted lids from silver chafing-dishes in search of her favourite kidneys. 'I must be back in Exeter for the spring concert at the Assembly Rooms – they look to me to support our city orchestra,' and would brook no change to her plans. What's more, she took Tansy with her, thus incurring Cook's wrath.

"Tis worse'n ever, this visit,' she declared, 'Now she's took my spare pair of hands,' and she fanned her red perspiring face and, suddenly feeling constricted by her corset, sat down with a bump. Hetty, not liking the look of Cook's high colour, fetched smelling salts from the medicine cupboard and held them under her nose.

Meanwhile, Tansy sat high beside Seth on the carriage as it bowled along the bottom of the Wrey Valley on their way to Lustleigh. She laughed aloud as the steep-sided valley unfolded in front of them; bluebells and late primroses grew in drifts down the fields which lined the road and clusters of grey granite farmsteads dotted the hillsides. Tansy scrutinised each gate as they passed, looking for the name of Martin's farm, without success.

When they reached Lustleigh, Beatrice took Tansy to visit Biddy Pidsley in her tiny cottage on the green. Small and neat, she sat in the window of the cottage, lace pillow on her lap. Tansy watched, fascinated as Biddy's fingers crossed and re-crossed bobbins, moving pins until a pattern of violets and roses began to grow on the black velvet.

'There's a pattern called 'Tansy',' she said, 'Make you a piece for your wedding day, shall us?' and Tansy laughed and shook her head. She left Biddy making tea for Beatrice Vallance and went to the Post Office on an errand for her mother. Bags of mail lined the counter, exuding the smells of fish and game. Packs of butter, honey and cream stood labelled and ready to be collected. Then, her errand completed, Tansy wandered about the village green. She looked in at the store and there was Rosemary Brimmacombe's cousin, the May Queen, Thirza Hill.

'Why, if 'tisn't Tansy Drewe,' she exclaimed, her round face breaking into a beaming smile. Then her eyes clouded and her lower lip quivered as she told Tansy, 'I'm going to Moreton into service with the Misses Palk and I doesn't want to leave home.' Now she broke into loud sobs and Tansy put her arms as far round the plump figure as she could, to comfort her.

'Moreton's not so far away, Thirza. You'll be able to walk home and see your mother on a Sunday when 'tis your day off. Think of the grand house you'll be living in, the experience you'll get. Once you've learnt how to light fires, make beds and wait at table – why, then you'll be able to get a position wherever you want.' But Thirza sniffed and grizzled and looked more miserable.

'Don't want to be a kitchen maid. They say 'tis hard work and, besides, I doesn't want to leave home.' Tansy, remembering how homesick she'd been during her first few weeks at Courtenay House, how her back ached with all the lifting, the black ingrained into her hands from cleaning grates, was at a loss what to say.

'How old are you, Thirza?' and when the May Queen told her, all Tansy could do was press her hands with hers and smile encouragingly. After all, fourteen was no age to be leaving home but then, thought Tansy, the Hills had ten children in the family which must be hard on anyone, having to keep that number warm, fed and clothed. Thirza's departure would be counted as a blessing.

'You must get them to write to you every week,' Tansy urged, but this proved of no comfort to Thirza who looked even more dejected.

''Tis only me and Henry can read and write and I can't see him sitting down to put pen to paper.'

Now Tansy linked arms with Thirza and drew her from the store to wander about the green. They stopped to watch Seth Howell as he talked to the blacksmith at the forge. They talked of weather, crops and the war in South Africa, and their voices were accompanied by the ring of iron on anvil as an apprentice gently blew the bellows and sparks flew dangerously near the damped-down thatch of the roof.

At last Beatrice Vallance emerged from Biddy's cottage with her parcel of lace and sat in the carriage patiently waiting for Seth to come. Tansy called him to 'Come quick,' expecting a tirade from the Holy Terror, but none came. Instead she opened the parcel and held out two triangular pieces for Tansy to see.

'Look at the pattern. Isn't it exquisite? Biddy tells me it's called 'Violet'.'

Tansy admired the dainty flower shapes pinned to the velvet backing. 'Where would I get such work in Exeter?' Beatrice went on, 'I shall get Janet to replace the inserts in my summer gowns with these.' She smiled, a look of peace on her face. 'You must have a piece made, Tansy. True Lovers' knot perhaps?' She looked at Tansy and asked, 'Are you walking out?' Tansy shook her head, blushing furiously, thinking of Martin Webber.

'No, Ma'm,' she said, then thought of her own grandmother's lace which lay in the cabinet beside her parents' bed. That was taken out on special days to be looked at as a treat. Looked at, yes, but never worn. The difference, she supposed, was that Beatrice Vallance could afford to wear her lace until it fell into holes. She could afford to replace it. Her mother could not. No, Sarah Ann Thomas' bequest remained untouched, to be passed on to Norah or herself at some future date.

Deep in thought, neither occupant of Absolam Vallance's splendid carriage noticed the quickening pace of the horses as a train raced beside them, rails and road separated by a narrow strip of spring corn. Neither noticed anything amiss until the engine thundered overhead as it crossed Caseley Bridge. And it was only Seth's shouts that broke into their respective reveries as he tried to control Bonny and Major.

'Whoa, come back. Whoa, hey up.' He hauled on the reins as the horses reared and plunged in fright at the black monster which seemed to be chasing them. Seth fought for their heads, pulled at the foaming mouths while bits dug into lolling tongues. He had almost brought the pair under control when they went round a bend in the road and the nearside wheel hit a stone at the bottom of the hedge. The wheel rattled then wobbled for a moment before it flew from its axle and rolled slowly across the road into the opposite hedge. There it lay, spokes shattered, iron sprung. The carriage ground to a sudden halt and sank sideways on to three wheels. Beatrice and Tansy struggled up from the corner of the carriage where both had been thrown.

'Are you all right, Ma'm?' Tansy asked as Seth hauled them up and out.

'Yes, yes. I'm perfectly all right, no bones broken.' Beatrice straightened her hat and veil and joined Seth and Tansy as they stood back in awe, looking at the crazy angle of the vehicle, its pole pointing towards the sky as the horses struggled to keep their feet.

'Quick, Tansy, hold their heads while I release the harness,' and she hastened without fear to the lathered mouths and held tight to their head collars.

'Best get help,' Seth said as he tied the sweating, shivering animals to a nearby gate and looked enquiringly at Beatrice Vallance.

'I noticed a track a little way back, just where the horses began to bolt. Drewe, go and find someone. I'll wait here.' And she stood, shaken but calm and erect, fanning herself with her parcel of lace.

Tansy set off up the rough track which ran between thick beech hedges until bits of straw on the ground and the clucking of hens told her she was heading for a habitation and that it was feeding time. The farm gate stood ajar and she slipped through into a yard where the last of the previous summer's hay stood in tumbling ricks along one side. On the other ran a row of linhay, tallett and barn which sloped gently downhill, ending in a tall granary. From inside the granary came the sound of singing. A sweet voice declaiming the joys of cuckoos in spring. Around the steps hens and geese clucked and gobbled, waiting to be fed. Tansy ran lightly up the steps but couldn't open the door.

'Please can you help me – we've broken a wheel on our carriage.' The singing stopped but there came no reply. Tansy hammered on the door until suddenly the latch inside flew up and the door swung out, nearly knocking Tansy off her feet. She came face to face with a vision in flowered cotton, a girl younger than herself with curly brown hair, pink and white cheeks and huge blue eyes over-topped by lashes as heavy as summer moths. A provocative cupid bow of a mouth completed the picture that presented itself.

'Where have you sprung from?' the vision demanded, standing arms akimbo, hands set on hips above a tiny waist – her figure so dainty as to make Tansy feel large and awkward.

'From Newton – no, I mean,' she felt flustered, unsure of herself, 'We're going back to Newton from Lustleigh, only our carriage's lost a wheel.'

'Our carriage's lost a wheel,' the pretty voice mimicked, 'and what do you expect me to do about it?'

Tansy's patience began to fade. 'Is there a man about to help?'

'You've got red hair,' the vision went on, ignoring Tansy's plea for help. Tansy felt her colour and temper rise together.

'How observant you are, Miss! Yes, I've got red hair,' she said, controlling her temper with difficulty. A picture rose in her mind of Beatrice Vallance waiting in the road, her foot beginning to tap in her elegant black laced boots.

'Will you please tell me where I can find the farmer.' She added sarcastically, 'This is a farm isn't it?'

The vision at last made up her mind to come down the granary steps and involve herself in conversation. 'That's right, 'tis Staddens and I can take you to the Missus, she'll know what to do.'

The shock of finding herself at Martin's family farm was so great that for the first time in her life Tansy was at a loss for words.

'I've a sister works over to Newton,' the girl rushed on, 'works at Courtenay House for they Vallances,' and Tansy received a double shock. She realised at once that the girl standing opposite her must be Janet Luscombe's sister.

'Are you Fanny Luscombe?' she demanded, and as Fanny nodded interest quickened between them. 'I work with your sister Janet.'

Fanny stopped and the expression on her face changed from friendly curiosity to one of animosity.

'So you must be Tansy Drewe.' She spat out the words and began to walk in a circle round Tansy. 'She've told me all about you,' she sneered, 'red hair and all.'

'Do hurry, please.' Tansy wrung her hands over this fresh delay. She paced up and down while Fanny leisurely and deliberately fetched a pan of mash from the granary and began slowly to throw it to the squawking hens. Tansy could stand it no longer. Dancing up the steps to the granary, she grabbed handfuls of mash and flung it far and wide across the yard. Upsetting the pan between them, it fell with a clang onto the stone yard. Both girls tumbled after it down the steps – the first to get up, Fanny seized a clump of Tansy's hair and pulled it hard.

'Ow! Ow!' Tansy reacted as soon as she was on her feet. Letting her itching fingers have their way at last she slapped the pink and white cheeks hard. Breathing fast the girls eyed one another, waiting for a new opening.

'What be goin' on here I'd like to know?' The warm slow drawl familiar in Tansy's memory arrested their actions. Both girls looked at Martin Webber who stood waiting, red cheeks matched by the 'kerchief at the neck of his work shirt. Red-faced, Fanny struggled for words.

'She's interfering with my fowls,' then paused for a moment before blurting out, as if it explained everything, 'She works with my sister Janet over to Newton. She's Tansy Drewe.'

And now Martin looked closer at Fanny's assailant. 'Why so 'tis. Fancy seeing you here,' and he laughed at the girls. 'Not much to fall out about, is it? A flock of fowls?' Tansy fought to regain her dignity. She pressed her lips to prevent the anger at Fanny from bubbling over. She confined herself to explaining her errand. Martin watched as Tansy tried to tuck tendrils of hair under the straw hat which had fallen off into the dust of the yard. He thought she looked adorable. He noticed the round bosom as it rose and fell under the plain grey frock. He hardly noticed Fanny, the prettier by far, who now stood glaring at Tansy. Fanny wondered if Janet had told Tansy Drewe that Martin was about to propose to her which, at the time she'd spoken the words to Janet, seemed a possibility. Martin, meanwhile, thought that Tansy Drewe looked every bit as lovely as she had on the day they met at Lustleigh. He wished heartily that he'd come round the corner of the granary a moment earlier. It was obvious that neither girl was telling the real reason for their fight.

'I'll get Father,' he said, 'and I'll tell Mother what's happened.' He strode easily away with Fanny and Tansy hurrying in his wake, yards apart. Tansy, who had only seen Martin in his Sunday best looking rather stiff and embarrassed, liked the air of confidence he wore with his workaday cords and gaiters. Liked the way the bowler sat on the back of his thick, curly hair. Fanny followed Tansy's gaze.

'Keep away from him,' she hissed as the trio reached the farmhouse, 'he's already spoken for.'

A middle-aged woman sat plucking a chicken among a pile of feathers while a pile of cats slept at her feet and a black and white collie dog growled and ran, head low, at Tansy the stranger. A word from Martin shut its noise and it retreated to lie once more on the sunlit porch.

'What are you doing now, Fanny?' the woman demanded. 'There's butter needed for supper. Haven't you finished feeding the fowls yet?' And Tansy's adversary, a sulky look to her pretty mouth, slunk away. After a few brief words Martin hurried away down the slope, through a gate into a field, while the woman beckoned Tansy.

'I'm Sarah Webber. Martin's gone to fetch his father. Please tell your mistress she's welcome to come and rest while the wheel's mended.' Her voice, low and melodious, acted like a warm embrace. Her smile produced an inner light which softened the severe face with its crown of dark brown hair, parted in the middle and drawn into a knot at the back of her neck. Tansy found herself looking into eyes a deep blue mirror of her son's and she knew at once where Martin got his warmth and strength of character.

⁕

Sarah Webber dropped a curtsey as Beatrice and Tansy reached the house.

'If you will please to come in and take a dish of tea?' she invited and Beatrice Vallance had to bend her tall figure to pass under the low beam and enter a passage between shippon and living quarters. Her head struck a bunch of mint hanging from the central beam of the dark room.

''Tis to stop they dratted flies,' Sarah Webber exclaimed, hastily wiping with her apron a settle, which stood invitingly to one side of the open hearth. Instead of taking the proffered seat Beatrice walked over to the fireplace, set back under a giant granite lintel. A smell of bread, peat and herbs hung on the air.

'Do you still use your bread oven, Mrs Webber?' she asked, and at Sarah's nod continued, 'And what fuel do you use nowadays?' Sarah Webber, who had hovered nervously by, forgot her inhibitions as she explained the changes that were about to take place at Staddens.

'Yes, I bake twice a week. My son, Martin, cuts ash for the oven. Makes a lovely loaf does that.'

Tansy thanked her lucky stars for the accident that had brought them here. Not a moment too soon if Fanny and Janet Luscombe were to be believed. Fanny was certainly pretty enough to capture the heart of any man, Tansy thought, as Sarah paced about the room explaining.

'Peat fire is goin' next month, Ma'm. Amos is bringing a range from Moreton. 'Twill make life easier for all of us.' And she opened the bread oven door to show the clean stone base. But now Beatrice was extolling the virtue of having sons, adding her account of how Charles Vallance had instigated the restoration of Absolam's carriage which now lay useless in the Moreton Road. This led to the mutual discovery that Absolam had grown up at Combestone Farm where, before marrying Amos Webber, Sarah had worked as a dairy maid. She and Beatrice exchanged looks of complete empathy.

In spite of the sun the room was cool, light restricted to a tiny window set in a deep recess.

'Amos has arranged for the stone mason to put in another window,' Sarah said and led them to the far corner of the room where a cupboard was set into the wall. She pulled open the latch to disclose a leather-bound bible. Beside it lay a small box. Sarah took the book from its place.

''Tis Amos' family bible, always kept here, but now we're having a new dresser built,' she pointed to the long panelled inner wall, 'why, we'll find a place for it there.' Next she took out a small box, shining with beeswax, and held it out to Beatrice for inspection. 'There's the children's baby curls. First time of cutting.' Tansy strained forward to see the coils of hair lying in the box and wondered which of the blonde twists had belonged to Martin. 'The dark curls belonged to my girls. Both lost, both gone with whooping cough.' She wiped her eyes with the corner of a snowy apron.

Beatrice laid a sympathetic hand on her arm and Tansy looked longingly at the settle. Her feet ached with all the walking of the last few days but Beatrice showed no signs of fatigue. Instead she turned back through the door into the passage.

'Do you still keep cows in the shippon?' But now Sarah shook her head, throwing open the door to reveal Fanny slapping thick clotted cream with her hand.

''Tis the quickest way to make butter if you're in a hurry,' Sarah explained as Beatrice inspected the rows of gleaming pans and milk pails.

'Been used as a dairy ever since I married Amos and came to live here. He built a byre next the linhay for the cows. 'Tis handy to have the dairy just across the passage – saves a wetting many a time.'

'If you wouldn't think it an impertinence,' Beatrice said, 'I would like to see the garden.' Sarah blushed with pleasure. The garden was her pride and whenever her chores came to a temporary halt she would take trowel and hoe and work on her beloved flowers and vegetables.

'These are my herbs.' She paused where sun-drenched plants grew in an aromatic pattern by the cottage wall. 'Would 'ee care to take a bunch?' she invited Beatrice, who thanked her. She picked rosemary, sage, tarragon, feverfew and fennel and bound them up with a piece of straw and handed them to Tansy to look after. Next they passed through a little gate into an enclosure, divided by a cobbled path – one side neat with rows of peas, beans and salads, rhubarb and gooseberries, the other side a mass of flowers. Sarah produced a pair of scissors from her apron pocket and snipped until a bunch of Beatrice's favourites grew into a fragrant bouquet.

'Thank you, thank you. How kind. I had forgotten such flowers were still grown. Such a blue the larkspur, the colour of a summer sky,' and Tansy muttered under her breath, 'The colour of my Martin's eyes,' while Beatrice continued, 'The parks in Exeter are so stiff and formal, heliotrope and salvias are not really to my taste. You have got a garden to be proud of, Mrs Webber. Cook shall have the herbs for her fish and the flowers will grace the dinner table at Courtenay House when my guests come on Wednesday night.'

As they re-entered the house they heard the crunch of boots and Tansy held her breath as the sound came nearer and nearer, then let it go as they faded away.

'There go the men folk,' Sarah said to Fanny, who hovered awkwardly in the doorway awaiting instructions from her mistress.

'Now you must surely be ready for your tea,' Sarah said, setting a small oak table in front of the fire, and at last Beatrice sat and indicated that Tansy should join her. Sarah brought out rose-patterned china from an old dresser, then added sweet bread rolls and a dish of treacle. Last of all came Fanny, bearing a large blue and white striped bowl of clotted cream.

''Tis all there is M'am, but you're truly welcome. Calls it Thunder and Lightnin' us do, here in the Valley.'

Beatrice beckoned Tansy to take a roll and spread it liberally with cream then treacle. The combined sweetness was not really to Beatrice's taste but she did her best, suggesting that perhaps Seth would welcome something when the men had finished with the wheel. She drank her tea and Sarah offered her the use of an upper room to make her toilet. Fanny, still furious and reluctant to help Tansy, showed her the earth closet built at the far end of the farmhouse wall and, after drinking two cups of tea, Tansy was very grateful for the relief. She and Beatrice thanked Sarah for her hospitality and slowly retraced their steps down the track to see how the men were progressing.

''Tis almost ready, M'am,' Seth reported as Amos Webber and Martin hammered home a wheel which fortune had seen fit to have available of just the right size and strength.

Tansy's heart beat fast as she stood as close to Martin as she dared, and was rewarded with a blush as he straightened up.

'There, 'tis done – that'll see you back to Newton. I can collect the wheel when next I comes to market,' Amos Webber said, and Beatrice thanked father and son.

'Mrs Webber has something for you at the house, Seth. We'll wait here quite happily until you've finished. Tansy will look after the horses,' she added, confident in Tansy's capabilities. Tansy was delighted to take this further opportunity to catch and hold Martin's eye.

'Fancy seeing you in this way,' she said as he came round beside her. 'Of all the places to cast a wheel, that it should have happened so close to Staddens!'

Their hands, hers small and neat, his large and rough, collided as he ran his fingers over the shining harness.

'Indeed, I never thought to see you here,' he smiled, a smile of such warmth that Tansy forgot her aching feet and the pile of chores that would be waiting for her back at Courtenay House. She held her breath, wondering if he would mention the Ram Roast again and, as if he could read her thoughts, he asked, 'You'm still coming to Kingsteignton Whit Monday?' and she answered in a voice low enough to prevent Beatrice Vallance from hearing. 'You'll not be taking Fanny Luscombe then?' Martin looked puzzled and replied 'Why ever should I be taking her?' Tansy shrugged. 'Someone told me you and she were courtin',' and was rewarded with his denial, which came swift and sure. 'No, no. There's nothing I'd be less likely to do. Take Fanny Luscombe anywhere.' The emphasis on the name Fanny filled her with a contentment that stayed with her until Seth returned and hitched up the horses.

'I'll ride outside, Ma'm, if that's convenient to you,' Tansy suggested. Then, permission forthcoming, she climbed up beside Seth in order that she could wave to Martin till he was out of sight, happy in the knowledge that both Fanny and Janet Luscombe had been lying when they had averred that Martin Webber was about to propose to Fanny. There and then Tansy made up her mind to say nothing, to keep her knowledge for use at a later date. Seth, who had been given two mugs of cider to slake his thirst, swayed dangerously from side to side as they rolled back down the valley through Bovey to Newton. He sang lustily in a deep bass:

> 'Tom Pearce, Tom Pearce, lend me your grey mare,
> Rife and all, jingle ay oh,
> Wi' Bill Ewer, Jan Brewer, Joe Davey,
> Philly Widpot, George Parsley, Dick Wilson.
> Old Uncle Tom Cobley and all, and all,
> Old Uncle Tom Cobley and all.'

Tansy held her breath, hung on for dear life, and expected at any moment to hear the bang of Beatrice Vallance's stick on the roof, but her stick remained silent and, when they arrived back at Courtenay House, they found the Holy Terror fast asleep, a gentle snoring issuing from her open mouth, her hat tipped over one eye. She awoke with an embarrassed start to discover the lateness of the hour. She declared that she needed no supper but would go straight to the concert.

So Caroline Vallance got her wish after all and arrived at 'The Messiah' in the somewhat dusty splendour of the family carriage. As they drew up outside the chapel Charles Vallance was heard to plead with his mother, 'Tomorrow I would prefer it if you kept your visits to town, Mama. You can have the trap after lunch. Howell and Drewe have their work to do, jobs are getting behind.' But Beatrice had other ideas.

'I'm a little tired, Charles, so perhaps a short visit to the Mill would be a better idea.' Charles sighed as she added, 'I will come down with you straight after breakfast – will nine o'clock be convenient?'

※

Meanwhile, when Tansy reached the kitchen Hetty Westcott, normally so sunny tempered, glared at her.

'Whatever next, Tansy. Meals is never on time when you and the Holy Terror go galli-vantin' about the countryside. Cook's been poorly. She had one of her turns just after you went off this morning. All because you weren't here to help.'

As much as Tansy protested and tried to tell of the accident to the carriage, the atmosphere in the kitchen stayed cold as ice. Cook made Tansy clean every piece of the Vallance family silver instead of letting her off for the evening to attend 'The Messiah', as she had promised earlier in the week.

Nothing, however, could dispel the aura of happiness surrounding Tansy as she looked at her reflection in the huge silver punch bowl. She imagined she could see Martin's warm suntanned face looking over her shoulder as she polished. She must hold Hetty to her word. She must go to the Ram Roast on Monday.

✢ Chapter Five ✢

Ram Roast

When Monday arrived Hetty needed a lot of persuading to change her day off with Tansy. Since her mother's death she had been moody and sad, missing the support Kezia Westcott had given her only child.

'I wish Jack could come home,' Hetty said to Cook, 'or write. If only I knew where he was. It seems so long since he sailed.'

As if by magic a letter arrived for her by the second post. Her pale wan face became animated, her eyes shone and her hands shook in her haste to open the travel-stained envelope.

'He says it's blistering hot. Here's a lot about the horses. Let's see. Yes, he's all right. With Kitchener in the Ashanti.'

Now there came murmurs from her audience. 'With Kitchener, then he'll be all right. Kitchener's our best General.' 'Fancy Ashanti – where be that to?'

Hetty went on reading. 'There's more about his blessed horses. Still in their winter coats!' Now Hetty turned the sheet of writing paper over. 'Says there's not enough forage for them, or water. Says they die of exhaustion and heat stroke after the battles.'

'That's terrible.' Tansy, soft-hearted as always when it came to any creature in trouble, tried to imagine the heat, the thirst, the pain. 'Tidd'n right,' she exploded, 'Men decide if they want to fight. Poor dumb creatures don't have no choice. Tidd'n right.'

Then the breakfast-room bell jangled and Tansy offered to clear for Hetty, who stood clutching Jack's letter, tears of relief pouring down her cheeks. It seemed as if the letter had acted as a catalyst for the pent-up grief for her mother that Hetty had kept to herself over the last weeks. She blew her nose hard and accepted Tansy's offer.

'Westcott have heard from her Jack, Ma'm.' She bobbed to Caroline Vallance before clearing dishes form the table and her mistress explained to Beatrice, 'Westcott's man is in the 2nd Devons. Left for South Africa in April.' She turned to Tansy. 'That's good, I'm very glad she's heard at last. That's very good.' Why, she'm human after all, Tansy thought as she carried the heavy tray downstairs into the kitchen and, seeing Hetty's change of mood, took the opportunity of pleading with her once more to change days off.

'Yes, Tansy. That'll suit me very well. I can go down to Torquay on the new motor bus tomorrow to see Jack's mother. She'll want to see the letter and know Jack's all right. Perhaps she'll have heard too. Yes, Tansy, you go.'

Tansy rushed through the breakfast dishes, made up fires and ran headlong down 148 steps to Southernhay. She stopped halfway to call for Rosemary, who had the Bank Holiday off from the Vallance's Mill.

'Come on, Rose, Hetty's changed her mind. I can go to the Ram Roast after all. She's heard from her Jack. Real cock-a-hoop she is.' And she badgered Rosemary to go and get ready. 'Come on, Rose, or we'll miss the fun.' She paced up and down the Brimmacombe's living-room where Bessie Brimmacombe sat nursing a sick chicken.

'Stop that, Tansy. You'm upsetting my Clara,' she declared as she rocked back and forth, holding the ailing bird. Tightly wrapped in a piece of old sheet, she held the startled bird close to her chest, its beady eyes were almost bolting from its head until, suddenly, Bessie decided it was better and released the unfortunate creature, who promptly fled out through the back door to join its fellow fowls in the garden.

'If 'ee's going to the Ram Roast then 'ee'd best take some bread and cheese with 'ee,' Bessie suggested, but Tansy shook her head impatiently – 'No, no. We're going to have roast ram. It tastes so good cooked outdoors, all crisp and brown.' She lifted her muslin dress to show neat feet shod in black buttoned boots. 'Come on, Rose!'

'You'm an optimist, Tansy,' Rosemary said, glancing at the gathering clouds. 'Don't look too good to me. You'm gonna get awful wet if it rains, Tansy.' But Tansy ignored Rosemary's dire warning and danced off across the garden and out through the gate.

At the bottom of the steps Tansy turned to Rosemary. 'Let's go and call for Blodwen Williams, see if she can come.' And the girls set off, leaving Jimmy sitting by the fire opposite Bessie Brimmacombe. As usual he had a piece of wood in his hands, preferring to spend the day, his day off, with his carving rather than go to the Ram Roast.

At the top of Bowden Hill, Gwynneth Williams was up and about. She was busy pegging clothes in rows across the backyard. Further lines were hung from posts at the edge of the field where Evan had built a pigsty. Blodwen and Myfanwy hung up socks and aprons.

'Yes, Blod, you go. Tied here all day, the change will do you good. Myfanwy will watch the clouds for me, won't you, my pet?' Now she turned to Tansy. 'Blodwen did enjoy coming up to the big house. Do you think Mrs Vallance would give her some more work?'

And when Tansy hesitated, Blowden pressed, 'I can sew well. Good at mending linen. Perhaps you would mention that to Mrs Vallance? Used to wash and mend for the mill owner's wife at Merthyr. I've references if need be.' Tansy promised to ask.

By the time the girls had left town and reached the racecourse they could hear the sound of an organ, and by the time they got to the Fountain at Kingsteignton the smell of roasting meat was strong enough to make their mouths water.

A large tent selling beer and cider was already crowded with men, some of whom swayed dangerously on their feet, even though it was only eleven o'clock in the morning. Stalls sold gingerbread and fairings.

A fortune-teller called to them as they passed her kiosk. 'Read your hands for a shilling, my beauties!' And after a moment's giggling and whispering Tansy was pushed towards the gypsy tent where Romany Rose gazed at her hands for a very long time.

'Aries aren't you?' she queried. 'All fizz and fire.' And Tansy nodded, impressed. 'A long life and a healthy life lies in store for you. You will have two great loves in your life.' She paused, searching Tansy's face. 'But one will outlast the other. Sorrow lies close to your door but,' she added when Tansy's mouth drooped, 'laughter will never be far away.' She looked along the right-hand edge of Tansy's right palm. 'Just the one child I see.' Then abandoning Tansy's hand for her crystal ball, she peered into its depths. 'Watch out, someone is out to make trouble for you in the near future.' Then she pocketed Tansy's shilling and held open the tent flap for Tansy to leave.

'You go, Rose, see what she says about you.' But Rosemary smiled her usual contented smile and refused. 'I know my future, a pianist I'm going to be. Anything else I leave in the lap of the gods.'

'Blodwen, here have this shilling. See what the future has in store for you.' But Blodwen shook her head. 'Thank you for the shilling but if you don't mind I'll buy some fairings for the others at home.'

'Come on then, let's have our treat.' And before they could stop her, Tansy had spent her last shilling on helpings of roast ram from the slowly revolving carcass. Fat dripped into a bath below the animal and small boys from the village darted forward with chunks of bread in their hands. These they dipped into the hot dripping and sucked, repeating the process until fat ran down their chins. Blodwen stood by amazed, and wanted to know why they roasted a ram every year in this way.

''Tis all to do wi' drought hundreds of years ago,' Rosemary explained. 'A ram was sacrificed and water began to flow from a spring at Rydon. This brought an end to the drought. The spring's been flowing ever since.'

'You know so much, Rose.' Blodwen was impressed but Rosemary shrugged, ''Tis Tansy's father tells us about things.'

Then Tansy, who had been looking about her, coloured up and hid between Blodwen and Rosemary. 'There he is,' she whispered as Martin came towards them with another young man, so like him to look at, it had to be his brother. But Martin had seen Tansy and hovered about waiting for her to speak. Rosemary gave her a push and whispered, 'Go on, silly, he's waiting for you to greet him.'

'Hallo, Martin.' Tansy blushed furiously but stood her ground. 'Is this your brother?' Martin introduced Adam to them all. Although the younger man had the same thick brown hair and blue eyes, there the likeness finished. He hadn't the same warmth of expression that communicated itself from Martin.

'There's a roundabout just waiting to fill up,' Martin offered Tansy his arm. 'Will you come and ride the horses with me, Tansy?' She accepted and they set off towards the sound of the hurdy-gurdy.

'Will you come too?' Adam asked, offering an arm each to Blodwen and Rosemary. They crossed the crowded field where ropes and stakes were being set up in preparation for the children's races in the afternoon.

'The others would have loved this!' Blodwen exclaimed, 'Just wait till I tell them. They must come next time. Ifor loves running, always won the races at Merthyr.' And she climbed up on the horse beside Adam. Rosemary turned away in time to see Evan Williams come out of the beer tent, then disappear among a crowd of men.

Martin lifted Tansy up onto the roundabout. 'Why, you're as light as a feather!' he exclaimed, as she tried to decide which horse to ride. 'I want this one' – she decided on a piebald with gilt pommel and blue saddle. Martin jumped onto the companion mount beside her. 'I've never ridden a horse before,' Tansy shouted above the sound of the organ, 'I mean a real one. Have you?' And Martin laughed as the roundabout gathered speed.

'Bless you, of course I have, had a pony when I was young.' Their knees touched as the painted horses surged forward and back and Tansy shrieked in excitement.

'I'm slipping, I'm slipping.' She hung on until Martin flung his arm around her waist and pulled her across to his own horse. 'Hold on tight, I've got you,' he yelled against the noise and flashing lights. Tansy enjoyed the sensation of speed, rushing air against her burning face, the closeness of Martin's strong body against hers – and when the carousel slowed to a stop at last, she wanted more. Martin parted with more coppers and they rode again.

'Your hair smells as fresh as Top Meadow!' he exclaimed as curls escaped from under Tansy's straw hat. She laughed and removed her hat to let her hair blow free until the ride ended and they climbed down from the wooden pegasus. Martin offered, 'Teach you to ride one day if you like,' and Tansy laughed with delight at the thought.

But, when she asked how often Martin rode and he replied, 'Whenever Father can spare us from the plough, ride to hounds in winter do me and Adam,' her face grew angry and she began to stalk away across the grass.

When he caught up with her she rounded on him, 'How could you, Martin? Chase innocent creatures. How could you?' And she stamped her foot at him.

'Hold on, Tansy Drewe,' he grabbed her arm, 'You might wait to hear what I have to say on the matter before you goes off half-cock. You've never seen a chicken house after Mr Reynard has paid his nightly visit.' Martin forced her round to face him. 'Just bites off their heads and leaves 'em. Kills for pleasure does that one, not for food. Christmas time he's after our turkeys. Then we have to sit up all night to watch.' Tansy felt silly. After all, what did she know of keeping fowls when she had lived in town all her life.

Rosemary limped up to them. 'What are you two discussing so serious like?' she wanted to know and when she heard the subject was foxes went on to corroborate Martin's account of a fox's habit. 'You must have forgotten the time Ma lost five ducks to a fox and couldn't afford to buy the Christmas groceries.'

Tansy listened but still looked doubtful. 'I'm still not convinced it's right to chase an animal to the death with dogs and men,' she said. 'Still, I would like to ride a horse one day,' she added wistfully. 'And so you shall,' Martin promised, 'I'll teach you when you come out to Staddens.' And Tansy had to be content with that.

They looked around for Blodwen and Adam and found them at the gingerbread stall. 'I've bought hearts for Myfanwy and Poppy and lions and tigers for Ifor, Emrys and Owen.'

'Did you know your father was coming here today?' Rosemary asked. Blodwen shook her head. 'He left for the clay pits this morning,' she said, but now Jack Avery appeared and climbed onto a nearby wagon. Motioning to the band to play a drum roll, he announced, 'Today we're to hold the second round of the Devon step-dance championships. Evan Williams, winner of the first round at Lustleigh throws down the gauntlet to any man who thinks he can out-step him.'

And now Blodwen paled. 'Oh no!' she exclaimed, 'I must stop him.' She hurried off, face set, chin determined, towards the wagon. Rosemary tried to keep up with her. 'What's wrong?' she demanded. 'He won at Lustleigh, didn't he?'

But Blodwen just shook her head. 'Men bet on him,' she retorted, 'that's what's wrong, because sometimes he's too sick to dance. Then there's trouble.'

But by the time they arrived at the wagon a large crowd of men had gathered and money was changing hands. It appeared to be a great deal of money, Rosemary thought. It was being collected by a stocky red-faced young man dressed in a yellow-checked waistcoat and moleskin trousers. A billycock hat sat jauntily on the back of his square head, a ginger beard framed his jaw. Now a small thin man pushed his way to the front and spoke to Jack Avery, who announced, 'We have a taker. Billy Baker has accepted Evan Williams' challenge. Come up Billy. That's right.'

Martin joined them. 'There's a lot of money riding on Evan's back. Can you persuade him to withdraw?' he asked Blodwen who stood, obviously distressed, twisting her hanky in her hands.

Tansy, surprised at the reactions of Blodwen and Martin, looked enquiringly at Martin. 'But he's a wonderful dancer. I saw him at Lustleigh. He won't lose, will he?'

Martin spoke in a low voice, looking round to make sure he wasn't overheard, 'Billy Baker's last year's county champion. He should win unless,' he paused, 'he's been nobbled.'

Adam, seeing the look of puzzlement on Tansy's face, took over. 'Bets are put on both of them but sometimes it's fixed for one of them to win. Some of the men have been tipped off. They know who the winner's to be. So they place their bets accordingly.'

Now Tansy realised what was happening and she looked with sympathy at Blodwen who stood, sick at heart, but resisting Rosemary's efforts to take her away from the scene. 'No, no, I must stay.'

And they stood together, Blodwen in their midst, Tansy and Rosemary, Martin and Adam. They stood tense and silent, waiting to see what the outcome would be. To test the air Martin asked the nearest punter, 'Who do you think's going to win here today then?' and back came the reply, 'Evan Williams of course. Best get your money on if you're to show a profit!' and Martin stood, not believing Evan could willingly be taking part in such a shabby trick. Martin thought back to May Day at Lustleigh. Evan was good but Billy Baker was even better. It must be fixed if they thought that Evan was going to win.

'As is the custom,' Jack Avery declared from his platform on the wagon, 'Billy Baker, last year's winner, will dance first,' and the slight figure jumped up onto the wagon and placed down his board. He nodded to the fiddler and the sounds of Family Jig began. He started well enough but stumbled twice in the second phase and ended out of time with the fiddle. There was a disgusted roar when he jumped down.

'What's the matter wi' 'ee, Billy Baker? Too much cider in thee's belly?' came from some of the public not in the know.

Then Evan stepped up and a repeat of his winning performance at Lustleigh began. After the initial stamp with either foot, there came the high jump, then flurry of steps so fast that the eye could hardly see movement. All went well for the first two minutes but then a spasm shook Evan's body and a series of coughs wracked his thin frame. He stopped dancing and tried to control the paraxysm, blood spurted from his mouth and he collapsed onto the floor of the wagon. He, the outsider upon whom rode long odds, had collapsed. The fiddler stopped playing and an eerie appalled silence filled the arena, broken at last by Jack Avery, who announced, 'Billy Baker wins by default. Billy goes through to the third round.'

The audience began to mutter. 'What do 'ee mean by it? We'm lost all our money. Who said Evan Williams was going to win, I'd like to know?'

And now Martin knew that the Welshman was in real trouble. 'Come, Adam, let's get him out of here,' and together the brothers dragged Evan from the wagon and carried him off in the direction of the fairground. Blodwen, Rosemary and Tansy provided a protective barrier around him, trying to shield him from the crowd of cheated punters who began to follow.

'Where can we take him?' Adam demanded and, as they drew level with Romany Rose's tent, Tansy, quick as a flash, pulled aside the flap and beckoned them to bring Evan in. They deposited Evan in the customer's chair and left.

'Take care of this man or he's dead.' Tansy kept her voice low. 'We'll pay,' she added, and left Evan swaying in the chair opposite the astonished fortune-teller.

'Run, run,' she shouted and the group ran between stalls and peep shows until the ugly crowd, seeking vengeance for their lost money, caught up with them.

'What have you done with him?' they demanded and one or two began to double fists and threaten Martin and Adam. Tansy, however, was a match for them. 'You're so drunk you don't know what you're doing. Look, he's not with us is he? Go back to your cider or I'll fetch the village constable.'

And, after hesitating a moment or two to assure themselves that Evan Williams wasn't with them, they turned away, still muttering threats as to what they would do when they caught up with Evan Williams.

Martin looked at Tansy, admiration stamped on his features. 'What a clever girl you are. Brave too, facing that mob,' he exclaimed and there, in front of everyone, placed resounding kisses on each of her flushed cheeks.

Now Blodwen came forward. 'Dadda, we must get him home to bed,' and once again Martin took charge, fetched the Webber trap, and he and Adam gently lifted the sick man into it. With Blodwen crouching beside him, they set off for Bowden Hill. Rosemary and Tansy followed on foot, all heart for the joys of the Ram Roast fair suddenly gone.

Clouds built, moving slowly but inexorably from the hills of Dartmoor until they opened and rain fell, not the soft rain of early spring, but the torrents of full summer. Halfway home Tansy and Rosemary were drenched. They parted at the end of Southernhay and Tansy entered the Post Office, her muslin dress clinging to her figure. She sneezed loudly and Eva banished Robert and James to the living-room, stripped off Tansy's dress and wrapped her in a blanket.

'Get the bath, Norah,' she commanded, and the bath was emptied of leaves and spiders and dragged into the kitchen. Eva lit faggots under the copper and made tea while Tansy related the events of the day, leaving out the drama of the step-dancing competition. Norah's calm face took on a look of envy when Tansy told of riding the roundabout.

'Next year I'm going to be there,' she said, but the next year Norah was at college and it was two years before she was able to attend.

'You know it always rains at the Ram Roast,' Norah scolded as Tansy steamed in the bath in front of the kitchen fire to which Eva had added mustard and lavender. It was only when Eva left the girls to get supper did Tansy relate the collapse of Evan and her meeting with Martin Webber.

'I'm afraid Evan Williams is going to get into trouble,' Tansy said. 'It was fortunate for him that Martin and Adam were there to rescue him when he collapsed.' Here Tansy's face softened. 'Martin's a good man, always playing the Good Samaritan. Perhaps it would be best not to tell Father, it might make things difficult for the chapel members if he knows about Evan's involvement in betting.'

And for once the sisters agreed.

⚜

When Blodwen found she had left the gingerbread fairings in Martin's trap she burst into tears. Gwynneth looked up from cutting thick slices of bread for tea. It wasn't like Blodwen to cry. Through all their troubles she had never given way.

'It's spoilt already, Mam!' she wailed. 'Just when we'd made a fresh start and some good friends.' Gwynneth left her board and held Blodwen close in an effort to comfort her. Blodwen only cried the harder.

'All our hopes for a new life ruined in one day,' she moaned, and Gwynneth was at a loss for something to say that would bring her eldest daughter real hope for the future. Blodwen had been such a tower of strength to both she and Evan at the time of the strike when, one by one, she had wrapped the family treasures and sent her with them to the pawnshop. Their value had been just enough to pay the high price for bread. Blodwen had stood by, dry-eyed, while their good sticks of furniture had been taken away to the sale-room to pay for the journey to Devon. But now, at the first evidence of real kindness and loyalty from Martin and Tansy and their friends, Blodwen had given way, dreading no doubt a repetition of the troubles which had come from Evan's betting and ill health.

When Blodwen and Gwynneth heard the children's voices as they approached up the hillside from school, Blodwen seized her mother's hands. 'Don't tell them about the Fair,' she pleaded, 'don't tell them about the Fair.'

And Evan, lying in pain on the sofa in the living-room, heard and turned his face to the wall.

❖ Chapter Six ❖

The Dinner Party

Tansy could sense a change in the atmosphere as soon as she entered the kitchen at Courtenay House the next day. Janet Luscombe, instead of ignoring Tansy, came up to her at once, a broad grin on her face.

'Guess what's happened?' she demanded of an astonished Tansy. 'I be going with Miss Emma to Exeter for the Season,' she paused, 'whatever that is.' she gloated. 'Holy Terror's insisting. Missus don't like it nor do Miss Emma but me, I'm over the moon.' With a toss of her head she picked up a pile of underwear and swept from the room.

Tansy looked to Cook for confirmation. 'Yes, 'tis true. Right ructions there was yesterday. Holy Terror announced her plan at dinner. Seems she thinks Miss Emma's not being brung up proper like, thinks a spell among city folk'll do her good.'

'And what does Miss Emma think about it?' Tansy wanted to know, remembering the recent trip to Dartmeet which had proved disastrous as far as Emma Vallance had been concerned.

'Sulked all day according to Hetty. Wants to spend summer here with Mary Westaway and her friends from Lawn College. Not locked up in Exeter wi' her grandma.' But now their conversation was terminated by a clanging of bells from the morning-room.

'Best go, Tansy. See what Missus wants, though I've enough instructions for tomorrow night's dinner, Lord knows. Fourteen places at the last count. We'm gonna have our work cut out sure as eggs is eggs and no mistake.'

Above stairs Caroline Vallance handed Tansy a sheet of paper on which was written the final copy of Beatrice Vallance's menu for her dinner guests. Place cards lay on top, written in the old lady's elegant copper plate. Caroline looked grim as she stood up from her desk.

'If my mother-in-law asks for you today or tomorrow, Drewe, please refer her to me. She will be going home on Friday and till then your place is in the kitchen.'

As Tansy took menu and place cards through the hall, Miss Emma emerged from the cloakroom.

'Tansy,' she hissed, 'come in here a minute.' And she drew her inside. 'Have you heard?' she wailed. 'I'm going to Exeter with Grandmama, just when College's finished for the summer. What shall I do?'

Tansy bit her lips in sympathy, not yet knowing what to say to her young mistress, who wrung her hanky which was already soaked with tears. 'Just when everything's starting up for the summer. There's Mama's garden party, the band concerts in Courtenay Park and Mary says her brother, Christopher, will be here for the river trip to Teignmouth. It's not fair.' She dissolved into tears yet again. Tansy hesitated but only for a moment, then put her arms around Emma, letting menu and place cards fall to the floor.

'There there, Miss Emma, don't take on so, it's not for ever, there's bound to be parties and dances there. Father went on a visit to Exeter last year and he went to the theatre and the Assembly Rooms. It'll be almost as good as going to London.' But nothing she could say would stem Emma's tears.

'I'm going to pick gooseberries in a minute, why not come too? There's nothing like a breath of fresh air to put a new face on things.'

Tansy retrieved menu and place cards and took them to Hetty who arranged to meet her in the dining-room later in the day to go through the service of dinner. Janet had been told to help and Tansy felt a tremor of anxiety at the thought of having to work closely with her. Normally their duties kept them strictly apart but any accidental encounter meant trouble for Tansy. She took up a basket and hurried off to the kitchen garden where Seth Howell's nephew Stephen dug new potatoes under the watchful eye of Beatrice Vallance who stood by, a bunch of herbs in her hands.

'All the same size now, Howell,' she commanded, then at the sign of Tansy and Emma declared, 'Well, you coming to pick fruit, Emma? That's right, make sure you get the best. Doesn't hurt to see things through from start to finish.' She marched away in the direction of the kitchen where Tansy didn't doubt she would set Cook's palpitations off again. Emma's efforts at fruit picking were short-lived. She pricked her finger and at the sight of blood began to cry afresh.

'I wanted to go to the Ball at Dartmouth College with Mary Westaway,' she said. 'Christopher's being given the Sword of Honour. Mrs Westaway's invited me to go with them. Now it's all spoilt.' And her tears fell onto the green fruit which began to fill Tansy's basket.

'Tidd'n far, Miss Emma. Only takes an hour on the new motor bus does Exeter,' but Emma shook her head. 'I might as well be going to the moon,' she said, 'as far as Christopher Westaway's concerned.' Tansy nodded in sympathy, thinking how she would feel if she was about to be denied sight of Martin Webber all summer.

But now she had an idea. 'Why not ask your grandma to invite the Westaways to Exeter?' she suggested and was rewarded by signs of recovery on Emma's part. 'She do like to give a dinner party don' she?' she said, and Emma hugged her tight.

'You're a treasure, Tansy Drewe. I wish you were coming to Exeter with me and not Luscombe.' But now Cook appeared at the door into the garden.

'Tansy, what be you a doing of? There's work to do in the kitchen.' And Miss Emma and Tansy parted immediately, Emma to begin sorting out clothes for her stay in Exeter, Tansy to begin preparations for the Holy Terror's dinner party.

⁂

At last all was ready. Cook had given of her best and the salmon, freshly caught from the Teign, lay in a blue and white dish garnished with lemon and herbs. She stood, flushed with her efforts but proud as she checked Tansy's uniform. Neat in black dress, white frilled apron and cap which hid most but not quite all of Tansy's riot of hair. Janet, who had served dinner before, stood by looking supercilious.

'Can't think what the fuss is about,' she sniffed, then as the drawing-room bell rang hissed, 'Come on, Drewe. Keep an eye on me, watch what I do and us'll be fine.' Her spirits rose, perhaps this time all would go well, Tansy thought as she followed Janet into the drawing-room.

Beatrice stood ram-rod straight, a little apart from Charles, Caroline and Emma. They made an elegant picture as they waited for their guests to arrive. Tansy noticed Biddy Pidsley's lace at Beatrice's throat, softening the Holy Terror's severe face and black bombazine gown. Emma looked fresh and pretty in blue moire taffeta, shadows beneath her eyes the only evidence of earlier tears. As was his habit, Charles stood studying his watch and Caroline, in salmon pink georgette, stood at his side looking resigned.

'They're late,' he grumbled and Caroline opened her ivory fan with a snap, then tapped it against her teeth in irritation.

'Your obsession with time is becoming more than I can bear,' she spat, and Beatrice remarked, 'Why are you young people always so concerned with the passing of time? They say punctuality is the habit of kings but our guests are coming a distance and who knows what might befall them. I had no idea when I set off for Lustleigh that it would turn into such an adventure.'

Now there came the crunch of carriage wheels on the drive and Seth and Stephen Howell, both pressed into service and impressive in silk stockings, knickerbockers and tunics, flung open the double doors. They hurried down the steps to help the guests to alight their carriages.

The first of the guests were Maude and Henry Westaway with Mary, who hurried at once to Emma's side. Caroline's parents, Gertrude and Reuben Widecombe, followed the Westaway's car in their brougham. Auctioneer, Jack Avery and his wife Susannah came next, then Dr Thomas Weekes and Alice. Last to arrive were Robert and Pachell Hood, who had journeyed from Combestone bringing Daniel Gill, once the Mine Captain at Hexworthy where Beatrice had gone to recover from Absolam's death in the Mill fire years ago. Now he bowed his silver head over her slim, time-worn hand, then straightened to take his place at her side and accept a glass of Madeira.

'You are looking well, Beatrice. Your visit must have wiped away the city's cares.'

''Tis the air on the Moor,' she laughed and the years dropped away as she simpered up at Daniel and accepted his arm when Caroline announced that dinner was served.

Tansy listened to Beatrice's guests as they talked through the patè and toast, as Caroline's parents spoke of the latest developments at 'Widecombe's Emporium'. She watched Caroline become more and more embarrassed, as she did whenever 'trade' was mentioned.

'Have you heard, Caroline,' Reuben Widecombe asked, 'shop closes at one o'clock from next Thursday?' Gertrude interrupted, 'I don't know what things are coming to. What do they think they'm doing? Reuben voted against it but 'twadden no good. We'll be bankrupt before long.'

'Chamber of Trade decided,' Reuben went on, ignoring Gertrude, 'but then I suppose change is inevitable, the old Queen can't last much longer. Things are bound to change once Victoria's gone. New king, new ways.'

'You must move with the times,' Charles interpolated, 'get left behind otherwise', but Gertrude wouldn't let the subject die. 'Get ideas above their station, they will. Our shop girls. All because Torquay shopkeepers have begun this half-day business.'

Caroline, in an effort to change the topic of conversation, turned to Robert Hood, 'Did you have an easy journey from Combestone?' He gave an account of their ride through Holne and Ashburton while Pachell Hood sat smiling and nodding.

'Do you remember when we met, Daniel?' Beatrice turned to Daniel who smiled. 'Indeed I do. Walking from the Mine to the Inn I was and there you were across the heather sinking slowly into the edge of Foxtor Mire!' There was an outburst of laughter at the thought of Beatrice in such an unexpected predicament. Tansy caught Seth's eye across the table, where silver epergne and crystal gleamed among Sarah Webber's country flowers and dessert fruits. He nodded at her and moved to the decanters.

Beatrice continued, 'I remember hearing your voice. It carried across the Moor. "Hold on, I'm coming."'

'And you took some pulling clear if I remember rightly!' Daniel said with a twinkle lighting his bright blue eyes.

'But you did. If you hadn't', she paused and looked around the table at the friends she had harboured over the years, 'why, we wouldn't be here tonight.'

Charles beckoned to Seth. 'That's worth celebrating. Fetch the white port, Howell. We'll drink a toast to my mother and our dear friends,' which led Beatrice to speak again of Hexworthy.

'It helped so much to walk where Absolam and I had stayed with his parents when we first married. I walked miles each day with only the larks for company.' She paused and laid her careworn hand on Daniel's arm, 'Except when Daniel left his Mine to accompany me.'

'I'd have married you Beatrice, but you would never say yes.' They both fell silent, deep in shared memories, as Charles carved fillets from the salmon and Tansy took helpings round the table. Smothered in butter and herbs, its delicious smell made Tansy's mouth water as she placed finger bowls at strategic places.

'Heard the cuckoo today,' Pachell Hood remarked, 'shows spring is on the way.' Beatrice nodded in agreement.

'I heard one call from the edge of Decoy Wood yesterday. But I still prefer the sound of the larks on the Moor. When I came over Haldon and saw the soft line of the hills, I felt I was coming home.'

The table's occupants fell silent until Jack Avery enquired of Daniel, 'Is the mine at Hexworthy worked out now? We've a miner from Wales who's looking for work.'

Daniel Gill shook his head. 'Hexworthy's closed but they're working at Vitifer. There's huts for the miners to stay during the week. They go home at weekends. Henry Wilson is the Mine Captain, I'll put in a word if you can recommend the man as reliable.'

Tansy paused in her serving to hear Jack Avery's reply. Janet gave her a sharp dig with her elbow, 'Go to the kitchen for the sauce,' she said, and Tansy could do nothing but obey. When she came back the subject had changed. Caroline was telling the party of Emma's proposed visit to Exeter.

'She's to do the Season with her Grandmama.' Emma sat blushing at receiving so much attention. She had talked of Tansy's suggestion with Mary Westaway and now, with a prod in the back from her friend, burst out, 'Can Mary come and stay too, Grandmama?'

Beatrice, mellowed by food and the company of old friends, reflected a moment. 'Why Emma, I wasn't sure you wished to come,' then as Emma nodded eagerly she gave her approval. 'I'm sure that can be arranged,' she said.

Tansy mirrored Janet's movements as they cleared plates and cutlery and brought in crisp, skinned Devon chickens. Talk changed to the coming summer with its pattern of market-days interleaved with fêtes, fairs and chapel outings.

'This year the chapel outing will be by boat from Town Quay to Teignmouth Pier, with a tea set up on the beach. It's bound to be popular so make a note of the date, 15th July.'

'Sounds expensive,' Beatrice commented. 'Will it cost more than the usual train? Will the congregation be able to afford it?' Charles continued to carve the succulent breasts of chicken. 'Can't have an outing that no-one can afford,' Beatrice remonstrated. 'How much will it cost?'

When Charles said, 'Two shillings each adult and one for each child,' Tansy felt her colour rise as she added figures in her head to arrive at the cost to her own family. Eight shillings for her parents, Norah and herself. Two shillings for the twins. Why, that was half their week's income. And they were among the better off among the working community.

'Move along, Drewe,' Janet hissed at her, bringing her daydream to an end. She recovered herself and stared at the amount left untouched on the dirty plates she carried to the kitchen.

She thought of the families she saw queuing at the Soup Kitchen. The line of poorly dressed women and children would have thought the dinner party leavings fit for Christmas Day. She scraped meat and vegetables into the kitchen waste bin, which was sent to Cull's farm. Why, Cull's pigs did better than many living right under the Vallances' noses.

She almost stumbled as she delivered the flummery, Janet as ever close behind her, so close that she could feel her quick breath on her neck. Quickly she recovered and held on grimly to the large dish as the pudding slopped on one side.

'I hear you're having a new bathroom put in, Caroline?' Henry Westaway asked and Caroline Vallance looked embarrassed. She had wanted to keep the work a secret until her mother-in-law had gone back to Exeter.

'Everyone should have one,' she blustered as Charles looked up surprised. 'More and more houses are being built with proper facilities,' she turned to Dr Weekes for confirmation.

'I would like to believe that one day every house will have clean piped water,' he said. 'Wells have been sealed off in Bradley Lane. Water's being laid on there so I hope this will bring an end to typhoid and Bright's disease. That's as much as we can hope for at present.'

'And not before time,' remarked Beatrice. 'Can you really confirm that everyone will soon have indoor water closets too?'

But here Dr Weekes shook his head. 'That would be a foolish promise. Ask landlords who rent to workers living in some of the town's terraces. Ask the men who're developing land to build new streets for the foundry and the railway.'

The occupants of the table fell silent as each grey head followed its own thoughts. Tansy raised one aching foot and rubbed it against the other, thinking of her weekly bath in front of the kitchen fire and trips outside at night to use the water closet. She remembered the image of Blodwen and her brothers and sisters lined up with buckets at the spring, their only water supply. Hard in summer's heat and rain, harder still when winter came with its frost and snow. Water to drink became the priority long before water to wash bodies and clothes.

'The poor don't feel it like we do,' said Gertrude Widecombe, and Tansy could stand by and listen no longer. How dare her Mistress' mother belittle the needs of working people.

'The poor don't feel it like we do,' she mimicked Gertrude Widecombe, her body pushed forward, her face aflame with anger. 'They're human beings same as you, aren't they? Families the other side of the Hill, they have to line up to collect every drop of water from a spring in the bank. Line up in summer and winter. Why, bathrooms!' Tansy exclaimed, 'Why, they would thank you for a pipe to bring a drink of water indoors. Never mind bathrooms!'

She stood, two bright spots of red inflaming her cheeks, arms on hips, chin stuck out in defiance. A silence descended on the table, a shocked silence so deep that the steady ticking of Absolam Vallance's grandfather clock could be heard from its position in the hall. Caroline was the first to recover. Her voice cut across the room, as cold as ice.

'Leave the room this instant, Drewe!' she snapped and Tansy, suddenly aware of the enormity of her sin, turned and fled towards the door. Her flight was arrested by Beatrice Vallance's voice, 'Just a minute, Drewe.' She turned to Dr Weekes. 'Are you aware of this family's situation?' and he shook his grey lion's mane of a head. 'My partner treats the people on the Hill.' He shifted uncomfortably. 'He did bring their problems to my attention but there's a waiting list...' His voice trailed off.

Beatrice beckoned Tansy to her where she sat at the head of the table. 'Is what you say true, my dear?' and when she assented, 'You'd better tell Dr Weekes where these homes are. Can she call at the surgery one day, Thomas?' When the doctor nodded she added, 'Can she finish her duties, Caroline?'

With all the eyes of the company upon her, Caroline could do nothing but give in. Tansy bobbed a curtsey of thanks to Beatrice and the doctor and cleared pudding plates, while Janet Luscombe stood transfixed in the background, open-mouthed in amazement.

'Please serve tea in the drawing-room, Luscombe,' Caroline ordered, and the ladies rose with obvious relief at the termination of this most embarrassing interlude and swept out, leaving the men to their port.

'You can call on me when next you're in town, Tansy Drewe,' Dr Thomas Weekes said, smiling in approval as he had on the day he attended Eva Drewe at the birth of this red-headed creature, who had been in such a hurry to begin her life that she hadn't waited for him to arrive.

Just as Tansy closed the dining-room doors behind her Janet hissed, 'Should be ashamed of yourself, Tansy Drewe. Who do you think you are, giving yourself airs and graces? Good thing Holy Terror was there or you'd have been walking out the front door by now!' As Tansy moved towards the service stairs Janet suddenly pushed her foot out in front of her and brought her down with a bang.

✣ Chapter Seven ✣

Martin Webber

Friday and the house lay quiet, the pulsing energy that had surged through its rooms had departed with Beatrice and Emma. Now Tansy climbed the stairs to Emma's room where she found Caroline sitting idle on her daughter's bed, Emma's favourite doll limp in her hands.

'Charles and I gave it her because it resembled her when she was young.' She sighed and put the doll back among the lace-edged bed linen. She wandered about the room, picking things up, then putting them down again, utterly lost.

Making a visible effort she remarked, 'We must make good use of Emma's absence. New wallpaper, I think, and curtains perhaps,' then burst out, 'It's so quiet without them both.'

Tansy, in an effort to console her mistress, said, 'Master Harry'll be home before you know it, Ma'm. The summer will soon pass,' adding, 'He'll be home in time for the river trip, won't he?' which reminded Caroline of the episode at her mother-in-law's dinner party two days before. She turned to Tansy.

'Your behaviour on Wednesday night was quite reprehensible. Don't let it happen again ever or I shall have no alternative but to let you go.'

But at the door she turned to Tansy yet again and, looking slightly embarrassed, announced, 'The Chapel Elders are trying to get up a subscription towards the river trip. I'm sure you will be glad to know that.' And then she was gone.

✻

Tansy called on Dr Weekes on her next day off but he only looked at her in an abstracted way.

'What are you doing at the Vallances?' he asked, commenting, 'A bright girl like you in service? Can't you get away to college like your sister?' This merely served to make her feel small.

'I'm working to help Mother and Father so Norah can go to Goldsmith's. She's taking the entrance exam next week. Then when she's finished it'll be my turn.'

But Dr Weekes merely grunted. 'How long will that take, pray? Two years or so. And how old will you be then?'

And Tansy, knowing what he meant, drew herself up and said proudly, 'There's more to life than just being a teacher. I'm going to travel and see the world.'

The doctor laughed at her pride and rang the bell for the next patient. 'Off you go.' And although she tried to introduce the subject of the Williams' water supply he merely waved her away. 'Need money for that, leave it with me.' and ushered her through the door

✻

The summer passed in a welter of change at Courtenay House. Dust filtered through room after room as workmen installed the new bathroom in what had once been the nursery. A William Morris wallpaper of tulips and willows in green and yellow was chosen for Emma's bedroom. Caroline showed it to Tansy who thought Emma would have preferred red hummingbirds in blue and pink but, as she was on her best behaviour, she bit her lip and said nothing. One by one the dark heavily-draped rooms were opened up and Caroline was overheard pleading with Charles Vallance to consider installing heated radiators. Now the Master called a halt to further expense, saying he had ordered a new Lanchester which had to be paid for and Caroline had to be content with that.

Meanwhile, Master Harry, hearing that Emma was staying with Beatrice at Exeter, pleaded with Charles that he be allowed to visit a school friend in Torquay for the holidays. He gave in reluctantly and Caroline, after shedding a mother's tears, consoled herself with visits to town with Maude Westaway to choose materials for the autumn and its changing fashions.

Each Sunday after chapel, Tansy met Martin Webber by the oak tree at the bottom of St Paul's Road. She liked to see him waiting, tall and solid, and liked the safe feeling it gave her to see him standing there. Liked the way his blue eyes shone with enthusiasm when he told her of his plans for the future as he walked her back to Courtenay House. They took the long way round, going up Bowden Hill past the Williams' house and the pigsty and up through the fields.

Each week they wandered along, Tansy trying hard to keep up with Martin's long country stride and dodge the cow pats which littered Farmer Cull's fields, and each week he kissed her gently when they reached the entrance gates to Courtenay House.

Today proved to be different. It was her Sunday off and Eva had invited Martin to dinner where he sat, nervous and shy, while Edward Drewe tried to find out what he wanted from life and Robert and James watched his every move.

'Going to have a place of my own one day. High up on the Moor. Keep sheep. There's good sheep runs up above Manaton on Black Hill.' When Edward pressed him about Staddens he shrugged and said, 'Adam can have the farm when Father stops work. More suited to the Valley he is. No, 'tis the hills for me.' And a determined look hardened the line of his jaw.

Suddenly he pushed back his chair, took up his hat and turned to Tansy. 'Will you come for a walk above town then?'

Eva smiled at the pair of them and pushed them towards the door. 'Go on Tansy, make the most of your day off. But keep away from Decoy Wood, they say traps have been set for the foxes.'

And so they went to Bradley Woods instead, following Courtenay Road through the churchyard, deep in white daisies, and across Steppes Meadow where couples strolled hand in hand.

'Will you be my girl, Tansy Drewe?' Martin asked and, when she hesitated, went on, 'I like your family and I hope they will approve of me. Now you must come to Staddens and meet my Father.'

But at his words Tansy's face showed alarm. 'We're not spoken for, Martin Webber. Just because my Mother asked you for dinner today – well, that doesn't mean anything.'

Now Martin stopped to look at her, anger flared on his face. 'Then why do you insist I meet you every week at Market and let me drive all the way in from Lustleigh to meet you after chapel on a Sunday, if we're not to wed?'

Tansy, not wanting to lose him, tried to placate him by reaching up and placing a kiss on his sun-reddened cheek. With that Martin, taking this as encouragement, drew Tansy off the path and into the green depths of a hazel copse. She felt his strong arms encircle her small body as his mouth, hard and insistent, smothered hers. She liked kissing, had kissed other boys briefly at fairs and dances, but as her body began to respond to his a feeling of panic took possession of her. As his hands touched her breasts she remembered gossip in the kitchen at Courtenay House, remembered talk of touching bodies leading to sudden weddings, and she struggled to break out of his embrace. She fought against his arms imprisoning her body against her will. She wrenched her lips from his.

'No, no, don't,' she cried and suddenly he let her go, so suddenly that she fell back, hitting the birch tree behind her.

'You're a tease, Tansy Drewe. That's what you are. Leading me on...' he said, his face sharp with disappointment. 'I'll let you go but you'll say No once too often. Then I'll have to look for someone else.'

But now Tansy felt a sense of real alarm. She thought of Fanny Luscombe with her cupid bow mouth and rounded body. Thought of Fanny seeing Martin every day at Staddens. She knew she wanted Martin, but in her own good time. Not now when she was held back by her fierce independent spirit which wouldn't allow her to give in to the growing demands of her developing body.

'We're only young, Martin,' she pleaded, 'There's the whole world out there waiting for us. We don't want to settle down yet and miss it all, do we?'

He relaxed at last, took up her small, neat hand and kissed its palm. 'All right,' he teased, 'first the world then you'll come back and marry me. I'll keep sheep and horses high on the Moor and you'll ride by my side.' And his black mood dispelled as they laughed and talked as they made their way back towards Ogwell Mill, never once looking back.

When he left Tansy at the Post Office to drive back to Staddens for milking he became serious once more.

'Do you still want to meet me?' he asked and Tansy, relaxed and happy after her walk exploded, 'Of course I do. Why, I...' then stopped at the words 'I love you' and bit her lip.

'If the day comes when you're not at the Oak then I'll know you've changed your mind,' he said, but even now she didn't want to commit herself and, deliberately pretending to misunderstand his meaning she said, 'Don't be silly, if I'm not here 'twill be because I'm kept late at Courtenay House, not because I don't want to see you.'

Martin, placated at last, kissed her gently and whispered, 'Then that's our bargain. We'll meet at the Oak every Sunday... if you'm not there four weeks running... then I'll know it's over.' She accepted his qualified kiss and went indoors content.

❦

It was the end of June before Tansy went to Staddens as Martin's guest. A mist hung, covering the town in a pink haze, the result of a week of hot sun on dew-drenched land and river. Martin waited for her at the bottom of Bowden Hill and for once Tansy was glad of Eva's old green suit which kept her warm against the chill. The bells of St Paul's came in a muffled sound and Tom's hooves were the only other noise assailing her senses as Martin drove Tom and the trap through the town, over the pack bridge to Highweek.

'Do let me have a go, Martin,' she demanded, 'I can see Tom's docile as a kitten,' and reluctantly he relinquished the reins.

'He'm not really docile, just lazy,' he said and, try as she might, she couldn't coax him into a trot. He laid his ears back and continued at a sedate pace between honeysuckle-scented verges of white cow parsley until they reached Bovey, where the mist cleared suddenly in an explosion of brilliant blue sky and bronze beeches. As they drew nearer Staddens, Tom sensed home and broke into a brisk trot and, when Norsworthy's mare whinnied from a nearby field, his trot became a gallop. Tansy fought to control the young gelding but he only went faster until Martin grabbed Tansy's hands, reins and all, and brought him to a standstill.

'Not so easy now, is it?' Martin reproved her, but she only laughed, excited by the incident, her face glowing under the green feathered hat.

'No,' she agreed, 'but 'twas exciting.' Now they turned up the track she had walked with Beatrice Vallance in the spring.

'Can I learn to ride today?' she asked, but Martin shook his head. 'Tom needs a rest afore I takes 'ee back home. I'll see if I can borrow Norsworthy's mare one day. Then we'll see if 'ee can learn to ride.' And when she protested, 'Why not Tom? He seems a horse of spirit,' he continued, 'Tom's too strong for 'ee. You'd never get him to obey.'

If Martin had understood Tansy better he'd have recognised the jut of her chin as she promised herself that one day she would indeed ride Tom.

They arrived to shouts of greeting from the rickyard where Amos leant against the long ridge of a hay stack. Adam held the ladder below while Fanny Luscombe watched Amos thatch the top. At the sound of the trap clattering over the cobbled yard all three looked round and it was Adam who greeted Tansy as she climbed down the steps of the trap.

'You'm just in time for dinner,' he said while Fanny scowled at Tansy, her face like thunder. 'Go you in and make yerself at home.' She left Martin to take off Tom's harness and put away the trap and hurried to the house where Sarah laid places on the long scrubbed table.

'Why is it hers never here when I needs her?' Sarah exclaimed to herself, then looked to see Tansy pausing in the doorway. She sighed. 'That Fanny's never around when she's wanted. Mooning about after Martin and if he's not about then she stands gawping at Adam.'

Then she smiled at Tansy and went on, ''Tis a blessing she'm good in the dairy and the hen house, that's all I can say, or she'd have to go! Set yerself down Tansy Drewe and tell me the news.'

Tansy took the cutlery from Sarah's hands and finished laying up while Sarah thickened gravy and tended the array of pots on her brand new stove. The men arrived together to wash up under the pump, followed shortly after by Fanny.

'Why you'm a wonderful colour,' Tansy couldn't help exclaiming and Fanny blushed and placed hands to hot cheeks. ''Tis from working in fields. Us've just finished the haymaking.'

Amos commanded Martin, 'Fetch up some cider, boy,' and they all drank the golden liquid and ate Sarah Webber's roast pork and crackling till Tansy felt she would burst. She struggled with her helping of apple-in-and-out, thinking that a suet pudding was the last thing she needed on such a hot summer's day. But she didn't wish to offend Sarah and when she had finished she asked, 'How do you like your new stove, Mrs Webber?' thinking at the same time that it didn't compare with the cheer of the open fire that had comforted her on her visit with Beatrice Vallance.

''Tis wonderful. There's hot water all day. Ovens for bread and ovens for meat. I can work in the garden while dinner cooks itself.' As she laughed her face shed the years and Tansy glimpsed the young girl whom Amos had married and brought to Staddens.

'Though takes a whole day to clean, but then I suppose you have a big oven to clean at the Vallances.'

'Yes indeed, 'tis twice the size and each day Cook insists I black lead it and polish the brass knobs.'

Now at last Amos, who had eaten his meal in complete silence, wiped his mouth, took a deep drink from his cider mug and looked at Tansy with the far-seeing eyes of a man whose days were spent out of doors.

'So this is the little maid as has taken our Martin away from his church to drive to Newton of a Sunday?'

Martin reddened and tried to change the subject. 'Hay's all in. Shall us begin on tatties tomorrow?'

Amos wasn't to be distracted. 'Set on living on Moor, our Martin is,' he declared. 'Staddens not good enough for him. Good enough for my feyther and his feyther afore him, but not for my son. So, young woman, if you'm set on being a farmer's wife I hope you'm used to a hard life.'

When Martin tried once more to interrupt he silenced him with an upheld hand. 'When snows come there you'll be shut in for days, even weeks, with only new-born lambs for company, praying for spring to come.'

Now Sarah interrupted. 'Nothing's settled, Amos. Leave the young folk alone, do.'

But still Amos went on, 'Fine thing when a son don't want what's rightly his. 'Tis as well I have another son to keep the Webber name alive at Staddens.'

Tansy struggled to quell her feelings of alarm that Amos seemed to take it for granted she and Martin were to marry, and Adam spoke up.

'You'm just a young 'un yet Feyther. Years of work in 'ee yet. Let Martin alone. If 'ee wants to go and live on the Moor let 'un go. Leastways I can have Staddens all to myself when the time comes.'

The tension which had built around the long scrubbed table dissolved and Amos turned to Tansy, 'Have 'ee been round the farm yet?' he asked and Martin rose and stood by the door waiting for her.

'I must help clear,' she offered but Sarah, like Eva Drewe, would have none of it.

'Fanny will see to it,' she smiled. 'You go now, make the most of your time.'

Fanny watched Tansy from her place close by the scullery door while Adam stared at Fanny with eyes which held her with a warm regard. Martin took down a gun from the rack by the door and, as they went out through the stone porch, Moss fell in close by his master's heels. Tansy laid her hand on Martin's arm.

'You're not going to shoot today surely? 'Tis Sunday after all,' she remonstrated, but Martin shook her off.

''Tis a habit. Never know when you're going to need a gun.' He tucked it under his arm and took Tansy first to the stables where the plough horses rested.

'The grey's called Hero and the cob Captain,' he said as she reached up to stroke their velvet noses. She admired the calves in the linhay as they gazed back at her from under white lashes and sucked the fingers she held out for them.

'Now you must walk the meadows,' Martin said, whistling up Moss who sat watching a mouse hole in the granary wall. They set off along the black loam valley where the earth was turned ready for sowing. Moss ran ahead of them, nose to ground, until he reached a group of pheasants feeding at the wood's edge. They watched as the birds rose in a blue and green glitter. She heard the gun catch released, saw his arms raise, aligning the shiny barrel to his eye. She watched him take aim. Then in an upward thrust her arm moved faster than his trigger finger. She hit the barrel towards the blue arc of sky. The hammer hit cartridge and shot pellets into the air. Moss barked as the birds escaped over a distant hedge into the wood. Martin swore. He broke the barrel, took the second cartridge from the breech and thrust it into Tansy's face.

'You little fool,' he shouted, 'You could have been killed.'

Exhilarated at the success of her action, she laughed into the fury of his face. He set down his gun and seized her, shook her until her curls swung, her teeth chattered. Her smile faded with his anger and his relief that she was safe exploded in a savage kiss. A kiss crude and sudden which bruised her lips until he let her go and she fell back onto the grass. Slowly he retrieved his gun and stalked away in the direction of the wood. Moss ran between them, sniffing at the fallen girl, then barking at Martin, who stopped to wait for her. She picked herself up, brushed leaves and grass from her clothes and marched across the field. Determined not to apologise, she chose instead to use the best method of defence.

'It's God's day and all you can think to do is to shoot at his creatures.'

Exasperated he replied, 'The pot would stay empty if you were around all the time, I can see. You must stay calm when guns are out. No sudden movements.' Then he hesitated. 'But I must say you acted with courage, even if those birds will soon be shot by the gentry if not by me.'

Tansy fell in beside him, saddened by his last remark, excited but confused by his sudden kiss. Why had he chosen the middle of an argument to show such passion, she wondered. Now he kept his distance, calm but still showing annoyance in the slight twitching of his cheek.

"Tis wrong to breed birds only to kill them for sport,' Tansy went on, 'Why don't the gentry give them to the poor? They can't possibly eat all they shoot, can they?'

Martin shrugged and turned to face her. 'You don't understand the ways of country people, you'm just a town girl.'

He called up Moss, who had disappeared into the wood. 'Come on, let's go down to the river, see if the fish are rising.' So they wandered along until they reached the Wrey, which swished and eddied among a fringe of spent summer leaves.

'Will you really leave all this for Adam and go up into the hills?' Tansy demanded, 'After all you are the eldest son. Isn't it your place to carry on the family's name? You must carry on – 'tis expected.' Now an obstinate look settled on Martin's face as he lounged against a tree and watched her throw sticks into the river for Moss. He laughed as Moss stayed firmly on the bank.

'He's too clever to be lured into water, only time he goes in is if I'm swimming.' Now he pulled the dog's ears and sat down beside him. Only then did he respond to Tansy's remarks.

'They say I must. Now you say I must, but my heart's set on the Moor and nothing can change it. It's pulling me away from Staddens and I must go.' Still Tansy looked doubtful.

'It's so beautiful here, what more could anyone want?' She began to wind her way in and out of the beech trees which grew in a row above the river bank. As her green-clad figure appeared and disappeared between the trunks Martin rose and followed her, shouting above the noise of the river.

'The Valley's well enough but some days it's stifling, not a breath of wind to fill the lungs. Then I saddle up Tom and ride up to Hunter's Tor and keep on until I can see the open Moor. It's only up there that I can breathe.' Then suddenly he caught her, turned her to face him, a sense of urgency filling his being.

'Come with me Tansy, come and see, tidd'n far. We can walk there and back in an hour.' Taking her hand he led her through a wicket-gate which led along the river path to the village and up the Cleave till they reached Sharpitor. Here they climbed the granite outcrop and Tansy clapped her hands in delight at the sight of the deep valley spread out below.

'Why, 'tis like heaven up here,' she exclaimed as she looked down beyond the rocks to the valley, where mist clung thick and white as a sheep's fleece. 'Look at that! It feels like we're high above the clouds.' She turned to Martin, who swung her down from her granite perch. 'Let's go on!' She danced ahead of him along the narrow path which wound between strong rocks and sloe bushes. Yellow gorse glowed, scenting the path as the sun drenched the hillside below. Suddenly, the path emerged onto open moorland where heather bloomed purple among bracken, and stonechats chinked from lookouts among the rocks.

'There's Black Hill. The pile of rocks which looks like a castle are called Hound Tor. Before them lies Hayne Down and there on the right is Bowerman's Nose.' As Tansy gazed across the valley Martin pointed to a jutting rock at the end of the ridge. 'Look see there, like a man's chest and head,' he said, pointing, one arm around Tansy's shoulders. She stood, silent for once, overwhelmed by the sight of hills stretching away before her, stretching away to a clear blue arc of sky, but recovered to enquire, 'And who was Bowerman?'

'Bowerman was a hunter who fell foul of the witches' coven. He intruded on their meeting. Was changed into a hare and one of the witches changed into a hound and pursued him across Hayne Down, then turned him into stone when she caught him.' Tansy fell silent again as she stood looking at the great tor edge in horror.

'Is it far?' she asked, 'Could we walk there?' Martin laughed and shook his head. 'When we get you a horse, then we could go. 'Twould be easy, there and back in a few hours.'

He led the way across Hunter's Tor and down steeply through Peck Farm to Foxworthy. As they approached the hamlet a small boy came running towards them up the lane. He was in great distress, his chest heaved and sweat stood out on his forehead.

'Mister, come quick, come quick. Granny's chimney's on fire and there's no one here to help us.'

Martin broke into a run, Tansy hurrying after. In through the gate they went and over the stone sill into a room where smoke billowed out from a huge stone hearth, where an old woman raked wildly at a blazing fire which roared up the chimney. Martin pushed her aside, pressed cartridges into the breech, aimed his gun up the chimney and fired both barrels. Soot fell in a great black cloud, extinguishing the fire and covering the four of them in a mantle of black soot and grease.

'Well, bless my soul, 'tis out!' the old woman exclaimed, then shook Martin and Tansy by the hands. 'Thank 'ee my dears. I thought the thatch was gone. 'Tis a blessing you were nearby.' Then, trembling with shock, she sat down suddenly on the settle. Tansy set about opening windows and doors, and swept soot into heaps for Martin to shovel out into the garden.

The old woman's grandson ran off to tell the neighbours, who came hurrying back from the fields, exclaiming, 'When us heard crackling then see'd smoke us thought the thatch would go up afore we could git back', and when they heard what had happened they crowded into the cottage to shake Martin by the hand. Mugs of cider appeared as if by magic and, after washing off the worst of the soot, Martin and Tansy said their farewells and left Granny Holman still celebrating.

'Where did you learn that trick?' Tansy wanted to know.

''Twas my Grandfather Webber told me that trick when he lived at Staddens afore he died.' Then Martin laughed. 'Guns can be quite useful at times can't they?' Tansy looked up ruefully.

'Seems to me your part in life is to rescue people in distress! Why Martin, I've only known you a few months and already you've rescued Evan Williams twice. Today it's been Granny Holman and her grandson. If ever I'm in trouble will you come and rescue me?'

She laughed but Martin looked down at her with serious eyes and solemnly promised, 'Of course, I'll come if ever you need me, Tansy.' He paused, 'You won't hesitate will you? Wherever you are just send for me and I'll come.' Tansy found, to her horror, that her eyes began to fill with unsought tears.

❧

Fanny Luscombe was feeding fowls when they entered the rickyard and she stared at their blackened clothes and faces. When Martin left Tansy to go to the linhay she turned to her, 'Whatever have 'ee bin up to now, Tansy Drewe? Why is it whenever you'm about there's trouble?' Her face darkened as she came close, pushing her face into Tansy's. 'I've told 'ee afore – leave Martin Webber alone or you'll be sorry.' But Tansy just ignored her and went in search of Sarah, who she found weeding her herb bed. As Tansy's shadow fell across the warm plot she straightened then laughed.

'You look as if you've been down a coal mine,' she exclaimed and after Tansy had told of their adventure she nodded. 'Martin seems to draw trouble to him. Even when he was a child. 'Tis a blessing he seems always to know how to handle it.'

Then the memory of Beatrice Vallance's visit came to them both, seemingly at the same time. 'How is Mrs Vallance?' Sarah asked.

'Mrs Vallance loved your garden,' Tansy commented, and they laughed in easy camaraderie. Tansy told her the news from Courtenay House, how Emma had gone with Beatrice to Exeter for the summer. They talked of the new half-day closing at Newton and the plans for the new library.

'There's not much time for reading out here,' Sarah said, 'Always mending and patching, but I do like my crochet.'

When she heard that Robert and James had just gone down with croup she looked sad. 'Took both my girls,' she said, 'my Meg and Belinda. Lie in Lustleigh churchyard they do. Just two years old each time.'

Then she bustled indoors to fetch a bottle of her home-made mixture. ''Tis the linseed brought the boys through. Tell your mother to give it every four hours.'

She also handed Tansy a basket of raspberries topped with marigolds, forget-me-nots and rosemary. 'Tell her to put rosemary among the blankets, keeps the moths away.' She smiled at Tansy and pressed her hands.

Amos joined them by the door of the farmhouse and watched Martin settle Tom for the journey back to Newton. 'Remember young woman,' he said with a twinkle, 'kissing's in fashion when gorse is in bloom'.

Martin whipped up Tom in unnecessary haste, thought Tansy, as she waved until they turned the corner into the rickyard and emerged out on to the Newton Road. Martin stayed silent while Tansy pondered Amos' last remark and they were almost back to Newton before she realised what the old man had meant.

'Why, gorse is always in bloom!' she said and laughed aloud, but Martin stayed silent until she could bear it no longer.

'I like your family, Martin. But I think you must be absolutely sure it's what you really want before you leave Staddens.'

Now he broke his silence at last. 'Something's pulling me away. Besides I've a mind to go.' He slowed Tom to a walk and asked Tansy, 'Are you sure you know what you want, Tansy Drewe?'

Tansy hesitated, realised the truth, that she really hadn't the least idea. She rushed on,

'I want to see the world. Go on the train to London. That's where the world begins. You must see, Martin, 'twouldn't be right for me to wed you when neither of us is ready. I may change my mind in a year or two, but not yet!'

'So,' said Martin, 'if I'm to have you then it seems I must wait.' He looked puzzled. 'But how will you know you've found what you want if you don't know what it is?'

Tansy tossed her head, a look of hope and confidence bright on her face. 'I may not know it now but when it arrives, why, then I'll surely recognise it.'

As they got to town the mist closed round them once more and as they neared Bowden Hill she could bear to be at odds with Martin no longer.

'If I'm to come to Staddens again, I'd like to go to the Moor with you.' Shyly, she laid a hand on his arm.

'As soon as you've been there you'll know what I mean,' Martin replied, and, clicking his tongue at Tom, the pony broke into a brisk trot and reached the bottom of the Hill in next to no time. Martin gently lifted Tansy down in the fast-darkening night. Suddenly his lips were on hers, a gentle kiss which stayed on her mouth while she climbed the last few feet to the Post Office.

She compared the two kisses Martin had given her during the day. The first so passionate, the second so gentle. The first his reaction to her spiking his gun, the second hinted of a promise. As she rang the bell she compared the power of the first, which had excited her in its unexpectedness, with the gentleness of the second. Was she being unfair in holding Martin to her?

Through the sound of slipping locks she heard the hard dry coughs of the twins. Remembering Sarah Webber's words, she felt a chill descend on the beauty of the day.

✥ Chapter Eight ✥

Sisters

Tansy Drewe looked across the room to the bed under the eaves where her sister lay sleeping. She watched the rise and fall of her chest and frowned as she admired Norah's cloud of dark brown hair, spread across the lace-edged pillow.

She sat up, swung down her legs and tiptoed across to a large brass-bound chest which lay open at the foot of Norah's bed. She looked at the neat piles of books, underwear, skirts, blouses and last of all the new blue gown their mother had made for Norah's first year in college. On top of the gown lay a mirror, brush and comb set, silver backed.

Tansy took up the mirror and traced the initials S.A.T with her finger then, taking it from the chest, brushed furiously at her mop of red curly hair until it stood out in a bush of frizz like a circus clown's.

'It's not fair!' she shouted in despair, flinging both brush and mirror back into the chest where the mirror shattered, spattering slivers of glass across the room and waking the sleeping girl. Norah shot upright and stared at Tansy, who stood petrified with fright at what she'd done. Norah's look changed from that of puzzlement to one of resignation.

'What have you done this time?' she demanded. Then, when Tansy kept silent, followed her anguished gaze, leapt from the bed and ran to the chest. She saw at once the broken mirror and, touching the broken shards of glass, immediately cut her finger, which bled in slow red drops onto her nightdress.

'You little beast, you've broken my mirror,' she shouted, furious.

'Granny Thomas' mirror you mean,' Tansy was quick to retaliate. 'Sarah Ann Thomas was my grandmother too.' She paused, adding sarcastically, 'But, of course, it's you who gets her things!'

'The mirror set Mother lent me to take to college you mean?' She picked up the precious keepsake – 'Now look at it, it's ruined and all because of your jealousy. I know you wanted it for yourself.' She sucked her bleeding finger.

Tansy's face changed from anger to contrition. 'Norah, I'm sorry, really I am. I was just trying to smooth my hair...' Her voice tailed off and she began to pick bits of glass from bed and floor, lowering her face to hide her shame, sniffing back guilty tears which overflowed from the bold green eyes. If only she hadn't touched the set Granny Thomas had received from Lady Morrison when she'd left service to marry Grandpa. If only she hadn't the beastly red hair which made her act the way she did.

Almost as if Norah could read her sister's thoughts, she straightened from washing blood from her nightgown and faced Tansy. 'And don't blame it on your red hair. It won't do, Tansy. It just won't do. One day your bad temper will get you into trouble, you mark my words. Serious trouble, I shouldn't wonder. You'll end up in prison if you allow your temper to run away with you.'

'Let me take it, Norah. Perhaps Martin Webber can mend it. He's good at fixing things.' But Norah ignored her outstretched hand, shook her head and placed the damaged mirror in her large black bag.

'Don't you think you've done enough damage for one day, Miss. Go back to bed and stay there while I get dressed.' Tansy gave way to Norah, climbed back into bed and took up a small blue book from the bamboo table by her bed. Ignoring Norah she held the book up to her nose, enjoying the smell of leather and tracing the title with her finger, murmuring aloud, 'Black Beauty by Anna Sewell.'

She'd borrowed the book four times already, accompanying Norah to the library in Market Street in the evenings and paying a penny each time for the pleasure. But today the story of the young horse's adventures couldn't lift her above the misery of her spirits. Using the book as a screen she watched Norah wash in the bowl on the blue tiled wash stand, her figure tall and slim in its cotton petticoat. Watched as she fastened her corset, pulled up pink lisle stockings, fixed them to suspenders, stepped into grey hobble skirt and striped blouse, and slipped her feet into round-heeled shoes. Tansy thought of her own clumsy boots and watched enviously as Norah plaited the cloud of thick brown hair and, twisting it into a knot, pinned it to the top of her head. Suddenly conscious of the younger girl's eyes on her, Norah's anger gave way. She smiled a rueful smile.

'Day off today?' she asked and, as Tansy nodded, continued, 'Haven't begun it very well, have you?' She softened still further to add, 'Going down to market?'

Nodding again, Tansy sat up in bed, moving to the bottom of the mattress and pulling back the curtains to peer out into the rapidly lightening day.

'Get me some hankies from the cheap jack, will you? Here's sixpence. Get as many as you can for that.' And she put the shiny coin down on the table by Tansy's bed, looking at her sister across a two-year gap. 'Going to see your sweetheart too I reckon!' she added, and Tansy's cheeks flushed a bright red as she shook her head vehemently.

'Mind your own business, Norah Drewe,' she exclaimed, 'or I shan't get your errand.'

'If you don't I'll have to tell Mother about the broken mirror,' Norah chided, then, good humour restored, she took her hat and coat from the wardrobe and left the room.

With the slamming of the door Tansy relaxed, rested her head on her freckled arms, and gazed across back gardens which stretched away beyond the stone wall of the Post Office's tiny backyard. She looked at the neat rows of broad beans and brussel sprouts set to stand the winter. She watched the Brimmacombe's cockerel with his red comb and black tail feathers gleaming in the early morning sun as he pecked at old cabbage stalks in Rosemary's garden.

Tansy dreamt of the time she would be the proud possessor of a set of silver-backed hairbrushes with her own initials, T.L.D. (Tansy Lillian Drewe), engraved on the back. The time when she too would leave Newton Abbot – not to go to college in London as Norah was to do in a few weeks' time, but to see the world. Only then, she thought, would she be content to settle down and marry Martin Webber.

❧ Chapter Nine ❧

Market-day

'Will you look after the twins while I go over to Ma Sellick's for some flour, Tansy?' Eva Drewe looked tired, her hair untidy, movements slow where normally she was bright and quick. Witness to yet another disturbed night. The seven-year-old twins slept in a rosy heap. Robert, the spokesman for them both, lay on his back snoring gently, his right arm cradling James, who lay curled into his brother's side. A fire burnt brightly, kept going day and night to warm the kettle which steamed gently to moisten the air and ease the hacking coughs that had kept the boys from school for a long month. Tansy smiled at the mops of red hair and scattering of freckles spattered across their neat noses.

'You'll not be long, Mother?' Her brow creased in anxiety. She wanted to get to market and look at the animals before ten o'clock when she had promised to meet Martin Webber at the Drum Clock.

'Let me go for you, Mother. Stay and rest.' But Eva Drewe merely smiled and shook her head.

'I must have a breath of fresh air, Tansy. Then I'll have to take a turn at the counter for your father while he goes down to the station. He's meeting the new minister today.' Then, seeing the look of disappointment on the girl's face she smiled and touched her shoulder. 'It's all right, my dear, you can go as soon as you've done your clothes. The copper's boiling, just keep an eye on the boys from time to time. I'll be back long before you've finished.'

Tansy scraped flakes of soap from the yellow block, whizzed it round in boiling water with a copper stick, then scrubbed collars and cuffs of her grey work dresses and dropped them with petticoats and knickers into the steaming boiler. She took her breakfast into the sitting-room, enjoying the fresh brown egg and home-baked bread her mother had left out for her.

By the time Eva Drewe came back she had hauled her washing from the copper, rinsed it under the pump in the backyard, squeezed it through the iron mangle and was pegging the last garment to the line.

'The boys are still asleep, why don't you try and catch an hour before they wake up? I'll not be long.'

Free at last, she hurried down Beaumont Road past gleaming stone doorsteps, joining a stream of women all flowing in the direction of the market, all trying to be first to get the best of the butter, eggs, pigeons, cream and fresh vegetables.

Tansy reached Courtenay Street to find it full of animals all being driven to market, the air full of honking and bleating. She hovered on the pavement edge, waiting for the crossing sweeper to clear away piles of animal droppings. There she met Rosemary's mother hurrying along, pushing a small handcart bearing a crate of Rhode Island reds and four baskets of brown eggs. She bumped into Tansy, almost tipping her load onto the road.

'Can 'ee watch the cart, Tansy. I wants to see superintendent – promised us a better place ave 'ee!' Tansy hesitated, not wanting to miss the arrival of the Webbers, but long habit and a natural kindness of heart led her to agree and it was nearly ten o'clock before she was free to wander among the pens where she petted lambs, holding out fingers for the young calves to suck.

Soon her attention was caught by a thick-set young man who prodded and hit a herd of young calves into pens, striking their backs with such force that he broke skin on young tender flanks. She watched, sickened by his behaviour, and picked her way through stalls till she was near enough to command his attention. The billycock hat, yellow checked waistcoat, and moleskin trousers seemed familiar. His face, red with the effort he was putting into controlling the terrified animals, registered enjoyment.

'Hey you – stop that!' she shouted. 'You've no call to treat animals that way!' But he continued to lay about him, seemingly unaware of Tansy's shouts. A group of lads drew near, intrigued by the sight of a pretty young woman standing, eyes blazing, hair escaping from under her hat in her fury.

'That's it, Miss, you tell 'un. Jess Hallett, do what the young 'oman tells 'ee!'

'So that's your name, is it? I remember you!' Tansy said, 'And what's more I'm reporting you to the market manager!'

At last Jess Hallett realised he was the centre of Tansy's attention. He looked up from his beating, surprise registering on his broad features. No one had ever interfered with his methods before. His hand, stretched in mid-air, held a thin willow stick, the end bloody from a wound in the back of a small black and white calf which ran away to burrow into a group of calves huddled as far from their torturer as was possible. He sneered at her.

'What's it to do with you? Mind your own business!' Then, realising for the first time that he had an audience, went on, 'Seems as if 'ee needs a bit of stick yerself, my beauty!'

He moved towards Tansy and tried to grab her as she twisted and turned between the groups of farmers which lined the animal pens to look over stock. It was only the arrival of Jack Avery and his team of helpers that brought an end to the chase. As bidding began, Tansy withdrew to Clock Corner. She straightened the new hat, its partridge feather brushing her creamy cheek, tucked strands of red hair back under its brim and looked around for Martin Webber. Her neat figure drew many admiring glances from the groups of men and boys gathered there. She began to tap one small booted foot. Where was Martin? The hands of the Clock were already past ten o'clock and she felt foolish standing there.

Suddenly there was a loud rattling over the cobbled street and the Webbers' pony and trap careered toward her. Martin, whip in hand, stood above the steaming beast and, seeing her standing there, called out, 'Hey, Tansy Drewe, here I be!' and, handing the reins to his father, jumped down at her feet. Then, oblivious of passers-by, placed both hands on her waist and swung her round until she lost her feet and her legs flew through the air, skirts flapping above the ground. At this Tansy reddened and hammered with her fists on his chest till he set her down, whereupon she stamped one foot in temper.

'Martin Webber, what do you think you'm doing? How dare you!'

This scene amused the crowd so much that they began to laugh and whistle. ''Tis the young maid as has been tellin' Jess Hallett off!' they shouted to each other.

'Don't git yerself in a stooer,' Martin said to her at once contrite, then, eager to make amends asked, 'What's all this about Jess Hallett?' and she, speechless with rage, glared as he went on, 'You don't want nothing to do with him. He's a bad lot! Don't you remember 'twas he held the book on the step dancing at the Ram Fair?'

'And I suppose you'm perfect, Martin Webber!' Tansy snorted, 'keeping me waiting...'

She would have told him what she thought of his behaviour, that of Jess Hallett and men in general if she hadn't caught sight of a large red bull which suddenly appeared behind his back. The huge animal stood swaying, held by a long pole with a hook through his nose ring. Martin, seeing the expression on Tansy's face change from annoyance to fright, turned to see the cause. He laughed, turned back and put a firm hand under her elbow.

'Don't 'ee worry, Tansy. He'm quite safe. Widow Bowden's selling him now her husband's gone. Feyther's going to bid for 'un later today.'

Tansy pulled away from his hand, but not too far for fear that Widow Bowden's bull would slip his ring and charge her. Norah had once told her they were inflamed by anything red and hadn't she red hair?

But now the bidding had begun and Martin's father called to him. 'I must go' – still he hesitated, reluctant to leave Tansy's side – 'Meet me at the Penny Arcade at two o'clock. I'll treat you to a fortune reading'.

Now she hesitated, knowing that at two o'clock she would be needed at home so her mother could take a turn at the counter. But ever since the machines had been installed Tansy had longed to have her fortune told. She made up her mind.

'All right, Martin. I'll be there and this time don't you be late.'

She walked away from the animal pens to the butter market, chose hankies for Norah from a stall crammed with cottons, needles, lavender bags and the new lisle stockings she hankered after but couldn't afford. Completing her mother's errands of crochet cotton and sock wool, she hurried home. She helped Eva until the living-room clock registered ten minutes to two, then slipped through the Post Office door to run downhill to the Penny Arcade.

She admired the glass booths, automatic machines lit by coloured lamps, but there was no Love Meter for her to try – and there was no sign of Martin. She waited. Surely he wouldn't keep her waiting twice in one day. Then to her horror she saw a group of men coming towards her from the Courtenay Arms. As they approached they sang 'Tara-ra-boom-de-ay' and in the midst of the group was Jess Hallett, swaggering along, the offending willow cane still in his hand.

Quickly she looked around for somewhere to hide. There was nowhere and nothing to do now but stand her ground. Her chin went up as her heart began to pound. Jess Hallett wasn't going to get the better of her. Besides, she thought, Martin would be here any minute. Jess Hallett saw her, came unsteady on his feet, put his face inches from hers and sneered, 'Well, if it isn't the beauty from the market. Tried to tell me my job this morning, she did!' he announced to his crowd of hangers-on. Then he turned back to Tansy and looked her over slowly, his eyes lingering on her hips, waist, then breasts until she felt a rush of blood to her face.

'Come for the Penny Arcade have 'ee? All on our own too?' He paused. 'Tell 'ee what, I'll forgive 'ee if 'ee'll give us a kiss,' and he bent forward to put his words into action. She twisted away from him, conscious of his beer-laden breath, blotchy face and stubble-covered chin. He pushed his face closer, closer. Desperate, she drew back her head and spat with all her might. Her aim was good, she hit him fair and square in the eye.

'Get away, Jess Hallett, get away from me. Just you wait till Martin Webber gets here, he'll soon put you in your place.' She spoke boldly while her knees shook and her hands were moist with sweat lest Martin didn't come.

'So that's it. Seems the beauty prefers Martin Webber to a 'andsome lad like me.' He looked around sarcastically. 'Don't see your fancy man anywhere hereabouts, do you?' As the group pressed even closer his eyes narrowed as he looked her over yet again. 'You bin in to see the Planascope?' As she shook her head he added, 'Like to see the pretty women would you?' He grabbed her arm tightly while she prayed that Martin wouldn't be much longer. Wherever was he when she needed him so badly?

'Just like 'ee, they are! Except for one difference.' And now he appealed to his audience. 'Us all knows what that is, don't us?!' Now he dragged her into the centre, clear of the men. 'They don't have no shimmies on!' He paused, then went on, 'Wonder if this 'un looks like they?' The crowd sniggered and dug each other in the ribs, watching Jess to see what he would do next. They moved even closer, hemmed in Jess and Tansy, laughing and grinning in anticipation.

'Only one way to find out!' came a voice from the back of the crowd. His face brightened, a leer forming on his besotted countenance. 'That be a good idea. Well done. Why didn't I think of that?' and he began to pull at the buttons on Tansy's jacket. 'Come on, lads, give us a hand. Let's find out if Miss Tansy Drewe be the same underneath all her finery!'

Fear lent a strength to Tansy she never would have believed she could have possessed. She fought with nails, elbows and feet, finally butting Jess Hallett in the stomach with such force that he howled and let her go. The group opened in surprise and she shot through the gap, running like the wind towards the station, crossing the park and home to safety.

✤ Chapter Ten ✤

The New Preacher

Edward Drewe stood behind the grille, his handsome face serious as he served Ma Sellick with stamps. He merely glanced at Tansy as she hurried, gasping through the street door but, just as she was about to slide through the inner door, he called out.

'Just a moment, young woman. I've something to say to you.'

She recognised the stern tenor of his voice, familiar through childhood whenever she obeyed the impulses of her wild temperament. Her heart sank as she stood, waiting for the old woman to leave.

'This is to be between you and me,' he said, 'Your mother has enough to worry about with the boys and their whooping cough, without hearing of your transgressions.'

'What have I done?' she asked, well aware that her hair was slowly shedding pins and falling down her back. Aware too that her face was hot and sweaty, that the back of her blouse stuck to her body.

'I was very surprised to see you being swung off your feet in a public place by Martin Webber this morning. Surprised and, I might add, embarrassed, especially when our new minister asked if I knew the young unruly pair behaving in such unseemly fashion. It pained me to have to admit that half of the "unruly pair" was my own daughter.'

He waited for her to speak. She swallowed hard, horrified to know that he had witnessed the scene with Martin. She prayed that no one had seen her outside the Penny Arcade.

'Martin was pleased to see me, that's all,' she blustered, 'That was why he swung me off my feet. I was cross with him myself.' Then she went on to explain, 'He and his father came to market to buy Widow Bowden's Red Devon bull.' Still her father looked cross so she added by way of appeasement, 'Thought he was dancing The Lancers at the Globe Hotel... good at dancing is Martin. He took part in the step dancing at Lustleigh May Day. Evan Williams beat him that day,' she paused, 'but of course you know all about that...' her voice trailed off.

Edward Drewe's mouth twitched at the corners as he stifled the burgeoning smile, leaving only the twinkle to soften his deep blue eyes. Tansy observed the softening of his expression and knew from past experience that she was more than halfway to being forgiven.

'Well, as 'twas only Martin Webber then I suppose I must put his and your behaviour down to youthful high spirits. But don't let it happen again. Now go and tidy yourself, young lady, and see if your mother needs any help. The new minister's a good man. He's coming to supper tonight and I wish you to be here to help entertain our guest.'

He turned away and began to fill mail sacks for the evening train. Tansy breathed a sigh of relief and crept up to her room to wash and change before her mother's eagle eye spotted anything amiss. Wednesday hadn't worked out a bit the way she'd planned and she threw herself down on her bed, letting disappointment spill out in a storm of tears. Now the evening, her only evening off, was to be spoilt too. This time by her father's guest. Instead of exchanging supper and news with Rosemary and the Brimmacombes she was to be on family duty with an old and no doubt boring minister. 'It's not fair,' she shouted, ripping off her soiled blouse and opening the wardrobe to find something to wear that was suitable for supper with an elderly and religious man. Then she changed her mind and slammed the door shut.

'I'm not going to dress up for some old fogy, just see if I am!' She put on a clean blouse but replaced the green skirt and jacket and studied her reflection in the mirror. Always green, her clothes, she couldn't persuade her mother to allow her to dress in any other colour. Quickly she re-pinned her hair and went downstairs, smiling wryly at the way her father had accepted Martin Webber's behaviour.

'Well, he didn't deserve it!' she muttered under her breath. 'Leaving me at the mercy of Jess Hallett! Just you wait till I see you again, Martin Webber!' She'd tell him just what she thought of him.

When she entered the living-room she was greeted with shrieks of delight from Robert and James. Both boys were dressed in grey knickerbockers and white shirts with frilled collars, their cheeks glowing with excitement.

'Well, you two, you do look smart. Up and dressed, that's good!' And both boys caught at her hands, swinging her round, looking up at her expectantly.

'Mother says we can stay up to supper. There's to be a visitor. Have you brought us anything from market?' adding as she turned away guiltily, 'Oh Tansy, you promised, you promised.'

'I've left it at Rosemary's. No, you can't come with me. Not yet. Not till Mother says you're completely recovered. I'll only be a moment or two.'

She hurried once more through the Post Office where her mother worked. She looked rested, her fair hair neat, smart in a navy frock with tucked bodice trimmed with lace. Eva noticed the tear stains on her daughter's face but made no comment. With Tansy it was best to wait until she was ready to tell.

'I've asked Rosemary to join us for supper. That way you won't miss your evening together. Your Father is making a fire in the parlour and says we can have music for our guest.'

Tansy brightened visibly, at least if she couldn't go out, having Rosemary to supper was the next best thing. She hurried across the road to Ma Sellick's with a lighter heart – perhaps the evening wouldn't be so bad after all.

When she entered the shop, Ma wasn't there. Tansy gazed round at the open sacks lining the floor beneath the counter – lentils, butter beans, porridge oats, flour, sugar and rice. She loved the smell of coffee and the picture above the counter advertising Mazzawattee tea. The lace-capped woman and small girl sitting beside her could have been Grandmother Thomas and me, she thought, regretting the years she'd grown up without her. She searched for something for the twins. Tops and whips they had, bags of marbles too. Kites hung, tails dangling from the ceiling, but they'd be disappointed if they weren't allowed out to fly them. It had to be something special. Then she saw the frogs, tin frogs painted green with black pop eyes. She picked one up and squeezed it – it leapt into the air with a croak! Just the thing, and when Ma Sellick came in answer to her call, she had her money ready.

Her family were already seated when she slipped in through the inner door, Rosemary between Robert and James. She thought the table looked a picture, lit by Cranberry glass lamps which sent a pink glow over her mother's best lace-edged cloth. Blue and white china was set at each place and a bowl of bronze chrysanthemums marked the table centre. Edward sat at the head of the table carving slices from a succulent leg of lamb and passed plates, first to Eva then to their guest.

This was no old fogy, she thought. He looked quite young for a preacher. His shoulders almost touched Edward's as they sat next to one another. She caught her breath. Freckled nose, green eyes and, could it be, red hair! Red hair which fell in thick waves to his shoulders, framing a face with wide mouth partially concealed by moustache and beard. Edward heard her gasp, paused in his carving, turned to the man on his right.

'Ah Tansy, there you are. This is my youngest daughter, Geoffrey. Tansy, this is Geoffrey Llewellyn who's just been appointed our new minister.' He regarded her with a long slow look, then smiled, and as she responded she felt a warmth rise through her body. Quickly she sat down and began to fiddle with her knife, waiting for him to speak. When he did the warmth reached her cheeks.

'I believe I saw you earlier in the day?' he enquired, and seven pairs of eyes stared first at the young red-haired man then at Tansy, awaiting her explanation.

'I'm sure you must be mistaken,' Tansy said, 'I'm sure I'd have remembered if I'd seen you before...' then stopped, covered in confusion.

But still he persisted. 'It was by the Drum Clock – I believe it's called. You seemed to be enjoying a dance. Was it in celebration of Market Day?' His words added even more to her discomfiture. How dare he tease her on such short acquaintance. Edward, seeing her embarrassment, came quickly to her rescue.

'Will you say grace, Geoffrey?' She felt the colour which had diffused her whole being gradually subside. If only her father had prepared her for their visitor, told her he was young and yes, she had to admit, handsome. She stole a glance at the calm, freckled face, watched as he composed himself, noticed how slim were the fingers folded in prayer.

'For health, for home, for food, for keep, for love and life – we thank thee Lord.'

Dishes passed and the twins, round-eyed till now at being allowed to stay up, began to giggle and attack their food. Conversation began, rather stilted at first, but under the benign influence of the new minister the party relaxed.

'What do you do here in Newton when you're not at work? I know that Norah teaches at Bell's School, that Rosemary's a clerk at Vallance's Mill and Tansy's in service. What I don't know is how you spend your free time.'

It was Norah who took it upon herself to supply the answers while Tansy sat biting her lips in frustration. Why did Norah always take over whenever anyone came? Always been bossy, Tansy thought. She'll make a good teacher. All she is good for, a teacher. Probably end up an old maid! Now she was telling Geoffrey Llewellyn about the Summer Fête in Courtenay Park, the Christmas Poultry Fair and the Michaelmas Dance at the Globe Hotel. As she thought of the dance she remembered Martin Webber and how he'd let her down. Let her down twice in one day! She'd have something to say to him when next they met. That she would! Suddenly she became aware that her mother was speaking to her.

'Will you fetch in the junket and cream, Tansy?' Eva said, and she was glad to escape to the kitchen. She took her time fetching down the best china bowls from the dresser. She piled clotted cream into a glass bowl and sprinkled the junket with nutmeg until Rosemary came through the living-room door and the girls were able to talk at last. Hastily, Tansy reached behind her friend to close the door and ensure their conversation went unheard. She met Rosemary's eyes and both girls began to laugh.

'Why, Tansy,' Rosemary exclaimed, 'he could be your brother, your colouring's that alike.' She put an arm round Tansy's shoulders and gave her a comforting hug. 'At least he's an improvement on our last preacher.'

Tansy burst out, 'I wish Father had told me he was young and handsome. I nearly died when he said he'd seen me in town with Martin Webber.' She ran cold water over her hands from the tap at the stone sink and pressed them to her cheeks, which had coloured at the mere mention of Geoffrey's name.

'What happened today? Did you meet Martin as planned?'

Tansy's brow creased into a frown, a frown that usually meant trouble for whoever had been the cause of it. When she'd finished telling Rosemary of her experiences with Jess Hallett she burst into tears and her friend produced a hanky and handed it to Tansy. In all their growing years she had never known her friend possess a hanky when she needed one.

'Never mind, Tansy. At least we've been able to meet this evening, after all. I thought I wouldn't see you and I've some exciting news.'

But the telling of her news had to wait as the door burst open and Robert stood there, legs apart, face red with importance. 'Mother says you're to hurry up with the pudding. We're all waiting.' The girls had no choice but to take the junket and cream through and resume their places at the table.

Tansy watched enviously as Norah rose to serve. Eva Drewe had begun to train her elder daughter in the art of playing hostess, but before Norah could begin there came a 'cronk, cronk' as the two green frogs hurtled across the table. One landed in the junket and the other in the cream.

'What the devil...' Edward Drewe jumped to his feet to peer at the offending objects as they slowly sank out of sight. All eyes stayed riveted on the bowl as Norah wielded a spoon and lifted the metal toys onto her plate while Robert and James giggled and exchanged looks of triumph at the success of their trick.

Edward turned a stern eye in their direction. 'If this is the way you choose to behave then you can go straight up to bed. I'll see you both in the morning. No pudding, Norah!'

As the twins slid from their places and slunk towards the door Tansy followed them, glad of a chance to escape. Feeling partly responsible for their disgrace she settled them into bed then climbed to the attic. There she changed her clothes, combed and re-arranged her hair and descended to the living-room where the table had been cleared and pushed back against the wall. She took her place by the piano, ready to turn the pages for Rosemary.

The girls made a stark contrast; Rosemary in soft blue with dark hair, calm and neat, Tansy now in green striped muslin, the material much too thin for November. She knew instinctively how her last summer's dress set off her tiny waist, her flaming hair. She had added a lacy shawl which had been passed down to her from Grandmother Thomas, the originator of the family inheritance, the detested red hair.

Chapter Eleven

Courtenay House

The next morning Tansy quietly shut the door on the dark living quarters so as not to wake her sleeping family, hurried past the long wooden counter and banged her ankle against a stack of mail bags piled high beside the outer door. She winced with pain, reached out to undo the heavy bolts of the outer door and pulled it to behind her, making sure it was quite shut so as not to incur her father's anger. He was forever expounding the responsibilities involved in being a postmaster.

She turned into Southernhay, walking away from the clay brick terraces which curved down towards town under a mantle of smoking chimneys. When she reached 148 steps she took a deep breath and began to climb the vertical flight that would take her to Courtenay House. Halfway up she stopped at Rosemary's gate in the hope of seeing her friend, but today she was late and there was no sign of her.

Apart from a 'tell you later' they had had no chance to talk the night before and now Rosemary had left for the Mill. Even as Tansy hesitated St Paul's church clock began to strike the hour and she leapt the remaining steps. At the top she was met by a strong wind coming straight off the Moor and her spirits lifted. Today, she thought, she would have no trouble getting the Master's fire to catch. She hurried across Courtenay Road and ran between stone pineapple-topped gates, along the drive and in through the servants' entrance and into the kitchen.

'You'm cuttin' it a bit fine ain't 'ee my maid?' Seth Howell paused in his shoe cleaning as Tansy reached for her morning overall and tied a white cap over unruly red curls.

'The new minister came,' she replied as she collected a water jug from the scullery and carried it through to the iron range, 'and we were late to bed.'

'Well you'd better hurry — you know the Master don't like being kept waitin',' and leaving his row of boots the huge man held the service door open for her. She lugged through the jug of scalding water, struggled up two flights to the first-floor landing and rapped on Charles Vallance's bedroom door.

'Come in, come in!' an irritated voice rang out as she wrestled with the heavy panelled door.

'You're late, Drewe!' Charles Vallance strode about the room, dressed only in nightshirt and slippers, gold watch open in his hand. A frown sat between thick black brows which matched the heavy waxed moustaches and centrally parted hair. She set off across the room, managing a bob from the waist on the way.

'Sorry sir, but the new minister came to supper and...' she began but he waved her apology away and watched as she struggled to lift the heavy jug on to the tiled washstand.

'Here, let me...' Large hands took over, pouring steaming water into the dainty violet decorated basin. Setting down the jug, her employer began to pull the nightshirt over his head then stopped, suddenly conscious of Tansy, standing frozen with shock as his sturdy hair-covered legs began to emerge.

'What are you waiting for?' he shouted, 'I'm sure there's plenty for you to do elsewhere!' She darted forward, seized the jug and ran from the room. His words floated after her as she made for the basement steps. He was right of course, she thought. There was a great deal to do, now she must light the fire in the breakfast room in just twenty minutes. Even in summer the Master insisted the shady room be warm for his breakfast.

Seth waited for her at the top of the steps with a trug filled with sticks, wood and coal. She seized this from the old man's strong hands, rushed back up to the ground floor to open shutters and clean out the day before's ashes. As she laid paper and wood she prayed aloud, 'Please, Lord, help your lowly servant,' and all went well. The wood burnt steadily as she piled on first small then larger pieces of coal. If there had been no wind but a damp mist drifting across the hill the fire would have faltered and gone out. Then she would have had to shout for Seth who would have placed a sheet of paper over a shovel balanced in the fire opening in the hope that the draught would set flame to paper. Many times Seth had rescued her from the Master's wrath. She worked the bellows gently and by the time she heard Charles Vallance's footsteps on the stairs a steady glow filled the hearth. Hastily she brushed ash from the ivy patterned tiles, collected her brushes and slipped from the room.

'Comin' to help me now, be 'ee, Tansy Drewe?' Seth was waiting in the courtyard, harness and brasses over his arm. Now was the time she loved, a time she looked forward to each day when she could take a few minutes' break. Since the new bathroom had been installed she no longer carried water to her Mistress, or Harry and Emma when they were home, but the Master remained stubborn and continued to wash in his dressing-room.

The house was quiet without the young Vallances but Emma was due back from her visit to her grandmother's at the end of the week and Harry would be home from his stay in Torquay soon. Then, thought Tansy, things would be more lively. Now she watched Seth harness Tinker into the smart gig Charles Vallance used to drive downhill to the Mill.

'Here Tinker.' She held out a handful of apple cores on her palm and enjoyed the warmth of his rough tongue as he ate. Then the pony's velvet nose searched her pocket for the rest of the treat he knew would be there. Next Seth slid the bit between the pony's teeth, buckled on the harness and set a gleaming brass bell high above its fringe.

'Come up, Tinker, come away now boy,' and Seth coaxed the lively five-year-old back between the shafts.

'Hold his head now, Tansy,' and as she gripped the bridle he slipped reins through rings and straps. 'That's right. You'd make a fine stable lad that yo'ud.' He led the trim outfit out from the courtyard into the garden. As they reached the front steps Charles Vallance's impressive figure, dressed in grey worsted, emerged from the house, watch in hand. He ran lightly down the steps, astonishing for one of such heavy build.

Seth touched his cap, 'Good morning, Sir!'

'Good morning, Seth. Right on time. Excellent, excellent.' He snapped shut his watch case and stepped smartly into the trap. Seth handed him the reins and sat down in the back of the gig.

'Walk on,' Charles Vallance commanded, clicking his tongue and slapping Tinker briskly on the back with the reins. The pony broke into a sharp trot, setting the bell jingling and drawing the gig away down the drive.

The moment they disappeared through the gates a figure emerged from the laurels, hurried along the drive and passed through the arch to the servants' entrance. It hesitated there as Tansy came out to shake dusters, ready to begin her weekly brass cleaning. Seeing the figure she stopped.

'Who's there?' she called, 'What do you want?'

''Tis I, Tansy. Martin.'

She drew back, looked round fearfully lest anyone should see him.

'Whatever are you doing here?' she demanded.

'I've come to apologise for yesterday,' he said, shifting from one foot to the other, turning his cap round and round between work-roughened hands. Surprise gave way to anger on Tansy's face.

'I should think so indeed. Leaving me in the lurch. Where were you when I needed you? Nowhere to be seen. Jess Hallett and his crowd molested me at the Penny Arcade and you were nowhere to be seen.' Then she stopped to draw herself up to her full height, even though the top of her head reached only to the middle button of Martin Webber's jacket. 'I showed 'em what was what!' she exclaimed proudly. She went on, 'You'd best be off or you'll get us into serious trouble, we're not allowed followers,' and as she said this she blushed and turned away.

Now Martin stopped her with a hand on her arm. 'Please Tansy, hear me out... we had trouble with Widow Bowden's bull. Slipped his ring he did and led us a proper dance.'

She hesitated at the door, awed at the thought of the huge creature breaking free, her curiosity and a morbid fascination getting the better of caution.

'What happened – did you catch 'un?' Martin's face lit up as he recalled the excitement of the chase through town, the moment when the bull jumped the low wall and landed in the river. The battle as men fought with ropes against the animal's strength.

'Cornered 'un in river but,' he added, 'by the time us got 'un tethered 'twas too late to come and meet 'ee...' His voice tailed off. Tansy looked slightly appeased, remembering how the massive animal had frightened her the day before, but she didn't intend to let him off lightly and, jutting out her chin, she insisted, 'And why couldn't 'ee have come to the Post Office after and told me what happened, I'd like to know?'

Martin now coloured up. 'It was such thirsty work us went down Market Inn and us forgot...' he stammered, 'Well, it sort of slipped my mind...'

At this Tansy remembered how Martin's absence had caused her acute embarrassment and, yes, even danger. She stamped her foot at him.

'If I mean so little to you that I can just "sort of slip your mind" then I want no more to do with you.' And at this moment, Cook came out to look for her.

'Oh, my dear soul!' she exclaimed when she saw Martin Webber. 'Whatever are you doin' here?' she asked. Then, turning to Tansy, 'Missus is asking for you – you'm to go to the morning-room straightaway.' She scolded Martin, 'You'd best be off if you don't want this young woman to lose her position.' With that she pulled Tansy back into the kitchen and shut the door in Martin Webber's face.

'Go on up, my maid, Missus has been asking for 'ee for past ten minutes. Hurry now, and don't let that young man come here again. You know the rules!' She pointed with one flour-covered finger to the illuminated sign close to the bell pulls. It read: 'No followers will be allowed at any time or for any reason – the breaking of this rule will lead to instant dismissal'

Caroline Vallance looked annoyed at being kept waiting by the lowliest of her staff. She sat erect at her desk, wearing a grey and white dress, its pleated bodice decorated with tiny mother-of-pearl buttons, her fair hair piled on top of her head.

'What were you doing that it took so long for you to come?' she demanded, but when Tansy opened her mouth to explain she waved her hand. 'No matter,' and went on, 'Cook tells me you are quick at cooking?' Tansy nodded. 'As you know Emma will be home at the end of the week and her birthday party is arranged for Thursday. I want you to help Cook.'

'But what about my brasses, Ma'm?' Tansy wanted to know.

'That's all right, you can do those another day. Now run along.'

❧

When Emma Vallance stepped from the station cab, it was a new Emma – dressed in a striped cotton skirt and tucked silk blouse, her hair up under a smart straw boater trimmed with ribbon.

She got out of the cab and flew first to her mother, then, with barely a nod in the direction of Janet Luscombe, she hugged Tansy then of Hetty Westcott and Stephen Howell.

'Oh, how I've missed you all!' she exclaimed, 'but you must see what Grandmama gave me,' and she turned to the cabby who opened the boot and took out a bicycle, complete with basket and bell, and set it down on the gravel. No sooner had the wheels touched the ground than Emma seized it and got on, pushing herself off with one foot and pedalling slowly and with a pronounced wobble round the circle of lawn. Tansy, Hetty and Stephen clapped their hands at her performance, but Janet Luscombe stood and sulked at the paucity of her young mistress's greeting. Caroline Vallance frowned at such behaviour but decided to overlook it as Emma got off in front of her.

'Here Drewe, take this round to the stables. You must come with me when I go out for a ride.'

Then she linked arms with her mother and they passed up the front steps and in through the door. Her voice floated back, 'It's lovely to be home, Mama. Exeter was wonderful but...'

Tansy picked up the bicycle, then with a quick look round to make sure no one was looking, placed one foot on the nearest pedal and clasped the handlebars, copying what she'd seen Miss Emma do. The feeling of movement pleased her and, finding it less difficult than driving Martin's trap, she grew more confident. She sat on the broad saddle and pushed the pedals round to gain momentum. She aimed the bike at the arch opening into the stable yard, wobbled wildly through it, then crashed into the water trough. Seth, who was cleaning the carriage in the coach-house, came running, picking up first the bicycle, then Tansy.

'What be 'ee doing now, my beauty?' he wanted to know as she brushed gravel from her skirt and hands.

And Tansy, finding herself none the worse for the experience, laughed.

''Tis Miss Emma's new bicycle. Isn't it splendid?' Together they admired the polished steel, gleaming bell and handsome leather saddle.

'She's promised us a ride next time she goes out!' Tansy said, stretching the truth a little.

'Well, I should take a few lessons afore I try riding 'un downhill to town,' Seth advised before he led the machine away to be cleaned and polished alongside Amos Vallance's gleaming carriage and Charles Vallance's gig.

⚜ Chapter Twelve ⚜

Chapel

It was Sunday morning and Tansy sat with the other servants from Courtenay House listening to the new preacher as he gave his first sermon. The three girls made a pretty picture. Hetty Westcott, serious in her best blue, Janet Luscombe fair and flirtatious in Miss Emma's cast-off red velvet, and Tansy as usual in green. Admiring Tansy from the gallery opposite sat Martin Webber, clean scrubbed in a black suit with stiff wing-collar, a bowler hat on his knee.

Tansy, however, had eyes for no one but Geoffrey Llewellyn and his words flowed over her unheeded as she admired his handsome face and large frame, which filled the plain wooden pulpit. She sat enjoying the novelty of knowing someone who appeared to bear the same cross in life. She must ask him how he managed to be a preacher when he possessed red hair and surely the temperament that went with it. Suddenly, she became aware of Hetty nudging her to bring her attention back to the service and Geoffrey's closing words.

'Today we have here in our midst a young man who on Wednesday last and in our town, saved the life of one of your chapel members. A woman, who was in danger of being crushed to death by one of the beasts of the field of whom I have been speaking. She is too shaken to come here today but is alive and, I am assured by Dr Weekes, will recover in a few days. I would ask you all to join in giving thanks for the courage of this young man, who put his own safety at risk to save someone of frail and advanced years.'

Tansy listened, intrigued as to who this hero might be till Hetty nudged her again and pointed across to Martin, who stood smiling in her direction.

'Is that your sweetheart then?' she wanted to know, but Tansy shook her head in denial. The last thing she wanted was to have her name linked with that of Martin now she had, at last, met someone she could really look up to.

By the time they had filed down into the vestibule a crowd of well-wishers had surrounded the man of the moment and Geoffrey Llewellyn was standing apart from his congregation to allow the young man his moment of glory. Seeing Tansy he came forward. 'Good morning Tansy, and how are you today?' he asked, taking her hand and pressing it while she blushed scarlet from head to foot.

'I'm quite well, thank you,' she hesitated, 'Sir', she added, not liking to call him by his Christian name in public.

'Aren't you going to congratulate your young man on his act of bravery?' he asked, eyes twinkling as he observed Martin trying to break free from the group of admirers. She hesitated, shocked that it was Martin who had saved Keziah Chard from the path of the bull. Geoffrey led her forward then placed her small hand in Martin's large rough one and smiled at them both.

'Now, Martin,' he said, 'Here is someone who I'm sure wants to speak to you. I'll leave you two together.' He turned once more to Tansy. 'Your parents have invited me to supper next Wednesday. I look forward to seeing you then.' And with that he moved away to speak to the Church Elders. Tansy turned to Martin, annoyed that she seemed to be the only one who hadn't been told of his brave act.

'Why didn't you tell me what really happened last Wednesday?' she asked, pressing his hands in both of hers in agitation. 'How could I have treated you so badly when you came to the house?' Martin shrugged. 'You know I'm used to handling animals all the time.' He changed the subject. 'Mother wants to know when you'm coming out to the farm again?' Tansy, still annoyed at being put in the wrong, retaliated, 'And you, do you want me to come out to the farm again?' she mimicked, then her expression changed to one of contrition when she saw the hurt expression in his eyes.

'Of course I want you to come.' He paused then went on in a rush, 'I've asked Joseph Norsworthy if 'n I can borrow Fairy for the afternoon – thought you might like to try riding. But if you'd rather not...' Now Tansy flushed with pleasure and put out her hands towards him.

'Why Martin that's wonderful, of course I'll come. But my next Sunday off isn't for ages. Can I come on Wednesday?' Now it was Martin's turn to look pleased.

''Tis Market Day but I could take you back with me afterwards.' Tansy was so excited at the thought of learning to ride at last that she reached up and kissed him on the cheek. 'See you Wednesday,' she said, and watched as Martin hurried off.

Geoffrey Llewellyn, who had been watching this exchange from the shadows, now came up to Tansy. 'I think he's finding fame hard to handle. Give him time.' He paused and looked down at Tansy, flushed and pretty. 'Be kind to him,' he said, and she blushed. It was as if Geoffrey could read her very thoughts and moods. He pressed her hand once more and his touch immediately banished Martin from her thoughts as she walked uphill, deep in thoughts, all of which were centred on Geoffrey Llewellyn.

Tansy wasn't allowed to forget Martin so soon. All the talk in the kitchen was of Wednesday's incident and his quickness of mind in sweeping Keziah Chard from the path of Widow Bowden's bull.

'That's all they'm talking about,' said Hetty Westcott, 'them upstairs. Why he's quite the hero, Tansy, your Martin Webber.'

She grew angry as she tried to deny that Martin was 'hers', at the same time feeling mean at her treatment of him. She was halfway through the huge pile of luncheon dishes when she received a summons to the drawing-room.

'You'd best change aprons, Tansy – perhaps the Master has heard about your young man's visit. Just you deny you knew anything about him coming – that's best,' and Cook gave her a gentle push towards the service stairs.

Tansy's heart beat fast as she mounted the basement stairs, where painted walls gave way to paper. Daily use had taught her that eight thrushes ate strawberries on each strip. She tapped on the drawing-room door, wondering if this was to be her last day at Courtenay House. How would she break the news to her parents that she had lost her job? – her very first job. Would the loss stop Norah from going to college?

'Come.' The Master's voice rang through the panelled door; she drew a deep breath and slipped into the room, the slight draught she brought in with her setting ruby lustre drops chinking on the mantelpiece. Polished brass reflected the sunlight which poured into the pretty room. She hesitated inside the door, bobbing to Charles Vallance who scrutinised this, the lowliest member of his staff, through pince-nez.

'Mrs Vallance tells me that you received a call here from a young man on Thursday morning?' He waited for her nod of affirmation.

'Can you tell me the reason for this?' he asked, producing his gold watch and dusting the glass with a hanky. Tansy's face began to colour and she shifted from one foot to the other. Briefly she explained the reason for Martin's visit then, as always a great teller of stories, rushed on with an account of her abortive visit to the Penny Arcade. At the mention of the Penny Arcade the Master's eyebrows rose high on his wide forehead and he exchanged meaningful looks with Caroline Vallance, who shook her head. Tansy's palms were wet with perspiration as she stood, awaiting sentence.

'You know the rules, Drewe. No followers and no callers at the house at any time.' He paused to replace his watch in his pocket then went on, 'However, as I understand this was none of your doing and,' he paused again while Tansy sensed a reprieve, 'as I have heard that the young man in question performed an act of great bravery last Wednesday, I will say no more on the subject except to advise you to obtain your parent's permission to court – Martin Webber is it? And to stay away from Penny Arcades in future.'

Here Caroline Vallance rose to her feet and smiled at Tansy. 'You may go, Drewe. By the way, Emma has been invited to a party next week and would like you to do her hair.' Tansy bobbed and nodded, surprised at this unexpected request.

'Yes'm. Thank you, Sir,' and fled, relief flooding over her at her narrow escape. Arriving back in the kitchen she met Cook's enquiring gaze.

'It's all right. I'm let off. They like Martin Webber because he's a hero.' Here Tansy stopped short of telling her other news, knowing that Janet Luscombe was going to be angry at being replaced in Miss Emma's bedroom. Suddenly she longed for the comfort of home, for the privacy of her room in the attic. Even when she had to share with Norah it was better than the cramped space at Courtenay House where Janet and Hetty took all the room in the wardrobe and chest and extinguished candles long before she had a chance to read. She wondered if Norah had found anyone to mend Granny Thomas' mirror, what the twins were up to and whether Geoffrey Llewellyn had called again. She felt a quickening of her pulse as she remembered his words after church.

'See you at supper next Wednesday.' Then she remembered that that was the day she had arranged to go to Staddens. She could send a message to Martin but the thought of learning to ride overcame her reluctance to miss the supper meeting with Geoffrey. Martin might be everyone's hero, she thought, but certainly he wasn't hers.

✣ Chapter Thirteen ✣

The Riding Lesson

When Wednesday came Tansy waited for Martin under Drum Clock, a feeling of pleasurable excitement filling her being. She sent up a prayer that he wouldn't be late, wouldn't forget their arrangement – and on the stroke of two he was there. She clambered up into the trap and sat happily while Martin drove through the Wrey Valley, which deep summer had turned into a tunnel of green. When she saw Norsworthy's mare tethered to the gate leading to the rickyard she was filled with delight.

''Tis Fairy. She'm gentle to ride and has a good mouth,' Martin said and cupped his large, square hands for Tansy to place her foot in. 'You must ride side-saddle... up you go,' and she swung her legs across Fairy's back and round the pommel, arranging her skirt as best she could. 'Now I'm going to walk you round the yard till you get the feel of it.' Tansy, excited beyond measure, allowed her body to go with the movement of the mare until Martin instructed her to kick her legs and make Fairy trot. 'Now kick again when you want her to stop.' Leading, rein in hand, he ran beside the girl whose hair matched the colour of Fairy's coat.

'Now take the reins and hold them loose in your hands. That's right.' Soon she had learnt to guide the pony through the orchard and round the trees. When Sarah Webber called them in for dinner, Tansy had mastered the rudiments of riding.

'She'm doing well, a natural born horsewoman!' Martin announced over plates of Likky Stew and Nackerjack, and Tansy ate her leeks, bacon and dumpling with relish. Her eyes sparkled with the excitement of discovering new skills and she asked him, 'Can we go for a proper ride after dinner?' After a moment's hesitation, he agreed.

They set off along the river, then climbed through Houndtor Wood, crossing the Bovey and following the bridle-path to Manaton Green, where Martin fetched glasses of ale from the Half Moon. There they rested Fairy and the cob under beech trees while a group of men teased Martin.

'Did'n know as you was sparkin'!' they called.

'Hey, you given up your cricket now, my buck?' Martin, blushing furiously, called to Tansy, 'We'm going on,' and hurried his mount on to the crossroads where Tansy demanded, 'Where are we going now?' and when he hesitated added, 'You promised to take me to Bowerman's Nose one day!' When he continued to look doubtful she pressed him. 'You know, the day we saw the fire at Foxworthy.' But still Martin demurred.

'We should go back, Hayne's too far for a first ride.' Tansy, eager for further adventures, dug her heels into Fairy's side and set off, ignoring his shouts for her to come back until there was nothing he could do but follow. Soon they were climbing Hayne Down and at the summit Tansy swept her arms in a wide arc, letting Fairy crop the sweet grass which grew between heather and rock. They tethered the horses to a hawthorn bush and he led her across the granite pile to stare at Bowerman's Nose. She looked at the stones rising in the shape of a torso, topped by a jutting chin and rounded nose, but Tansy was disappointed.

'Don't look like a hunter at all. 'Tis more like Jess Hallett 'cept he's wearing a flat cap instead of a bowler.' She laughed and ran off to hide in a cleft of the rocks, startling a rabbit which ran from under her feet. Martin didn't come and find her. Instead he called, 'Come out, Tansy. Come and see the view.' She found him at the tor's edge, looking down on the Green where half an hour before they had drunk ale. White figures moved about the cricket field close by the church and she realised Martin was more interested in the game than her. She tossed her head and stamped her feet.

'I'm going on.' she declared. 'You can stay here all afternoon for all I care. I'm going over there.' She waved her hand in the direction of a pile of rocks which stood out, black against the shimmering heat haze of the bilberry-strewn valley floor. She hauled herself onto Fairy's back, kicked the pony with her heels and took off. Martin shouted at them to stop but the pony flattened her ears and carried on, trotting off along the track then breaking into a gallop. Martin leapt to his feet, hastily untying the cob who was whinnying and stamping his feet in his desire to be off after the mare. They caught up with them at the foot of Hound Tor.

'You'll get yourself killed if you're not careful,' Martin shouted angrily as he caught Fairy's reins and hauled them to a standstill. But Tansy was gazing in awe at the caves and columns of granite which rose in a long ridge in front of them.

''Tis wonderful!' she exclaimed, then turned to Martin, 'I saw rabbits and lots of birds. Why, they don't fly away when you'm on a horse.' Martin was captivated by her energy, her body, aglow with excitement, and further words of caution stayed on his tongue. Instead he led her down to Hunter's Gate and on to Becca Pool. Here they stopped to unsaddle their mounts and drink deeply from the cold moorland water. After they had rested Martin offered to teach Tansy how to tickle trout and she tucked up her skirt and waded into the pool after him.

'Don't move.' he commanded, and they stayed immobile in the still hot afternoon until she could hear Martin's breathing as he held his hand under a spotted fish as it hovered, almost invisible over a stone. Suddenly he moved and his hand came up with a trout wriggling in his grasp. Now Tansy was upset to see the creature's mouth open as it gasped for water and she pleaded with Martin to put it back. Reluctantly he let the fish slide back into the pool. He looked puzzled.

'There's no pleasing you, is there, Tansy Drewe? I kin catch enough for supper in an hour.' Disgruntled, he returned to the bank where mosquitoes hummed and damselflies lit reeds with brilliant blue and green.

They sat silent, each busy with their own thoughts, till suddenly they became aware of each other's bodies. Close and yet not close. Martin took her hand and traced the fortune lines. She let him. He moved close, slid his arm round her waist. Tansy found it pleasant and closed her eyes, enjoying the heat of the sun, the heat of his body next to hers. They lay back on the bank, listening to the buzz of a bumble-bee. It stopped and she opened her eyes, aware suddenly of Martin's breath on her face. His blue eyes regarded her, full of passion, deepening as his lips descended on hers until her mouth was trapped in his. She closed her eyes again and allowed him to caress her body. She allowed him to undo the row of buttons on her shirt and felt relief from the August sun as he slid off her skirt and she lay in her chemise, enjoying the sensual feeling that was beginning to steal over her. But when she felt his hands warm on her breasts her eyes flew open, she pushed him away and jumped up.

'No, no, you mustn't!' she shouted at his naked figure.

'Why not?' he pleaded, 'You'm my sweetheart or you wouldn't be here with me like this.' Tansy began to put on her skirt, fasten her blouse and, with a look of fury and disappointment, Martin turned from her and dived into the pool. She finished dressing and sat watching him move effortlessly through the water. Suddenly she was overcome with a misery so profound that her stomach knotted with an emotion she could not understand. Finally he came out of the water and back to her and began to put on trousers and shirt while a silence grew into a wall between them.

'Get Fairy,' he said, 'We'm going back.' He saddled the horses, mounted the cob and waited impatiently for her to drag herself up onto the mare. The journey home was accomplished in total silence until they reached Heaven's Gate when Tansy, exhausted by the long hard ride, slipped sideways from the saddle onto the hard road and Martin, softening at last, lifted her up onto the saddle in front of him. Leading Fairy they covered the last mile home, the sun's heat begining to lessen, creatures scuttled away from them into banks and holes. A barn owl overflew the hedge beside them on its evening hunt and when they rode into Staddens Tansy almost fell when Martin lifted her from the cob and set her down. For a moment their bodies collided and Tansy breathed two words into his ear – 'Forgive me'. When he didn't respond she added, ''Twas a wonderful day, Martin. The best day of my whole life...' Her voice trailed away as she left the sentence unfinished and he looked at her gravely.

'Then why did 'ee spoil it?' She shook her head. 'I don't know, I wanted you but something stopped me... please,' she repeated, 'forgive me. I need time, time to know myself, only then can I give myself.' At last he smiled.

'You'm a puzzle Tansy Drewe and no mistake.' He went on, 'You'd best go indoors while I take Fairy back. Mother'll give you some tay.' She was grateful for the comfort of Sarah Webber's warm presence but Martin's mother didn't smile when she handed the cup to Tansy and her words when they came were serious.

'Don't break my Martin's heart, Tansy.' she said, 'He thinks so much of you, 'tis cruel to play with his affections.' It was as if she knew what had taken place up on the Moor. Tansy blushed as she remembered Martin's embraces at the pool. Why had she stopped him from loving her? And even as she remembered, Geoffrey Llewellyn's face grew before her. Would she have held back if it had been he who held her in his arms? Conscious of Sarah watching, waiting for her to speak, she said gravely, 'I will never accept Martin unless I can do so with my whole heart and that time hasn't come.' Then she went on, 'I have a strong feeling that I need to go away from here, to journey to another place. Until then I can't commit myself to anyone.' Sarah accepted her promise and waved them off in the trap.

Neither she nor Martin spoke on the way back to Newton but when he lifted her down at the bottom of Bowden Hill she spoke out with passion, 'You'll not want to see me again will 'ee Martin Webber? Not want to see a girl who doesn't know her own mind from one day to next?' Yet even as she spoke she wished with all her heart that he would deny it, and when he did she felt a rush of gratitude for his generosity of spirit.

'Seems as if 'ee don't know what 'ee do want!' he said. 'That I will try to understand but perhaps until you do find out t'would be best if us don't meet.' He bent and kissed her lightly on the cheek and was gone, leaving Tansy with a sense of loss so deep that tears slid from her green eyes and she paced up and down Southernhay as she tried to compose herself before going in to face her family.

⚜

Thursday came and with it Miss Emma's party, her eighteenth! Tansy and Cook rolled up their sleeves and began on the baking.

'Can we make Chudleighs, Cook?' At first Cook demurred.

'That's for country volk' she said, 'You don't make that sort of thing for the likes of they toffs.' But in the end Tansy won her over and was proved right later, when the splits filled with Cook's strawberry jam and clotted cream disappeared rapidly from large plates.

By four o'clock the house was ready, a smell of baking filtered up from kitchen to hall, where Tansy hovered ready to take coats and wraps. Hetty Westcott stood behind a rose-patterned Round Betty ready to fill the twelve china cups.

'You do look nice, Miss Emma.' Tansy couldn't stop from speaking her mind at the sight of her young mistress in a new red taffeta gown with tucked bodice and leg-of-mutton sleeves which showed off dainty wrists and soft white hands. Tansy, suddenly conscious of her own work-roughened hands, hid them behind her back.

'Thank you, Drewe. Mother says you can show me how you arrange your hair.' She bent towards Tansy, adding in a whisper, 'Luscombe can't make mine look as good no matter how hard she tries.' She tossed long blonde ringlets back behind tiny ears while Janet Luscombe glared malevolently at Tansy.

The rapid click of hooves, followed by the sound of an automobile horn, announced the arrival of Emma Vallance's guests and almost at once the hall filled with the swish of taffeta as a crowd of young girls in colours as bright as peacocks filled the hall. They laughed and giggled and handed over packets and envelopes. Tansy was kept busy hanging coats and wraps in the small ante-room where she smoothed and touched silk and velvet. On a sudden impulse she gave in to temptation and tried on a dark blue wrap. She admired the way it swung out from her shoulders in the new cape line. Excited, she stared at herself in the Cheval mirror. It was the first time she had seen herself in blue, not the green her mother insisted was 'her colour'. Her eyes however, instead of reflecting the colour of the wrap stayed obstinately green while her hair fought to free itself from the confining cap and her freckles stood out in large blobs as they always did when she got excited. Suddenly she heard Caroline Vallance's voice calling her name. She hastily took off the wrap and hung it up.

'There seems to be no end to your talents, Drewe!' she exclaimed, 'I am given to understand from Cook that you know lots of party games?' As Tansy's eyes widened in surprise she added, 'I want you to help Westcott and Luscombe after tea. Blind Man's Buff and that sort of thing. Nothing rough, the conjuror will come at the end to bring the party to a climax.' Delighted, Tansy nodded her head vigorously at the prospect of actually taking part in the party herself, quite unheard of, and Caroline added, 'Ask Luscombe to lend you one of her afternoon gowns, that grey just won't do. Don't want Emma's friends thinking we can't afford proper livery.' And she swept past her into the dining-room to supervise tea.

'Trade' Tansy muttered to herself as soon as her mistress was out of earshot. Later, as she and Cook shared the little pile of treats in the kitchen, she told Cook how Eva Drewe always sniffed when Caroline Vallance's name was mentioned.

'Mother says Caroline Vallance used to be Hilda Widecombe when they were at school together. Her father owns Widecombe's Emporium in Courtenay Street.' Tansy sniffed, 'Caroline indeed! Giving herself airs and graces when everyone knows she's only trade.' Tansy's imitation of her mother set Cook off. She liked a laugh and if it was at the expense of the people she worked for then so much the better.

'You're a real little caution, Tansy Drewe,' she said, 'and no mistake.'

As the time for Norah's departure grew near a growing sadness crept over Tansy. She spoke her thoughts aloud as she polished silver at the long table in the kitchen at Courtenay House.

'Norah leaves for college next Friday,' she said, absent-mindedly dipping a finger wound round with cotton into whiting powder. 'I wish there was something I could give her to take to London for luck– something to remind her of me when she's up there and among all those famous people and places.'

'That's what I'd like,' exclaimed Janet as she pressed Emma Vallance's red party frock. 'My Cousin Annie works up London for one of they toffs. Walking out with a Sergeant in the Lancers she is.' She sighed and replaced the iron with a fresh one from the range. She held it up to her face to test the temperature then spat on the black face and watched it sizzle. Then she rubbed one aching foot against her calf. 'Have steam presses in her place, not these old fangled things!'

Hetty looked up, her face darkened with memories. 'My Jack was stationed in London afore they sailed for South Africa.' She sounded wistful, her voice full of longing. 'That was way back in May and now here 'tis August and still no more news.'

'Haven't you heard since then?' Tansy wanted to know.

'Just the two letters I've had.' Here she took crumpled pieces of paper from her pocket and smoothed them out on the kitchen table. Tansy looked down at the letters, discoloured and wrinkled, while Hetty looked up and quoted their contents as one who has learned the words by heart.

'First is about his beloved horses,' she said. 'In a state they are, short of forage, water and no grazing. Still with their winter coats on in all this heat, lots of them die after the fighting.' She peered at the scrap of paper as if willing it to say more. 'This one says he's at Mafeking. That they're shooting the horses for food. Says if it was left to him he would like to sweep the Boers off the face of the earth. Says the Generals on both sides have an arrangement not to shoot on Sundays. Waiting for General Buller to relieve them. Says he sleeps with a round of ammunition and a rifle for a pillow. Says the Boers have invented a gun called a Mauser and the bullets explode inside you.'

She shivered in spite of the hot day. Suddenly she straightened, cleared her throat and put a comforting hand on Tansy's shoulder, asking of the girl who stood weeping freely at the account of the animals' suffering, 'What would you like to give Norah if you could afford anything in the world?'

Tansy hesitated for a minute, then her face brightened. 'Why that's easy – a gold fob watch with pin bow, all set with rubies just like the one the conjuror tricked us into believing he'd smashed at Miss Emma's party last week.' The three women paused in their tasks, remembering the awesome moment when bits of watch lay disclosed in his silk hanky.

'Wasn't it dreadful?! You should have seen Miss Emma's face – for one moment she thought that were the end of her birthday present.' Cook, who had been listening to the girls' chatter, laughed and shook her head.

'You'm aiming high Tansy Drewe and no mistake – a gold watch indeed!' She clicked her tongue and poured steaming water into the large teapot and set out a fruit cake for their afternoon tea. Hetty turned to Tansy.

'Missus says Master Harry's coming home next week. Wants us to clean his room, wash the curtains and paintwork, freshen up the bed linen.' She stopped, thinking hard. 'May have to change your day off if we'm to get it finished by Friday.'

'Oh no, Hetty, I must go home Wednesday or I shan't be able to say goodbye to Norah.' She stood, appalled at the thought. 'Unless I can change to Friday, we'll be bound to have done by then.' She brightened. 'Then I could go to the station.' And Hetty took pity on her.

'I'll change with you, Tansy, so there can be no objection. Would you like me to mention it to the Missus?' As Tansy nodded she added, 'Don't forget you're to do Miss Emma's hair for Mary Oliver's party.' She looked round quickly to see if Janet had left the room. 'Janet's in a real pet about that, I'd try and keep out of her way till 'tis done. Lucky for you Missus has arranged for her to go into town on some errands.'

But when Thursday came round Janet returned just as Tansy pushed a mother-of-pearl comb into the pleat of hair at the back of Emma Vallance's head. Tansy had curled her young mistress's blonde hair into a softly curling fringe above her excited blue eyes and creamy skin.

'Why, you look a real treat Miss Emma,' said Tansy as she stood back, head on one side, pleased with her efforts. She admired the watch which rose and fell on Emma' softly rounded bosom, the rubies set in the gold bow which matched the red taffeta dress. Emma took hold of Tansy and danced her round the bedroom, stopping only when the door opened to admit Janet.

'I hope Mary's brother is there. He looks so handsome in his naval uniform. He's on The Falcon and they're due in at Devonport any day now,' Emma paused for a last look at herself in the mirror.

'Trap's at door, Miss Emma.' Janet intervened grimly. She put a dark cloak round Emma Vallance's shoulders and pushed her gently towards the door. Tansy stayed to tidy away the curling tongs and brushes but as she turned to leave Janet came and barred her way, two spots of colour rising in her cheeks.

'I know what you'm after, Tansy Drewe – you wants my position here as lady's maid, don't 'ee? You've always wanted to be above stairs ever since you come. What's more you don't care how you get there. I know your sort,' she went on, 'trading on your hair...' With that she pushed Tansy hard against the heavy iron bedstead where her face struck the ornate ironwork flowers. Tansy's scream rent the air as her hand flew to her face, where blood spurted from her split cheek. Janet paled. 'Stop that! Someone'll hear.'

'You ought to have thought of that before you pushed me. It's not my fault the Missus told me to do Emma's hair. You'm jealous 'cause I'm good at doing things.' She broke off to dab her hanky at the flow of blood which splashed down onto her white afternoon apron.

'My sister was courtin' Martin Webber till you come along – now he wants nothin' to do wi' her.' Janet went on, 'She'm fair broken hearted!' and Tansy retaliated, ''Tis not my fault Martin Webber prefers me to her. Fanny can have him for all I cares. He's nothing to me...' and she howled with pain at the split cheek reflected in the mirror.

'Stop it for goodness' sake. Someone'll come and I'll get into trouble.' She wrung her hands in fright in case she got caught.

'You deserve to get into trouble, Janet Luscombe. Spiteful, that's what you are – just look at what you've done to my face.'

'Don't tell anyone it was me that done it,' Janet pleaded. 'I'll fetch ice from the pantry,' and she hurried out, leaving Tansy to make her way to the room high in the attic where she tried to staunch the wound at the washstand in the corner.

❦

It was gone seven o'clock by the time Tansy hung up cap and apron and set off for the Post Office. She looked forward to seeing Norah and patted the small package in her pocket. She crossed Courtenay Road and hurried down the flight of steps until she reached Rosemary's gate, where she hesitated. She knew she shouldn't stop, knowing the twins would be waiting to hear her news. Then she heard the unmistakable sound of her friend's feet, the thump of right foot against the left, iron-clad right against booted left. Rosemary put up a hand and Tansy pulled her up the step beside her.

'Thought you'd never come,' she said. 'Still waiting to hear your special news.' Her friend smiled from a face which exuded weariness from every pore.

'I hoped you'd be here. 'Tis such a climb, going down's not so bad but at the end of the day,' she brightened visibly, 'but that's going to change. My news,' she paused to underline its magnitude, 'is that Hester Mudge wants me to take the music exam – then I can teach myself. Can you imagine! No more Mill, no more twelve-hour days. Just imagine, Tansy – playing the piano and being paid to do what I love!'

Tansy's eyes widened with shared excitement. She grasped Rosemary round the waist and whizzed her round until they almost overbalanced in their delight at Rosemary's news.

'I'm so happy for you, Rose,' Tansy said. ''Tis the best thing could've happened for you. When's the exam?' They sank down on the steps where they shared so many secrets.

'Oh, 'tisn't for ages yet. Next spring I think.' And they sat, arms around each other, and contemplated the future.

'Perhaps something good will happen for you, Tansy.'

Then Rose noticed the bruised and swollen cheek. 'What've you done?' Tansy, not wanting to spoil the moment, brushed aside her friend's concern and hurried away, leaving Rosemary to limp through the wicket-gate into her mother's garden where Bessie's hens settled to roost in the laurel hedge. At the Post Office Tansy hammered on the door impatiently, then listened for her mother's quick steps and the rattle of bolts.

'Come on, Tansy, you'm late. The twins are all ready for bed,' her mother chided as she pulled her through the door, re-bolted and went ahead, the lamp reflecting in brass weights and scales behind the shadows of the grille.

'Your father and Norah have eaten but I've left something out. What kept you so late?' Then she saw the split cheek and exclaimed, 'Whatever have you done? Have you been in a fight?' Tansy laughed and dismissed her injury, she decided there was no point in arousing her mother's anger. Nothing to be gained by causing trouble for Janet just now, and Eva Drewe accepted Tansy's explanation that she had tripped on a rug and fallen against a bed end. She winced as her mother dabbed linament onto the open split. 'You mustn't be such a harum-scarum my maid!' she said, leaving Tansy to enjoy the simple food she'd left out on the table by the fire. She enjoyed too the warmth of the fire in its surround of ivy-patterned tiles, the flicker of flames on fire dogs, the leap of shadows on overmantel where portraits of Thomases and Drewes stood in silver frames next red earth pottery and china dogs. As she pushed her plate away Eva Drewe reached for the tea caddy, admonishing the twins, 'Now, now boys, let Tansy have her tea, then perhaps she'll read 'ee a story'.

'Don't want a story, wants to know about heaven,' demanded Robert, who as usual spoke up for both himself and James. The latter nodded his head vigorously.

'You wouldn't call it heaven if 'ee worked there.' retorted Tansy, but Eva placed a finger to her full red lips.

'Don't spoil it for them Tansy,' she murmured, 'they look forward to your accounts of Courtenay House so much. Besides it'll settle them down for bed.' She moved the kettle back onto the fire dog and Tansy settled down on the sofa between Robert and James, putting an arm around each of them and began.

'Last week,' she said, 'Miss Emma had her eighteenth birthday party and her posh friends came.'

'How lovely!' Robert exclaimed, wriggling closer.

'A party, a party! Wish I could go to a party!' shouted James, for once forgetting his bashfulness.

'Be quiet or I shan't tell you anything.' Tansy scolded. 'Seven girls came, two in a trap, three in Westaways' brougham and,' here she paused, 'guess what the others came in?' When they shouted, 'Tell us, tell us!' she rolled out the words, 'an automobile!' Here the twins' eyes seemed about to pop out of their heads.

'Tell us, tell us, what was it like?' and Tansy considered, trying to recall the look of the strange contraption as it arrived outside Courtenay House, remembering how both guests and servants had run down the steps to gaze in wonder at the vehicle.

'It looked like, a sort of huge pram, two small wheels at the front and two larger ones at the back. The girls sat high at the back and the driver drove it from the front with a sort of handle,' she paused for breath.

'Did it have a name?' Robert asked and she shook her head.

'I don't know. I'll ask Master Harry when he comes home. He's mad about the new machines, I'm sure he'll know.'

'What did they have to eat at the party?' James wanted to know. There was no end to their questions, which only stopped when Tansy produced two pieces of cake wrapped in serviettes and two screws of paper full of dolly mixture. Now Eva got up and made tea and while Tansy drank she shushed the boys upstairs to bed.

'You go up, Norah's finishing off her packing, she wants to talk to you. See you in the morning.' Tansy dropped a kiss on her mother's forehead and wearily climbed the stairs to the attic.

'You're lucky to be going away.' she said to Norah. 'I wish it was me.' Norah looked up from the pile of shirts she was folding.

'Your turn'll come one day, you'll see. Before you know it, you'll be filling your own trunk and setting off.' But Tansy was not to be comforted.

'What chance have I got? It's not fair, you've had all the luck. Getting a job straight from school as pupil teacher, now college! You've had all the family's help and now there's nothing left for me!'

Norah laughed and said, 'Don't be such a silly goose, you should know better. Mother and Father have high hopes for all of us, for you as well as for me, and the twins.'

'How can I get away from Newton? Stuck in service that's what I'll be. Stuck here forever while you...' and now Tansy's jealousy threatened to choke her.

'Your chance'll come one day. They'll find ways and means to help you just as they've helped me...' But Tansy refused to look on the bright side.

'I wish I looked like you, dark hair is so much better than red...' she burst out. Now Norah sighed impatiently and took the last garment from her side of the wardrobe.

'I think it's high time you stopped blaming your looks for everything. You may not know it but your hair is the envy of lots of girls in town.' And she laid the garment down on Tansy's bed.

'Look at the new preacher,' she went on, 'he's the same colour hair as you and everyone thinks he's handsome.' Now Norah blushed. Tansy sat up, shocked to see her cool, calm sister looking flustered. Why, Norah never had time for sparking. Always been deep in marking homework and study. Surely she wasn't keen on a man she'd only seen a few times.

'Are you keen on Geoffrey Llewellyn?' Tansy demanded, then as Norah ignored her question she stormed on, 'I'm glad you're going away, you'll have to leave him for me!' She crashed down on her bed, surprised at the strength of feeling flooding through her. Norah turned to face her, shocked by her sister's last words.

'Why, Tansy, I thought you liked Martin Webber? Thought you wanted to be a farmer's wife, live high on the Moor, ride horses?'

Now it was Tansy's turn to look flustered as she fiddled with the buttons of her nightdress. She looked up and announced, 'That was before Geoffrey Llewellyn came to Newton. Now I'd like to be a minster's wife and travel the country doing good.'

Norah burst out laughing at the thought of her volatile sister 'doing good'. Tansy picked up the book from the table by her bed and flung it with all her might. Norah ducked, the book missed and hit the wall, bringing down a picture which fortunately landed on the bed.

'Stop that, Tansy Drewe. I've told you before, your temper will get you into real trouble one day. You'll have to learn to control it if you want to win a man like Geoffrey Llewellyn.'

Now Norah pointed at the garment she had laid on Tansy's bed. 'Aren't you going to see what I've given you?'

Tansy picked up the soft cotton blouse and held it to her face. It was the one she had always admired and envied. Its pink stripes scattered with roses, its sleeves trimmed with broderie anglaise. Suddenly she felt ashamed of her outburst. 'Oh Norah, this was new this spring. It still fits you. You can't give it away.'

Norah just smiled and shook her head. 'Take it, you know you've always wanted it. Perhaps Mother will make you a skirt to go with it. It will come in later for Christmas parties.' and Norah began to unpin her long dark hair. Then, when Tansy still said nothing she looked at her accusingly.

'You're glad I'm going away aren't you? You can't wait for me to be gone!' At this Tansy's eyes filled with hot tears and she crossed the room to take Norah in her arms.

'Of course I'll miss you. It will be so strange here without you. You promise to write every week?' Norah dried her own tears, her face calm once more, as Tansy added, 'Thank you for the blouse. I'll think of you whenever I wear it.' Reconciled at last, the girls lay down to rest. Sleep didn't come quickly to Tansy or to Norah as they lay exhausted with the emotion of parting, apprehensive and excited about the future.

✣ Chapter Fourteen ✣

London

Tansy did her best not to cry as the Drewe family lined the platform to see Norah off. 'Don't forget to write every week and tell us what it's like!' she admonished, pressing Norah's gloved hands. Norah looked suddenly small and vulnerable against the huge steam monster which waited to carry her out of their lives. Robert and James raced back and forth along the length of the train, marvelling at the crates of rabbits being loaded into the goods van.

Edward Drewe had arranged for Norah to travel in the company of an elderly lady and Eva placed a sovereign into her daughter's hands 'in case of emergency, mind.'

Norah turned to Tansy before stepping into the carriage. 'Thank you for your present – I still can't believe you could have afforded such a lovely thing. I'll take care of it always.'

Norah's eyes grew bright with unshed tears as she leant from the window and waited for the guard to wave his green flag. The stationmaster blew his whistle and, with an explosion of steam and a clanking of iron, the train left in a cloud of flying soot.

※

'I'm to send you to the Missus as soon as you gets in.' Cook greeted Tansy gravely when she arrived some two days later.

When Tansy asked, 'What for?' she pressed her lips together, folded her stout arms and shook her head. Slowly Tansy climbed the basement stairs to be met by Janet Luscombe who hovered there in the hall, a look of smug satisfaction on her face.

'You'm for it now, Miss High and Mighty. Master and Missus are both waiting for you in the morning-room. Now we'll see who's the clever one!'

She stood watching as Tansy tapped at the door of the room where by rights she should be lighting a fire ready for the Master. What could be so urgent that both he and Caroline Vallance were wanting to speak to her?

When she was bid 'Come in' she was surprised to find a fire burning brightly and Caroline and Charles Vallance sitting among the remains of their meal.

'Good morning, Sir, Ma'm.' She bobbed then stood waiting, a slim figure in her grey work dress. When Charles Vallance took his watch from his pocket and began to polish the gold case Tansy knew whatever it was, it must be serious.

'Drewe, we have something very serious to ask you.' He paused, shifted uncomfortably, then continued, 'Yesterday evening Miss Emma went to her jewel box to show her watch to Master Harry.' Tansy exclaimed with pleasure, 'Master Harry's home then?' and Charles Vallance cleared his throat nervously and went on, 'Yes, yes, he's home. Emma found the watch gone, the box empty, and although we and the staff have searched her room and, in fact, the whole house, no trace of it has been found.'

'Oh my, that's dreadful!' said Tansy, clearly puzzled as to what she could do about such a loss.

'We wondered if you could help us?' Caroline butted in hastily.

'Well, of course, I'll do my best M'am but I don't ever need to go into Miss Emma's room.' Surely, she thought, it should be Janet standing here, not her.

'When did you last see the watch?' Charles Vallance went on. Tansy's mind cleared. Of course, she'd been off the day before. The other servants had already been asked the same questions. Just like a mystery in *Woman's Realm*.

'Why, it was the day of Miss Emma's party – the conjuror tricked us into thinking he'd smashed the watch up. Then he said "Hey Presto" and there 'un was, good as new!'

She paused, thinking hard, then added, 'Oh yes, and I did see it again on the day of Mary Oliver's party. You remember, M'am. I did Miss Emma's hair. She looked a real treat in her red gown with the watch pinned on...' Her voice trailed away, Tansy realising the enormity of the situation but pleased at her feat of memory. But seemingly this remembrance was not enough to satisfy her employers, who continued to look at her sternly. Caroline Vallance pulled the bell rope and when Janet appeared asked her, 'Luscombe, can you tell us again of the conversation that took place recently in the kitchen?'

Janet, a look of triumph on her face, recounted the moment when Tansy, in answer to Hetty Westcott's question, 'What would you like to give Norah if you could afford anything in the world?', had answered, 'Why, that's easy – a gold fob watch with pin bow all set with rubies just like the one the conjuror tricked us into believing he'd smashed at Miss Emma's party.'

'That's all thank you, Luscombe.' Janet turned to go, a look of triumph still on her face.

When Charles Vallance added, 'Please ask Westcott to come up,' Tansy realised at last that it was she who was under suspicion. Surely they didn't believe she had stolen Miss Emma's watch. She felt her mouth go dry and her hands became wet with perspiration as they waited for Hetty to climb the stairs. But when she saw Hetty she felt her spirits rise. One word from her and all would be well again; but after an anguished look in her direction Tansy heard Hetty confirm that that was indeed the conversation which had taken place in the kitchen two weeks since. Then it was Cook's turn and Tansy began to feel as if she was taking part in some kind of nightmare. If Cook was prepared to blacken her name then she was finished. But, after corroborating the account of the conversation between Hetty and Tansy, Cook burst out, 'I'd stake my life on it that Tansy didn't steal Miss Emma's watch. Honest she is, honest as the day's long and the hardest worker I've ever had in my kitchen. Begging your pardon, Sir, M'am.' Dropping a curtsey, she shot a look of compassion in Tansy's direction and waddled out.

The door closed behind Cook and Charles and Caroline Vallance exchanged a long confirmatory look. He rose to his feet, taking his watch in and out of his waistcoat pocket. He cleared his throat and began, 'I'm afraid I have no alternative but to dismiss you from your post, Drewe. Unless you can prove beyond doubt that you didn't take Emma's watch.' As Tansy moved towards the table he held up his hand, 'If you can bring it back to me within the next week with an apology... well, then we would have to reconsider the situation. I can understand the temptation of such treasure to someone like you. If not, then there's no more to be said. Now please leave this house at once.'

His words seemed to come from a long way off to Tansy, who stood trying to take in what he was saying to her. At last she spoke up in her own defence. 'But I didn't take Miss Emma's watch. You must believe me, I would never do such a thing.'

Now Charles Vallance's tone changed to that of anger. 'That's quite enough. Seth will deliver your box to the Post Office. Now you may go.' His words, so cold and harsh, dismissed her and, as if in a dream, she passed through the doorway into the hall, suddenly conscious of a row of accusing faces staring at her. Slowly she walked across the hall and out through the doorway. She went without collecting hat or coat. She walked down the drive, automatically turning left, hardly conscious of directing her feet. When she reached the top of the Hill she met the full force of the west wind and with it rain, and as she hesitated, trying to accept what had happened to her, her clothes became saturated. Still she stood looking towards the Moor, not seeing the clouds as they filled in the valleys beyond the Hill. She couldn't go home and tell Eva and Edward that she had lost her position, been accused of theft. Without a reference she knew she would never get another job. She stumbled away from Courtenay House and through the kissing-gate where she'd been so many times with Martin. She walked towards the church then plunged off the path and crossed Cull's field until she found herself dropping down the fields to Evan Williams' pigsty. There she stopped and sat on the fence, watching the large white sow until Myfanwy came to feed it potato peel and found her there.

'Tansy! What are you doing here? You're soaked!' She took Tansy's hand and led her downhill and into the house.

'Look Mam, 'tis Tansy caught in the rain!' Gwynneth took one look at Tansy, normally so vivacious, now seemingly in a state of shock, and acted.

'Fetch towels, Myfanwy, and a blanket,' and as the girl hesitated, 'Go on, be quick'. As soon as they were to hand she stripped Tansy of her wet clothes, wrapped her in towels and rubbed her hard until the colour returned to her pale face. She asked no questions but dressed her in her own spare clothing, wrapped her in the blanket and sat her down by the fire. Gynneth brewed tea and at last Tansy began to speak. The words came in a whisper, her face set.

'Don't tell Mother you've seen me. If anyone else asks tell them...' she paused, 'tell them you've not seen me.'

'Whatever's happened, Tansy?' Tansy just shook her head. 'I'm going away.'

Gwynneth exclaimed, 'You can't go anywhere in this weather without a coat and hat. You'll catch your death.'

Tansy jumped up, a look of determination filling her eyes. 'Then lend me something, a shawl will do. I'll let you have them back as soon as I can. But I must go from here.'

'But where will you go if you don't go home to your Mam?' Gwynneth asked, concerned for this girl who had championed her family on more than one occasion. Rescued her Evan when he got into trouble at the Ram Roast. But Tansy set her mouth in a determined line and shook her head and Gwynneth, seeing that she was not to be dissuaded, reached down her only winter jacket and shawl and gave them Tansy, while Myfanwy stood protesting in the background.

'At least take something to eat with you.' Gwynneth said, but while she went to fetch bread from the crock Tansy hugged Myfanwy and slipped from the house. She hurried downhill to town and entered a black-painted door she had once been through with Beatrice Vallance. Twenty minutes later, her head wrapped close in Gwynneth's shawl, she got on the London train. In the early hours of the morning she knocked on the porter's door at Goldsmith's College. Aroused from sleep he opened the door to Tansy's bedraggled figure.

'What do you want, waking a body at this time of night?' he demanded.

She replied in a voice so low he could hardly hear, 'I want Norah Drewe. Please fetch her.' When he looked doubtful she pressed him. 'She's a student here. Please fetch her.' Then he consulted his list and reluctantly let her in.

Norah was working late when the porter came for her. 'You've a visitor Miss.' he announced and Norah looked up from her books in disbelief.

'There must be some mistake. Who would call at this hour?'

But he insisted and she rose, curious to know who it could be, believing there must be some mistake. At first she didn't recognise the dark figure, then as it turned to her she caught the familiar look.

'Tansy? What are you doing?' Her question went unanswered as her sister gave a slight moan and swayed towards her. She caught her in her arms and with the porter's help half carried, half dragged her upstairs to her room. Gently they lifted her onto Norah's bed and, as the shawl fell away, Norah gasped. Gone the riot of red curls, the mass of strands, and in its place was a tight cap of hair cut to within an inch of Tansy's scalp. Distressed beyond words she motioned the porter away. Gently she removed Gwynneth's jacket and the working boots. Tenderly she bathed the blistered feet and as she worked tears fell as she remembered times they had argued fiercely over Tansy's hair. Tansy, who now lay semi-conscious on her bed, breathing in a strange, jerky fashion. Norah looked at the clock. It was three o'clock, she could do no more till morning. She wrapped herself in Gwynneth's shawl and settled herself by the bed until light began to filter through the high window.

In the morning Tansy looked at Norah without recognition. Her body burned with a high fever and Norah sent for the college doctor. He took Tansy's temperature, examined her and declared her to be in a state of delirium.

'Her lungs are congested too. Needs to be kept warm,' he commanded, looking pointedly at the grate. 'I'll make up some medicine and get it delivered to the porter. Do you know how she came to get into such a state?'

Norah could only shake her head. 'She's not spoken yet but I did find a train ticket in her pocket. She must have walked from Paddington.'

'Paddington! That must be fifteen miles at least!' he exclaimed and Norah replied proudly, 'We'm used to walking in Devon.' She took hold of her sister's hand, adding, 'But why she's here and why she cut her hair...' she bit her lip to hold back the tears which had threatened her ever since she saw her sister standing in the porter's room.

'You must get word to your people,' he suggested and Norah nodded. 'Do it as soon as possible,' he added, then closed his bag and was gone.

Norah sent a note to her tutor excusing herself from lectures and fetched wood and coal from the caretaker, spending some of her precious hoard of coins. She made soup and kept it simmering on the hob, ready for the moment Tansy was strong enough to eat.

She sat up again that night and watched Tansy as she tossed feverishly and babbled a stream of words, none of which made sense. At midnight she stopped and fell at last into a deep, unbroken sleep.

Hetty arrived at the Post Office at the same time as Norah's telegram, two days after Tansy had fled Courtenay House, and quickly she told Eva and Edward all that had happened.

'We'm all upset at the House. No one believes Tansy took Miss Emma's watch.' She paused. 'Leastways all of us except Janet Luscombe, but then she'd do anything to get Tansy into trouble. 'Tis all to do with her sister wanting Martin Webber for herself I do believe. 'Twas Caroline Vallance as accused Tansy in the end.'

Eva, appalled at Hetty's news, exploded in a burst of fury. 'Just what you'd expect from someone's who's been brought up 'trade'?' she snorted. 'But you say Tansy left two days ago.' And the full horror came to her. 'Then were is she?' Now she was conscious of Edward coming through the door, a telegram in his hand.

"Tis all right, Eva. She's with our Norah!' He handed the paper to Eva who read and re-read Norah's message, as if by doing so Tansy would be restored to them.

'I must go at once.' He said, 'Tell her we love her no matter what she's done.' And Eva struck him fiercely on the chest.

'She's done nothing. Our Tansy a thief! How can you, her own father, stand there and accept someone else's judgement?'

Edward grasped her hands and led her to a chair by the fire. 'I didn't mean, 'twas just a manner of speaking. I must fetch her home, Norah won't be able to keep her there. The silly girl. She should have known she could tell us anything.'

As he left the room Eva, abandoning all her normal calm, threw her apron over her head and wept.

Edward, meanwhile, headed downhill to Charles Vallance's office at Bradley Mill. He forced his way past Rosemary Brimmacombe, brushed aside Jim Tozer, the foreman, and burst into the room.

'You've made a great mistake in accusing my daughter Tansy of theft. I shall hold you responsible for any harm that may befall her. When the watch comes to light, as I'm sure it will, I shall expect a full public apology. Her name must be cleared, as I know it will.' With that he turned on his heel, leaving Charles Vallance startled and uneasy.

❦

Late on the second day the doctor called and pronounced the fever broken. 'She's been fortunate to escape pneumonia. Keep her warm and give her something light to eat whenever she wants it. You've done well! I'll not need to call again.'

But as he left Tansy called out, 'Norah, don't leave me, don't leave me!' Norah took her sister into her arms and together they rocked back and forth with the joy of being together again. Then they shared a bowl of soup and Norah asked the question that had been on her lips ever since Tansy's dramatic arrival.

'What happened? Why did you come like that?' Tansy looked down at her hands, a flush rising in her face. She hesitated, reluctant to tell Norah of the scene at Courtenay House, knowing it would call for a long explanation. When she didn't reply Norah's expression changed to one of familiar accusation.

'What have you done?' she demanded and Tansy exploded, 'Surely you're not going to accuse me too! I've not done anything yet I'm being treated like a thief. It was bad enough to be accused by the Vallances but I can't believe you will take their side too!' At last she knew there was nothing to be done but explain all that had happened up to her arrival at Norah's college.

'And your hair...' Norah prompted gently. Tansy's face looked tragic as the full realisation came upon her. She could only guess how long it would take to grow.

'I'm best off without it. I've always hated it.' She paused then burst out, 'Besides it was the only thing I had to sell!' When Norah looked puzzled she added, 'Gave me the chance to get away when I needed to, the money paid for the train ticket.'

When Norah still seemed not to understand she explained, 'I sold it to Beatrice Vallance's wig maker in Newton. I went there with her once for a hairpiece. The wig maker told me if ever I thought of selling my hair to go to him. He said it was really hard to find red hair!'

Norah, relieved at the simplicity of Tansy's explanation, began to laugh and Tansy joined in. They talked of home and of all that had happened since Norah had left Newton to come to London and college.

✿

The next day Tansy felt well enough to sit out and Norah attended lectures, leaving her installed by the fire, kettle close to hand. After a while she put down *The Woman in White*, still not well enough to concentrate on Wilkie Collins' plot. She studied the room, thought it bare and ugly with not even a picture on the walls, just bookshelves and a hanging wardrobe. On a small table stood a box and a blotter in the centre. Curious, Tansy got up and picked up the box. Made of wood, it was carved in a pattern of fans and circles and carried initials on the top. She read them and a surge of anger coursed through her veins. Her grandmother's initials, yet again. Was there to be nothing left to pass on to her? And when Norah came back at lunchtime she greeted her with an accusation.

'Where did you get this box? I've never seen it before.'

Norah, surprised and hurt, retaliated, 'Don't shout, Tansy. Two days here being looked after and causing a great deal of inconvenience and suddenly you're up to your old tricks again – causing trouble!' She turned away to unlace her outdoor shoes and slip feet into black plimsolls. As she straightened she explained, 'Mother gave it to me on loan to keep writing things in... you mustn't be so jealous. I've told you before your turn will come.' Tansy, feeling slightly ashamed, put the box back onto the desk, then opened it and looked inside.

Now it was Norah's turn to show a flash of temper. She crossed the room and snatched the box from Tansy's hands, but not before she had seen the sloping writing on the top envelope. Writing familiar from Chapel Minutes on her father's desk.

'What's Geoffrey Llewellyn writing to you for?' she demanded. Norah blushed and turned away.

'Why shouldn't he? He's sent me the address of a friend who lives in London. This man has sent tickets for a Magic Lantern Show tonight. We could go if you feel up to it?' Tansy looked up, a pleased expression on her face. 'It would be good to go out – what's it about, this lecture?'

''Tis about the War,' Norah replied. 'Professor Broughton saw it advertised in *The Times* and recommended we should go. We'm lucky to have been given tickets.'

Now Tansy's hand flew to her head where a red fuzz was beginning to sprout. 'I can't go out like this. What am I to do? I've only Gwynneth's old dress and jacket to wear.'

Norah sighed. 'It hasn't taken you very long to regret cutting your hair,' she said, then repented. 'I'll go and see Helen, she's about your size. Maybe she'll have something to lend.' She was back in a few moments accompanied by a slim small girl with dark hair and brown eyes who reminded Tansy of Rosemary Brimmacombe. Immediately she felt a warmth grow between them, even before they spoke.

'Tansy, this is Helen Drayton, from Kent. My sister Tansy.' Helen clasped Tansy's hands in hers and smiled.

'I've heard so much about you. Norah has missed you all so much, she's been quite homesick. She's loved having you here, even it it's been a bit unexpected.' Tansy felt ashamed of all the trouble she had caused Norah and determined to make up for it during the rest of her stay.

She took Helen's coat and skirt and when she put them on found them a perfect fit. The brown tweed fitted into her neat waist and set off her colouring when she slipped them over Norah's tucked cream shirt. As she fastened the tiny buttons Helen offered her a velvet cloche which Tansy pulled on – it came low on her forehead.

'Look, it completely covers my head!' she exclaimed and turned this way and that in front of the mirror, smiling at her reflection. 'What a change from green!' she said and they all laughed and agreed that Helen's suit could have been made for her. The noise of a bell came pulsing through the building and Norah pushed Tansy out into the corridor where they joined a stream of hurrying women.

'Where are we going?' Tansy asked.

'To eat.' Norah replied as they made their way to the dining hall where they sat at a long, bare table and ate boiled beef, pease pudding and carrots, followed by lumpy rice pudding. Tansy made a face.

''Tidd'n a bit like home, is it?' she said, comparing it with meals at the Post Office and Courtenay House. Helen laughed and patted her arm.

'You eat anything if you're starving!' she exclaimed and went on to explain, 'This is one of the first colleges for women and is not very well funded. We need some more patrons to provide bursaries for people like Norah and I. The girls who pay help fund the ones who don't. So we mustn't expect roast beef for dinner.'

'Did you get our letters?' Tansy asked, and when Norah nodded added, 'Then why haven't you replied?'

Now it was Norah's turn to apologise and at last she spoke of life at college. 'The days are never long enough. After lectures there's work to do. Every evening there's preparation for the next day. We work after supper to ten o'clock, lights go out at eleven. To keep up I have to spend every free minute reading in the library or writing essays for tutorials.'

'Don't you have any fun at all?' Tansy wanted to know, remembering how she had envied Norah leaving home and coming up to London. Norah laughed and gave her a hug.

''Tis not all work, we go to each other's rooms for tea and talk even after lights out, although you get gated – not allowed out – if a monitor catches you. Sundays we go up West to see the sights. We're saving up to go to a music hall. Don't tell Father, he'd be shocked!'

Talking and laughing they spilled out into a long bare corridor and made their way through the gate to cross the park and catch a bus. True to form Tansy was first on and she flew upstairs to capture the front seat and peer down into the dark streets. Instantly the glow on her face faded.

'London's not a bit as I imagined it. All those ugly buildings. Lots of children running about barefoot. When I walked from Paddington I saw them begging outside public houses. Everywhere looks poor and so dirty!'

'London's not all palaces and parks, Tansy! There's more factories and mills here than anywhere else. That's what makes it so dirty. Tomorrow we'll take you to St James' Park and we can walk through by the lake to Buckingham Palace.' She paused and glanced at Tansy, trying to gauge how she would react to her next piece of news. 'Then on Monday someone's coming to take you home.' Now Tansy's face took on a look of real fear and she clutched at Norah's arm.

'Must I go back so soon? How can I face them all after what's happened?'

Norah hugged Tansy's arm to her side and tried to comfort her. 'You didn't steal Emma Vallance's watch and no one who knows you will believe that you did. Your hair will soon grow and Father will find you a new position.'

But Tansy still dreaded the prospect of returning to Newton. 'Is it Father who's coming?' she asked and when Norah nodded her face crumpled and tears slid beneath the ginger lashes. 'I didn't think about going back when I ran away. I've caused everyone so much trouble, haven't I?'

Now Helen and Norah were getting up. 'We're here, it's Fetter Lane, hold tight Tansy.' The moment they got off the bus a crowd swept them along the street and up gas-lit steps into the Birkbeck Institute. Rows of seats quickly filled and they sat as close to the front as they could get. A huge banner fastened across the platform proclaimed 'The Boer War Day by Day' and a screen was set up in front of it. A row of distinguished gentlemen lined the platform, dominated by a tall handsome man with a monocle in his left eye. The doors were closed and he stepped forward and began to speak.

'We are here this evening to watch newsreel of our gallant men fighting for their Queen and country in South Africa against the Boers. This film show is given to raise relief funds for our soldiers and their families!' Here he fixed his audience with a look of steel from his one good eye. When he bent in her direction, Tansy felt it bore into her very soul. She shivered with anticipation. The line of gentlemen disappeared and their place was taken by a tall thin man who held a pointer in one hand and a sheaf of papers in the other. Monocle turned to him.

'I give you Professor Esdale, who will introduce the film and give the commentary.'

'Ladies and Gentlemen, good evening,' he began, watching the screen which remained obstinately empty. He looked to the back of the room where a great deal of activity was going on, then after the strong smell of paraffin filled the room, followed by a cloud of smoke, lights were dimmed and images of tented campsites and lines of horses appeared waveringly on the screen. He pointed as squads of troops marched before General Roberts.

'These men have all taken part in the Ashanti and Matabele Wars,' he announced. Campaign maps were flashed onto the screen and Tansy's mind changed to thoughts of the next day and the meeting with her father. She wondered if anyone from Courtenay House had been to see her mother and this train of thought brought her back to the room and pictures of the Highland Light Infantry in kilts and bush hats crawling across the veldt. When this changed to pictures of wounded soldiers being carried onto ships she searched faces for Hetty's Jack. Next followed pictures of Queen Victoria visiting more wounded at the East London Hospital. Then Norah was nudging her and whispering, 'There's General Buller – he's from Exeter.'

The professor's voice droned on, 'On his way to relieve Ladysmith and Kimberley with its diamond mines. General Baden-Powell is still holding out at Mafeking. These reports have been sent to you from our own Conan Doyle, Winston Churchill and Rudyard Kipling.'

Tansy began to fidget, they could have gone to see something more interesting, she thought as she stifled a yawn. The professor was introducing yet another soldier but this one was handsome with huge eyes and a drooping moustache. Tansy sat up, she could tell by his picture that he was the possessor of red hair.

'Lord Methuen,' said the professor. 'And here is the General's force in action.' The screen came alive with scenes of close combat. Tansy's pleasure was short-lived as she watched horses galloping towards the Boers' guns, only to be mown down by the enemy Mausers. She saw horses shot from beneath their riders. Travelled dusty tracks lined with broken guns and dead animals, their limbs rigid, pointing to the sky. She was on her feet in spite of Norah's hissed warning, 'Sit down Tansy – behave.'

'Stop this!' she shouted, 'Stop this slaughter of innocent creatures.'

Professor Esdale's voice ceased, heads craned towards her as she continued, 'Look at their eyes!' She raised one arm and pointed to the screen. 'Look at the terror in them.' Now she turned to appeal to those sitting in the audience. 'Animals have no choice. They didn't choose to fight. They didn't choose to die.'

The professor appealed to her. 'Please sit down, young lady, and let me finish my lecture.'

Two men came from the back of the hall and began to make their way towards her. The man with the monocle leapt onto the platform as the last images faded from the screen.

'A retiring collection will now be made. Give all you can. Help our wounded and their families. There are souvenirs on sale at the exit. Thank you.'

Tansy was not to be quelled and she climbed onto her chair and appealed to the audience, who began to make their way from the hall. A group of young sympathisers formed round her in a protective phalanx and began to struggle with the two men as they reached up to pull Tansy from the chair.

'Give your money to stop this war! Stop the slaughter of innocent creatures. Save them from this horror.'

A fight broke out between those wishing to give money to soldiers and their families and those trying to stop them. Someone seized flags from the platform and began to sing 'Goodbye Dolly Gray' and a rough-looking man turned over the table bearing handkerchiefs printed with regimental flags and boxes decorated with battle scenes and ran off with the money. The police were called and Tansy was forcibly removed while Helen and Norah stood by and watched helplessly as she was arrested and taken away to the police station.

❦

It wasn't Edward Drewe who came to fetch Tansy, but Martin Webber. Missing seeing her on market day, he had called at the Post Office and, on being told of her flight to London, volunteered to go at once. Edward, who was having difficulty getting someone to stand in for him on his rounds, accepted Martin's offer. However, when Martin called at the college the porter told him that both the Misses Drewe were at Cannon Street Police Station and not expected back till lunchtime.

When Tansy saw Martin waiting outside the college she thought he looked handsome in his best suit and bowler hat, but out of place among the clerks and teachers. She gave him a long look which dared him to say anything.

She still wore Helen Drayton's suit and velvet hat on her close-cropped head and Martin, innocent of the truth, thought she looked quite adorable.

'What be ye doin' at the police station then?' he enquired, after touching his hat to Norah and Helen.

''Twas just a misunderstanding Martin, that's all.' Tansy said and Norah added sardonically, 'If you can call being arrested and charged with starting a public affray 'a misunderstanding'!' Martin's eyes opened wide and he would have questioned Tansy further had she not rushed in with her own account.

'The magistrate was a very kind old gentleman, he sympathised with my efforts on behalf of the horses. Let me off with a caution.'

'Said if ever you was caught again behaving in the same manner it would be six months in jail,' added Norah wickedly – then the three girls laughed with relief that the incident had ended so well.

'I'm come to take 'ee 'ome' Martin stated simply and Tansy replied with a flash of temper, 'And what if I'm not ready to come yet?'

But she couldn't get the better of him. 'Then I'll wait until you are,' he said coolly. 'I've promised your Mother and Father that I'll not go back without you so I think it best if we set off now.'

Tansy went back into Norah's room for the last time, changed back into Gwynneth's old coat and dress and, once again, wound the shawl round her head. She emerged to hug and kiss Norah and Helen.

'Any messages for home?' she asked and Norah gave her an envelope.

'Keep it safe – and no more pranks, Tansy. Just go home and I'm sure things will sort themselves out soon. Helen will come home at Christmas with me. Now don't forget to write.'

Tansy nodded and implored, 'And this time you write back.' Helen and Norah watched from the gate as Tansy slipped her hand into Martin's arm and they set off.

As soon as they were out of sight Martin teased her, ''Twas a near thing I didn't come visiting you in the Tower then!' and Tansy, pleased to see him, hugged his arm and said, 'You said you'd come if ever I needed you – and here you are.'

Martin touched her hand and stared about him with great interest. 'What do you think of London then?' Suddenly he pulled off the shawl. 'You don't need...' and stopped at the sight of her shorn head. 'Who did that?' he demanded. 'Just take me to 'un and I'll settle their account.'

Tansy snatched the shawl from his hands and rewound it about her head. She stuck out her chin and stalked away from him across Greenwich Park till they reached the market, where women cried 'Lovely sweet lavender!' and vegetables and offal were piled high on stalls. They watched a sheep being shorn and Martin was duly amazed at this and all he saw. He bought apples for them and they sat by a fountain and ate and again he asked what she thought of London.

Her brow darkened as she recounted the long walk through streets teeming with people, when without money for bus or cab she had stopped continually to ask the way. She recalled the terror of being accosted by men who offered her money to go with them.

'I stopped to speak to a newsboy and he had nothing on beneath his jacket and no socks beneath his boots.'

Martin shook his head. ''Tis no different to Devon then, is it? Look at the people at home who've no boots, let alone socks, and have to go to the Soup Kitchen when there's no work.'

Then they heard the sound of a band floating towards them and ran to look at blue-clad ranks of the Salvation Army coming into the Square. A girl, the same age as Tansy, handed out pamphlets while the others set up music stands. 'Beware the demon drink' the girl shouted as she collected pennies. Soon the strains of 'Onward Christian Soldiers' over-whelmed the cries of the street vendors and Tansy and Martin, self-consciously at first, then with increasing confidence, joined in.

Singing the familiar words took Tansy back to the chapel at Newton with the Vallances in their family row, Hetty Westcott and Janet Luscombe singing with her from the gallery. She saw again Geoffrey Llewellyn's flame-covered head above his inspired face and wished herself home with Eva and Edward, reading to Robert and James by the fire.

She turned to Martin and with tears in her eyes said in a level voice, 'I'm ready now Martin, let's go home.'

❧ Chapter Fifteen ❧

Geoffrey Llewellyn

Meanwhile at Courtenay House Emma complained to Caroline Vallance, 'How could you get rid of Drewe – she was the only one who could manage my hair. You should have sacked Janet instead.' And she stamped her foot and sulked for days.

Master Harry asked repeatedly for Tansy, liking her because she was used to young boys and could always be called upon to play games when no one else was available. She knew all the parks and walks nearby and sometimes took him to the Post Office for tea, where Eva made a great fuss of him and the twins laughed at his clothes. They thought a sailor suit was sissy, but enjoyed the sweets he inevitably brought for them.

It was Cook who missed Tansy most of all. In the year she'd worked at Courtenay House she had become indispensable – always there, whatever needed doing. She waited, hoping for Tansy's return and poured scorn on Janet's efforts to help when she was pressed for time.

At The Manse, Geoffrey Llewellyn heard of Tansy's dismissal and flight and called at the Post Office to enquire for her.

'Would it help if I asked her to accompany me in my walks about the parish?' he asked. 'It would save time if I took someone with me who knew the way.'

Eva looked uncertain. Should she allow Tansy to go out unchaperoned with Geoffrey? Since she had returned from London, Tansy had moped about the house looking forlorn and miserable and Eva longed for the return of her vivacious fun-loving daughter.

'Just a moment, Geoffrey. I'll have a word with Edward. Please do sit down, it will only take a minute.'   Soon she was back, smiling and nodding. 'Thank you, that will be most kind. Edward thinks it will be quite suitable as long as you keep to public places and do not stay out too long,' adding, 'I'm sure it will be of great help to Tansy. I can't get her to leave her room... she's missing Norah too. Even more so since she saw her in London. Now she's nothing to keep her occupied. The Vallances are adamant that she can't return until the mystery disappearance of Emma's watch has been solved. The only good thing to come out of the whole business is that Blodwen Williams has been given Tansy's position as kitchen maid.'

She went to the stairs and called for Tansy to come down, returning to entreat Geoffrey, 'Please persuade her to accompany you. Anything would be better than to see her in her present state. Tansy's the last person in the world to steal anything,' she burst out, 'and Caroline Vallance must be a poor judge of character to believe otherwise.'

Now Tansy came into the room. She looked pale, deep shadows made blue patches beneath her eyes as if she hadn't slept. Her growing hair formed a halo round her face. When she saw Geoffrey standing there in brown corduroy trousers and Norfolk jacket, holding in his hands the cloth cap of a working man, her expression changed from misery to surprise. Surprise kept her standing there and Geoffrey seized the opportunity to appeal to her.

'I've come to ask for your help, Tansy.' he said and she replied in a voice so low that he had to bend towards her to hear what she was saying. 'My help? However may I assist you?' and she hesitated, one hand holding the door handle, intrigued yet ready for flight.

'I'm told that you know the town and its surroundings very well.' Geoffrey paused to let his words sink in. 'Do you think you know them well enough to be my guide?'

Carried along by the unexpectedness of his request, she nodded. 'Why, I suppose I do, after all I've lived here all my life and I do like to walk about.' She looked across to Eva for her approval. When she nodded, Tansy asked, 'When do you want to go?' and Geoffrey smiled and held out his hand. 'What about today – now?' Before she could demur Eva had fetched coat and hat, hustled Tansy into them, and pushed them through the Post Office and out into Southernhay. Automatically, she turned left and when they reached 148 steps she turned and from force of habit began the long climb to the top. There she hesitated, looking fearfully towards the stone gates of Courtenay House, but Geoffrey placed a firm hand under her elbow and took up a position between her and the road. As if on cue the Vallance family gig came out between the gates. Master Harry held the reins, backed up by Seth, who stood close to the young boy, ready to take the reins in case of difficulty. The moment he saw them Harry Vallance hauled on Tinker's reins and tipped his hat in their direction.

'Drewe. I must speak to you...' he called as soon as he saw them and Seth held tight to the reins and tipped his hat in their direction.

'Why have you gone away just when I've come home? No one will tell me. I need you to play Mafeking. Luscombe's no good, she's dull. Please come back.'

Tansy stood, blushing from deep embarrassment, not knowing how to answer. She felt Geoffrey's presence strong beside her, felt the firmness of his supporting hand under her elbow.

'I need Miss Drewe to show me your town today but I'm sure you'll be able to play Mafeking (was it?) with her again very soon. How would it be if, until then, I came in her place?'

Harry Vallance looked doubtful but smiled politely and took the reins back from Seth.

'Well, all right, I'll give you a try, although no one could be as good at it as Drewe.'

'How would it be if I called on you this evening?' offered Geoffrey with a smile and Harry, still looking unsure, nodded slowly. Then as the trap moved away he looked back and repeated, 'I do miss you, please hurry back,' and Tansy, somewhat cheered by his words, smiled and waved at her young Master.

'Thank you Geoffrey,' she said in a low voice. 'I'm most grateful for the way you helped me out. Fancy no one telling him why I'd gone.'

Geoffrey laughed. 'I'm sure Harry Vallance has as much faith in you as many of us have. Perhaps his parents knew he wouldn't believe that you stole his sister's watch, that's why they've said nothing.'

The road levelled out, affording views of smoking factory chimneys, railway sidings and houses which decorated the hillside like coloured ribbons, and they stopped to look at the churches made miniature by distance.

'This is my favourite place, high above town. Look, there's the chapel and that patch of green, that's the cricket field.' She turned to ask him. 'Do you play?' and when he nodded went on, 'There's the Teign going down to the sea. That's where we go for our Chapel Outing!'

Geoffrey noticed how the freshening wind was dispersing the early morning mist, whipping colour into the cheeks of his companion.

'Is that where Martin Webber comes from?' he asked, genuinely interested, but this question brought a change of mood.

'Webbers' farm is at Lustleigh, I went there with Beatrice Vallance and Sarah Webber gave her bunches of flowers and herbs.' And that was all she would say. Instead of telling

Geoffrey about her ride with Martin she hurried ahead to the kissing-gate. She turned to Geoffrey, her forehead wrinkled in thought.

'Mafeking no longer seems suitable as a game to be played by young children. Now I know what war is really like,' and in answer to Geoffrey's enquiring gaze she went on to explain. 'I went to a Magic Lantern Show with Norah and Helen in London. The title of the lecture was 'The Boar War Day by Day'. I'll never forget the sight of the wounded, the horses...' and she lapsed into silence as her thoughts went back to the evening she had ended up in the hands of the police.

Geoffrey regarded her thoughtfully, then said, 'I can see the pictures made a deep impression on you. You are right when you say war shouldn't be the subject for children's games. But Harry Vallance will come to learn the truth soon enough. Don't deny him the chance to treat it as a game while he's still young.'

They walked on across the field where Tom Cull's team ploughed straight furrows and a cloud of seagulls followed in their wake. Tom Cull bent to the plough and blades turned red soil, ready to be sown with seed.

'It's a different landscape altogether,' Geoffrey said, his voice tinged with bitterness. 'In the Valley we played cricket against a background of coal heaps!'

She turned to him. 'Our nightmares are of a different kind. If a child survives its first year 'tis a miracle!' She hesitated, one hand on the lych-gate. 'Would you like to go to Bradley Woods? We can cross Steppes Meadow to the river.' The grave look left his face and was replaced by a slow smile.

'I'd like that very much,' he agreed, and they took the church path downhill between hedges draped with old Man's Beard and hawthorn berries. A robin alternately sang and flew beside them until they crossed the road into the meadow.

'And how do you like living in Newton?' she enquired. 'Do you miss your last place?'

He laughed, remonstrated, 'Two questions in one sentence!' Pausing, he went on, 'To the first I can truthfully answer yes. I find the people friendly if a little slow. However, the slower pace of life gives one plenty of time to think!'

Tansy immediately sprang to the defence of her townspeople. 'They're not slow when it comes to money and enjoying themselves,' she retorted as they crossed the meadow where the river mist lay, their only companions a herd of Devon Reds munching steadily.

'On Sundays it's full of people,' she said. 'Young people bring their sweethearts,' she blushed but struggled on. 'They bring cups to drink from here,' she stopped at the spring which flowed from the side of the bank into the leat. 'Spring's supposed to have magic powers!' she added, then stopped, covered in confusion while Geoffrey looked at her with a twinkle in his eye.

'And have you brought a cup for us?' he asked. When she shook her head, he knelt on the bank, cupped his hands, filled them with fresh water and held them toward her. 'Then you'll just have to drink like this,' he said.

Before she could recover from her surprise Tansy found herself bending to slurp water from his slim brown hands which lifted liquid to her parted lips. She held them steady until the cold water slid down her throat then stood and brushed leaves from her skirt, blushing at the contact of his hands on her skin.

'You haven't answered my other question,' she said as she dried her hands on the green velvet of her skirt. Now his face darkened and he looked away from her towards the soft grey stone huddle of Bradley Manor.

'I miss the people but not the blackness of the valleys, the never-ending fight for life that goes on above and below ground.'

'Whatever do you mean?' she asked as they stepped through a curtain of leaves that divided the meadow from river bank, 'Fight for life?' He didn't answer but left her side, striding away along the path.

'You've not told me anything about the people at Merthyr,' she persisted as she hurried to catch up with him, but now his face took on a closed look which discouraged further questions.

'I'll tell you about it one day,' he paused, 'but not now.' And Tansy had to be satisfied with that.

'This,' she began as he slowed his stride to match hers, 'is the Lemon. Father says it rises on Dartmoor near Haytor. Then it rushes down through the newtake, that's the strip of land between moor and farm, through valleys and woods till it arrives here.'

Together they stood on the bank to peer into the clear water. 'Look,' she breathed, 'there's an eel.' They watched till the long, wriggling shadow disappeared beneath a sandy ledge at their feet. When they came to a bend where the meadow narrowed, a bridge took the path across into a wood. She hesitated. 'I haven't been any further than this on my own,' she said and together they looked across to where trees, clothed in the brown and gold of autumn, climbed away from the river to thicken and darken, a hint of a path disappearing into their depths.

'Are you afraid to go any farther?' he asked as she still hesitated. When she didn't answer, he teased 'Or are you afraid to go there with me?' Now she rose to the challenge, straightened her hat, stuck out her chin, plunged across the bridge and began to climb the path.

'No, I'm not afraid,' she shouted back. 'I'll try and find the Pit where William Yeo preached. He was put in prison for his beliefs.' She stopped to see if he was following. 'Would you like that?' she called back, then stood waiting for his answer.

'Why that would be wonderful,' he said as he came up beside her. 'I should certainly like to see a place with such associations.' Thus encouraged she went on, stopping from time to time where sycamore and bramble had grown over the path. Here Geoffrey produced a knife and cut a hazel stick to beat a way through. They climbed up from the river until suddenly the ground fell sharply away from the path at both sides. Two pits appeared, the one on the right shallow, that on the left deep, plunging eighty feet to the floor below.

'This is it!' Tansy panted, 'Now look for the steps.' She ran back and forth, searching for a break in the undergrowth. At last she found what she was looking for. 'Look Geoffrey, down here.' When he caught up with her she asked, 'Can you break through?' He stopped, breathing hard from the stiff climb, and laid about him with his stick, exposing the width of the path.

'Come on.' She took his hand, excited. 'Let's go down.'

When they emerged onto the path he exclaimed, 'This is marvellous! Just like a cathedral.' He allowed her to lead him down the rough-hewn steps which obtruded from the side of the pit. 'Why, it's a natural amphitheatre.'

When they reached the bottom, they stood and looked up at huge trees which soared towards the sky above them.

'They're just like the columns of Exeter cathedral,' Tansy said as she ran from side to side, reaching up and pressing her hands against the exposed roots of giant oaks.

'The caves are like chapels, dark and mysterious,' Geoffrey enthused, his voice echoing round the open theatre. 'All we need are the candles of confession.' As if in response to his words, the mist cleared and a gleam of winter sun shot through the foliage above them to light the stone face of the cave opposite. Excitement gripped them. Geoffrey took her hand, led her to a stone platform at the centre of the pit.

'Kneel and confess your sins,' he commanded, his voice vibrating. He pushed her roughly to her knees. She struggled to free herself but his hands held her down, his grip of iron, his face contorted with zeal. She hardly recognised him as her companion of a moment before.

For the first time since they entered the wood Tansy felt afraid. Afraid, not of the atmosphere of the pit, but of Geoffrey. He towered over her, huge and strong, his hands weighing down her small frame. The only way for her to escape this stranger was to obey him, then perhaps he would let her go.

'I confess,' she began in a quavering voice, 'to the sin of vanity.' As her voice gathered strength it grew stronger. 'I confess to the sin of jealousy.' Now the pain and tension of the past weeks were freed in a flood of tears. 'But I'm innocent of the sin of theft,' she shouted, suddenly defiant. With that he pulled her to her feet. The look she had hated dissolved suddenly into one of gentleness and he cradled her body in his arms.

'I believe you Tansy,' he said gently, 'but I wanted to hear it from your own mouth.' He led her to a fallen tree which made a natural seat. 'Sit here and tell me what you think could have caused such a disaster?' and she told him of her spoken wish to give a watch like Emma Vallance's to Norah.

'But I didn't take it, Geoffrey. I didn't! I didn't!'

'Then you must have an enemy at Courtenay House. Is there someone there who dislikes you? Someone you may have upset without knowing it?'

She hesitated for a moment, reluctant to tell tales, but when he pressed her she told him of Janet Luscombe's jealousy and the cause. He sat silent, deep in thought, while she felt comforted and easy in her mind for the first time since Charles Vallance had dismissed her.

'Do you think this Janet jealous enough to have taken the watch and hidden it?'

At this suggestion Tansy brightened. Could this be the possible explanation, she thought? A solution which hadn't occurred to her through the journey to London and back, through the nights when she lay unable to sleep, tortured by worry? He got up, took her hand in his and led her back to the steps, to begin the hard climb up and out of the Pit.

At the top he turned to ask, 'Tell me, what did you give to Norah to take to London?'

She smiled, remembering the look of delight on her sister's face as she had undone the small package. 'It was a pin cushion. A pin cushion with her initials picked out in coloured pin heads, lace at the edges and decorated with mother-of-pearl sequins. So pretty. It took me ages to save up but it was worth it. Two shillings out of my wages. Bought it from the cheap jack at the Michaelmas Fair and I've not seen another like it since,' she finished proudly, and he bent forward to kiss her flushed cheeks.

'I can't think of anything less like a gold watch,' he laughed, adding, 'but I imagine just as useful.'

As they began to walk away from the Pit he asked, 'Will you allow me to try and solve this mystery?' She sighed and shrugged as her problem returned to tax her once more.

'I don't see what you can do but thank you for your faith in me.'

Cheered beyond measure, she began to run forward towards the river. Now the path became full of potholes, caused when the river rose and ate into the banks in winter. They heard the chink of water over stone, heard the occasional plop as a water rat slipped into the river at their approach. As they progressed the volume of sound increased until it became a roar which grew into a crescendo as they reached the weir.

'A boy drowned here last year,' she said. 'Balancing on the sluice gate he was, then fell in and was drowned.' They hovered there a moment, saddened at the loss of a young life.

'It looks so gentle and harmless today,' Geoffrey replied, and when they got to Ogwell Mill he bought glasses of milk from the miller's wife, who added teacakes, hot from the oven, for his sixpence.

'Let's cross over the ford, go back to town the other side,' Tansy cried. She set off over moss-covered stones which, magnified by their covering of water, offered false footing. She slipped sideways and would have fallen in had Geoffrey not caught her from behind. As his arms enclosed her she felt a warmth pass through her clothes to caress her body. She stood still, not wanting him to let go, until she could keep up the pretence of fright no longer for fear he would guess her feelings.

Neither of them noticed the small, stooping figure approach from Chercombe Bridge, stopping to watch them as they struggled across. Neither of them were aware of her standing there as Tansy stepped off on a safer path to the other side where Geoffrey steadied her once again and, offering his hand, helped her climb up on to the field path. The woman waited no longer and hurried towards town, an expression of shock and disapproval on her face.

※

Eva, forewarned of her daughter's escapade, noted Tansy's skirt hem, muddy and wet, her hair escaping the green hat, the dried leaf sticking to her shoulder. But as a remonstrance rose to her lips she was stopped by the glow on Tansy's face, the way she followed Geoffrey with her eyes as he crossed the room to warm his hands at the fire. Now he turned to Eva.

'Tansy has taken me to see the Puritan Pit – it was most rewarding. A rough walk but full of interest.' Here he smiled at Tansy. 'I'm afraid you must blame me for the state of her dress,' and as Tansy returned his smile, he asked, 'Will you come with me to visit the village chapels – we could walk to those close by? Are you engaged tomorrow?' As she nodded her head and accepted this new invitation, Eva experienced a sudden sense of misgiving. When the tall figure of the preacher had gone she turned to Tansy.

'Do you think that's wise, Tansy? Your Father's already received an account of your behaviour at the Ford. You may be sure it won't stop here. I think you should stop and consider your father's reputation as a lay preacher.'

Tansy looked shocked, tossed her head and declared, 'We didn't do anything you wouldn't have approved of, Mother. Geoffrey's a good man. He's going to try and catch the thief who took Miss Emma's watch. Clear my name.'

Eva looked up in surprise from her pile of ironing. 'Won't that be wonderful?' Tansy went on, 'Show those Vallances they're wrong.'

'And how is he going to do that?' Eva wanted to know and, as she pressed iron to linen, a smell of scorching rose from a too hot iron.

Tansy replied airily, 'We met Master Harry and Seth going to town... Geoffrey's arranged to call on the Vallances later today. You'll see,' she went on, full of hope and confidence. 'If anyone can solve the puzzle I'm sure it'll be him!'

Her hurt and distress abated and, in their place, a growing excitement took hold of her. Perhaps, she thought, her dismissal from Courtenay House was meant to be, for how else could she have got to know Geoffrey Llewellyn so quickly. They had reached a point of intimacy that could have taken weeks of family suppers, she thought, recalling their conversation earlier in the day. She wondered about his past, what had caused his sudden change of mood when she asked about Merthyr and the people he'd known there.

She climbed the attic stairs, took off wet stockings and skirt, and lay down on the bed, feeling again the touch of his skin against hers as they'd drunk from the spring. She felt again the weight of his hands on her shoulders as he forced her to confess at the Pit. Forced her to admit to vanity and jealousy.

Now she looked across at Norah's empty bed and longed for her sister's presence. Longed to have someone to confide in and missed her more than she'd ever thought possible. *Black Beauty* lay unread beside her, her favourite horse, the awkward snappy Ginger, completely forgotten. Instead she dreamt of walking the high moor with Geoffrey. Of taking the train to Teign Valley with him at her side to pick primroses in spring. Dreamt of the next summer, standing deep in the Teign to catch sticklebacks while he watched her from a sunlit bank.

Her dreams were interrupted by the arrival of the twins from school. They burst into her room with pleas that she should go downstairs.

'Tansy, what are you doing? Come down and hear us read. Then you must play with us!' Reluctantly she abandoned her musings, following Robert and James downstairs to hear them read their parts in the Christmas nativity play. Then she shuffled and dealt from the well-worn pack and, as they began to play 'Beat Your Neighbour', Geoffrey, dressed once more in professional attire of black jacket and striped trousers, rang the bell of Courtenay House and asked for Master Harry.

ꞏ❀ꞏ

The gossip had been thorough in spreading the account of their behaviour at Ogwell Mill and there wasn't an empty seat in chapel as the congregation waited to hear Geoffrey Llewellyn speak.

'Today,' he began, 'instead of taking a quotation from the Bible for my sermon, I will tell you a little of my background and of my impressions of Newton Abbot since I came here to live a few months ago.'

Tansy's interest heightened, perhaps she would have the answer to her question at last. Know the reason for Geoffrey's reticence the day they'd walked into the Pit. She felt a stir of interest among the people sitting close by.

During the weeks following her return from London she had accompanied Geoffrey to the dank festering Courts close by the river where the poorest among them lived. She had waited in the background while he'd interviewed the Superintendent of Schools and Workhouses, Hospitals and Almshouses. And, much against her Mother's wishes, had gone with him to the prison at Princetown where the worst of the country's criminals were incarcerated.

Now she watched him as he waited for the hum of conversation to subside and thought he looked pale under the shock of red hair. She looked lovingly at the familiar hands which rested on the polished mahogany pulpit, knuckles tensed. At last all was silent.

'I have found a town,' he began, 'a town much the same as other towns throughout the land. A town composed of rich and poor, healthy and sick, good people and bad.' Here Tansy looked round to see the effect his words were having. All eyes were fixed on his face, all bodies shocked and still. 'A place existing since Saxon times, set between two hills and within sight of one of the last great wildernesses.' He paused and looked round his congregation slowly, as if to imprint each and every one on his mind.

'You are fortunate indeed to live in such a beautiful place. Where I have come from people live overshadowed by waste tips. Men wrest a living underground in temperatures as hot as Hades. Danger attends each minute of their working day. Death can come with the striking of a spark to a pocket of gas. Our hearths are fuelled by such men – their hearths often attended by widows and fatherless children.'

Tansy drank in every word as he painted pictures with his eloquent descriptions. She leant forward so as not to miss any nuance.

'Here the town is divided between rich and poor. The former live on the south side of the hills, enjoy the warmth of the sun.' He paused, rocked back on his heels in the pulpit. 'The poor live on the north side, suffering depths of cold and shade.' Now there rose a murmur of approval from the poor and dissent from the rich. 'The rich live in airy, spacious houses, while the poor survive in crowded courts and terraces. Outside the confines of the town stretch woods and river valleys.' Again he stopped, looking around slowly at the sea of faces. Tansy held her breath, sensing a change of mood. The strong, sharp scent of fresh chrysanthemums reached her from the lectern. Geoffrey leant forward, his voice deepening in tone, swelling in volume as it had done in the Puritan Pit.

'One day last week I had the good fortune to be taken by one of our members to a place that influenced this community two hundred and fifty years ago. I refer to the Puritan Pit where William Yeo, dismissed from his position as Rector of Wolborough, preached non-conformist views to his followers. Defying the law he led them in worship, at dark of night in Bradley Woods.'

Now Tansy felt excitement generate in the people close by as they turned to their neighbours to nod and whisper.

'As an act of faith, as an act of worship, as an act of commitment to improve the lives of this community.' His voice changed yet again, this time to the note of one who had decided on the course ahead. His eyes blazed with a burning zeal and she was back kneeling on the stone altar, his hands pressing down on her shoulders, searching for the truth.

'I propose that an Anniversary Service be held in Puritan Pit on the first Sunday of December. The path is steep and overgrown but I am sure that with determination on our part, and with help from the strongest of our members, it will be possible to clear the way.'

Tansy, conscious suddenly of eyes upon her, felt proud that he had come to her at the outset for help in his work. No longer did she feel a failure. She sat straight in her seat as he continued.

'Let us unite in this venture and mark Puritan Pit as a place of dedication to God and Man. To heal the sick, to teach those who cannot read or write, to clear the names of those wrongfully accused. To share our own good fortune with those in need.'

Now there was movement from the Vallances' pew across the aisle to her right. Charles Vallance, grim-faced, had risen and left his pew and the chapel, followed by Caroline, Emma, Harry. The young Vallances smiled apologetically at Tansy as they passed her and this token of affection lifted her spirits even higher. A sudden disturbance in the gallery mirrored the Vallance withdrawal as Hetty, Janet and Blodwen hurried down to follow their employers from the building.

As the doors of the chapel closed behind them a babble of excited talk rose from the congregation. Geoffrey Llewellyn made a sign to the steward, who announced the final hymn. 'We will sing Onward Christian soldiers, Marching as to war...'

A hundred voices rose and filled the lofty building. Robert and James stopped playing their surreptitious game of 'I Spy', Rosemary Brimmacombe's feet flew over the organ pedals with renewed vigour, and Tansy felt as though she would burst with pride at having such a man as Geoffrey for a friend. Unconsciously, her hand flew to her hair, now growing in tight curls. This time her hand didn't try, as was its habit, to push it out of sight, but for the first time in her life to touch it with pride.

⁂ Chapter Sixteen ⁂

Puritan Pit

The following week Charles Vallance, as chairman of the Chapel Elders, called a meeting to discuss Geoffrey Llewellyn's sermon.

'This newcomer to our town has taken it upon himself to criticise its social structure. I do not think it part of a minister's role to interfere in the education and enlightenment of the working classes. I propose that he be asked to confine himself to the ordinance of the Ministry. He must be prevented from spreading subversive ideas from the pulpit.'

But when the motion was put to the vote it was defeated by six votes to three. Henry Westaway went so far as to suggest it would be a good thing to have an independent person take an interest in the welfare of the town.

'No harm can come from having an educated man like Geoffrey Llewellyn play a part in the affairs of the town. For one thing,' he went on, 'it's high time that the Courts were cleared up. If an epidemic happens where does it usually begin? In the Courts. And why? Because there's no mains drainage, no sanitation and water from the well there is tainted.'

Now Edward Drewe rose to give his opinion. 'I feel an Anniversary Service such as that proposed by our new minister could act as a source of inspiration to all of us. But work on clearing the path to the Pit must begin straight away if it's to be ready in time for December 9th. That's a mere two weeks away. So with the Elders' agreement I will take on the task of recruiting workers. May I have the Committee's authority to pay for this to be done?'

A show of hands produced the necessary majority and Edward, ever a man of action, left Courtenay House and set off for the Courts.

⁂

Flames flickered and sent shadows across the platoon of Hussars, showing blue tunics and white plumed helmets as horses stepped across the parade ground. Following their proud display came the 2nd Devons, bayonets fixed, marching six abreast and, last of all, the Gloucesters, renowned for their ability to fight with such ferocity that few could withstand them. Bringing up the rear came four field guns, and, controlling them all, the hands of Harry Vallance.

'All present and correct, General Kitchener.' His voice rang through the morning-room where he lay, full-length in front of a fire lit specially for him by Blodwen Williams. Now he waited for Geoffrey Llewellyn to join him as he had done on the last three Tuesday evenings when he took the place of Tansy who had, before her dismissal, been let off kitchen duty especially to share in Master Harry's after-supper recreation.

'Your next assignment, Captain Brown, will be to go to the relief of Mafeking.' Now Harry tried to wheel the six Hussars and failed. 'It's no good,' he sighed, 'my hands aren't big enough.' Suddenly losing patience, he scattered his troops to the far corners of the room. The door opened and Geoffrey Llewellyn stood, looking down at Harry, who immediately leapt to his feet.

'Hurrah, hurrah! Mr Llewellyn you've come at last. Password?' he demanded, and after Geoffrey had tried 'Custard' and failed, Harry crowed in triumph. 'It's cauliflower today. Cauliflower! Cauliflower!' Geoffrey laughed and rumpled the boy's thick brown hair.

'Who will you be today?' Harry demanded, 'British or Afrikaans?' Geoffrey dropped down beside him on the hearth rug, doubled up his long legs and looked at Harry with a quizzical expression.

'What's happening in the war today, young man?' he asked, and Harry began to explain.

'You should have come earlier. General Kitchener was taking the salute after the raid at Rorke's Drift. Shall I set it up for you again?'

But Geoffrey remembered Tansy's description of the newsreel and stopped Harry with a hand on his arm. Gravely he looked at the figures lying prone on the floor, the scattered guns and abandoned horses.

'I think I prefer this scene, it's more like the real thing,' he said, and Harry's eyes widened with surprise.

'But they were winning. We're British, we always win,' he hesitated, 'don't we?' Geoffrey smiled ruefully, 'If only that were true. At the moment the British Army is far from winning. Men are dying in the veldt. Dying under a blazing sun in a foreign land and for a cause they don't understand.' Slowly he picked up soldiers one by one and arranged them in a double row.

'What are you doing?' Harry demanded.

'I'm making a guard of honour for those killed. We will bury them with full military honours.' Harry watched, fascinated as Geoffrey lay four soldiers on the rug and covered them with his handkerchief.

'When I give the command, we will fire a fusillade over them, like this.' He raised an imaginary rifle to his shoulder and made the sound of an explosion. Harry brightened at the sight of action and joined in.

'Bang! Bang!' he shouted. His cheeks grew rosy, his blue eyes animated.

'What about the others?' he gazed down at the figures lying by the fire.

'The walking wounded will go to a tent near the front line. The badly wounded will be carried on stretchers. Once they've been attended to by a doctor they'll go back behind the lines for emergency surgery. Then they'll be brought home to England on a boat.'

'Christopher Westaway's going into the Navy. Do you think he'll be sent to South Africa, Mr Llewellyn?' He pushed his arms through the air in imitation of waves.

Suddenly the door flew open and there stood Charles Vallance. He stared at Geoffrey in surprise.

'What's all this noise?' he demanded. 'And what are you doing here, pray?' He turned to Geoffrey, taking his watch from his pocket in his agitation, and Geoffrey rose to his feet in response, his face serene in contrast to the high colour of the face of Harry's father.

'I was invited here by young Master Harry. I have been to visit him these past three Tuesdays. Mrs Vallance seems to approve as it seems your son needs someone to share his manoeuvres with.' He waved his hand at the battlefield below him. 'I believe Tansy Drewe used to fulfil this duty before she was dismissed.' The colour deepened in Charles Vallance's face. He replaced the watch in his pocket.

'I would like a word with you in my study, if you would be so good,' he said, and left the room. Geoffrey touched Harry's shoulder.

'I'll be back as soon as your father has finished with me.'

'Please don't be long. I want to know what happens next.'

Geoffrey smiled and said, 'Just look after the wounded till I get back. See how many of your troops have survived the Boers' attack.'

He walked towards the door, meditating as he crossed the hall on the words Tansy had uttered on her return from London. Perhaps it was time Harry learnt that war was not all fame and glory. He thought she would have approved of his handling of Harry's battle.

He tapped on the study door. 'Come in!' The response was sharp and when Geoffrey entered the room he found the older man pacing the floor behind his desk in some agitation. He stopped, turned to face Geoffrey and pressed his hands on the gleaming mahogany where gas light reflected in a silver-topped inkstand.

'This won't take long,' he said shortly, 'so I won't ask you to sit down. I have just two things to say to you. 'The rich' as you called them in your recent sermon, include those of your congregation who have become so due to hard work and wise investment. They support many of the town charities. Were it not for them the poor would be even worse off than they appear to be.' He straightened. 'We provide work for many of them,' and he leant across the desk to glare at Geoffrey, 'and don't you forget it.'

The smile on Geoffrey's face faded and was replaced by a look of steel.

'And how much do you pay your workers, may I ask?'

'We pay them the rate for the job.' Charles retaliated.

Geoffrey smiled a long, slow, insolent smile and perched his large frame on the corner of Charles Vallance's desk.

'One last question, if I may?' He paused and Charles nodded impatiently. 'And who fixes the rate for the job?' Charles looked taken aback. No one had ever questioned him like this before.

'Why the employers, of course. Who else?'

'Exactly!' exclaimed Geoffrey, a look of triumph on his face. 'And is it enough to feed and clothe a family when work is scarce? Enough to heat homes in winter? Is it enough to support them when they're too sick to work? And,' he straightened his back, 'when they die because they can't afford to pay a doctor, who buries them?'

Charles Vallance's face became suffused with rage. He spoke in a harsh voice and with a look of finality he crossed the room and, opening the door, indicated Geoffrey should leave.

'I shall be glad,' he said coldly, 'if you will confine contact with my son to subjects suitable to his age and your sermons to the religious aspects of your Ministry. I do not wish my family to have to leave the place where we have worshipped for many years. You may leave.'

Geoffrey followed him to the door and then turned to face Charles. 'If I am not to involve myself with the well-being of my congregation, then can I depend on the affluent members to right the wrongs that seem to be apparent, not only to myself, but to other thinking people?' He paused to allow the weight of his words to strike home. 'If you cannot give me such an assurance then I must do as God tells me.' Charles stood, speechless with fury. In the hall, Geoffrey bumped into Blodwen Williams, who carried coals through to the drawing-room. She bobbed a curtsey and smiled shyly.

'Blodwen, what are you doing here?' Geoffrey asked.

'I work here now, Mr Llewellyn, in Tansy's place.' She seized his hands and pleaded, 'Please come home and see Father. He's off work again. He's sick. He would be so pleased to see you.'

Geoffrey promised to go as soon as he left Courtenay House. 'But now I must go and say goodbye to young Master Harry.'

Caroline was dressing for dinner when Charles burst into their bedroom. He stopped at the sight of her as she sat at the dressing-table, trying to fasten a necklace.

'Is that new?' he enquired, staring at the soft black velvet dress which emphasised the creamy skin. She turned to meet his gaze.

'No,' she snapped, 'it's not new. Even your Mother was aware of the paucity of my wardrobe.'

Charles reddened. 'She didn't remark on it to me!' he said indignantly and Caroline, sensing her advantage, went on, 'Now Emma's eighteen she'll be going out more. She'll need a good suit and evening clothes.'

Charles advanced towards her, his eyes admiring her reflection in the mirror.

'Here, let me,' he said and took the gold chain out of her hands. His fingers touched her neck and she jerked away from him, letting the necklace fall to the glass-topped table.

'I couldn't afford a dress like this on the allowance you give me!' she stormed, and picked up the necklace once more. In spite of himself Charles burst out, 'Diamonds would look splendid with this!' then instantly regretted it when he saw the change come over Caroline's face. She snorted with rage.

'You talk of diamonds when you can't even provide a carriage for me to visit my friends and go into town. How much will you pay for the Lanchester? And how are we to pay for a chauffeur?'

Charles shifted awkwardly. 'The automobile has already been paid for,' he said.

Her lips tight, her face white, Caroline's voice was waspish. 'Already paid for? So you could find the money for an automobile which may or may not go but you can't find the necessities for your wife and children.'

Now Charles broke into a sarcastic laugh. 'Don't be ridiculous, Caroline. Who has paid for the house to be redecorated and modernised this summer? I thought that was your priority – or did I misunderstand? Perhaps you'd rather I hadn't paid for the work but given the money to you to put on your back?'

Now it was Caroline's turn to look guilty as she remembered the last winter spent in cajoling and wheedling constantly to get her way over the bathroom and William Morris wallpapers. She half turned and smiled up at Charles, holding the necklace out to him.

'Of course I'm grateful, Charles,' she conceded. 'The house is much improved and I know it cost a great deal of money.' She paused, then invited, 'Please fasten this for me, I can't seem to manage.' He bent over her, connecting the tiny links about her neck. When his fingers came in contact with her soft skin, they hesitated there. He bent down, brushed his lips against her coiffured hair and she put up a hand and caught his.

'Harry will be so excited with the new automobile, I'm sure,' she placated him and this reminded Charles of the reason he was here. He stood away from her, the expression on his face hardening.

'I would prefer you to find company of his own age for Harry. Geoffrey Llewellyn has some strange ideas and his politics are far too radical for someone growing up in our society. Hasn't Mary Westaway another brother as well as Christopher?'

Caroline sighed and shook her head. 'There's Robin but he's only seven. A three-year gap is too great for a ten year old. Besides, now we've taken over the nursery for a bathroom, where would they play? No, Harry needs someone of his own age in the holidays. You remember he stayed at Torquay with Arthur Proudlove last summer. They get on really well, but how am I to take him back and forth without a carriage of my own? Unless,' she spoke slowly and with great emphasis, 'you intend to take the gig for your daily journeys to the Mill and leave the Lanchester for me.'

'No, no!' Charles exclaimed and began to pace excitedly up and down the room. 'That won't be possible. You see Caroline,' he paused then rushed on, 'I intend to learn to drive the car myself.'

Caroline jumped up in astonishment. 'Drive the car yourself?' she exploded, 'And when will you find the time to learn, I'd like to know?' Before Charles could answer she laughed scornfully. 'Can't find enough time to play with your son but can find time to learn to drive the new vehicle!' Now Charles stopped in his pacing and seized her hands in his, a look almost of ecstasy on his face. She hadn't seen him so animated since the first of the contracts for the Army in South Africa had arrived in the spring.

'I've been studying the manual,' he said. 'Now the Prince of Wales has bought one, the Daimler engine is being produced in great numbers. Lanchesters are fitting them in all their vehicles. I think it'll be quite straightforward. Howell will have to fetch petroleum and oil from the engineering works until we have a garage here in Newton. Perhaps that nephew of his would like to learn to look after it.' Here he paused. 'It will free the gig for your use whenever you need it. That will solve the problem of taking Harry to Torquay.

But Caroline's mouth fell into a pout and she stamped one small silk-shod foot. 'That's all very well in the summer or when the weather's fine but it won't do now. Why, it's done nothing but rain for the last ten days. No, you'll have to arrange for Blodwen Williams to go with him on the bus and that means she'll be absent from her duties and Cook will have one of her tantrums.'

Charles sighed. Really, Caroline was becoming excessively demanding these days. Not content with the alterations he had carried out to Courtenay House, now she wanted her own carriage. Spending too much time with Maude Westaway, that was the trouble, he thought. There seemed to be no limit to the depth of Henry Westaway's pocket, well-lined from the clay mines. There was always a need for clay, especially now homes were being fitted with bathrooms and water closets and sewers were being installed throughout the land.

'Until you can provide me with suitable transport I shall continue to ask Geoffrey Llewellyn to come and visit Harry on Tuesdays. It's not much to ask, is it?' She took a lace hanky from a drawer and dabbed it to her eyes. 'Unless you can make time to play with Harry yourself,' she finished.

Charles' brow darkened and he shook his head. Although proud of the sturdy little boy who did well in school at games and lessons, he'd never grown as close to him as he had to Emma. It had been at his insistence that the boy had been sent away to school.

'You spoil the boy, Caroline.' He crossed to the dressing-table once more and now Caroline surrendered. She felt she had sewn the seeds for a future which would include an automobile to take her to concerts and dances if not for shopping and visits. She gazed up at him through long lashes, then back at her reflection in the mirror.

'You're right, of course, Charles,' she said. 'Diamonds would be perfect but until you can afford them my amethysts will do very well.' And Charles, trapped once more by his own words, made a half promise.

'Perhaps,' he hinted, 'if the Army order's repeated...' She lifted a parted cupid bow mouth towards him and their lips met. Charles slid his arm round her, drawing her body up to meet his, his tongue searching hers. The dinner gong sounded. Caroline drew back.

'I'm sure you'll make a wonderful driver, Charles,' she murmured, brushing his ear with her lips. His body responded to the invitation in her eyes.

'I'll see what I can arrange for Harry,' he promised and went to open the door for her. He paused, one hand on the door knob.

'I'll not be going to the Club tonight, Callo,' he said, using his pet name for her. 'Perhaps an early night would suit us both!'

✧

Edward had gone down to the Court at the back of Wolborough Street, where men hung around the entrance. They stood aside for him to pass and as he emerged and straightened up from the low passage stinking slops just missed him, thrown from an upper window. The stench of offal from a nearby butcher's filled the narrow terrace where sun and air never reached. Children with twisted limbs played barefoot, the absence of boots denying them access to Bell's School where the poor might attend for free lessons in reading and arithmetic. Water closets lined the side of the Court opposite the stone dwellings. Edward retraced his steps.

'Who wants to earn sixpence a day clearing paths in Bradley Woods?' he asked, and six immediately volunteered including Tom Moore, whose wife Avril expected her fifth any day.

'How many days work can 'ee give us?' Tom wanted to know, thinking that here, for the first time in months of searching town and outskirts for work, was an offer that seemed too good to be true. Edward hesitated, to promise more days than proved necessary could mean disaster for the population of the Court. With the promise of money, they would send out to buy meat or cheese on tick and end up further in debt.

'Two days sure, maybe more. Bring your own hooks and spades.' Tom Moore's face fell and he ducked under the passage, making for number five Moon Court and Avril. His four little sons sat in a heap around the front door playing five stones. They sensed the excitement emanating from their father.

'What's happening, Father?' William Moore wanted to know, but Tom pushed him aside in haste. Avril sat resting by the open hearth before a small coal fire, a pile of mending in a basket by her side. She looked up as Tom hurried into the room.

'Where's the pawn ticket, Maid?' he demanded as she struggled to get up. 'Postmaster from Southernhay's offering work. Sixpence a day but we've to take our own tools. Where's the ticket?' he repeated.

A look of anger flushed Avril's pale face and she shook her head fiercely. 'What's the good of a ticket if there's no money to pay it off? 'Tis no good looking, Tom. There's nothing in the tin.'

Still he searched among the few pots on the mantelpiece, a look of desperation on his thin face. In the far corners of the gloomy room sat Tom's parents, Alice and George, one in each alcove. George looked up from sucking an empty pipe, watching Tom searching for the vital piece of paper. Alice let her tatting fall into her lap and shook her head at Avril's remonstrance.

'Told you not to pawn your spade, didn't I?' Avril declared sarcastically. 'You'm a fool, Tom Moore.'

The young man turned and left the house to find Edward Drewe. 'I've lost my tools, Gaffer. Is it possible you can lend me some?' And Edward, knowing that tools and clothes were pawned to pay rent and for food, considered for a moment.

'If you will sign a paper and return the tools to me when the work is done?' Tom nodded vigorously and made his mark on a piece of paper produced from Edward's pocket. They

111

were watched by the children who, catching the air of excitement Edward's presence had brought to Moon Court, went to fetch their mothers. Women emerged from narrow door-ways, good news travelling equally as fast as bad.

'Are you giving cider, Sir?' Nancy Mitchell asked, knowing that if cider was supplied the chances of wages reaching home were less than if it wasn't.

Edward hesitated, this was proving more difficult than he had imagined. 'Cider will be given only at the end of the job.' He paused. 'I will bring it here myself.' The women turned away, satisfied.

At the sound of a familiar voice Edward turned to see Geoffrey Llewellyn enter the Court, his bright hair lightening the shadowed terrace.

'The paths to be cleared are for the purpose of attending a special service in Puritan Pit on December 9th. If your men make a good job of it you're all invited to attend. The young ones are assured a place in the front row and food will be brought and given out.'

A buzz of talk broke out, women sent children with messages to their men, who waited for the Half Moon to open. The promise of pasties and cider as well as an outing for the inhabitants, who had no money to stray far from the cramped rooms of the Court, was indeed something to gossip about. Wives wrapped what little bread they had and filled stone jars with water from the pump. They gathered at the entrance to watch their men depart.

The Pit was half a mile from the bridge over the Lemon and the men toiled all the first day and on through the second until a path, three feet wide, wound up between the trees to the rim of the deep hole where Tansy had taken Geoffrey on their first shared walk.

When the night of the 9th came, bright and clear, the same men lined the path with torches which sent shadows dancing in the wind above in Lang's Copse. Chapel Elders went on ahead to prepare. Edward Drewe and Rosemary Brimmacombe walked anxiously beside the harmonium which wheezed and sang in accompaniment to the breathing of the men who carried it. They stopped frequently to set down the organ and wipe sweat from their faces. Arriving at the Pit, they set stones to form a level platform for the instrument and Rosemary tried out hymns on it and prayed that it wouldn't rain.

Those of the congregation fit enough to undertake the mile-long walk gathered at St Leonard's Tower. Geoffrey Llewellyn had asked Jimmy Brimmacombe to carve a small cross and the boy carried it proudly. He had decorated it with thorns and added, at the last minute, a wren from his collection of bird carvings. He led the procession and as many children from the Court who had shoes, and a few who hadn't, ran and skipped around him. Next came Geoffrey Llewellyn, serious and official, in black, carrying a bible and, just a step or two behind his left shoulder came Tansy with hymn sheets.

As she followed, Tansy struggled in her mind with the task he had set her. How was she to get Stephen Walters to see her, let alone listen to what she had to say. Norah Drewe had found him a difficult Head when she worked at Bell's School as a pupil teacher. He had told her he didn't approve of women in positions of authority and it was only due to the absence of a suitable young man to fill the vacancy that he had taken Norah on. Since her return from London, Tansy had led each day in a suspension of her true self until Geoffrey had rescued her.

'I need a helper,' he had stated that day after they had visited the Puritan Pit. His steely eyes had bored into hers and she had accepted the proffered invitation immediately – much to the outrage of Aurelia Brown, who had fulfilled the role of clerk-housekeeper to the previous minister and had hoped to go on performing these offices for Geoffrey Llewellyn. Aurelia had arrived with Havelock Childers from Eastbourne twenty years before and held the minister in a firm grip until he had suffered a stroke and died. Now she tried to exert the same control over Geoffrey Llewellyn. She kept The Manse clean but cheerless, the food adequate but dull, and salted away a small profit from the housekeeping each week. With the arrival of Tansy Drewe things had begun to change. A stream of callers kept her attending the front door throughout each day and the demand for tea and coffee at all times was beginning to make inroads into her nest egg. Each morning she awaited the arrival of Tansy who came in breathless from her excited rush across town and climb up Knowles Hill. At the gate of The Manse, Tansy would pause and look back at the Post Office on the opposite side of the valley. She looked at the line of shadow formed by the sun, dividing the hill neatly in half. She knew the sun's warmth wouldn't reach Bowden Hill and the Williams' family until late afternoon, wouldn't warm their homes as did the sun the houses of the rich families on the other side of the hill.

Tansy felt excited by her new existence, looked forward each day to greeting Geoffrey where he waited for her in the gloomy study with its worn carpet and dusty bookshelves, left untouched for years by Aurelia. Each morning she brought him flowers. Although it was December, she still found handfuls of harebells in stone walls in Southernhay, or she would beg a bunch of chrysanthemums from Bessie Brimmacombe's abundant plot. There they glowed on Geoffrey's desk until Aurelia's jealousy got the better of her and she flung them out each Monday with the wasted sheets of Geoffrey's sermon.

Tansy and Geoffrey had fallen into a state of easy camaraderie, each day had taken on a certain pattern. First they knelt in prayer for a few minutes, dedicating the day to God. Then Tansy fetched tea from the kitchen, where Aurelia glowered at her. They discussed letters from parishioners and he suggested the replies he wanted her to send. Following his visit to the Courts he greeted her with a fresh request.

'I want you to list the families who live in the Courts. All the Courts, not just the Wolborough Street one, but those at the back of East Street.' Tansy began to write in a small notebook. He went on, 'I want to know all their needs. How many share the pump. If there are sewers. How many children attend Bell's School. Any suggestions you have for benefactors to provide scholarships to the Grammar School for the brightest.'

When she had looked up, unsure, and asked, 'How will I know who would be willing to give money?' he patiently explained. 'Make a list of the owners of engineering works, mills, brick works – perhaps lawyers and the wealthy. I'm sure you and your family will know who they are. Then we will write to each one and invite them to make an offer.'

She wrote busily, understanding at last the depth of information he wanted. As the list of tasks grew her face clouded. 'I know what you want but how am I to gain entrance to all these places and meet all these people? No one's going to take notice of me, are they?'

Geoffrey laughed and stood up to usher her out. 'Where's the fierce young woman who spoke out for the army horses in South Africa? Where's the brave young woman who was taken away by the police in London? And where's the soldier who breached the woods with a fiercesome stranger?'

Stung by his teasing challenge, Tansy closed her notebook with a snap, stuck out her chin and marched through the study doorway.

Now, as she followed Geoffrey to the Pit, she patted the letter of introduction he had given her. She would begin on Monday, starting with Stephen Walters, and prove to Geoffrey Llewellyn that she was capable of justifying his confidence.

She was hardly conscious of Martin Webber joining the procession at her side until she heard him greet her mother. 'Good evenin' Mrs Drewe. A fine evening for it! You two, up and about at last!' He smiled down at the twins, who kept close to their mother's skirts, yet refused to hold her hands. Their eyes, huge with excitement, darted into the darkness on either side. Eva watched Martin greet Tansy with a feeling of relief. Whilst she was pleased that Tansy's appetite had returned at last, pleased that Geoffrey Llewellyn had provided Tansy with an occupation, a purpose for her bright intelligence, she felt that Martin, with his steady supportive ways and calm nature, would be better for Tansy and her mercurial temperament. Edward, she knew, didn't share her approval of Tansy's association with Geoffrey. He had received an expression of doubts from the Chapel Elders, who feared their congregation wouldn't accept a relationship which seemed so radical. Murmurs were heard about town.

'Calling at The Manse every day.' 'He's no wife there to act as chaperone.' 'Aurelia Brown says they spend hours together in his room,' which transformed their hours of social duty into one of suspicious liaison. Aurelia took care to bring back town gossip to her employer, who looked at her levelly and spoke slowly, 'And what do you say in answer to these false accusations?' which turned her thin face red and sent her hands to her untidy hair in a gesture of nervous defiance. 'It's just that it gives people the wrong impression, Sir,' she murmured.

'Because,' he said rising, 'if you prefer to believe gossip-mongers, rather than the evidence of your own eyes, perhaps it would be better if you found a new position, one where guarantees of loyalty are exchanged at the outset.'

She bridled at his words, her sallow bony face flushing at the implied accusation. 'The Reverend Childers never found anything to complain of in my work or behaviour,' she protested. 'He always found everything to his satisfaction.' Here she drew herself up with pride. 'And he didn't feel the need for extra help.'

Geoffrey smiled. 'Then if you will behave in the same manner while I am minister here I shall be very grateful. But I shall expect you to make an effort to become friends with Miss Drewe. She will, I am sure, help you in any extra domestic demands which result from my Ministry. I intend to get to know my congregation and having them come to The Manse is a good way of doing so.' He paused to see the effect his words were having on his house-keeper, who stood pulling at her skirt. 'If you think this is beyond your capabilities, then perhaps it would be best if you were to seek alternative work.'

Aurelia shook her head vehemently. 'Please don't ask me to leave,' she begged. 'Where would I get a position at my time of life? Besides,' she burst out, 'the Reverend Childers promised me that this would be my home for the rest of my days.' She turned and scuttled away to seek refuge in her room, high above in the eaves.

Geoffrey had felt it wise to report this conversation to Edward who, in turn, had transmitted it to Eva. She drew in her breath. 'Just let anyone say anything to me about Geoffrey and Tansy,' she had responded. 'Only just let them!'

Now Eva hurried along, trying to keep up with Geoffrey's long strides. The Chapel Elders and curious townspeople followed behind and, last of all, the women from the Courts and their children. They walked at a discreet distance, the women shawled and carrying the baskets of food and drink provided by the chapel.

Charles Vallance, a reluctant participant in the outdoor service, had said he would meet the procession at the bridge and lead it up the path to the Pit. A steady hum of anticipation accompanied the walkers until they arrived there. Then a silence fell as they descended the torchlit cavern, overhung by a canopy of stars. Charles Vallance had no difficulty in making himself heard as he stood high on a platform of rock to declaim,

'This service is in memory of those who desired liberty to worship God according to the dictates of their conscience. Those who were compelled to leave the church they loved and find a place here among the quiet of these rocks and woods in God's own temple.'

Then they sang one of the Reverend Baring Gould's hymns:

'Through the night of doubt and sorrow
Onward goes the pilgrim band
Singing songs of expectation
Marching to the promised land'

Even the children were quiet, joining in when they knew the words, staring about them when they didn't. Now Geoffrey Llewellyn took Charles Vallance's place on the stone pulpit and began.

'We are here as a result of the hard work by the men of Moon Court. It is they who have, in clearing the path, cleared the way for this night's pilgrimage. A pilgrimage to remember William Yeo who founded our Church by his action 200 years ago. Born at Totnes in 1617, he was priest in charge of Wolboroguh Church. From there he was cast out because he didn't agree with the prevailing clerics. He brought his followers here to this deep cavern at night to worship God, free from persecution.'

Shadows leapt from rock to rock and Geoffrey Llewellyn paused, looking around at upturned faces, rapt in the mood of the moment.

'We are going to use this pilgrimage to launch another,' he paused, 'but of that I will speak later. Now I want to quote John Ruskin, painter, philosopher, radical thinker. He wrote these words in 1868 and they apply as much today as they did then. But first I will ask Tansy Drewe and Martin Webber to distribute the food and drink. When you are all supplied and comfortable then, only then, will I begin.'

There was a hum of talk and movement as families settled down together as best they could on the rough ground. At last all the pasties and cider mugs were distributed and Geoffrey Llewellyn took his place once more on the stone pulpit and began, while Tansy sat almost beneath his feet. She gazed up at his face, enthralled, waiting on his words. A deep silence fell on his attentive audience as they wondered what this man of action had to say.

'John Ruskin said 'Whatever our station in life may be, at this crisis, those of us who mean to fulfil our duty ought first to live on as little as we can; and secondly, to do all the wholesome work for it we can, and to spend all we can spare in doing all sure good we can.''

'Hear, hear!' came a voice from the back of the congregation.

'And sure good is first in feeding people, then in dressing people, then in lodging people, and lastly in rightly pleasing people, with arts, or sciences, or any other subject of thought.'

'What be arts and science?' another voice broke in.

Geoffrey abandoned John Ruskin's words for a moment to explain. 'By arts and science we mean music, poetry, painting and making things from wood and stone.' He broke off to point at Jimmy's cross, propped between stones on a makeshift altar. 'Here we have a fine example, carved by one of our own members.' He continued. 'Science is the study of medicine and all those things which improve health and life.' This explanation seemed to satisfy many. Geoffrey held up his hand to silence the babble of talk which had broken out among the craftsmen in the crowd.

'Many of us here tonight,' he went on, 'know what it is to live on as little as we can, for wholesome work is not easy to come by.'

'That's true, sure 'nuff!' exclaimed Bessie Brimmacombe then, realising her voice had carried to the top of the Pit and bounced back again, giggled and covered her mouth with her hands.

'John Ruskin,' Geoffrey continued, 'went on to offer solutions and again I quote, 'Lodging people, which you may think should have been put first, I put third, because we must feed and clothe people where we find them, and lodge them afterwards."

'Tell us something we don't know!' came with sarcasm from a tall, grey-haired man. But Geoffrey ignored him, his voice rising in volume, his body leaning forward towards the audience. 'And providing lodgment for them means a great deal of vigorous legislature, and cutting down of vested interests that stand in the way, and after that, or before that, so far as we can get it, through sanitary and remedial action in the houses that we have.'

Now, at last, all the heckling stopped and men and women were silent, straining forward intent so as not to miss a word.

'And then the building of more, strongly, beautifully, and walled in groups of limited extent, kept in proportion to their streams and walled round so that there may be no festering and wretched suburb anywhere,' his voice rose in the cadences of lyrical Welsh and roared and thundered round the Pit, 'but clean and busy streets within, and the open country without, with a belt of beautiful garden and orchard round the walls, so that from any part of the city fresh air and grass, and sight of far horizon, might be reachable in a few minutes' walk.'

He paused and many clapped their hands together in sheer delight at the picture he painted for them. Slowly, he looked at each section of the crowd to underline the fact that he spoke to each and every one of them.

'We, in Devon, have the belt of beautiful garden and orchard round our town, fresh air and grass and, yes, sight of the far horizon of Dartmoor. Let us strive, those of us who have it in our power, to mend roofs and floors, provide clean piped water and indoor sanitation until the inner lines of our town match the outer lines of God's provision.'

A spontaneous cheer rose from the mass of people, from those who understood John Ruskin's words and from those who didn't. All were enjoying the splendour of the occasion.

'Don't he speak proper!' Bessie Brimmacombe exclaimed to Eva. 'Never heard anyone wi' such a gift of the gab!' But before Eva could reply, she became conscious of a movement high above, a glimpse of a missile dropping towards them. Geoffrey fell to the ground, blood pouring from his head and it was Tansy's scream that brought a sudden end to all the babble around him.

'Geoffrey, you're hurt!' she exclaimed. Then she was on her knees beside him, examining the gash, pulling her petticoat from under her skirt to rip in her haste to staunch his wound. A shocked silence ensued and Martin stared in disbelief at Tansy as she took Geoffrey in her arms and cradled him against her breasts. Then all was hubbub. More stones and clods of earth rained down. Mothers seized children and ran for shelter under overhangs of rock and ivy. Martin looked up, searching the rim of the Pit for their assailants. Tom Moore pointed at flares and figures moving high above and, handing their own torches to the Chapel Elders, both men signalled those from the Court to follow.

Edward and Charles Vallance assisted Geoffrey to his feet, where he stood, pale and swaying. He murmured his thanks, a livid bruise beginning to swell on his forehead. Charles was the first to speak, exploding in anger, 'I was against this tom-foolery all along. You could have been killed, Llewellyn!'

Edward Drewe turned to Rosemary, who stood by the harmonium, wringing her hands in distress. 'See if you can find a suitable hymn, Rose. Something that will stop the panic. I'll not have the meeting ruined by a lot of drunken louts.'

Geoffrey returned to the platform and called to his flock. 'Come, let us continue with our service. The culprits will be caught. Miss Brimmacombe will find a hymn for us to sing as we return to the Clock Tower. The new pilgrimage I mentioned earlier is to be one of self-help to our own people. I ask you to pledge your help to those in the Courts of the town. We will not cease our efforts until all children are booted and schooled, all men have honest toil from which to support their loved ones, good clean water flows through pipes and main drains are supplied to every man, woman and child in this town. Only then will we turn our efforts to providing recreation for their leisure hours. The struggle will be hard and may be long but we will succeed.'

Charles Vallance leapt up beside him to add, 'I, on behalf of the Elders of the Chapel, thank you for your support. We shall not be deterred from worshipping here. The next night meeting will be announced in chapel on Sunday.'

It was then they saw a struggling mass of men and captives as Jess Hallet, for it was he who led the reprobates, was dragged into the Pit with his followers. Tansy recognised him at once from their confrontation at the market and from the fracas at the Ram Roast which had been so disastrous for Evan Williams. He, in turn, recognised Tansy.

"Tis the witch 'erself,' he snarled as Tom Moore forced him down to his knees at Geoffrey Llewellyn's feet. 'I didn't mean no 'arm,' he stuttered with beer-laden breath, the shock of being discovered having a sobering effect on him.

'Fetch the police, Llewellyn,' Charles Vallance commanded, but Geoffrey shook his head. He knew an appearance before the magistrates, probably to be let off with a caution, was all that could be expected for these troublemakers. He came down from the platform and walked along the row of men, looking long and hard at each in turn.

'Why did you do it? You do realise that from such a height you could have killed me? Let alone women and children.'

The men hung their heads and looked sheepish. Jack Steer, a regular attendant at chapel, tugged his cap and apologised. 'We was drinkin' at Aunt Gin's,' he said, 'and Jess said to come and watch. We didn' mean no harm. 'Twas Jess that threw the first stone... drunk too much cider, he had. 'Twouldn't happen ever agin Mr Llewellyn, Sir.'

Geoffrey nodded his head. 'Very well, but remember I shall know you again, each and every one of you. Don't let me catch you in further trouble or I will hand you over to the Law. Tonight we'll settle for instant justice. I'm going to hand you over to Tom Moore and Martin Webber. They caught you and they'll deal with you as they see fit.'

He resumed his place and took the hymn sheet Tansy held up to him. For our march back to the town we'll sing 'He who would valiant be, follow the master'.'

A few minutes later there came the noise of loud splashes and shouts of rage as the sound of heavy bodies hitting water came from the river. Eva smiled down at Robert and James, who clutched each other and danced a jig. Edward and the men from the Court took up their torches once more and slowly led the people up and out of the Pit. Voices rang through the woods and Gwynneth Evans told Eva next day they could hear the sound from the top of Bowden Hill. As the march passed Mackrell's Almshouses and advanced along Wolborough Street, people emerged from their homes to join the procession and the words of the hymn were repeated until a great throng stood singing around St Leonard's Tower.

'There's no discouragement shall make him once relent, His first avowed intent to be a pilgrim.'

Tom Moore shouted, 'Hurrah for the preacher. Hurrah for Geoffrey Llewellyn.' This was followed by a flurry as caps were flung high in the air, and Charles Vallance, who had been swept along by the excitement of the evening, recovered his dignity at last and turned to Geoffrey.

'Well done, Llewellyn,' he said. 'Anything that breaks the lethargy of the unemployed has my support,' and he shook Geoffrey heartily by the hand before disappearing into the crowd.

Now Martin caught hold of Tansy, excited as always by the look of her vivacious face, glowing now with the events of the evening. Perhaps, he thought, she would have knelt over him had he been the victim of the stone thrower. He pulled her to him.

'Be 'ee comin' out Staddens Sunday then, my beauty?' But the face that turned to him was distant, detached, dreamlike. 'I've arranged for 'ee to ride Fairy.' Martin pressed her hands to his, but although she turned to look at him, she seemed as if under a spell and when she spoke it was only of Geoffrey.

'It's been splendid, hasn't it?' she said. 'I've never felt more alive in my whole life. At last I know where I'm going.' Her face glowed below the halo of fast-growing hair. 'Isn't he just the finest person you've ever met?' she said and, without waiting for a reply, she hugged Martin abstractedly and hurried off after Geoffrey Llewellyn.

✤ Chapter Seventeen ✤

Eleanor Moore

At Moon Court, Alice Moore watched for Tom. 'Avril's time's come!' she greeted him. 'Your feyther's upstairs with the boys.' She laid a hand on Tom's arm.

"Tidd'n goin' well. He've had to send for Doctor Jones...' Tom pushed past his mother and crossed to the bed where the young doctor struggled to bring Avril's confinement to a conclusion. He looked up as Tom bent over to kiss his wife's perspiring face. Their eyes met, Tom's holding a question.

'Baby's upside down. We're progressing,' Alyn Jones told him. 'It'll not be long now.' He turned back to the bed where Mabel Prettijohn, the midwife, laid a cloth on Avril's forehead. Tom turned away, his face pinched and afraid.

'Go outside, man. I'll let you know the moment it's over.' The doctor returned to his task. 'Come now, one last push. Push on the pain, Mrs Moore.'

Tom walked out of the house to pace the cobbles back and forth, back and forth. Half an hour passed before the doctor emerged to declare, 'You've a fine girl, Mr Moore.' Tom seized his hand and shook it.

'And Avril?' he wanted to know. Alyn Jones hesitated.

'She's as well as can be expected after a difficult birth. Might be a good idea to end your family here. You can go in now. I'll be back tomorrow to see her.' And he took up his black bag and was gone.

Tom looked down at Avril, holding the tiny form, and tried to find words to express his relief and pleasure.

'Well done, my love,' he crooned. 'Our first daughter.'

The smile of pleasure left Avril's face. 'Doctor says there's to be no more, Tom. Says there's no guarantee next would be all right.'

Tom lifted her hands to his lips and kissed them. 'One girl's enough for me. Especially if she takes after her mother!' he declared, then hurried on, 'I'm going up to Vitifer Mine. There's work there and good pay for it. Work every week from Monday to Saturday and somewhere to sleep too. Chapel man has fixed it up for us.'

Avril's face brightened. Tom had seemed to lose hope after he'd lost his job at the clay works, but tonight he was a different man. 'This new preacher has promised to make things come good.' But now a look of doubt spread across her face. 'I believe this one,' he said. 'He's been here just a short time and already he's got a following. He's promised that all the children shall have boots and schooling. We'm to have water laid on indoors and water closets too!' he added.

Avril's face changed to the shut-in look she constantly wore. She leant back against the pillow. 'Us've heard it all afore and we'm still fetching every drop of water from the pump and using chamber pots at night, ain't we? Now go away and let me rest.'

Tom took the baby from her, placed it in his mother's arms and crept away to share his news with the men who had now returned from the Pit. Men who leant against house walls, full of the food and drink Geoffrey Llewellyn had dispensed with his sermon of hope.

Alyn Jones walked home with a heavy heart. He had noticed the distorted limbs and pale faces of the four Moore boys. Not long come to Newton, he had recognised the familiar signs of undernourished bodies, familiar from the Rhondda where the striking miners' fight for better wages had caused an increase in deprivation to their families. He thought he had left all that behind. He must talk to his partner Alan Weekes, see if pressure could be brought to bear on the Local Board. He climbed the steps to Powderham Terrace where he and Jenny had settled. She heard him come in and appeared almost at once in the Chinese wrap Alyn had bought her on their honeymoon earlier in the year. The wrap set off her vivid colouring as she took in the weariness of his thin face. She noticed the sombre expression in the grey eyes she loved so much. Quickly she opened the doors of the iron stove to let out a burst of heat. She pushed the kettle back onto the hob, where it began to simmer. Then she knelt and lovingly began to unlace her husband's boots. As she did so he touched her hair, felt the spring in its jet mass. She set his boots beside the stove and ran square practical hands across his forehead until he closed his eyes and lay back in the chair to fall asleep instantly. Not until she had brought him fresh tea and a plate of bread and cheese and had shaken him awake did either speak.

'A girl – first after four boys,' he said in answer to her questioning look. 'Both alive but, Jen, you should have seen the place. Overcrowded, no light or air. Not even adequate...' his voice fell away in despair. 'Four young boys sharing the only bedroom with their grandparents. I though we'd left all that behind in Wales...' Jenny reached for his hand and smiled, a smile which brought an inner warmth into the protruding blue of her eyes.

'Society isn't separated neatly into prosperity and poverty, Alyn. Towns will always be a mixture of both.' She hesitated. 'Why not let me help?'

He straightened and shook his head. 'No, no, you've done enough nursing. We agreed when we married that you would keep our home and care for our children.'

He rose and came to her, placed his hand on the swelling that held the new life to be. The new life conceived on an idyllic day when they'd walked the cliffs near Salcombe and made love in a high meadow. Idly they had watched a sparrowhawk hunting along the cliff and there and then had vowed to come back for one reason only. To live and work in the warmth and delight of South Devon.

Tansy enjoyed each day, was up bright and early, in a hurry to begin the next task set for her by Geoffrey. Every day she called at The Manse, because not to see Geoffrey every day had become unthinkable. She liked to arrive as he finished the simple meal which was his breakfast. Then she hovered around him, trying to find excuses to delay her departure. She dusted shelves of books and at his invitation began to read Rousseau, Karl Marx and Dickens, until he took Capital from her hands and substituted Elizabeth Gaskell's book on *The Life of Charlotte Bronte* and a volume of poetry by John Clare.

'Too much industry can be a bad thing,' he said, tipping her chin with his hands and looking deep into her eyes. 'Today I'm going to see Evan Williams and I would like you to call in at Moon Court and see Avril Moore. I'm told there's a parish layette – can you find out where it is? Then take it to her. You'll need to exercise tact. Avril Moore's proud but needy.'

It was Tansy's first visit to the Courts and as she walked through the low entrance passage into the dark cobbled terrace she gripped the flowers and herbs she had found in the overgrown garden of The Manse. A late waxy rosebud formed the centre of a ring of early forsythia, blue harebells and rosemary leaves which provided fragrance to combat the stench of urine and fetid air hanging around the Court. Tansy thrust the bouquet at Avril, who sat nursing the tiny newcomer.

'What are you going to call her?' Tansy wanted to know, concealing the real reason for her visit until confidence in each other had been established between them. Avril looked proud as she told her, 'Eleanor, we'm going to call her Eleanor,' and they both gazed at the tiny scrap.

'A big name for a little person!' Tansy laughed but Alice Moore clicked her teeth and muttered in the background, 'Unsuitable name for a baby born in the Courts. Should have called her Joan or some such. Fancy names breed fancy ideas.'

Avril turned on the old woman, a red flush rising on her neck. 'Hold your tongue, old woman. 'Tis time you went to the Workhouse and made way for Tom's children.'

Tansy looked up, horrified at the bitterness in Avril's voice. Intercepting her look, Avril went on, ''Tis all very well for those that doesn't live here,' she exploded, 'but she's going on at me all day and doesn't do a hand's turn. 'Tis hard, Miss, with Charlie and Ted still so small. Tom's father, he takes William and young George along by the river to catch minnows and I trust him. He wouldn't let nothing harm neither hair nor hide of 'em, but she,' and she turned to Alice who rocked unceasingly by the fire, 'she gives me nothing but tongue all day long.'

Tansy felt it time to hand over the parish box. Avril's face filled with suspicion until she opened the box, then it changed to one of pleasure as she lifted out the little cotton caps and bootees, sets of flannel nightdresses and napkins. She looked up at Tansy.

'How long am I to keep them?' she asked and Tansy, to whom the errand was a new experience, shrugged then rushed on, 'Until she'm growed too big,' and then set about helping to dress Eleanor Moore from the skin out, while Eleanor's grandmother sat, silenced for once by the novel experience.

❖ Chapter Eighteen ❖

The Proposal

The Sunday after the service at Puritan Pit, Tansy and Martin resumed their meetings at the Big Oak but their walks back to Courtenay House were spoilt for Martin as she talked of nothing but her work with Geoffrey. When he bent to kiss her, her response was more that of a loving sister than lover. Martin gritted his teeth and sought a way to win her back and on the Sunday before Christmas he called at the Post Office with an invitation for dinner at Staddens. Tansy demurred at first, not wanting to miss seeing Geoffrey at chapel, but when he added that the invitation had come from Sarah, of whom she had become inordinately fond, she began to waver.

'Surely you've earned a day off from chapel and chapel affairs,' he pressed, then added with a sneer, 'Or are you afraid of what Geoffrey Llewellyn will say?' She rose to the challenge, her independent streak not allowing him to think she was any but her own creature.

'Very well,' she agreed. 'I'll come on one condition,' and when Martin sighed and shrugged she pressed home her advantage, 'that I take the reins.'

So it was that a triumphant Tansy directed Tom down through town with its frosted roofs to trot along lanes lit by berried holly trees. Along the valley sheep wintered in orchards and mistletoe hung from apple boughs. One side lay in shade and wore a mantel of frost while the fields opposite rose, exposed to bright winter sun which drew out the cold in wraiths of mist.

When they arrived at Staddens and Tansy saw Fairy tethered to the farm gate, she exploded with delight. 'Martin! Have you brought her for me to ride?' When he smiled and nodded she leapt down from the trap in an instant. ''Tis a man's saddle!' Then she looked up at him, a question in her eyes. 'How am I to manage?' Again he smiled and led her across to the linhay.

''Tis all arranged. Adam has lent you a pair of his corduroys. You can change here,' he indicated a corner behind a hay wagon. 'Give me your skirt and I'll leave it indoors.'

By the time Martin returned she had mounted the pony and was impatient to start.

'That's better! Now I'm really in charge, ain't I Fairy?' She bent forward to stroke the mare who, sensing her excitement, danced on the straw-strewn yard and pricked her ears in a hurry to be off. 'Hurry up, Martin,' she shouted as he took the harness from Tom and let him loose to crop among the sheep in the orchard. Quickly he caught the cob and soon he and Tansy were climbing through Lustleigh to Rudge.

'They suit you, Tansy,' he commented as soon as the path allowed them to ride side by side. 'Lucky for you Adam is smaller than me,' and he ran his eyes over her boyish figure, neat in brown trousers which went well with the green jacket of her mother's old suit. The velvet hat with its barred partridge feather set off her creamy complexion. 'Though Mother was shocked – "Don't go through the village" she said.' He laughed at the puzzled expression on Tansy's face. 'You hadn't thought of what other people'd say, had 'ee?'

They set off down through the Cleave among amber bracken and skeletal birch until they arrived at Hisley Bridge, then crossed the Bovey and arrived at last on Black Hill. The breath of both riders and horses steamed in the cold air and Martin rose in his stirrups to point to a red streak disappearing away from them towards Haytor.

'Fox, see 'un?' - his voice laconic. Tansy, who had never seen a fox before, felt a thrill of excitement course through her veins. 'Done his huntin' and is off home, I do reckon,' Martin added, then rode on and, as they rode, the harnesses jingled beneath their hands. Suddenly a lark rose beneath their horses' hooves. It rose in vertical flight, its wings beating in time with its song until it became a black speck in the heavens. Tansy let go of the reins and clapped her hands in delight.

'Tell me, Martin,' she cried, pointing across rolling moorland down pastures to a silver slash beyond Newton. 'What's that?'

He laughed at her naivety. ''Tis the Teign on its way to the sea. See the break in the coastline?' When she nodded he said, 'That's Teignmouth.'

'That's where we go for our Chapel Outing in July,' she exclaimed, turning to him. ''Tis the best day of the year. We run barefoot on the sand and dig in the sea. This year,' she added proudly, 'I'm going to learn to swim.'

A pair of buzzards circled away to their right, rising slowly on a thermal. Martin hauled in the cob and waited for Tansy to join him. He turned to her, his face a picture of calm content.

'Do 'ee understand now why I wants to live up here? Here where the air is clear, the land open – not closed in as it is in the valley?' When she nodded he went on, enthusiasm exuding from every word. ''Tis not to spite Father. I can't help myself. 'Tis all I've ever wanted. A ram, a ewe and a sheep run to begin. A simple stone house and a woman to share it with me.'

He leant forward and seized Tansy's hands in his. 'There's a farm going for rent over to Chagford. I've saved enough for a year. Enough saved for to start a flock. Enough to start a new life.' He gripped her hands even tighter and asked, 'What do you say?'

Tansy, who had been but half listening, was startled by his sudden question. She sat, comparing his brown wavy hair with Geoffrey's amber locks.

'You do like the Moor?' he pressed and she, feeling the tension grow as he waited for her response, left her hands in his while Fairy shifted feet beneath her.

''Tis wonderful up here,' she placated him. 'I could ride all day and never tire of it!' And, taking this for encouragement, Martin took a quick breath and plunged on.

'Then marry me, Tansy. Marry me in the spring when we've all summer ahead of us.' His blue eyes deepened with passion and he held her hands so tight that she felt the blood leave her fingers in the pain of his grip. She pulled away.

'Martin, you're hurting me.' Suddenly he let go. She turned Fairy away to avoid his gaze while she tried to summon the right words. Words to refuse him yet not hurt his feelings. She gathered up both reins and courage and turned Fairy about.

'I've told 'ee afore, I'm not ready to wed. The life you want is tempting but I'm not sure it's for me.' And as Martin's face fell into one of disappointment she hurried on. 'Now I've met Geoffrey Llewellyn, he's shown me there are other goals in life besides marriage. Besides,' she added, 'he needs me to help him in his work.' Her voice rose on an ascending spiral of enthusiasm. 'He's going to improve the life of the poor in Newton...'

Now Martin broke in, his voice bitter, his eyes angry, 'Don't tell me again. I've heard his sermons too, remember. We'll wait and see if'n he's all bluff and bluster. See if'n he kin turn words into deeds!' And he kicked the cob into a gallop across fast-melting frost towards Haytor. Tansy did her best to keep up, enjoying the rolling motion of her steed as they followed the cob along the sheep track and down into a steep gully. Martin stopped at the edge of a quarry where granite slabs lay at crazy angles, sharp ends pointing sky-wards among hoists and blocks where iron rings were embedded. Willows grew at the edge of rain-filled workings, now iced over and sparkling in winter sun.

''Tis a magical place, Martin, for sure!' she exclaimed as they dismounted and tied their horses to a derelict hoist.

'Been worked out a long time has this,' Martin explained, 'but they'm still cutting stone from t'other side. Going for to build London Bridge they do say.' He opened a leather pouch and produced food Sarah had given them. They ate and Tansy let her mind wander to the months ahead when the quarry would be clothed in green, the water melted and warmed by the sun, protected from wind by the towering sides.

'No one would know us was here!' she exclaimed and Martin nodded, his good humour restored by their shared adventure.

''Tis a good place for swimming in summer. Then Adam and me come here skinny-dipping.' But once more Tansy's mind had wandered far from him and she couldn't resist blurting out, 'Geoffrey would love it here.' She turned to Martin. 'Could we bring him here one day?' She went on, not waiting for Martin's reply. 'Although I expect he'd want to change it into a meeting-place and bring the Moor men here for a service on Midsummer's Night.'

Martin turned away, his face darkening with jealousy. He stooped to pick up loose stones and hurl them angrily across the ice. Tansy, never to be outdone, tried to emulate him but couldn't get the knack of it. She cast about for two more stones and, finding none, darted onto the ice to retrieve her spent supply. As her figure flashed past him Martin gasped and tried to catch her.

'Come back, you little fool – tidd'n safe!' But even as he spoke there came an ominous cracking and a gap opened up between them. He started forward but the ice sank beneath his feet. He leapt back onto the bank. 'Hold on,' he shouted. 'I'll get you out.' Tansy grabbed at a wooden plank as her body sank beneath the ice. She felt her legs dragged down into weed, felt a deep chill grip her body as she struggled to retain her grip on the wooden bolt. She could hardly breathe and Martin's voice seemed to come to her from a long way off. He fought to tie leather with hands that shook. He must get Tansy out immediately or she'd drown in the deep water. He ran back, poised on the edge.

'Tansy, do you hear me?' And when her voice came back faint from cold and exhaustion he instructed her, 'Catch the line – now!' Taking careful aim he threw the reins across the ice, buckles flashing in the sun, to descend above her head. She let go of the wood and grabbed the reins as they fell past her into the water. Martin felt her weight take hold and hauled steadily until she broke free of weed and ice and came towards him through the water to collapse at his feet. The terror of the last moments broke from him in an explosion of anger.

'You little fool!' he shouted. 'Never venture on ice when sun's high. Get up!' He put his arms under her shoulders and lifted her to her feet, then began to drag her back and forth while she gasped for breath.

'Let me be,' she pleaded, but Martin continued to walk her to and fro until her teeth stopped chattering and the blood began to run again through chilled veins, setting her body burning. She tried to pull away from him to end the agony.

'Stop it, Martin! Just let me lie here.' She collapsed once more onto the rocks.

He ran to the horses and released the cob from the hoist, harnessing them roughly as best he could. Then he came back and began to drag her, this time back up the gully.

'We'd best get 'ee home afore 'ee gets pneumony,' he said, adding grimly, 'Now 'ee's gonna walk, my beauty.' When she moaned in protest he repeated, 'You'll catch your death else.' She staggered as they set off and would have fallen had he not grasped her round the waist. Holding the reins in one hand and Tansy with the other, Martin led them off the Moor while she cursed him as she stumbled along over heather and rock, back the way they'd come.

'Just let me be,' she moaned. 'Let me die!' But Martin continued on down Black Hill and never stopped once till they reached the bridge. The sun stayed hot above them and as its warmth reached them a cloud of steam enveloped Tansy as she half ran, half staggered beside him. She collapsed against the wall of the bridge.

'I can't go no further, Martin,' she moaned, and now he took pity on this girl whose sheer guts had got her this far. He turned to her.

'You've done well. Now let's see if you can remember all I've taught you about riding.' He lifted her up and set her on Fairy's back. 'Hold on tight and don't let go.' Tansy was surprised to find the chill had left her bones and that her body was aglow.

'Follow me,' he commanded and began to climb the cob up and out of the valley. He stopped from time to time to make sure she was close behind. She clung to Fairy's mane and when they reached Heaven's Gate, laughed with sheer enjoyment. Martin, amazed at her recovery, praised her and trotted along beside her to Staddens.

'Well done, my beauty. Most girls would a been prapper mazed by now.'

᳙᳙᷾

Dusk fell as they rode the track into Staddens where Amos held a lantern high to see who was coming. 'Come on bye, you'm late. Us be wondring where you'd got to.'

Martin explained that they had had a slight accident and Tansy, now swaying in the saddle with exhaustion, was grateful for him covering up her foolishness. Amos set down the lantern to lift her from the pony's back then, as her legs gave way beneath her, he carried her into the warmth of the kitchen. Sarah Webber took one look at her bedraggled clothes and white face and spoke.

'You look as if'n you've been near drownded in a dew pond!' she exclaimed. 'Let's get 'ee out of they wet clothes, my dear.' She led the way upstairs to a small room under the eaves where two beds stood, one against each wall. When Tansy stepped out of the muddy trousers and green jacket and began to tell what had happened, Sarah placed a finger to her mouth.

'Let's get 'ee warm first, my maid. I'll fetch hot bricks and some broth, kindle a fire. You can tell me what happened when you've recovered.'

Tansy sank back into the crisp clean sheets and as her eyes closed suddenly remembered the Post Office and her waiting family. She started up.

'Mrs Webber. Please – can you get word to Mother and Father. They'll be wondering where I am.'

Sarah nodded her head and promised, 'Adam'll go. He's to fetch Fanny from visiting Janet Luscombe at Courtenay House so 'tis no hardship.'

At last Tansy, dressed in one of Sarah's voluminous flannel nightgowns, sank into troubled dreams. She woke to toss and turn in the strange bed. She thought back to Martin's proposal. Remembered how he'd saved her yet again. She fell asleep and dreamt she rode beside a man rounding sheep towards a pond which at the last moment turned into a quarry. She screamed as the sheep fell over the top and turned to find it was Geoffrey riding beside her, not Martin. She woke once more, half conscious of someone bending over her, but it was not till dawn lightened the room that she realised she was sharing a room with Fanny Luscombe. A Fanny who sat on the bed opposite regarding her with a look of utter hatred.

'Seems there's no end to the trouble you do bring, Tansy Drewe. Leading my Martin a dance from what I do hear. Well, 'tis his lookout if'n he wants a thief for a wife. If Mrs Webber knew you stole Emma Vallance's watch I doubt you'd be sleeping here so snug.'

Tansy retaliated. 'At least I've made no secret of the Vallance's accusations. One day I'll find out who the culprit really is and then we'll see. At least,' she added, 'I'm not a liar!'

'And what do you mean by that I'd like to know,' Fanny demanded, yet turning bright red at the same time.

'Making out Martin wants to marry 'ee when only yesterday he asked me to be his wife.' But before Fanny could recover from this riposte the door opened and Sarah came in with Tansy's green jacket and skirt.

'Up you get Fanny, the cows is waiting,' she said and Fanny slipped on her rough grey work dress, tied back her blonde hair, slipped feet into pattens and reluctantly left the room.

Tansy started up, intent on following suit, only to find a delaying hand placed on her chest.

'There's no hurry yet, my maid.' Sarah gazed down at her, a serious expression on her face. 'There's no cause to fret. Adam called at the Post Office last night. Your Mother sent a message asking you to call at Lustleigh and collect a parcel from Mrs Retallick. 'Tis wanted in town urgent like.' Then she sat on the edge of the bed and smoothed her apron with brown wrinkled hands.

'Spending a lot of time with the new preacher, Martin tells me?' she enquired and Tansy blushed and began to stammer an explanation. Sarah ignored her broken phrases and went on, 'Become quite the church worker I do hear!'

Tansy burst out, ''Tis wonderful work, Mrs Webber. Geoffrey's so keen to change things, make life better for the poor people of Newton...' she tailed off.

'Don't forget Martin will 'ee?' she pleaded. 'He's a hard worker too and he'll still be here when Geoffrey Llewellyn has moved on to another parish.'

At her words Tansy's heart turned cold. Move on. Geoffrey. Why he'd only just arrived in Newton. She remembered her father's words when he had introduced Geoffrey at chapel. 'Please welcome your new minister who will be with us for the next two years.' Then she brightened, there was still time to make him fall in love with her. Now she turned to Sarah.

'I will never forget Martin. How could I when he saved me from drowning in the quarry? He's a good friend to me. Why, he's taught me how to ride and shared such days with me. Days' I'll never forget. I had a wonderful day yesterday, even,' she added with a rueful smile, 'if I nearly drowned.'

She and Sarah laughed with relief. Sarah that she had had the chance to cast doubts on Tansy's infatuation with Geoffrey and Tansy at the thought that in two years a lot could happen. When Geoffrey left them, why, he would take her with him. Wouldn't he?

These thoughts filled her mind and kept her silent on their return to Newton and Martin put her silence down to fatigue and didn't press her to tell what she was thinking as he usually did. When he lifted her down from the trap at the bottom of Bowden Hill her kiss settled on his cheek like the brush of a summer moth and she didn't hear him when he called, 'See you next Sunday.'

✤ Chapter Nineteen ✤

Christmas Eve

It was Christmas Eve and Edward and Eva Drewe worked hard to empty the Post Office of cards and letters from far-off members of the town's families. There were precious missives from the Devon Regiment bringing belated accounts of Black Week, when tens of thousands of British soldiers died on the African veldt. Ladysmith and Mafeking were still cut off from the British Army and, among the piles of mail, came one from Hetty Westcott's Jack.

'The wounded keep coming down each day. 'Tis horrible to see them. It makes you feel as if you'd like to shoot all the Boers you could,' he wrote. He went on, 'If 'twas left to me I'd sweep them off the face of the earth.' Hetty turned the page. 'They go about marauding helpless women. We have to sleep with our rifles and ammunition beside us for instant use. 'Tis quite a novelty to have 100 rounds for a pillow!'

In spite of the grim words Hetty's face glowed with relief at hearing from him. She held the thin sheet of paper in her hands as if it was a piece of fragile china, the only contact with the man she loved.

Geoffrey organised a carol-singing party which Norah and Helen, home from college, wanted to be part of. They refused to stay at home with Robert and James and at the last minute Eva relented. She tied woollen scarves across their chests against the night air and the family set off to join other members of chapel to sing at all the big houses on the Hill.

So it was that Tansy found herself standing next to Geoffrey in the hall at Courtenay House, where the singers had been invited in by Caroline Vallance to entertain her house party. Tansy felt strange. It seemed a lifetime since, day after day, she had crossed and re-crossed the tile-patterned hall, dressed in grey uniform and white cap and apron. Now the hall was hung with berried holly and twines of ivy. A huge tree bearing coloured glass balls and gaily wrapped gifts took up the corner between stairs and sitting-room where the door stood ajar in order that the company could hear the singing.

In the weeks running up to the festival and by dint of working hard Geoffrey had arranged transport to Vitifer Mine for Tom Moore and as many men from the Courts as wanted to go. There they worked from Monday to Saturday, sleeping in specially erected dormitories. On Saturdays they returned home to a joyous reunion with their families – except for the one or two wives who felt themselves to be well shot of troublesome husbands!

Tonight's carol singing was to raise money for their children. The aim was to fill socks with an orange, a handful of nuts and a chocolate penny. Tin soldiers for the boys and clothes-peg dolls for the girls lay in piles, waiting to be distributed. All had been acquired 'on tick' by Eva and Tansy, who was nothing if not persuasive, using her charm to touch all but the hardest heart.

She hadn't wanted to sing at Courtenay House, the choir's last call, but Geoffrey had whispered, 'Come on, my soldier. You've nothing to be ashamed of. We all know you're innocent. Fly the flag!' Now his warm hand touched hers as they shared a hymn sheet and joined in 'God rest ye merry gentlemen' until the sound filled the hall and stairs where the servants had been allowed to stand. Hetty, Cook and Blodwen had waved and smiled at Tansy but Janet Luscombe glowered at her from the top stair.

Suddenly a small, slight figure rushed from the sitting-room, hesitated a moment, then hurled itself at Tansy.

'Master Harry!' She looked down at the suited figure. 'I do declare you have grown!' Harry smiled and hugged her in his pleasure at seeing her again. Caroline came after him, followed by Charles, who gazed, appalled as Harry began to pull Tansy clear of the choir until they stood in the centre of the hall.

'That's enough, Harry!' Charles Vallance spoke sharply and the choir faltered to a stop. 'Return to your guests this minute!' he ordered. But Harry, defying his father, stood his ground, raising pleading eyes.

'Please, Father, mayn't she stay? And Mr Llewellyn? She's always been at my parties before. It won't be the same without her.'

Charles exchanged looks with Caroline. He hesitated, embarrassed in front of such a large company, and that moment's hesitation proved his undoing. Fans were lowered and lorgnettes raised as Harry dragged Tansy into the centre of the room. Emma Vallance immediately rose from a stool at her Aunt Hortense's feet and ran to greet Tansy.

'Have you come back?' she wanted to know. Tansy blushed and shook her head. An outraged rustling stirred among the older members of the party.

'I was taught to speak when spoken to!' clucked Aunt Hortense, and her neighbour nodded vigorously. 'And servants knew their place!'

But Harry was not to be deterred and he announced to the room at large, 'This is my friend, Tansy Drewe, who's the best person in the world at games.' Then he took Geoffrey's hand and led him forward to join Tansy. 'And this is my friend, Geoffrey Llewellyn, who comes to play Mafeking with me every Tuesday.'

Charles and Caroline stood dumbstruck in the background at this unexpected turn of events.

'Dismissed for theft and now here being treated like Royalty!' Aunt Hortense bristled with shock and a steady murmur rose from the astonished company. Harry Vallance ignored them all and remained firmly in charge.

'Come on, Drewe, let's play spinning the trencher.' Tansy slipped back into the role she had played when she'd worked at Courtenay House. Quickly she circled the room and gave each of the young people a number. The outer ring of settees held the older generation who watched, hardly able to believe what was occurring before their eyes. The inner circle of young relatives and friends became animated and, at her invitation, rose from footstools and chairs to form a ring. The bright taffeta dresses of the girls alternated with the Norfolk jackets and breeches of their cousins, making an ever-changing pattern as Tansy called out 'seven' and spun the wooden platter lent by Cook. Tamsin and Montague White bumped into each other, then staggered back into the clutch of uncles gathered by the buffet for mutual support.

'She said Eleven,' Tamsin protested.

'No, she didn't, it was Seven,' rejoined her brother. And with witnesses taking sides, the game would have come to an end there and then if Geoffrey Llewellyn hadn't intervened.

'Seven. It was Seven,' declared Uncle Bertram. 'Spin the trencher, Montague.' Everyone settled down and the game proceeded. There was a whirling and rushing about the room as boys and girls ran to catch the spinning platter before it fell to the floor when a chorus of 'Out' rang through the room. After ten minutes Geoffrey called an end to the game and Hetty and Janet circled the room with sweetmeats and sherbet for the young ones, Madeira and mince pies for the adults and mulled ale for the choir.

Tansy and Geoffrey stood by until Caroline whispered to Hetty who approached them with refreshments. Tansy declined, still unsure, and Geoffrey, with a fine understanding of her feelings, also shook his head in refusal. They turned, about to rejoin the choir who stood about the hall, not knowing what to do without their leader. Harry came to her once more, pleading, 'Blind Mans Buff, Drewe. Just once!'

Tansy looked for direction from Caroline Vallance who, pleased that the party had taken on life, which had been absent until the arrival of the chapel choir, nodded her approval.

'Very well, Master Harry,' Tansy gave in, 'but you must be the first to be blindfold.' She removed her own scarf and tied it firmly round his head, holding up three fingers in front of his eyes. 'How many fingers am I holding up?' Satisfied he couldn't see, she spun him around then gave him a gentle push into the centre of the room. The young people ran about the room eluding his grasp until Mary Westaway moved towards the fire, overbalanced and caught her hand on the overmantel in an effort to steady herself.

'Mary, watch what you're doing...' Maude Westaway called, but her warning came too late. Droplets tinkled as the ruby lustre vase crashed to the floor. Janet Luscombe tried to cover the distance between the buffet and the spot where the vase fell, but failed. The game came to an abrupt end. Geoffrey bent to extricate a round object from among the shards of glass. He held it high above his head for all to see.

'Does this belong to anyone here?' he asked, looking slowly around the room.

'It's my watch!' Emma exclaimed. 'My birthday watch! How on earth did it get there?' She held out her hand to take the golden orb, suspended from Geoffrey's hand by its ruby-studded brooch. But he was looking at Janet Luscombe as she stood ashen-faced beside him. 'You knew it was there, inside the vase, didn't you?' he demanded of her, and now Charles Vallance advanced towards them.

'Is this true?' he asked of the terrified girl, who burst into tears and, turning, fled from the room.

Hetty appeared with a dustpan and brush and began to sweep up slivers of red lustre as a murmur of astonishment filled the room. Geoffrey now held up a hand for silence. He turned to Charles and Caroline Vallance who stood together, a picture of embarrassment.

'It seems that it was Janet Luscombe who stole Miss Emma's watch and not Tansy Drewe.' He spoke the words slowly and with emphasis so that none should misunderstand what had just taken place. 'I think there can be no better moment than now for your apology to Miss Drewe.' His voice made the words into a statement, not a question, while Tansy, cleared at last from the cloud of suspicion that had hung over her, smiled and smiled.

Then in a sudden feeling of release she ran from the room to tell Eva and Edward the good news, only to find the choir dispersed and gone. She ran back and stood at Geoffrey's side, eager to hear what Charles Vallance would say. Her late employer seemed to be having difficulty finding the right words. His face flushed an embarrassed red, his hand polishing his watch case in extreme agitation. Geoffrey repeated his request for an apology and at last Charles spoke.

'Please accept our apologies, Drewe – I mean, Miss Drewe – for drawing the only conclusion that seemed to be the possible one at the time.' He looked around at the interested assembly. 'Circumstantial evidence was strong against Miss Drewe but I realise now that our – Mrs Vallance and I – our decision was the wrong one.'

But still Geoffrey wasn't satisfied and spoke up for Tansy again. 'That's all very well as far as those present are concerned, but, in the light of her dismissal from her position here and all that she has suffered because of it, Miss Drewe is entitled to a public apology.

Newton is a small town where gossip travels fast and, should her innocence not reach all ears, this cloud could remain over her future for all time.' He paused to let his words sink in. 'A written apology to be published in the *East & South Devon Journal* only will be judged sufficient. And as soon as humanly possible. The first issue in the New Year would be the ideal opportunity.'

Then he turned and offered his arm to Tansy. The servants gathered to offer their congratulations to Tansy as she swept through the hall and out onto the drive. Geoffrey smiled with satisfaction as he strode downhill while Tansy danced along in front of him singing at the top of her voice.

'I'm free, I'm free, no longer do they think it's me! 'Twas Janet Luscombe as did for me!' When they reached the Post Office, where lights still blazed from every window, Tansy turned to him and said, ''Twas the best Christmas present you could have given me, Geoffrey!'

She reached up on tiptoe to pull down his face to hers for the kiss that had been waiting from the day she first saw him. Taken off guard Geoffrey responded – his lips opened to hers. Then he clasped her about the waist and whirled her off her feet in celebration.

'I knew it was only a matter of time before the truth came out,' he said, then promised, 'Your real present comes tomorrow.'

As she rang the bell and indicated that he should come in, he shook his head. 'Tomorrow I am invited to Christmas dinner by your Mother. Now I'll leave you to tell her the good news.' He walked swiftly away downhill, across town to The Manse and the supper Aurelia Brown was keeping hot for him.

⚜ Chapter Twenty ⚜

Christmas Day

Tansy and Geoffrey watched eyes grow big with excitement in pale faces as they delivered stockings after chapel. Tom Moore insisted they share a glass of mulled cider and Avril offered Tetti Cakes she'd baked with currants and sugar bought with Tom's wages. They lay in a pile, golden brown, straight from the oven. She smiled shyly at their visitors.

'We've chicken for dinner and pudden. Cooking in the baker's oven this very minute,' she went on, then turned to Geoffrey. 'And 'tis all due to you!'

Tom Moore looked down from his great height and added, ''Tis the best Christmas we've ever had.' He shook them both warmly by the hand. As they left the family to their celebrations, Geoffrey invited Tansy to climb Knowles Hill to the Manse.

'Aurelia is cooking lunch. It wouldn't be Christian to leave her to eat it alone would it? I'm sure Eva can spare you for a couple of hours.'

Tansy's face grew bright at the thought of having him almost to herself. But when they stepped inside the dark hall there was the smell of baking, but no Aurelia. A note lay beside the cold cut of ham and dish of potatoes. It read, 'My good friend Maudie Pengilly was recently widowed. I'm sure you won't mind my joining her. Otherwise she will be all alone.'

They laughed at this turnabout and, hungry from their morning's work, they tucked into the food while Geoffrey asked, 'What will you do now?' When she looked up, puzzled, he prompted, 'Now that your name has been cleared.'

'What do you mean?' she wanted to know.

'You must realise you're free from the stigma of being dismissed. So what are you going to do now?'

Her face changed from one of surprise to one of pleasure. 'I'll always remember they Vallances, standing there apologising. Apologising to me, a servant, for the first time in their whole lives.' She laughed and began to pile up their dirty plates.

Geoffrey took down a parcel from a shelf and handed it to her. 'You may as well have your present since you're here.' Her fingers shook with excitement as she opened the strong brown paper. She cried out with pleasure as a bottle of perfume emerged, then smiled at him over the fly leaf of Jane Austen's *Pride and Prejudice*.

'Thank you, Geoffrey. What wonderful presents! A book I've always wanted and Bradley Woods bouquet.' She hesitated. 'It'll remind me of our first walk together,' she said as she withdrew the glass stopper and sprinkled drops of scent onto her hanky. She breathed in the smell of celandines and violets and he smiled at her delight and pressed her once more.

'Stop avoiding my questions, Tansy. Now you're free to find work, what are you going to do? You can typewrite, compose letters in good clear English and talk to people on an even footing. I'm asking what use you're going to make of these newly-found skills?' When she said nothing his look became quizzical. 'Only you can decide what you want of life. Do you want to become a first-class secretary to an able mind? Or help the Church? Carry out social work? Improve the life of the poor?' When still she stayed silent an edge of sarcasm entered his voice. 'Go back to service with the Vallances?'

At last the needs of her innermost being erupted into expression. 'Why would I want to go away?' She leant across the table towards him. 'Why would I want to find work when I've work here,' she hesitated, 'with you?' She got up and ran round the table to him. 'I love you, Geoffrey,' she said, then blushed deeply while he pushed back his seat.

'I love you too Tansy,' he replied, getting up. 'I love you as we should love all God's creatures, but,' he added hastily, 'our aim in life shouldn't be to make of love a thing in itself.'

She was puzzled then hurt that he should compare her love for him with that of the animals. Still she pleaded, 'I want to be with you, always. To work with you here in Newton. Please...' She threw her arms around him.

The heady effect of the scent affected them both and her body against his set him alight with desire. His arms stole around her and they sank down together on the Chesterfield. Her closeness carried him back to another moment. The mouth beneath his was transformed from Tansy's youthful bow to the generous curves of a mature woman. Her slim body pressing against his became the fullness of another man's wife. Her eyes had been of the deepest blue, her hair fallen in waves of jet. Geoffrey opened his eyes to meet not blue but green, saw hair of auburn not black, and was shocked to feel Tansy's boyish breasts beneath his hands. His face, hot with passion a moment before, now cooled to an ashen white as he pushed her away and strode to the window.

'I think you had better leave.' He paused. 'At once.' His voice was thick with emotion aroused by Tansy's touch, memories of a past love surfacing even now. Tansy stood, shocked into stillness by his sudden withdrawal from their close embrace. 'You must forgive me,' he went on, 'this is the result of our spending too much time together. You're young, you've so much to learn. I had no right...'

Tansy's hands flew out towards him as if he had struck her. 'But Geoffrey, I love you. I want you to touch me. There's no one here to see...' Then followed words which surprised even her. 'I want you,' she said, hardly knowing what she meant.

But Geoffrey won his fight with temptation and walked away from her to turn as he reached the door.

'If you won't go then I must,' he said, adding, 'I've some books for Evan Williams.' As she started across the room to stop him leaving he put out a hand in protest.

'No, no, don't follow me... I've obviously allowed you to become too involved in my work. Perhaps it will be best if you find something more...' he paused, searching for the right word, 'suitable.' And before she could voice the protests which rose in her throat he was gone.

When she heard the heavy outer door of The Manse shut behind him she ran to the window and watched his tall, lean figure stride away downhill, the parcel of books under his arm, his red hair glinting in a flash of winter sun. Slowly she turned from the window, cleared away their dinner plates and washed them in the kitchen sink. Surely, she thought, he wouldn't have kissed her if he didn't love her? She hugged her body, pretended his arms still encircled her. She went back to the study, missing his presence, and wandered about the house. She picked up the silver-framed photograph of Geoffrey's hero, John Ruskin. He had a humorous face, Tansy thought as she studied his features. The wide-set eyes, blue surely. The thick hair parted in heavy waves. The sideburns framing a generous mouth, its lower lip sticking out in a gesture of determination. *The Stones of Venice* lay beside the framed portrait, a marker at Geoffrey's favourite quotation.

She read the words aloud. 'You must make either a tool of the creature or a man of him. You can't make both. Men were not intended to work with the accuracy of tools, to be precise and perfect in all their actions. If you will have that precision out of them and make their fingers measure degrees like cog wheels and their arms strike curves like compasses, you must unhumanise them!'

Tansy re-read the words, tried to understand, and looked back at the man in the frame. He wore a white bow-tie over the starched shirt front and a heavy overcoat. She wondered, where he had been going. This man who thought medieval life with its craftsmen working in communities preferable to the factory sweatshops of the industrialised nineteenth century. Perhaps he had been going to a men's dinner for women were still not, even today, allowed to play a real part in society, were they? She laid down the photograph and passed through the doorway into the dark hall. Perhaps this was the message Geoffrey was trying to give her. Was he encouraging her to take up a way of life, even now new to women? The unaccustomed silence hung heavy. It was the first time since she had come to work for Geoffrey that Aurelia Brown hadn't emerged from the kitchen to stare at her, demanding to know what it was she wanted. Tansy looked up at the curving stairs, wondering which room was his, knowing she should leave. The need to stay near him carried her slowly up the stairs and onto the landing. She could hear her mother's shocked remarks – 'Tansy whatever do you think you're doing?' – but, ignoring her upbringing, she crossed the wooden floor to hesitate outside the first door. Some instinct told her that this room was his. She opened the door and peered in. A huge bed took up half the room. It was covered by a white cotton bedspread. Over the bed hung the picture of a man with long thick hair, his head crowned with briars, a lantern in his hand. She stood and looked down. Imagining Geoffrey's head cushioned there. On the table beside the bed lay a bible, a large leather-bound copy, the words engraved in gold leaf. He had a small bible which went everywhere with him, carried in his inside pocket, next his heart. Tansy felt that if she was to win him she would have to use the holy book to reach him.

She looked around the room, her eyes resting on the dressing-table. She picked up the brushes, one by one. She brushed her hair with his brush. She looked into his mirror, longing for his image to appear there beside hers. Did he have as much difficulty controlling his mass of auburn as she did herself? A large mahogany wardrobe stood against the wall opposite, its red veneer needed a good polishing. Suddenly she felt like an intruder and yet still she opened the doors and looked inside.

She ran her hands along the row of dark chapel suits and the brown corduroys he'd worn the day they first walked in Bradley Woods. She laid her cheek against the Norfolk jacket, set his tweed cap on her unruly curls, breathing in the smell of his body.

Then the magic faded and she wanted him, not his possessions, not his clothes, not his smell, but his presence. She wanted his arms around her, his mouth on hers. She ran downstairs, her eyes scalded with tears, to let herself out into the garden. She picked creamy Christmas roses from the dark border of shrubs, breaking off branches of scented Witch Hazel and placing them in a jug beside his bed. She paused suddenly and fancied she heard movements in the room above. Running out onto the landing, she called, 'Miss Brown? Are you there?' But her call met only silence, a silence which enclosed the house. She left and ran away downhill without looking back.

Aurelia Brown had watched her from the study window, coatless and hatless, a grim smile hovering about her mouth as Tansy had watched Geoffrey leave.

❧

When Geoffrey left Tansy he didn't go straight to Bowden Hill but walked in the opposite direction, hardly noticing where he was going until suddenly he found himself at Town

Quay. There he followed the river path, the long liquid call of a curlew mirroring the tumult in his heart. He seemed fated to fall in love with unsuitable women, creatures of great attraction he thought, but of forbidden identity.

His thoughts travelled back two years to Anna Cartwright, the mine owner's wife at Merthyr, younger than her husband by ten years. She had shared Geoffrey's sympathies for the struggling miners and their families. Divided loyalties had placed them on opposite sides of the fight when Evan Williams had led his men out of the pit in protest at a cutting of wages below the poverty level on the pretext of a falling market. Then George Cartwright had brought in miners from Yorkshire to break the strike. He paid them a guinea a week, twice as much as the Welshmen were fighting for. Anna had helped Geoffrey start a Soup Kitchen until her husband had protested at her disloyalty, and their association, a shared passion which had edged over into love, had ended.

Now it was Tansy Drewe, fifteen years younger than Geoffrey, with her high intelligence and strong potential to become a fulfilled woman in all ways. Why had she had to fall for him? He stopped at a bend in the river to gaze across marshes to Hackney where, had it been any day but this, lightermen would have steered clay barges down river. His thoughts returned to Tansy. He had responded to her advances in spite of himself. Her youth and beauty were almost irresistible. Yet resist her he must. He knew, in his deepest consciousness, that he and Tansy were too much alike in temperament ever to become partners in life. Since coming to Newton he had exercised firm control over his mercurial temper but recognised a mirror of it in Tansy's colouring, her impetuous behaviour. No, no, he thought, I mustn't give way to temptation, mustn't spoil Tansy's life before it's really begun.

He thought of Martin Webber, who would make her a good husband – kind, strong and devoted. Why, you had only to see his eyes whenever he was near Tansy to know that there was a lifetime's devotion waiting for her if she wanted it.

He resumed his pacing until he found himself at Coombe Cellars, its alehouse closed for the day. He stood, deep in thought, looking over the sea wall and hearing the singing of the tide as it began to turn, watching the gradual seep as water bubbled up through the estuary mud and freshwater crabs scuttled away.

He knew that if he didn't turn back now the river path would be covered and he would have to make a wide detour through Netherton. Now salt water began to lap the shore and he turned and hurried back, slipping on slime-covered stones and ducking under beech branches. Ahead lay Newton with its smoking chimneys, where families gathered to celebrate the birth of Jesus Christ, the miracle worker. Beyond the town the twin humps of Haytor stood out against a rosy sunset. He increased his pace, intent on reaching Bowden Hill and the sanctuary of Evan Williams' home. He needed to confide in the friend with whom he had shared so many crises in the dark days of his ministerial apprenticeship at Merthyr.

As he strode uphill gas lamps sent shadows across streets and alleyways, their hissing the only sound to break the silence of the year's great festival.

❧

'Come you in.' Gwynneth welcomed him to the little room where Evan sat, restored to health from working above ground in the warmth of a Devon summer. Regular employment had put a temporary halt to his need to gamble and now he sat content, smoking by the fire. He rose and shook Geoffrey by the hand, although something in Geoffrey's face told him he was in trouble. Quickly he rounded up the girls.

'Go you now and see if you can find Owen and the boys. They'll be up the hill rabbitting, like as not.' Reluctantly, Myfanwy and Poppy left the room as Gwynneth entered with a joint of pork. She placed it on the table and carved it into thick, succulent slices, arranged them in a baking tin and took the tin back to the kitchen, where they heard the splashing of water accompanied by her voice as she sang 'All through the night'. Evan rose, took down a pipe rack from the wall and offered it to Geoffrey, who handed over his parcel of books in exchange.

'New are they, Evan?' he asked, examining each bowl and stem. The Welshman responded, 'Made from clay we're digging out at Decoy.'

The two men fell silent while they shared tobacco from an earthen jar and slowly filled bowls, lighting the mix of herbs and tobacco leaves. They drew in and exhaled smoke in the relaxed manner of men who had spent much time together. Evan opened each book to read its title, while Geoffrey's thoughts returned to Tansy. The need to tell someone what had happened had brought him here but now he sat trying to dispel the encounter from his mind. He failed, however, even in Evan's presence, to banish the feel of her warm body against his, the look of her face eager for his lips, her declaration that she loved him and finally her invitation that he should take her. Suddenly he became aware of Evan regarding him quizzically through the haze of smoke.

'I said it's been a blessing finding work so close to home! Owen has taken to it as well, even though he had set his heart on being a 'proper' miner'. He leant forward to touch Geoffrey's knee. 'What is it?' he asked, but Geoffrey now made a supreme effort to concentrate on Evan's earlier remarks, ignoring his question.

'That's splendid, Evan. You look so much better than when you first came to Newton. How is the chest?'

Evan blew smoke rings and struck his diaphragm. 'Couldn't have done that a few months ago, could I, man?'

'And you shouldn't now!' Gwynneth interrupted as she brought in a large plate of Welsh bread and a bowl of butter. 'Here's bara brith, Geoffrey. Help yourself for old time's sake. 'Twas the best move we ever made to come here. If you hadn't got the Ministry here... my Evan would have joined the men in the chapel garden...' The smile left her face as she remembered their life at Merthyr, overshadowed by the black diamonds beneath their feet. 'Do you remember the explosion at Manmoel?' she continued, and Evan and Geoffrey nodded, removing pipes from their mouths in deference to the memory of men buried, not in the chapel garden, but deep beneath the Valley, sealed in graves of coal. 'And do you remember the phrase that rang through the Valley when the owners wouldn't pay compensation to widows unless the bodies of their men could be produced?' Geoffrey completed the memory. 'No corpse, no cash!' he uttered the cruel words, remembering the pathetic trail of women who had come to tell him of their loss. Not only of loving husbands but fathers of their children gone forever, leaving them with no provision for the future and no compensation to ease the burden of the bills for food bought during the strike 'on tick'. Geoffrey broke the silence.

'Best to let go the past, Gwynneth. Put bad things from your minds and celebrate your new life here in this gentle place.' He turned to Evan. 'What's this I hear about your plans to begin allotments for the tenants here and down in the Courts?' His friend's face changed and became animated as he explained the need of the tenants for land to grow vegetables for their large families.

'The pigsties have been a great success. We've killed three pigs for Christmas and shared them. Later in the year another three will be slaughtered and we'll share again.'

'And what does Farmer Cull say to the row of sties?' Geoffrey wanted to know.

Gwynneth laughed and answered his question. 'Turns a blind eye, although sometimes when I'm up there feeding the animals I look up and see him standing there, watching. I don't know what he'll say to Evan's plans to dig up his top field!'

Evan jumped to his feet and began to pace about the tiny room in his excitement. 'Never uses it himself, too small for the herd he keeps above St Mary's. We'll begin to dig as soon as the ground becomes soft enough. There's more than enough space for fifty allotments. Keep fifty families from starvation, boyoh!'

Geoffrey felt a sense of alarm as he listened to Evan talk. His friend's brand of radical thought and action filled him with admiration. At the same time he sensed trouble ahead and remembered shared times back in the Valley where Evan had sung solo in the Bethesda choir and he, Geoffrey, had held his first post in the Ministry.

Evan put his pipe aside and turned once more to Geoffrey. 'Enough of our plans,' he exclaimed, 'You still haven't answered my question – I feel you came to speak to me about something important, yet you still haven't talked of it.'

Gwynneth, sensing their need for privacy, left to return to her preparations. Still Geoffrey hesitated, and Evan pressed him. 'Out with it, man! If there's something bothering you, then share it!'

At last Geoffrey laid down his pipe and began. 'Do you remember Anna Cartwright?'

Evan looked up, shocked and surprised, and now it was his turn to abandon his smoking. 'Then, it's serious,' he said, and Geoffrey nodded as both men fell silent while their thoughts travelled back in time to shared events.

'There's someone... she's attracted to me... and, if I'm honest, I to her... but,' he stopped, already feeling disloyal to Tansy.

Evan leant forward. 'Go on, man. Your secret's safe with me.'

But Geoffrey was afraid anything he might say would give Tansy away, even if Evan hadn't already guessed the subject of their discussion. So he said, 'I think it best I keep my own counsel.'

Again Evan offered, 'Haven't we shared enough problems in the past?' But Geoffrey rose and he in turn paced about the room, knowing that at any moment the children would return, yet still desperately needing to share his anguish with someone. A picture of Tansy alone at The Manse rose in his mind. Who would she go to in her distress, he asked himself, and this decided him.

'It's no good, Evan. I'm not suitable for her, too old and dissolute. I appreciate your sympathy but honour forbids me to tell even you – you understand?'

Evan rose and held out a coal-pitted hand to Geoffrey, who clasped it as each regarded the other with the warmest of feelings. Gwynneth came in and looked questioningly from one to the other.

'You do look serious,' she laughed and the men released hands, and abandoning the topic of women and attraction, turned to smile at her as she stood there, flushed from her cooking.

'You'll stay and share our meal, Geoffrey?' she asked as the door opened to admit their children, rosy cheeked and eager.

'Thank you Gwynneth, but I have already accepted an invitation to the Post Office. I wish you all a happy Christmas and success to all your plans.' He patted Ivor and Emrys on their heads, shook hands with Own and kissed Myfanwy and Poppy.

'Tis a pity our Blodwen can't be here to complete the circle,' Gwynneth said as she opened the door. 'Still, her job at Courtenay House has been a godsend.'

Her parting words reminded him that Tansy, now absolved from the accusation of theft, regarded him not only as her employer but also as the key to her future. Reluctantly he knocked at the Post Office door, trying to gather courage for the evening ahead, when he and Tansy would be thrown together once more.

⁂

Meanwhile, Tansy looked ahead to the evening's festivities with mixed feelings. This day, Christmas Day, which should have been the happiest of the year, now appeared clouded by her experience with Geoffrey. She felt uncertain of the future, uncertain of how she should greet Geoffrey when she saw him. Perhaps he would not come after all?

Thoughtfully she passed through the silent Post Office and began unnecessarily to polish stainless steel, comparing it to the heavy silver of Courtenay House, where Blodwen Evans would, she thought, be preparing for the Vallances' dinner. Tansy counted places and laid up for eight, planning how she would sit next to Geoffrey, but, when the moment came, it was Norah who slid into one seat beside him and Helen who took the other. Tansy sat between Robert and James, near enough to help Eva fetch and carry dishes of steaming vegetables from the kitchen and carry plates of turkey carved by Edward where he sat at the head of the table. This placed her opposite Geoffrey who deliberately avoided her eyes whenever they both looked up from their meal.

As the conversation flowed she sat, feeling alone, but when finally the plum pudding had been set alight and served on thick white plates, Geoffrey asked Robert and James to fetch a bag from the Post Office, where he had hidden it with Eva's connivance. From inside he produced diabolos for the twins, their delighted faces turning thoughtful when he added Robert Louis Stevenson's *A Child's Garden of Verses*, its sixpenny copyright stamp affixed to the back cover.

'I'll read you something from it tonight when it's time for bed,' Norah promised, but the twins protested, 'It's Christmas and we're never going to bed!' – which brought a laugh from everyone.

Norah opened her present from Geoffrey, a copy of *Tess of the d'Urbevilles* by Thomas Hardy. There were bobbins in ivory and mother-of-pearl for Eva, who was always promising herself an hour or two's lace making, and a copy of George Bernard Shaw's essays for Edward. Even Helen hadn't been forgotten and she cried out in delight at the print executed by Elizabeth Stanhope Forbes of two girls dressed in white, playing dominoes.

'This will be perfect for my room at college!' she exclaimed while Tansy tried to banish feelings of jealousy as she couldn't help but notice that each and every gift had been chosen with as much care and genuine affection as had her own. Only Eva noticed the question in the green eyes and the steady blush which rose in her face whenever it was necessary for Tansy to hand food or drink to Geoffrey. Once she intercepted a searching look between them, noting it was Geoffrey who was first to lower his gaze. The usual bantering was absent today and a mood of tension seemed to hang over the table. Eva felt disturbed. Perhaps Edward had been right after all, she thought, when he'd said he believed no good would come of Tansy's working so closely with Geoffrey. 'Too much alike in looks and temperament,' he had said. Perhaps now Tansy had been cleared of theft and she would have good references from Charles Vallance, it would be advisable for her to seek a new position. She decided then and there that she would go and see Caroline Vallance in the New Year and ask if Reuben Widecombe would offer Tansy a job in his Emporium.

The tension was dispelled at last when Rosemary Brimmacombe called with simple presents for all the family and was herself the recipient of a score of *The Messiah* from Eva and Edward, which was tantamount to a promise that she would be asked to play at the next performance in chapel.

She looked up, her face bright with pleasure. 'Thank you, thank you so very much. I'll go home now and begin to learn the score.'

But the twins wouldn't let her go until she'd seen them send their diabolos flying up through the air and catch them in the cups. Then she was asked to play by Norah and they rose and pushed back the table along one wall to join in singing, 'Silent night, holy night, all is calm, all is bright.' Rosemary settled down at the keyboard, Vallances' Mill and her crippled leg forgotten, to accompany whoever was prepared to perform. Edward sang in a warm baritone, 'Drink to me only with thine eyes, and I will pledge with mine; Or leave a kiss but in the cup, and I'll not look for wine.'

But when Geoffrey and Norah rose to sing 'The Keys of Heaven' Tansy could not bear it any longer. Their voices floated up the stairs as she made he way to the attic:

'I will give you the keys of heaven,
I will give you the keys of heaven,
Madam, will you walk, Madam will you talk,
Madam, will you walk and talk with me?'

She shut the door tight and flung herself down on the bed, covering her ears with her hands in order not to hear her sister's sweet voice respond. She regretted the wasted years when she had refused to attend piano lessons, refused to learn the words of songs lying in the piano stool. Now she turned to the panacea for all ills that befell her. She opened Geoffrey's present and began to read.

⁕

A few days after Christmas it snowed, falling in soft flakes which turned Bowden Hill into an ice slide. Evan Williams' children came to call for Robert and James, armed with new tin trays which Gwynneth had been reluctant to see leave the house. Tansy and Norah built a bank of snow where the Hill met Southernhay, curving it up into a barrier to save them hurtling into the shop on the corner.

'Don't go past this or you'll end up among the wagons at the bottom,' Norah admonished before going back to join Helen in the Post Office. Tansy watched the boys glide downhill, her body itching to join them.

A black shape climbed towards her and materialised into Geoffrey. He wore his off-duty clothes, the ones which changed him from a minister into her Geoffrey, the one who'd held spring water in his cupped hands for her to drink. Since the lunch they'd shared at The Manse on Christmas Day a constraint had come between them. He had taken to working in the chapel vestry, leaving her his desk at The Manse. She missed their daily exchange of news, the shared hours, she missed him. So when he arrived at the foot of the Hill she addressed him hesitatingly.

'They'm enjoying themselves, ain't they?' she said, and he smiled and watched the boys struggle uphill ready to slide down again. 'Johnnie Brimmacombe's made a sledge for the twins. I'm to take it up to the top field and try it out.' She paused then plunged on, 'Would 'ee like to come?' She went on nervously, 'The Moor looks grand on such a day.' He hesitated for a moment, knowing he should refuse, then, unable to resist the sparkle in her eyes and the opportunity to shed his official cloak, he agreed.

'You'll need someone to help you,' he justified his position and in a few moments they set off up Courtenay Road, through the kissing-gate to where Cull's fields fell away in a huge white curve lit by a golden ball as the sun rose beyond the dark green turkey oaks.

'Push me off!' Tansy implored as she settled herself on the toboggan and, as Geoffrey began to push, she shouted, 'Faster, faster!' until the runners began to slide on polished snow. The toboggan gathered speed and he leapt onto the back and together they hurtled downhill, going faster and faster until they hit a tussock near the bottom. The toboggan tipped up, sending their bodies colliding into a heap, their red hair tangling together, the breath knocked from their bodies. Two pairs of green eyes mirrored their delight and their lips met as naturally as lovers. He hauled her to her feet and together they pulled the toboggan back uphill.

When they reached the top Tansy was annoyed to find Norah and Helen watching them. Tansy's joy faded. Was there nothing her sister wouldn't spoil? Why did she always turn up when she wasn't wanted?

'How long have you been here?' she demanded, wondering if they had witnessed the embrace she and Geoffrey had shared. 'I didn't know you were coming,' she grumbled as the twins broke away from Norah and grabbed Tansy's hands.

'We've come to ride the toboggan!' they said. 'Johnnie's coming up after work.' They were kept busy for the next couple of hours until their faces grew scarlet in the wind and flurries of snow. Exhausted, they returned to the Post Office where the little boys cried as the fire's warmth set toes and fingers burning. Eva served up tattie and leek soup followed by thick slices of Christmas pudding, fried in hot dripping, but Geoffrey excused himself to return to The Manse. He left without once meeting Tansy's eyes while he arranged to accompany Norah and Helen to London on their return to college the following week.

※※※

Charles Vallance's automobile arrived in the week following Christmas. Tansy and Rosemary had been for a walk in Milber Woods, climbing high to the banked Roman camp, and the automobile passed them as they made their way home. The unusual noise stopped them by the railway bridge and they watched the four-wheeled open-topped vehicle pass them and turn into Courtenay Park.

'Look at that Tansy!' They set off after it, keeping pace with its slow progress while Charles Vallance, his face aglow with pride and excitement, doffed his hat to them. All propriety was forgotten as the girls kept pace with the polished wooden body and admired the gleaming brass lamps which exuded a glow into the January dusk. At the wheel sat a mechanic in brown work suit, and snow fell as they climbed the hill and disappeared up the drive of Courtenay House. The smell of kerosene and paraffin hung on the air as the girls retraced their steps and paused to exchange reactions before parting halfway down 148 steps.

'Wasn't that the most amazing thing you'm ever seen?!' Rosemary declared. 'I do envy Emma Vallance riding in that.'

Tansy laughed. 'I doubt the women folk'll have much use of that. I remember the commotion that went on over the carriage when the Holy Terror came last May. She and the Missus fought like cats over that then and Charles Vallance, he just used the trap all the time and took no notice of the women.'

But nothing could bring Rosemary back to earth. Her eyes held a dreamy look while she went on, 'I'm going to ride in an automobile one day, Tansy, you see if I'm not!'

'And how are you going to do that?' Tansy wanted to know, ''Tis hardly likely anyone we know will be able to afford one.'

But Rosemary was adamant. 'Well, tomorrow I'm going to buy one of they new motoring hats at the Emporium like I seed in the *Woman's Realm,* you see if I don't. You might as well get one too, be ahead of the fashion for a change. Not wait for it to come down from London like as usual.'

The next morning saw the girls setting off for Widecombe's, Rosemary positive and Tansy reluctant. Madie Shillabeer clucked her tongue and frowned when Rosemary demanded to try on her complete range of hats, but when she showed her two shillings lying in the palm of her hand, she could do nothing but stand by until Rosemary chose a blue straw, tied under her chin with pink chiffon, and Tansy was persuaded into a cream velour tied with a pink and cream satin bow.

'I'm sure I don't know where you'm goin' to wear such fancy hats.' Madie exclaimed as she folded bills and placed money into the cylinder, pulling the handle to send it flying across the shop to the cash desk high above the rolls of material.

'That's made a big hole in my savings,' Tansy remarked. 'Geoffrey got me an honorarium from chapel but, after I've paid Mother there's not much left.'

But nothing could dampen Rosemary's spirits as they set off home, wearing their new headgear, self-consciously at first but growing more brazen with every minute.

'Us'll be up with the nobs,' she declared, adding, 'We can always wear them to chapel of a Sunday' and with the simultaneous turning of heads that occurred as they walked to the front of the chapel, they agreed was worth every penny.

When the twins heard that Charles Vallance's automobile had at last arrived they hung about the top of 148 steps every day in the hope of catching sight of the gleaming conveyance. Charles Vallance was learning to drive. They squeaked with excitement when they heard the engine, 'parp parped' with the horn, and held their breath when he put the clutch into the wrong gear and the engine stalled and began a backward slide until Stephen Howell made a grab for the handbrake and arrested its progress. Then Charles Vallance, red-faced and perspiring, corrected the gear and slowly and painfully arrived at the foot of the house steps, where Caroline pleaded to be taken for a drive.

'Wait, just wait. Soon I'll have mastered it then we'll drive down to Torquay. Till then you have the use of the gig, my dear. Be content with that.'

Caroline sulked and moaned to Maude Westaway that there was no end to the frustrations of never being able to have a say in matters which affected their standing in the town. 'I need a motor, not a pony and gig. People will think we've no money.'

Maude laughed. 'I must say, driving up in an automobile is far superior to the indignity of arriving for luncheon somewhere behind a pair of horses with dirty hocks!' She patted her friend's hand. 'Think how handsome Stephen Howell will look when you get him a uniform – do you think pale blue would go well with the red of the automobile?' Then she suggested, with a twinkle in her eye, 'Of course you could always withhold your favours!' Caroline blushed and looked shocked at her friend's suggestion.

Snow fell steadily and deeply as Geoffrey got off the London train, to discover that the Wednesday market had been cancelled and the post van was left at the bottom of the hill, mail being carried up on foot.

At a meeting of the Wolborough Local Board it had been decided to begin relief work for the unemployed. A line formed outside the Soup Kitchen in Union Street and Geoffrey slipped and slid on his way to The Manse, where he arranged for Jenny Jones to work with Tansy in his study. Thus suitably chaperoned he returned to work there also and called on Aurelia Brown to keep a good fire burning in the gloomy room.

Geoffrey had heard of a Mrs Emily Caine who lived in Chicago and worked her servants only eight hours a day. He was very enthusiastic on this score but Tansy, used to working a twelve-hour day at Courtenay House, was sceptical – and said so.

'I'm prepared to put my new motoring bonnet on it!' she proclaimed. 'Why, you'll be saying she's in favour of Unions next.'

No more was heard about an eight-hour working day but Geoffrey did find a place for Tom Moore's parents at Mackrell's almshouses. Tom expressed his delight in no uncertain terms. 'They be certain to spend the rest of their days together now!' Although Avril, much to her surprise, missed them from the alcoves by the fire.

Tom and Geoffrey carried Alice the short distance to the bright new home in its stone terrace, carrying her over the snow with George hobbling along beside them with the aid of a stout ash stick. Edward Drewe welcomed them into a room made cosy with a coal fire. Gifts of furniture had come from chapel members, a scrubbed table and two sturdy Windsor backed chairs stood beside it and an armchair for each was set, one each side of the fire. Geoffrey had donated a large iron bedstead from one of the many unused rooms at The Manse, much to the disapproval of Aurelia Brown. As soon as Alice was set down in her new home she set about unpacking her sheets, which had lain gathering mould in her box at Moon Court. New life seemed to surge through the pair of them. She bustled about, polishing brass fitments on the iron stove and cleaning small paned windows. 'We mun put up some gilly flowers in the windows, George,' she said, looking forward to spring.

But still snow fell and a snowplough cleared the line to Moretonhampstead, from where Tom Moore walked to Vitifer Mine since it had become too deep for the motor van.

✢ Chapter Twenty-One ✢

The Flood

In the fellmongering shed at Vallance's Mill, Johnnie Brimmacombe hung cleaned sheep skins high in brick cells to dry. Geoffrey Llewellyn had tried to get him apprenticed to the wood carver who was restoring Lustleigh church, but Bessie had protested that they needed him to earn a man's wage. Now Johnnie listened to the sound of the River Lemon as it rushed past, filling the leat just twenty yards away.

Outside the sun shone fitfully, lighting up the town and moor beyond, where snowdrifts had buried a postman near Princetown. Relief had come at last, not only for farmers' wives almost out of tea and sugar, but also for British families besieged in South Africa where tea had reached a price of £30 a quarter, as on 23rd February General Buller had entered the gates of Ladysmith and became a local hero overnight.

A week later it began to rain, first in large separate drops, then more quickly, thickening until it became strong enough to wash melting snow away from Haytor to mingle with the source of the Lemon. Then it swelled the river till it became a torrent which poured downhill, rushing headlong through Ilsington to Bickington. It paused for a moment to send mill-wheels hurtling at Ogwell and Bradley. By now it had grown into an unstoppable force, picking up branches torn from trees during the previous autumn gales and tossing them across water-meadows into orchards. There it plucked grazing sheep and drowned them, wedging them fast in willow crucks.

At Newton gaitered men stood about shaking their heads. ''Tis showing all the signs of the Great Flood,' they said, remembering past experiences. 'Let's hope 'un stops afore the moon changes.' 'Let's hope neap tides is low,' they said while men filled bags with sand from Aller and the Local Board representative measured water levels at Hero's Bridge and the Roman causeway at Teigngrace.

Each day the twins, with Ifor and Emrys Williams, went through town to Baker's Park to play in the spring water close by Bradley Manor, until the day when the rushing sound of the river drew their attention.

'I'm going over to the bridge,' Robert announced boldly, and when he and James stood on the parapet and gazed down into the roaring water, he added, 'Let's drop sticks in, see how long it takes them to come through.' They rushed from side to side, excited by the speed with which the branches disappeared in the foam. So caught up were they in their new game that Eva began to worry as it got later and later, and still there was no sign of them.

'I wish they'd come straight home from school like they did when Norah was teaching there.' She bit her lip and stopped ironing to listen to the sound of rain hammering on the coal bunker.

Edward laughed. 'They'm just doing what all lads do. Finding out about life.' But as he caught her anxious expression he promised, 'I'll tell them to keep away from the river if that'll set your mind at rest.'

Eva smiled with relief, knowing that one word from their father was always worth six from her. She lowered the rack from the kitchen ceiling and began to take down the sheets which had hung there drying for days.

After Edward's warning the twins came straight home but after a few days they missed the excitement of their game with the river and Robert suggested, 'Let's go to the park. Just for five minutes. See if the river's down.'

James protested, 'But we promised Father we'd go straight home.' But Robert, always the leader, set off and James, always the follower, went too. 'Mother won't mind if we'm just a few minutes late,' Robert said. 'Us'll be home dreckly!' But when they got to the river it was running faster than ever and before they could cross between parapets the sticks were gone from sight. They were just on the point of abandoning their game when George Shillabeer and Walter Mortimore came sauntering along.

'Why, 'tis twins from the Post Office.' George Shillabeer caught each of them by the scruff of the neck and lifted them, wriggling and squirming, in each of his large fists. He and Walter Mortimore, the oldest boys in school, only attended when there was no work to be done on the land. Both large for their years, they were brawny and muscular and had a reputation for teasing the younger children.

'What be doin' here then?' Walter Mortimore wanted to know when at last George Shillabeer set the boys back on their feet. Robert and James stood, petrified, wanting to run but finding their legs wouldn't carry them. Walter held Robert and George held James, shaking them gently at first when they didn't answer, then suddenly Walter picked up Robert and suspended him over the parapet above the roaring water.

'Put me down!' yelled Robert while George and James peered at him over the bridge. 'Don't struggle or I'll drop 'ee in water, see if 'ee can swim?' Walter said and turned to James "Ee can swim, can't 'ee?' James, goaded into speech through sheer fright, wrenched himself from George's grasp and shouted, 'No, no, he can't swim, fetch him out, please, please!' Walter just laughed and lowered Robert until his head touched the water.

'Shall us drop 'un in then, George?' he asked, as James hammered at his legs. Then, as the weight of the boy began to test his muscles, his sneer faded.

'Please, please, get him up' James stuttered, and at last Walter responded – but now Robert's boots began to slip through his hands.

'Give us a hand, George,' he gasped, 'I can't hold 'un much longer.' George stood, mouth open in terror, as he reached over for the little boy who was gradually slipping from Walter's grasp.

'Haul him along towards the bank,' he shouted, and then to Robert, 'Push your hands against the bridge.' Robert pushed his body away from the wall with his hands as he was dragged towards the bank. In a last desperate move Walter flung him towards the bank with all his might. Slippery mud impeded his progress and Robert clung to the branch of a willow until George and Walter reached down to drag him to safety. Then they stood, horrified. Robert lay on the bank, his once neat suit filthy from river mud, his eyes holding their look of terror. The older boys seized the twins once more, giving each a final shake.

'Don't tell on us or 'twill be drownded in the river you'll be.' And they hurried off, looking back occasionally to make sure the boys were following.

When Robert and James reached the Post Office, Edward drew in his breath, took each by an ear and hauled them out to the kitchen where Eva stood ironing.

'Straight into the tub for these young scoundrels,' he announced grimly, 'and bread and milk only for supper.' Then, noticing that James was comparatively clean, he asked, 'Why are you so clean when your brother's so dirty?' But James would only shake his head.

'You must learn to do as you are told,' Eva scolded as she filled the copper and lit faggots underneath. But when questioned further Robert and James exchanged frightened glances and refused to answer.

※

'February fill dyke,' Alice Moore muttered as she peered at the rain through the leaded windows of her tiny room, and George replied, ''Tis the new moon and spring tide coming together that's done it.' He left to walk into town and gaze at the level of the Lemon, now almost at the top of the walls at Hero's Bridge. Then, worried for Tom's family, he called in at Moon Court.

'River's up,' he told Avril, who sat mending clothes and rocking Eleanor's crib with one foot. 'Where are little 'uns?'

She looked up at the note of concern in her father-in-law's voice. 'They'm just round corner, at the baker's.'

'Why not bring 'em along to Almshouses, at least we'm above water-meadows there,' he suggested, but Avril's memory of overcrowding and squabbling was still fresh and she hesitated.

'I'm sure we'll be all right here. I'll watch out,' she promised. 'If it gets bad then we'll come up.' She stepped outside into the narrow alley to peer at the moon, which appeared fitfully between scudding clouds. She shivered and, making sure that Eleanor was still asleep, hurried off to bring home her brood of boys.

※

After school that day Tom Coish and Harry Brooks set off for the river, followed by a crowd of boys. 'Us've made a raft. 'Tis hidden in woods,' announced Tim. 'Us be gonna float 'un down river, see if us doan't.' Robert declared, 'Us can't miss that, be worth a bread and milk supper.' But James protested, 'You know what Father said. Next time it'll be the strap.' Yet when Robert set off after the other boys, James still followed. When they got to Steppes Meadow the water was beginning to creep up and over the field path and form pools in the long grass.

'Give 'ee a ride if'n you like,' Tom Coish offered and Harry Brooks, sensing the opportunity for profit, added, 'Halfpenny a time.' But when they reached the river both were frightened at the height of the water. They hesitated then, afraid to lose face among their schoolmates, repeated the offer, 'Halfpenny a time.'

Robert and James shook their heads and looked down at the water, which was rising swiftly up over their boots.

'Us hasn't got no halfpennies,' Robert said, and shivered suddenly as they watched the river, now the colour of the toffee Eva made them on Bank Holidays, cross the bank while Tom Coish and Harry Brooks fought to launch the raft into the roaring water.

※

At Vallance's the men stopped work to listen as the river changed its note yet again. It changed from the deep roar to a quiet swishing and began to seep under the doors of the fettling room. Jim Tozer, the foreman, left his post and, cap in hand, tapped on Charles Vallance's door.

'Come in.' Charles Vallance looked up as he came into his office. 'Yes, Tozer, what is it?' The man spoke out, direct and confident. 'Begging your pardon, Mr Vallance Sir, but river's over and leat's coming in.'

Charles Vallance rose to his feet at once. 'You know what to do, Jim. Hang as many skins as possible then send everyone home. If there's time to put sandbags along the doors do so, but if the leat's over then don't wait.'

Then he put on his hat and coat and passed through the outer office, where Rosemary Brimmacombe sat writing in a huge Day Book. He hesitated just one moment, then made up his mind.

'Come along, Miss Brimmacombe, I'll take you home – where's Johnnie? You fetch him while I start the Lanchester.'

So Rosemary got her wish to ride in an automobile sooner than ever she could have hoped! She hurried to find Johnnie, who still worked high in the roof.

'Come quick, our Johnnie, leat's flooding, river's up and Master's to give us a ride home in his automobile.'

Johnnis shouted 'Hooray!' at the top of his voice, then swung down from the rafters on a pulley, his face breaking into a broad grin. 'Hooray for the river!' They joined the men streaming out of the building to wade through the rapidly rising water, while tenants of the Bradley Lane cottages desperately tried to dam front doors with blankets and mattresses.

'Best get out now,' Jim Tozer told them, remembering the Great Flood of 1894 which had risen to first-floor windows.

'But where would us go?' Maudie Pengilly wanted to know, as she shut her door firmly and prepared to sit it out.

Charles Vallance met Geoffrey Llewellyn as he drove axle-deep through Wolborough Street.

'What happens now?' Geoffrey asked. 'How high will the waters go?' His only knowledge of flooding was confined to the mines at Merthyr. He tipped his hat to Rosemary and Johnnie, who sat in the back of the Lanchester thoroughly enjoying the excitement.

'Only our Maker can answer that, Llewellyn. I'm going to the Quay to alert the boatmen, we'll need every boat that's available if the water goes on rising as it is at present.'

Geoffrey climbed up beside Charles and went with him past Tucker's Mill and under the railway bridge to the head of the river where boatmen stood motionless, awaiting the incoming tide.

⁂

Eva Drewe stood at the top of Beaumont Road watching for the twins. She had already been to see Gwynneth Williams in the hope of finding them there.

Gwynneth shook her head. 'No, they've not been here. Ivor and Emrys are home. Usually come home from school together, don't they? Would you like Evan and Owen to look for them when they come home?'

But now they saw Edward climbing the hill. 'No Gwynneth, it's all right. Here's Edward, he may know something.'

But he had only bad news. 'River's up, Teign Marsh is flooded. Mail train may be delayed if sea's over the wall at Dawlish.' Then he saw the expression on her face. 'What's wrong?'

'The boys aren't home, Edward. I must go down to Baker's Park, that's where they'll be.'

Edward put out a hand to stop her as she began to remove her apron. 'No, no, 'tis best you stay here. They may come back while you're gone. You keep an eye on the counter, I'll go and get them.'

But by the time Edward had retraced his steps to East Street the Teign had stormed the town's defences and the Courts were under water. Edward thought of the women there, their men working away on the moor. Instantly torn between the urgent need to find Robert and James and his Christian duty to help the women, he hesitated and in that moment the water deepened until it reached his thighs. A boat came rapidly towards him with Geoffrey Llewellyn standing at its bows.

'Get in, man!' he shouted to Edward, and no sooner than Edward had scrambled in than they heard shouts coming from the direction of Moon Court.

'The twins are missing,' Edward explained. 'I was on my way to try and find them but it seems there's trouble at Moon Court now.'

Between them they steered the boat into Wolborough Street where their attention was drawn by Andrew Bearne, who leant from the upper storey of the bakery.

'Can you help us? Avril Moore's trying to get back into the Court. There's a baby there in the house.'

Avril appeared at the window, holding Teddy in her arms, her face distraught. 'Mr Drewe, thank God you've come. Please help me. I've got to get Eleanor out... if anyone can help it must be you!'

Edward put the thought of the twins from his mind and helped Geoffrey and the boatman manoeuvre along the front of the buildings to Moon Court, where they found the passage door shut and held firm by the weight of water.

'Is there another way?' Geoffrey asked and Edward shook his head. 'There should be, if there was a fire they'd all be trapped like rats.' He paused, thinking hard. 'Perhaps we could climb over the roof and get in that way.' They turned the boat and rowed hard back along Wolborough Street and round the rear of Moon Court.

'Hold the boat steady, Edward,' Geoffrey ordered, 'this is a job for a younger man. I'll try and climb that gutter and go over the roof.' He placed his hands on the gutter and hauled himself up, hand over hand, struggling to gain foothold on the rough cob walls. He reached the roof and began slowly to climb up the tiles. He slipped and hung there for a long moment, regained his balance and disappeared from sight over the ridge. His voice floated back to Edward. 'Don't wait. Go and look for the twins.'

The boatman persuaded Edward that there was nothing more they could do by waiting there. Taking an oar each they rowed strongly past the almshouses to Steppes Meadow, now covered completely by water. They rested for a moment, then Edward held high his lantern and called, 'Robert, James, are you out there? Don't be afraid. Just shout!' But there was no response, no sound save the noise of branches hitting concealed objects as the river flowed and swirled around them. The last vestiges of daylight began to fade.

'I'll row 'ee to the higher bridge,' the boatman said. 'Perhaps they've climbed up into the woods.' A few minutes later Edward jumped from the boat and, lantern in hand, began to search the woods.

✧

Alyn Jones arrived at The Manse with a message from Geoffrey Llewellyn. 'He's told everyone who's home is flooded to come here!'

Tansy looked up from Geoffrey's desk, immediately alarmed. 'Is it getting worse then?' then bit her lip, not wishing to alarm Alyn. When Aurelia Brown had come back from town with the news that the river was rising fast, Tansy had told Jenny to go home. Now she bit back the truth.

'Where's Jenny? I've come to fetch her home,' the young doctor continued. 'No one told me the town was subject to flooding when I came for my interview!'

'Jenny wasn't feeling too well so I suggested she go home. She should be there by now.'

Alyn picked up his bag and prepared to leave. 'It's not her time yet.' Tansy hurried after him to the door. 'If the centre of town's flooded, go up past the station, then you must climb Courtenay Road and go along to Powderham. Good luck!' she called after him as he left The Manse and ran down the drive.

Tansy went into the kitchen where Aurelia was preparing food. 'Stop that, Aurelia, and come and help me.' The old woman looked up, an angry frown growing between her eyes. 'How dare you order me about! I'm getting the minister's supper and nothing is more important than that.'

Tansy rapped the table with impatient fingers. 'Geoffrey's told anyone who's home is flooded to come here. What do we need to do?'

Now Aurelia Brown came into her own. She straightened up, abandoned her pastry and quickly wiped her hands on her apron. 'They'll need beds for the night and hot food. Come with me.' And together they worked with a will, emptying airing cupboards of linen that hadn't seen the light of day since before the Reverend Childers had come to minister to the town. As each pile of sheets came tumbling out, the smell of mothballs issued forth into the hall but, after an hour, every bed in the house was ready and waiting. And an hour after that a new smell was added, that of hot vegetable soup which wafted from kitchen to hall just in time to greet the first of the flood victims.

❦

As night came an eerie silence fell over shops and houses, broken only by the sound of dipping oars and juddering engines as boatmen rescued people from upstairs rooms. Geoffrey's message given earlier had brought a swift response as families made the decision either to sit it out or leave their homes.

'There's hot food and beds at The Manse, come as you are. A welcome awaits you,' he had announced. Now nothing had been heard from him since he disappeared over the roof into Moon Court. Shop workers who had carried elderly customers across the flood in the late afternoon, causing shrieks of embarrassment as skirts lifted to show petticoats and ankles, now returned by boat and tried to repel water with brooms. They were defeated finally when the insidious creep of water was suddenly swollen by the high tide which had gained momentum on its journey in from the sea. As the water rose strange sights occurred. Boots floated out of Hammetts the shoemakers and a group of women propelled a raft down Bank Street, trying to fish them out of the torrid water.

''Tis a six I'm looking for,' one shouted, 'hev got one, needs another for my Jamie,' as they risked death to harvest the unexpected crop. The strength and power of the water was such that a piano was swept from Ebenezer Chapel and carried along East Street till it came to a halt at the Turk's Head where it floated, its keys tinkling like bells. Then, at first light, the flood began its retreat from town almost as rapidly as it had invaded homes and workplaces.

Avril, who had been forcibly held back by neighbours from venturing into the deep water, broke free as soon as it dropped below waist height. She struggled towards Moon Court to be met by Geoffrey who had forced open the door to the passage and now appeared, carrying a bundle in his arms.

'Is it my Eleanor?' Avril cried. 'Tell me she'm all right.'

But Geoffrey's face held no joy. 'I only found her when the water began to subside.' He spoke slowly, his face haggard as he handed the little bundle over to Avril. She covered it with kisses and began to croon, 'There, there, my little precious, did 'ee get lost then? Let's get 'ee indoors in the warm.' Geoffrey put his arm around her and assisted her to retrace her steps to the shelter of the baker's shop where her companions of the night's long vigil crowded round.

'I couldn't find her in the dark,' Geoffrey explained. 'The crib must have floated at first, then the water overwhelmed it and she drowned.'

Avril looked up, not seeming to understand what he was saying. 'Bless you, Mr Llewellyn,' she said. 'You'm a saint and no mistake. Just wait till my Tom gets back. There's nothing us can do 'ull be too good for 'ee'. She sat down on the nearest chair, undid her blouse and pressed the baby's body to her, milk beginning to flow from her breast. When there was no response she looked up, puzzled, then exclaimed. ''Tis sleep you be wantin', my little maid, then you'll be ready to sup.'

Geoffrey stood over her, at a loss what to do, while the women began to exchange worried glances. 'Eleanor's gone beyond your loving, Avril,' he said, his voice gentle. He held out his arms to take the baby from her but Avril clutched Eleanor's body close and shrank away from him.

'Tidd'n true!' she cried. 'You'm lying. All she wants is a sleep. Wants her own home she does, that's all.' As she got up and hurried towards the door, Geoffrey held up his hand to stop the horrified cries of the women. Now they looked to him for guidance.

'Give her time,' he pleaded. 'She'll come to accept what's happened before long. I'll get word to Tom as soon as I can. Don't leave her alone. Go with her.' And as the women went after Avril he added, 'I'll be back as soon as I've changed,' and he left to wearily tread mud-coated cobbles. He called at the General Post Office to send a telegraph to the mine captain at Vitifer. Then he climbed Abbotsbury Hill to The Manse but when he tried to insert his key in the lock his hands shook so much that he couldn't manage it and it was Tansy who, hearing his fumbling efforts, opened the door to him.

The sight of Tansy reminded him that the twins were missing but he said nothing as she greeted him. 'Get Aurelia for me, will you?' he asked her, needing to regain his strength and find out what had happened to them. No point, he thought, in alarming her if they had been found.

'She's been asleep this last couple of hours,' Tansy said, then asked, 'Where have you been? We got your message and the house is full. Aurelia was splendid. We've fed thirty people and they'm all in bed asleep or just resting.' She laughed on a rising note of hysteria, almost at the end of her resources. 'This is where I've been,' she said, leading him to the study, indicating the Chesterfield. 'There's nowhere else to go now. But I was too excited to sleep...' Then it was she noticed the pallor of his face, the wetness of his clothes, the shaking that had begun in his limbs.

'I'll get 'ee some dry clothes, hot soup...' Soon she was back to feed him from a steaming bowl. She helped him strip off his wet jacket and trousers and wrapped him in thick blankets, but still he shivered. She climbed up beside him and held him close. After a while the warmth of her body dispelled the chill from his and they fell asleep in each other's arms. When the sky lightened and Aurelia came in to pull the blinds she found them there, Geoffrey's clothes and boots lying on the floor, both sleeping the sleep of exhaustion.

*

When Widecombe's Emporium opened its doors that morning Maudie Pengilly cried out. Her hat display lay stranded, soggy and limp, on top of mens' suiting. She watched in amazement as Caroline Vallance and Maude Westaway came through the doors dressed in heavy work aprons, sleeves rolled up to the elbows, and began to scrub walls and floors.

'Just look at the muslins and crêpes, my dear! Whatever shall we do for spring outfits now?' Maudie wanted to know, while Caroline replied sharply, 'Whatever will my Father and Mother do? They must have lost a great deal of money.' Gertrude Widecombe arrived to stand about wringing her hands and moaning, 'Whatever will become of us? Your Father wasn't insured! Us'll be ruined.'

⁕

After Edward had parted from Geoffrey the night before he had spent an hour searching the far river bank for the boys and he would never know what unseen hand guided him up through Hangman's Wood to Puritan Pit. Without hope he called their names yet again, waving the lamp to and fro. He stood listening then repeated the performance a second time, then a third. He was just about to turn back when a faint cry reached his ears.

'Over here. Us be over here.' Edward hurried down the rough steps into the well of the Pit. He held the lamp high in an effort to pierce the dark.

''Tis Mr Drewe,' he heard. 'We be over here,' came faintly and he moved towards the sound. It came from Tom Coish, who he found standing in front of a curtain of ivy. Edward felt a rush of hope. If Tom Coish was alive then perhaps... Tom pulled aside the leaves and Edward peered under a natural roof of stone and tree roots. There, blessed relief, sat eight boys, all huddled together and in the middle were Robert and James.

'Thank God you're safe!' he exclaimed, bending over to touch the boys as if he could hardly believe they were alive. They grinned up at him from blue faces.

'I knew you'd come,' Robert said, turning to James, 'Didn't I, James? I told 'em you'd come for us.'

Edward noticed the chattering teeth and shivering bodies. 'What happened?' he demanded of Harry Brooks. When he got no reply he contiued, 'Never mind, that can wait. Let's get you all home.' They all rose and prepared to follow him.

'We brought them up here away from river, Mr Drewe,' Harry Brooks explained. 'Tom wrapped them up in our coats to keep 'un warm.' Edward laughed out loud in the sheer joy and relief of finding the twins alive and well.

'You did well, my lads. Indeed you did. Now follow me, we'll climb up to the road and make our way over the hill. Your families will be scared witless,' he said, then set off, holding the lamp high, the other boys close at his heels, up through the soggy woods to safety.

⁕

Tansy woke to the sound of Aurelia's voice, the place where Geoffrey had slept beside her now empty.

'Here's your father, Tansy Drewe.' Edward came to her and put his arms around her.

'The twins, they're safe!' he said, then drew back, puzzled by the look of surprise in her face. 'Didn't you know they were missing?' she shook her head.

'Geoffrey didn't tell you?' he continued. 'Obviously he had other things on his mind.'

'Where are they now?' Tansy demanded.

'At home with your mother.'

'Then I must see them.' Suddenly she felt the need to touch them, reassure herself that her little brothers were alive and well. But now Geoffrey, freshly dressed, came into the study. Quickly he crossed to Edward, clasping his hands in his.

'Aurelia tells me the twins are safe! Thank God!' Then the smile left his face, leaving it white and drawn, his eyes bleak. Edward immediately showed concern.

'What's happened, Geoffrey?' Slowly Geoffrey told them of his night of horror, how Eleanor Moore had drowned when the flood water rose above her crib.

'It was only when first light came and the water receded that I was at last able to find her.'

'Avril's baby's dead!' Tansy stood stunned by the news. 'That can't be!' Geoffrey brushed a hand across his eyes.

'I wouldn't believe it either had I not held the little body in my arms.' He paused and Tansy sat down suddenly as if the strength had suddenly left her. 'I must go back, I promised.' He hesitated.

'What is it? There's something you're not telling us?' Edward pressed him and Geoffrey walked about the room with quick jerky movements, then turned to face them.

'Avril,' he said slowly, weighing every word, 'won't accept that Eleanor's dead.' A picture came into Tansy's mind of the day she took them down the Parish Box, held the tiny fingers in hers, laid her cheek against the soft down of Eleanor's face. She looked up to see Geoffrey moving towards the door.

'If you can think of anything that would help her?' he implored Tansy, 'Please tell me...'

Edward shook his head and exclaimed, 'What we need is a miracle!' then, as Tansy moved to go with Geoffrey he offered, 'I'll go with Geoffrey. Go and see your mother, Tansy. She's had quite a shock. To see you will do her good.'

Tansy climbed the hill to the Post Office, her heart heavy. She felt guilty at not being with her mother during the hours the twins were missing. How long a night it must have been for the mothers, Eva and Avril, while she, Tansy, had administered to the needs of strangers. Could she ever be a mother? Then she was inside the living-room where Eva sat, arms encircling Robert and James as they huddled beside the fire. Robert and James jumped up, rushing over to hug her and she smiled across the room at her mother, whose eyes were smudged with black shadows, a mirror of the night's long ordeal.

It was only after they had coaxed Robert and James to go to bed for a short sleep that they made tea and sat together, cradling cups in hands, enjoying the comfort of the warm liquid. Tansy hesitated, wondering if she should break the news of Eleanor's death to her. Was it too soon after her mother's own agony? But the habit that had sustained her since childhood was too strong and, at last, she told her mother of the tragedy.

'No! Oh no!' Eva exclaimed, her fingers suddenly nerveless, her cup sliding to the floor. 'That's terrible! I can't believe it! Why, she can't be but two months old.' Then she stood up. 'Poor Avril, I must go to her. She'm from away. She'll have no family to comfort her.'

Tansy caught her arm as she reached for her shawl from the back of the door. 'Mother, wait. There's something else...' and, after hesitating a moment she drew a deep breath and went on. 'Avril won't accept the baby's dead.' And they stood, bound together by the catastrophe.

''Tis hard indeed to lose one so soon,' Eva said. 'Seems only a few weeks since the night of the service at Puritan Pit.'

Tansy nodded, remembering. 'I can hear Avril's voice now telling me she was going to call her Eleanor and old Alice Moore saying "Fancy names breed fancy ways...".' Her voice broke as tears gathered in the green eyes. Eva put her arm around her.

'Don't cry, my love. Save your tears for Avril.'

Tansy brushed them aside fiercely and swallowed hard. Her need to pour out her feelings came out in a stream of disjoined words. 'So pleased she was when Geoffrey told me to take down the Parish Box. Dressed the little baby together... she did, Avril and me.' At the second memory of the Parish Box her face changed, a look at once positive and bold banished that of sorrow.

'Mother!' she exclaimed. 'I've thought of a way to help her.' Quickly she explained to her mother who nodded, her face brightening. She went upstairs to return moments later with a parcel.

'Shall I come with you?' she offered, but Tansy shook her head. 'No Mother, you stay here with the twins. You've been through enough as 'tis.' When Eva looked doubtful she promised, 'I'll come and tell you if it works.' She kissed her mother and hurried back across town to The Manse. When Geoffrey came back for lunch he shook his head in answer to her questioning look.

'There's no change,' he said, and eagerly Tansy explained her plan. At once he agreed. 'It could work. How clever of you to think of it. I'll come with you.'

Tansy took the empty box from the cupboard in the hall, placing Eva's parcel inside, and together they set out for Moon Court. As they entered the passage they met women sweeping the last of the water from the narrow cobbled court, freeing gutters of debris, and when they entered number five they looked about them in amazement. Neighbours had built a fire with dry sticks fetched from the loft at the Major's stables. The room had been scrubbed till every trace of water and sludge had been removed. The flagstones gleamed white and Avril sat there by the fire, still rocking Eleanor. There was no sign of her brood of boys. Tom stood by her, a look of utter weariness and loss lining his face. He came forward when he saw who it was. He and Geoffrey clasped hands.

'You got home quickly!' Geoffrey remarked and Tom nodded.

'As soon as your message came I walked to Moreton and caught the post van from there.' He broke off to look at Avril, where she sat crooning to the lifeless bundle in her arms. 'I knew it must be something bad,' he hesitated. ''Tis no good, she won't let the little 'un go.' He dropped his head in his hands and Geoffrey touched his shoulder.

'The boys?' he asked and Tom responded, 'Feyther's taken them to the almshouses, Mother's looking after them.'

Geoffrey beckoned to Tansy, who had stood just inside the door, waiting for his signal. She stepped forward, carrying the box. Tom placed a stool for her by Avril's side and she sat down, the box on her knees. She touched Avril who looked up and stopped her rocking, surprised to see Tansy.

'What are you doing here?' she asked.

'Avril,' she began nervously, 'Do you remember the day I bought you the Parish Box and we dressed Eleanor?' Avril nodded, a smile of happy remembrance crossing her face. 'Now I've come to take the clothes away. Now that Eleanor doesn't need them any more.' A shadow passed over Avril's face.

'Not need them any more?' she asked. 'But you said to keep them till she grew too big for them...' Tansy, realising the hard task she had undertaken, tried again. 'We must have them for the next baby, Avril. Eleanor won't need them now God's called her home.'

Still Avril held the little body close. She stared at Tansy, a look of disbelief on her face, and Tansy tried her last ploy.

'Open the box, Avril,' she ordered and Avril, overcome at last with curiosity, handed the tiny creature to Tansy, then opened the lid and took out Eva's parcel. 'Look at it,' Tansy insisted and, like a sleepwalker, Avril obeyed. She unwrapped a tiny gown made of fine linen, trimmed with lace, bodice smocked.

'Why,' she exclaimed, ''tis the most beautiful thing I've ever seen,' and she held it up to the light.

''Tis the christening gown Granny Thomas made for our Norah,' Tansy explained. 'We've all worn it in our turn. Myself, Robert, James, and the little one who lies in St Mary's churchyard. Yes, even little May. She died of the croup when she was little more than your Eleanor.'

Avril, a look of delight on her face, nodded. 'It would fit my Eleanor perfectly.' Tansy seized the moment and bent forward. 'May wore it for her laying out,' she said. 'Let me use it for Eleanor,' she pleaded, 'then we can take her to church, give her back to Jesus. Let her lie, Avril. Let her lie at peace in St Mary's churchyard.'

She held her breath and the silence that filled the small room was such that a spider could have been heard weaving its web. Tansy was conscious of Tom and Geoffrey standing motionless in the background. If Avril didn't respond to this, her last plea, Tansy thought, then she would have failed. She had nothing left to offer. No other means to persuade Avril that her baby was dead. A sound brought her back, the sound of Avril crooning to the baby.

'Goodbye, my precious,' she cried. 'Not to run in the field with your brothers, my little maid...' Her voice broke and the tears fell, gathered and fell as without another word she began to remove the still damp clothes from Eleanor. Tansy took them from her and replaced them in the Parish Box, then handed Avril the christening gown. She watched as Avril dressed the child for the last time and laid her in the crib. Now Geoffrey came forward, Tom close behind.

'Avril,' he said gently, 'I've asked Johnnie Brimmacombe to make her a little coffin.' He paused, waiting for her to take in what he was saying. 'Shall it be of oak or pine?' Avril stood looking down at the crib, then turned to Tom as if aware at last of his presence.

'Oak from the King's forest,' she said, holding out a hand to Tom. 'I heard that somewhere, when a royal baby died, a tree was cut down special like.'

Then Tom took her in his arms and led her, sobbing, from the room. Geoffrey looked at Tansy, relief showing plainly on his face. Neither spoke. They left the house and he stopped to speak to the women who stood outside awaiting the outcome of their visit.

'It's over,' he said. 'The service will take place tomorrow at chapel, afterwards we will walk up the hill to St Mary's. We will come at nine.'

It was only when they reached The Manse that Tansy's grief, held back for so long, was released in a flood of tears. Geoffrey held her in his arms, held her close and stroked her hair in an effort to ease her distress.

'I'm proud of you,' he murmured, brushing her hair with his lips. 'You're the most splendid creature in the whole world.'

⚜ Chapter Twenty-Two ⚜

Benjamin Brealley

Three weeks later Geoffrey called Tansy and Aurelia to his study. 'There's to be a meeting here today and I want you Tansy, to take Minutes, and you, Aurelia, to receive the gentlemen, give them coffee or, if the meeting should go on till lunch time, then perhaps a glass of sherry.'

Tansy, nervous at being asked to do something she'd never undertaken before, asked, 'What do I have to do?'

He laughed. 'Just make notes of the conversation, especially any decisions, then I'll edit them later. I must go out now but I'll be back in good time. You can arrange the seating.'

He handed her a pile of cards, which she arranged after debating the advisability of placing Dr Alan Weekes, who though a friend of his mother, was anathema to Charles Vallance beside him. She tapped Andrew Billington's card against her teeth. New to Newton Abbot, Rosemary had told her of his visit to the Mill where he'd found the sanitary arrangements sadly lacking. Had been appalled that she, the only woman, had to cross Bradley Lane and use one of the privies of the terrace. Tansy smiled and placed his card beside that of Charles Vallance. Give him a chance to do something for her friend, she thought. Finally she put the doctors together so they could confer if necessary and, with a hint of mischief, she placed Benjamin Brealley opposite Geoffrey with whom he'd crossed swords over the proposed allotments. This left two cards, her father's and her own. These she laid down with a flourish, one each side of the preacher.

Everyone was seated by half past ten, everyone except the Chairman of the Local Board. Charles Vallance produced his watch, tapped the glass and placed it to his ear.

'Trust him to be late!' he said impatiently and Geoffrey added, 'I believe it makes him feel important, this keeping people waiting. It seems to be a habit!'

It was nearly eleven before they heard the sound of heavy footsteps crossing the hall. Benjamin Brealley burst into the room, dressed in striped trousers and waistcoat which strained against his enormous stomach, a frock-coat and overshirt with wing-collar, nudging rolls of red-skinned flesh. With one hand he fingered the diamond in his tie, while the other rested on the back of the chair and his cold blue eyes looked at the attendees one by one. His gaze came to rest on Tansy and a frown immediately grew.

'I'm not in the habit of attending meetings where women are present!' he boomed, glaring at Tansy who looked at Geoffrey for guidance. He leapt to his feet at once. 'Miss Drewe is here to take Minutes,' he said smoothly and sat down.

Benjamin Brealley remained standing. 'Can't you take Minutes, Llewellyn? Chit of a girl listening to parish affairs. Not in my book. Get rid of her!'

This time Charles Vallance intervened. 'Miss Drewe,' he said coldly, 'is more than capable of fulfilling the role of clerk. Tell them what you've been doing on behalf of the chapel.' Tansy rose, trying to control her blushes, and stated, 'I have just completed a report on Moon Court, the number of children living there., the numbers of children at Bell's School and how many vacancies there are. I have also listed various people who would be willing to act as beneficiaries to assist children to attend, perhaps also to give gifts to the brightest so they may attend the Grammar School.' She looked up at his towering bulk and added archly 'Perhaps I may add your name to my list?'

His frown threatened to turn into apoplexy as the folds of his neck swelled ominously. He sat down and the chair, too frail for his weight, broke, sending him backwards onto the floor. Edward Drewe rose and hurried to remove the broken remnants of the once elegant chair and set off to scour The Manse for something sturdy enough to accommodate the now-rescued Councillor.

Tansy stuffed her handkerchief into her mouth to stop the bursts of glee escaping and Geoffrey banged the gavel on the table.

'I call the meeting to order and invite Charles Vallance to take the Chair.' The latter rose at once.

'We are already more than twenty minutes late so I will waste no further time but call on Alyn Jones, Dr Weekes' partner, to give evidence on the state of Moon Court at the time of Eleanor Moore's birth.'

Alyn stood, his slight figure dwarfed by that of Benjamin Brealley who sat, struggling to regain his composure. 'Coming from away, I was shocked at the state of the accommodation there which reminded me of some of the worst slums of Cardiff. The twisted limbs of some of the children suggested they were suffering from rickets through malnutrition. Some of the inhabitants bore signs of consumption and the kidney complaint, Bright's disease.'

At this point Brealley leant forward to interrupt. 'Surely you're not blaming the landlord for the state of his tenants?' But Alyn continued firmly, 'The poor provision for sanitation, lack of light and air, and water from a well, which I tasted and proved of poor quality, cannot be ignored as being a contributory factor.' Here he turned to his partner and Alan Weekes nodded in encouragement.

'I understand from Dr Weekes that the Local Board offered to seal the well, install a water supply and lay main drainage last year at a cost of £150 but that the landlord, who has remained anonymous, refused.' He sat down, ran thin fingers through his mop of dark wavy hair and looked at Benjamin Brealley who moved angrily in his chair and shouted at Charles Vallance.

'Get on with it. I'm a busy man!'

Charles motioned to Tansy. 'Will you fetch Tom Moore, my dear?' he asked and Tansy rose to admit Tom. He entered the room and hesitated by the door. He was wearing his work clothes, a black mourning ribbon stitched to the sleeve of his jacket. He removed his cap and waited nervously, folding and unfolding it. Benjamin Brealley glared at him, but addressed the chairman. 'It would have been polite if this witness had had the courtesy to dress in a respectful manner before he came before us,' he said.

Geoffrey sprang to his feet to speak in Tom's defence. 'Mr Moore,' he said, steely-eyed, 'has taken a day off from his employment to attend here today. For him loss of a day's work means loss of a day's wages. But he feels the matter to be of such importance that he has taken on this loss in order to tell us what happened on the night of the flood.'

Here he smiled encouragement at Tom who began, haltingly at first but then with growing confidence. He told his story simply, pausing from time to time to swallow away the emotion the recounting of Eleanor's death brought. When he had finished Geoffrey rose and crossed the room to shake him by the hand.

'We're sorry to have had to put you through this ordeal, Tom, but I'm sure you will appreciate that it was necessary.' Tansy went and held the door open for him. 'Well done,' she whispered, touching his arm in sympathy.

'Is that all?' Brealley wanted to know. 'I've another meeting to attend.'

Charles Vallance turned to his neighbour. 'There's only one other witness to call and that's our newly appointed sanitary engineer, Andrew Billington.'

The young man rose and proceeded to tell the meeting, 'One of my first duties for the District Council was to inspect Moon Court and after inspecting it thoroughly I came to the conclusion that, had it been open at the end opposite the entry passage from Wolborough Street and had main drainage been in existence, flood waters would not have risen to the height they did. Since the flood recommendations have been made to improve the town's drainage system.' He paused to look through the sheaf of papers in his hands, then continued. 'I can also confirm Dr Jones' remarks about an offer for connection and improvement to Moon Court made last year. The offer's still open to the landlord. The cost however has now risen to £200...' He paused while Brealley glared at him and ran a finger round the edge of his collar. 'I am ordered to state that, should he decline to pay there is the possibility that the Court will be condemned as unfit for human habitation and an order passed that Moon Court and its dwellings be demolished.'

With a scraping of his chair, Brealley was on his feet, his face contorted with rage, his chest heaving. 'I've never heard the like,' he blustered. 'Those Courts have housed the poor for as long as I can remember. If they were good enough for them in my feyther's day, then they'm good enough for them today...' He stopped and abruptly left the room. The sound of a door slamming was followed by the tinkling of glass. A silence filled the room while the full import of his words came home.

Charles Vallance, his face sombre, rose to his feet. 'I think we can declare the meeting closed unless,' he stopped to look at each of the participants in turn, 'anyone has anything to add.'

Geoffrey rose and said wearily, 'I think we have a fight ahead if Moon Court is to be improved. However, nothing can be gained by further discussion until we know what action, if any, the landlord takes.' He held up a hand to arrest the departure of the meeting, adding, 'I would like to know who it was closed the entrance door to the Wolborough Street passage the night of the flood. If anyone hears anything please report it to me. Thank you.'

Aurelia Brown came into the room, swaying a little with her tray of Madeira and glasses. From the colour of her face and sound of her voice when she announced, 'Glass of Madeira, Sir?' (sherry indeed!), it was obvious to all that she had partaken of a glass or two herself!

Later in the day when, still angry at her continued exclusion from meetings, Aurelia called on Maudie Pengilly, she grumbled, 'Good enough to cook, clean and wash his socks and pants but not good enough to take Minutes any more. 'Twouldn't have happened in Havelock Childers' day. Then we all knew our place!' As Maudie nodded her head in agreement Aurelia went on. 'Just a skivvy I am since that Tansy Drewe came on the scene,' and her friend commiserated with her.

'Pity there's no way you can get rid of her, 'Relia.'

Aurelia's eyes narrowed, her lips tightened. 'Seen enough to have him sent packing too,' she went on. 'My time'll come you'll see.'

✢ Chapter Twenty-Three ✢

Return to Courtenay House

Tansy chose a day when she knew Jenny Jones would be absent from The Manse and laid down the Minutes on Geoffrey's desk.

'Thank you, Tansy,' he said, smiling at her. 'I'm sure these are in your usual faultless style,' and he put them aside, reached into a drawer and took something from it. He got up and walked round the desk, holding out to her a small box. She hesitated, surprised, wondering what it could be.

'But you haven't read them yet!' she protested. He ignored this and began on what seemed to her like a well-rehearsed speech.

'Now your job has come to an end, I have great pleasure in giving you this on behalf of the chapel and myself.' As Tansy tried to take in what he was saying he picked up her hand and placed the box in it. 'We wish you good luck in the future.'

Hurt beyond measure at the formality of his words, she cried out, 'But I haven't finished the list you gave me...'

He looked embarrassed and shifted his feet uncomfortably. 'It doesn't matter any more Tansy.' He hesitated. 'The tasks you have undertaken have served their purpose...'

Her eyes widened, her face growing red with rage. 'You mean you made up the list to keep me occupied after I was sacked from Courtenay House?' She paused, then went on. 'The list was one of your acts of charity!'

'No, no,' he protested. 'I don't mean that at all. Stephen Walters tells me he's offered you a position as pupil teacher next term?' He waited for her to speak and when she said nothing went on, 'You'll take it, won't you?'

At last she burst out, 'Me, follow Norah? Become a teacher? No, that's not for me, to be shut in all day with children who are too hungry and cold to be able to concentrate.' She could not be dissuaded from the thought that he had made up the job specially for her. 'And the work at Moon Court? Did you think of that just to keep me occupied too?'

The smile left his face, a sure sign that his patience was beginning to run out. 'Now you're being silly!' he exclaimed. 'Jenny Jones is to finish the list,' which only added to Tansy's hurt.

'Jenny? But she's having a baby in a few months' time! What will you do then?' She added sarcastically, 'If the list is so important who will finish it after Jenny's gone?' Now she saw a muscle twitch in his lower jaw and knew from experience that her remarks had hit home. 'You're ashamed of having me work for you, aren't you? Don't want to be associated with me any more? Are the old women gossiping about us in town?' He struggled to control his anger. 'It has nothing to do with what people think or making work when there was none. The study you've done on Moon Court will be an important part of the case we'll be presenting to the Local Board next week.'

He indicated the box she still held. 'Aren't you going to open it?' he asked sharply and she, recognising the finality of his words, opened the box and took out a silver chain from which hung a medallion. Upon its face was a raised figure, St Christopher, and on his back Jesus Christ. St Christopher, the saint for travellers! So he wanted her to go away did he. Still she wouldn't be placated. 'I don't want your bribe, Geoffrey Llewellyn! It's just an excuse to get rid of me. You don't want me working for you any more and haven't the courage to tell me.'

She hurled the medallion at him with all the force she could muster. Then she fled the room, stopping neither to collect her belongings from the hall or say goodbye to Aurelia. Instead she ran across the market and on through Steppes Meadow to climb the path to Puritan Pit. There she flung herself down on the stone altar where Geoffrey had forced her to tell him about Emma Vallance's watch. She lay there and cried out the despair which filled her heart. Not to see Geoffrey every day. Not to share in his work, to be part of his life. How dare he try and send her away when all she wanted was to be with him for the rest of her life.

⚜

A few days later Tansy met Aurelia Brown in town. The latter took up a belligerent stance in front of her.

'Not so high and mighty now, are we?' she sneered. 'Not cock of the walk now,' adding darkly, 'and there's another that's heading for a fall too avore long.'

Tansy gritted her teeth for fear of letting fly with the first words that came into her head and saying something she would most likely regret. Instead she asked coldly, 'Are you quite well, Aurelia?' And then, not waiting for a reply, hurried home to shut herself in her room. Downstairs, Eva worried over her daughter's pale face, her air of not caring what she looked like or what happened to her. For a week she listened to Tansy pacing the length of her room, back and forth, back and forth, then she climbed the two flights of stairs to demand of her, 'Isn't it time you stopped this, Tansy? Thought about your future? Do you want to follow Norah to college? If so, I'm sure your Father and I could manage somehow. We'd hoped to do something once she had finished.'

She was surprised at the vehemence of Tansy's reply. 'No, I don't want to follow Norah. And I don't want you to borrow money on my account.'

'Well then, we must look closer to home.' She sat on the bed and held out a hand which Tansy ignored. Eva sighed and went on. 'Had you thought of Widecombe's Emporium? You love clothes. Wouldn't you enjoy selling them? I should think that would be better than producing reports for Geoffrey, running his errands, doing work for which he gets the credit?' The challenge evoked a tirade from Tansy, 'I'm not working for Geoffrey Llewellyn any more as you well know. Was it your idea to give me the St Christopher?'

Eva looked up, surprised, and shook her head. Tansy laughed, a high-pitched laugh, verging on the edge of hysteria. 'I knew it!' she declared triumphantly. 'The gift wasn't from the chapel at all.' She went on fiercely. 'Where do you suggest I work? There's lots of positions in town for women with my training, aren't there? The steel works, the railway, the clay pits. I've tried them all and every position is held by a man!'

Eva, sensing the real reason for her distress, said gently, 'Your job with Geoffrey had to end sometime, Tansy. It's the first time a woman as young and attractive has ever worked with the minister. Aurelia Brown did all the work for Geoffrey's predecessor. I have worried about you. There's been talk...'

Tansy smiled in triumph. 'It was nothing to do with my work at all! But I'm not following after Norah now, whatever you say. Or going to work for Gertrude and Reuben Widecombe for a pittance and half a day off a week. I'd as soon go back to skivvying at Courtenay House. At least there I see the other side of the Hill, the side where the sun always shines. And I'd be working with friends.'

She left Eva to climb the Hill and stare at the field slope where she and Geoffrey had tobogganed down to collide at the bottom and kiss in the snow.

☙❧

Eva Drewe left the Post Office and toiled up the Hill to Courtenay House. The twins, with the aid of Sarah Webber's linseed oil, had at last shed winter coughs and returned to school in time for the Easter treats. Each week they were awarded coloured papers to stick into a cardboard lantern, a different colour for each aperture. Tansy missed them and hid herself away in the attic with a book.

Eva had called upstairs, 'Watch the counter for me Tansy. I'll not be long.' She had taken extra care with her appearance and looked smart in a chapel suit of navy with gloves and cloche hat to match. The door of Courtenay House was opened by Hetty Westcott.

'Why, 'tis Mrs Drewe. How's Tansy?'

'She's fine,' Eva replied, and hurried on, 'I wish to speak to Hilda Widecombe,' and when Hetty's mouth dropped open in surprise she corrected herself. 'I mean Mrs Vallance, I knew her as Hilda Widecombe when we shared a desk at school.'

Hetty nodded and preceded her across the hall to tap on the morning-room door, where Caroline Vallance sat over her household accounts. When she saw who it was she looked flustered but recovered enough to offer Eva a seat.

'Will you have some coffee, Mrs Drewe?' she asked, trying to establish a degree of formality. Eva shook her head.

'I prefer to stand,' she said. 'I'll come straight to the point.' She took a deep breath and plunged on. 'I've come to ask if there could be a position here for my Tansy?' She smiled grimly as a slow blush grew on Caroline Vallance's face.

'But I would have thought...' she stammered, 'after the most unfortunate affair of Emma's watch...' and she paused, her hands fluttering among the bills in front of her. Eva's eyes lit with a satisfied gleam.

'Yes,' she agreed, 'so indeed would I, after the treatment she received here. I too would have thought this is the last place she would have wanted to come back to,' and felt a glow of pleasure that at last she had been able to give vent to her feelings in the right quarter. 'But,' she continued, 'it seems we're both wrong. She's formed an attachment to Miss Emma and Master Harry and expressed a desire to come and work for them.' And, having accomplished the reason for her visit, she relaxed and waited to hear what Caroline Vallance would say. She now stood up, faced Eva and began, 'I must say, we have missed her, such a capable girl and she does get on extraordinarily well with my mother-in-law as well as Emma and Harry.' She drummed with her fingers on the edge of the table. 'I'll speak to Mr Vallance, see what he has to say. I'll let you know within the next few days.' She rang the bell for Hetty. 'Please show Mrs Drewe out, Westcott,' she said.

'Give our best to Tansy, Mrs Drewe.' Hetty opened the door, adding, 'Cook says to tell her she do miss her and her antics although Blodwen Evans is training up something real good.' Then Hetty added with a blush, 'My Jack's in hospital in London. Had a visit from the Queen herself. No more fighting for him what with his leg and that. We'm getting wed as soon as he comes home.' Eva wished her well and promised to tell Tansy and give her Cook's messages.

☙❧

A few days later a letter was delivered to the Post Office, addressed to Tansy.

'Who can it be from? 'Tisn't Norah's handwriting!' She looked up, puzzled, then her face brightened. 'P'raps it's from Martin!' Eva stood by anxiously waiting to see if it was from Caroline Vallance, while Tansy thought how good it would be to see Martin. She wondered what had happened to him, why he'd been absent from both chapel and the Big Oak for so long. She picked up a brass paper-knife, inserted it between envelope and flap and drew out a sheet of cream-coloured vellum. She looked up at her mother, startled.

''Tis from Mrs Vallance!' she exclaimed and quickly scanned the paper. 'They're offering me a job, Mother! Offering me Janet Luscombe's old job. Asking me if I wish to become Lady's Maid to Caroline and Emma!' She looked accusingly at Eva. 'Is this your doing, Mother?' Then she looked back at the missive. 'It goes on "I understand you're desirous of working at Courtenay House again." Did you tell them that?'

Eva smiled and nodded. 'Well you did say you'd as soon work at Courtenay House as anywhere!' Tansy's face was a study of mixed emotions. She went back to the letter, her hands shaking with excitement. 'If I accept I'm to have a room of my own!' She put her arm around her mother and waltzed her round the kitchen. 'Just imagine, no sharing tiny wardrobes, putting the light out when I'm ready. Reading in bed! And two dresses to be made to my measurements, not made over from hand-me-downs! Goodbye cap and apron!' she exclaimed and her eyes grew round. 'They've offered me three pounds a month! Twice what I got when I worked there as kitchen maid! Fancy that!'

Eva watched her with delight, pleased that her visit had produced such swift results. 'Then you'll take it?' she asked, and the look on Tansy's face told her the answer.

'Take it? Of course I'll take it! I've nothing to lose. I can pay my share towards Norah's college expenses once more and with dresses of my own I can save some of the money for myself. I shall never have to wear grey serge or the green suit ever again!'

Again she hugged Eva, who stood back from her and suggested, 'I should send a reply at once. You don't want to lose it for lack of a quick response, do you?' A look of relief filled her face at the solving of Tansy's problems, at least for the present.

Tansy's delight was complete when Charles Vallance sent Seth to collect her and her box the following Monday morning.

Cook welcomed Tansy back to her kitchen with open arms. She enveloped her in her ample bosom and planted great smacking kisses on her cheeks.

'I never thought to see 'ee back here again, Tansy Drewe. Thought you'd a gone and married that young Martin Webber as come here that time!'

Tansy laughed and denied he was ever likely to be her husband. 'He's no more mine than he was last year. He'm just a good friend and I love going out Staddens to ride Fairy and have tay wi' Sarah Webber.'

But Cook laughed at her and winked knowingly. 'I never knowed a young man and 'oman spend as much time together as you'd 'a used to and not git wed.' With that she began to hum Mendelssohn's 'Wedding March' and set about flattening a skirt of beef with a rolling pin.

Later, when Tansy was hanging her few clothes in the wardrobe, there came a soft tap at the door. She opened it to Blodwen, who hovered there looking shy and self conscious.

'Come in, Blodwen. Don't be shy. 'Tis the same Tansy. Just climbed the stairs.' She hugged the young girl and cleared a chair so she could sit and watch as Tansy set Geoffrey's scent and book on the bedside table, and her grandmother's hanky and shell box on the mantelpiece either side of a gilt mirror. She looked into the mirror, touched the scar put there by Janet Luscombe on the day she, Tansy, had dressed Miss Emma's hair for the first time. She returned to Blodwen.

Now I'm here in Janet Luscombe's old room I can't help wondering what happened to her. Have you heard?'

Blodwen nodded her dark wavy curls. 'Gone to work on her Uncle's farm at Bovey.' She hesitated then said, 'Cook says I'll get you into trouble if the Missus catches me in here!' Smiling, Tansy went and sat on the bed beside her. ''Tis one of the unspoken rules I believe but I'm sure you'll take care not to get caught, won't you?' Blodwen nodded again, her face relaxing, her eyes beginning to sparkle. 'It's good that you're here again.'

Tansy blurted out, ''Tis like a dream. A room of my own. Now tell me all the news! What's happening on Bowden Hill? But,' she added, 'keep your voice down.'

'You know that awful Jess Hallett?' Tansy's hand hovered over her hair as she practised fastening it into a coil on top of her head, 'Yes, go on...'

Blodwen's eyes grew big. 'He was hanging around the allotments when Dad and Tom Moore were working there the other night. What's more the baker told Dad he see'd him near The Passage the night of the Flood.'

Tansy put her arm around the small figure. 'Go on,' she encouraged her.

'Well Dad said he was sure he was up to no good. Thinks he's every reason to get even with Tom and Martin after they dumped 'un in the river that night at the Puritan Pit!'

Tansy remembered her own experience with Jess Hallett the day she went to meet Martin at the arcarde and he and his gang had tormented her. She felt Evan Williams was right to be concerned – Jess Hallett had never been known to do a good deed in his life.

'They'm going to plant tatties and onion sets Good Friday, Tansy. Everyone's going from Moon Court and Bowden Hill. Mam's taking the little 'uns and dinner and staying the day.' She looked wistful. 'I do miss home, Tansy.' Suddenly her eyes filled with tears. 'I know 'tis silly. Why 'tis only just the other side of the Hill but it could be the other side of the world for all I see of it.'

Tansy put her arms round her and comforted her. 'You can come up here whenever you can get away,' she said, then changed the subject to the forthcoming festival. 'It'll be like old times, you and me sitting with Hetty in the chapel balcony. Have you anything new?'

Blodwen looked down for a moment. 'Not properly new but Mam has made new drawers and shift and embroidered them with forget-me-nots.' She went on with a rush, 'With so many of us we has to take turns. Myfanwy has a frock, Poppy boots, Ivor and Emrys trousis 'cause the seats were wore out...' She shrugged away her own disappointment. Tansy thought of Gwynneth Evans struggling to see that each child had something new. The pity of it was no one would see the forget-me-nots, would they? She remembered the stigma of having nothing to wear to chapel on Easter Sunday. It had happened to her the year Norah needed school books. But Blodwen shrugged and rose from the chair.

'I must go down, there'll be the dishes to do.' And she added proudly, 'Owen has bought his own suit. Dad says he looks quite the dandy. And Tom Moore's William has boots for the first time so he'll be off to school after Easter.'

Tansy stopped worrying over what Jess Hallett was likely to do to the allotments and said, 'Would you like to borrow my new motoring hat?'

Blodwen looked excited for a moment but then her face fell. 'But what will you wear yourself?' she wanted to know, and Tansy laughed and said, 'Miss Emma's promised me her last year's straw so I can wear that and the blouse Norah left me when she went off to college!'

Blodwen's face glowed with pleasure at the thought of wearing a new hat, even if it wasn't hers and would have to be returned when Easter was over. Tansy took it from the wardrobe, set it on the dark curls and tied the ribbons under her chin. She led Blodwen to the mirror.

'It needs a touch more... primroses! Yes, they'd be fine. I'll trim it for you if'n you like!' She opened the door and looked out to make sure the coast was clear before shushing Blodwen away to the kitchen. She lingered in front of the mirror, wondering what Geoffrey's reaction would be when he discovered she had gone back to work at Courtenay House. She hugged herself with glee and awaited the moment he came knocking at the front door.

⁕

After Caroline Vallance had first seen Tansy in her new work dress, soft blue with tiny white flowers on it and a tucked bodice which set off her neat waist, and noticed how it clung to the soft curves of her body, she commented to Maude Westaway that she must find a new dressmaker for the servants' livery.

'Martha Bidgood's forgotten servants' dresses should be serviceable, long lasting and, above all, decent!' Her friend laughed and raised an eyebrow. 'Attracting the Master's eye, is she? Handsome young thing with that colouring – need to keep an eye on her. Watch her when my Christopher's about! Don't want any slip there, do we?' Both fell silent, contemplating their plans for uniting the two families in both marriage and business.

While they talked and sipped tea in the sitting-room Tansy shortened Miss Emma's new bicycle skirt in her room on the second floor, which overlooked the front steps and part of the drive. When she heard the sound of wheels she would rush to her window, never tiring of the novelty.

So today, as soon as she heard wheels on the gravel, she laid aside the tweed to peer through the net curtains and, as soon as she glimpsed red hair and saw the long, lean figure descend from the trap, she ran from her room, along the landing and down two flights of stairs to arrive at the door the moment the bell rang. She tried to stop the pounding of her heart, smoothed her dress and prayed her hair was tidy. She opened the door and Geoffrey Llewellyn stared back at her, noticing the air of confidence that exuded from her, how the blue dress clashed with the blazing emerald eyes.

'So what I've heard is true,' he said, his voice tinged with impatience. 'You have come back!' She nodded and held out her hands to take his coat. 'Do you not want to make the best use of your intelligence? Use your new skills?'

At the edge of sarcasm in his voice she spoke up in her own defence. 'How dare you criticise me!' she said, looking him straight in the eye, 'after sacking me. At least here I've a room of my own, better wages and position!' Her words smacked of a challenge. 'At least the work I do here is every bit as useful as addressing envelopes for you!'

He drew in his breath as if she'd struck him and the familiar movement of muscle in lower jaw began, but before he could retaliate, Charles Vallance appeared at the door of his study.

'What's going on?' he demanded. Then when he saw it was Geoffrey, he advanced across the black and white floor. 'Ah Llewellyn, come in. I was expecting you. I want to know how you got on with the Board.'

He turned to Tansy and said, 'Have tea brought up Drewe, please.'

She relayed the message to Cook and went back upstairs to her sewing, a smile playing around the curve of her mouth. She was pleased that Geoffrey had looked so upset at finding her here at Courtenay House once more. He obviously thought she was throwing away all the training and experience he'd given her. If she'd have accepted the position Stephen Walters had offered he'd have felt justified in ending her involvement with chapel affairs. Yes, she thought, that was it. The fact that she'd taken what to him would appear to be a subservient role instead of putting into practice all the principles he'd tried to engender in her. Him and his John Ruskin, she snorted. Well, if it maddened him to think she'd come back to work twelve hours a day for a low wage then he'd have to come and rescue her. Offer her... what? And her hands were suddenly still as she dreamt of Geoffrey storming into Charles Vallance's study to announce that he'd come to take her away. To offer her something better, like being a minister's wife – and the thought of all that entailed quickened the pulse in her breast and brought hot blood rushing to her face.

Her dream was interrupted by a whistling on the servant's tube and when she put her ear to it Miss Emma asked, 'Have you finished the skirt, Tansy? Christopher's coming to take me for a ride this afternoon. Quick as you can.' She came down to earth with a bump.

✤ Chapter Twenty-Four ✤

Easter

March came in like a lion, with gales and torrential rain which washed newly planted seeds from the allotments on Wolborough Hill, but went out like a lamb with bursts of hot sun which encouraged chapel members to leave coats and jackets at home. Tansy sat in the middle of the row of servants from Courtenay House in a new cream skirt, made by her mother, topped by Norah's blouse. Hetty Westcott wore pale grey linen in which, she confided to Tansy, she was to be married. On Tansy's other side sat Blodwen, her dark Welsh looks set off by Tansy's old green suit and new cream velour trimmed with fresh primroses and tied under her chin. At the end of the row was Stephen Howell, resplendent in the uniform he had worn to drive the family to church.

The Vallance family sat in their new spring outfits in the front row and Tansy felt a surge of envy at the sight of the ruby and gold watch gleaming on magenta worn by Emma. She longed for a keepsake of her own to wear in chapel. She regretted throwing the St Christopher back at Geoffrey and wondered if she should go and call on him, ask him to give it back. Her cheeks flushed at the thought of it and she put her hands up to cool them. Her sudden movement caught Geoffrey's attention as he climbed the steps to the pulpit. He looked at the straw hat, set at an angle on Tansy's curls, and thought she looked adorable. He began to arrange his notes as the strains of 'When I behold the wondrous cross' came to an end.

'There is no wealth but life,' Geoffrey began. 'I quote from John Ruskins's *The Veins of Wealth* written in 1862, but as always as much applicable to today as when it was written.'

For once, Tansy's mind wandered. She looked across the void to the place Martin Webber had made his own. She hadn't seen him since the flood, he hadn't been at market nor at the Big Oak and she missed the warm solid comfort of his presence.

Geoffrey's voice came to her. 'The farmer who cuts his hay at the right time, the shipwright who drives his bolt well home in sound wood...' Tansy made up her mind to take the train to Lustleigh on her next Sunday off to visit Staddens and find out why Martin had stopped visiting Newton. Having made the decision, she gave the sermon her full attention.

'The housewife who takes good care of her furniture in the parlour, and guards against all waste in her kitchen, are all political economists in the true and final sense, adding continually to the well-being of the nature to whom they belong.'

Geoffrey finished and Edward Drewe announced the final hymn and collection. Blodwen reminded Tansy that there were to be guests for lunch and they hurried down from the gallery and crossed the lobby where Geoffrey greeted his flock.

'You look very pretty, Tansy. Are you happy to be back in service?' Tansy stuck her nose high in the air and said, 'Perfectly, thank you', then enquired on a serious note. 'What was the result of the meeting of the Local Board?' He asked her to wait while he greeted a group of elderly parishioners as they left. Then he came back to her and explained, 'Ben Brealley has been ordered to cap the well in Moon Court, and pay for piped water and closets to be installed. He's very angry!' They both laughed. Geoffrey added, 'You can't stop helping people now, Tansy. You must try and get the hours changed at Courtenay House. Now you're one of the servants you could talk to them, ask for their support.' But she looked doubtful. 'Do you mean try and get them to go on strike?' and when he nodded, continued, 'I know what result that would bring! The Vallances would give us all the sack and get in others to do our work!' But when he pressed her hand and suggested she try talking to the servants first then broaching the subject with her employers as and when the opportunity occurred, reluctantly she promised to bear it in mind.

'How is Martin Webber?' Geoffrey enquired. 'I haven't seen him at chapel for some time.' Tansy shook her head and replied quite truthfully that she really didn't know.

'It seemed to me that you and he were made for each other,' he said, adding, 'You must bring him back.' He paused. 'Let that be your contribution to chapel 'affairs'.' At this assumption a rage began in Tansy and threatened to explode.

Now he turned to Kezia Chard and the sight of the old lady Martin had rescued from Widow Bowden's bull brought back his presence in a way no amount of words from Geoffrey could ever have done. It brought back visits to Staddens, the walk when he'd put out the chimney fire at Foxworthy, and reminded her of the day he taught her to ride Fairy, first side-saddle then later astride like a man. That had been the day she'd fallen through the ice at Haytor quarry and nearly drowned.

Immediately, she left the chapel and hurried to the Big Oak to lean against the trunk. She noticed the beginning of yellow shoots on the lower branches and missed Martin. Shutting her eyes she saw him clearly, diving naked into Becca Pool. Unaccountably she wished him here beside her. Longed for his warmth and steady purpose. He hadn't Geoffrey's fire and ability to inspire all around him, she thought, but nothing could take away from his strength and calm temperament.

When she called in at the Post Office on her way back to Courtenay House there was a letter waiting for her from Norah. 'We're so looking forward to Geoffrey's visit after Easter,' she wrote. 'Helen's family have been kind enough to ask him to join us at Rochester.' And further on it read, 'What's all this about you going back to Courtenay House? You won't conquer the world up there, will you?' This made Tansy so angry that she tore the letter into shreds, carried them to the top of 148 steps and there scattered them to the four winds.

✤ Chapter Twenty-Five ✤

Teignhead

Sarah Webber was surprised to see Tansy when she appeared in the doorway of Staddens on the last Sunday in April. But she smiled and bade her to come in and sit a while, and waited to hear what had brought her. She didn't have to wait long. As soon as they'd exchanged news of Courtenay House and Tansy had told her to expect a visit from Beatrice Vallance, who was expected at Whit, she blushed and asked, 'Is Martin about?'

Sarah kept her waiting a moment or two while she went to the pantry for a basket and began filling it with tatties, carrots and onions. She straightened, then stood where she could see Tansy's face.

'He'm gone, my maid.' Sarah was rewarded by the disappointment which grew on her face.

'Gone, Mrs Webber? Gone where?' Sarah took pity on her for her long journey and explained. 'Gone out Teignhead these past eight weeks.'

Tansy felt a sense of relief to know that there was a good reason for his absence from chapel and the Big Oak. A reason why he hadn't been in touch with her for so long. 'I wondered if 'ee was sick, that's all,' she said, to cover her embarrassment.

'I'm getting ready to go out there dreckly,' Sarah said, as she fetched sugar, tea and flour, and added it to the basket. She wrapped a cake and pasties in a cloth, and looked up. 'I expect you'd like to see his place, wouldn't 'ee?'

Tansy, startled by the idea, was at once filled with a need to see Martin again. Why would I be here, she thought, if I wasn't meant to go? She nodded and accepted.

'Yes,' she said, 'I'd like to come with 'ee. You'll not be back later than eight, will 'ee?' Sarah shook her head and laid clean, ironed shirts on top of the basket. Amos had harnessed Tom in the trap and as they moved off down the track he shouted after them, 'Tell him when he's finished with this foolishness he'm welcome to come home.'

Sarah called back, 'Won't 'ee change 'ee's mind and come along of us?' But he turned and stalked away in the opposite direction and Sarah sighed and whipped up the pony. Soon they were passing through hedges where the green sheen of early spring was beginning to show, willows hung draped with yellow and everyone they met shouted a greeting. When they got to Chagford, Sarah drove up past the church and they entered a hinterland of hamlets and farms where dogs barked and ran at them, escorting them past each property. At Fernworthy they took the track out onto the open moor and Sarah slowed Tom to a walk. Sheep stared at them as they passed and Sarah bent a serious gaze on Tansy.

''Ee won't say nuthin' to Martin 'ee doesn't mean?' Tansy shook her head and promised, wondering at the same time exactly what she meant and yet fearing to find out.

When they reached the clapper the sound of axe on wood came to them over the clean air. Sarah took Tom from between the shafts and led him across the stone slabs while Tansy carried the basket. Now Moss leapt the wall of the courtyard and ran, barking furiously at them, wriggling along the track in obvious delight. He jumped around them until they were penned like sheep in his circling. Now Martin appeared to open the gate for them. He held Sarah in a close quick embrace, then turned to where Tansy stood, uncertain of her welcome.

'I hadn't thought to see you here!' he said, his words a reproach. 'Has Geoffrey Llewellyn no work for you today?'

She flushed and retorted, all greetings banished by his sarcasm, 'I don't work for him any more.' Relinquishing the basket to Sarah, who disappeared through the porch and into the ugly stone house, she continued, 'I've gone back to Courtenay House.'

'Well, that does surprise me! Thought you was off to see the world!'

She found herself trying to justify her actions, his last proposal coming back to taunt her. 'Lady's maid to Caroline and Emma Vallance I am!' She stuck out her chin in an effort to restore her injured pride. 'Three pounds a month and all found.'

Now he laughed, this was more the Tansy he knew, and said, in spite of himself, ''Tis good to see you, Tansy.'

'I've missed you from chapel,' she responded. 'I mean, we've all missed you.'

He, not taken in by her change of direction, asked, 'Who else has missed me then?' And she, not wanting to mention Geoffrey again said, 'Cook was asking after you only t'other day.' She blushed, remembering the exact words Cook had uttered about she and Martin getting married. He dropped his teasing tone and, taking her arm, turned her toward him and dropped a gentle kiss on her cheek.

'I'm glad you decided to come.' He hesitated then rushed on, 'I've missed coming to market,' adding, 'Sometimes it's that lonely that I sing just so I hears a voice.'

In an expression of sympathy she replied, 'Well, I'm here now and I want to see everything.' She took his hand in hers, felt him wince, turned it over and touched the blisters crossing his palm. He took his hand away and showed her the leat which fed a pot well by the front door.

'You've no chickens? They'd do well here with all this grass to scratch. There must be hundreds of worms.'

He laughed at her ignorance and retorted, 'I've no time to keep an eye on fowls when Master Reynard's out stealing whatever he can. At night I stay awake and guard the sheep.' He picked up his gun from inside the porch and, stepping clear of the building, took aim and fired, sending a row of cans tumbling from the linhay roof.

'Then when do you sleep?' she wanted to know, and he shrugged. 'Take it whenever I can, after a meal, out on the Moor, on my feet sometimes. I'm going to buy a cob come the Chagford Sales in summer. Make it easier to cover the ground.'

Now Sarah appeared at the porch opening. 'Come you in. I've made dinner.' They crossed the cobbles and entered the living-room. They sat at a freshly scrubbed table where Sarah had laid out pasties and mugs of cider and while they ate Sarah told Martin the price of rams at Newton Market and Tansy looked about her. She noted the alcove full of tools, hooks, a scythe, stone breaker and large pincers, the purpose for which she could only guess. The other alcove which flanked the peat fire held a bed covered in rough blankets and work clothes, and while she struggled with the huge chunks of beef and potatoes Martin watched her, never taking his eyes from her.

'I caught Adam and Fanny Luscombe courtin' in the tallet week afore last,' Sarah was saying. ''Tis likely there'll be a wedding come autumn.'

Martin nodded, then asked, 'When be Feyther coming out?'

Sarah shook her head. 'Give 'un time, Martin. He won't be able to keep away much longer!' She hesitated and Tansy waited to see if she would deliver Amos' message but all she said was, ''Tis his pride won't let 'un come but I reckon he'll be out avore round up.'

Tansy rose and offered to wash the dishes but Sarah wouldn't allow it. 'No, my beauty, you go with Martin. 'Ee wants to see lambs, don't 'ee?'

'Lambs!' Tansy exclaimed. You didn't tell me there were lambs already!'

He laughed and led the way to the shippon where a ewe stood guarding twins. 'The first,' he said proudly, 'born three nights ago. First of the three ewes I bought from Chagford. In August I'm getting a ram then my flock will start in earnest.'

Tansy admired the little creatures, leaning over the hurdle to touch them, only to find Martin pulling her away. 'Don't touch 'em Tansy, lest the mother rejects 'em. They doesn't like a strange smell on their coats.' But he smiled as he regarded the first fruits of his labour and the lambs ran back to the ewe to suck her teats and waggle tails in a shiver of ecstasy.

He left the shippon and as she followed she noticed how the clothes hung on his large frame. A feeling of tenderness began to grow and for the first time Geoffrey Llewellyn didn't intrude on her thoughts.

'I'll show you the fold, 'tis up here.' Together they climbed heather and grass to where stone walls enclosed a large area.

'See this opening, 'tis just large enough for one sheep to pass through. When it's full they number a hundred. That's what I aim to do. Fill it.' She hugged his arm in congratulation while he led her across a newly-cleared patch of earth, a pile of stones and bracken evidence of the effort needed. 'Here I be goin' to plant cabbage and turnip for the cow.' Tansy thought of Evan Williams and the plot high above Wolborough Hill, where Tom Moore fought spring gales and Benjamin Brealley to establish allotments for the poor.

'Come on, Martin, let's climb to where the leat begins.' He took her hand in his, leapt across tussocks and bog cotton until the leat ended in a stream and finally a huge wet patch of moss, from which bubbled a spring. She bent, ankle deep, to dabble her hands. 'Wherever does it come from?' she asked.

'From underground,' he explained. 'The rain feeds the earth and it gives it back in springs like this.' They climbed on past a tinner's hut to the top of Little Varracombe and found a fresh breeze to cool them after their climb.

'Do you remember when we went to Haytor?' he asked, pulling her close to his side. As she nodded he continued, 'I showed you the Teign going down to the sea? Well, just now you saw where it begins!'

'You know so much!' she exclaimed, then broke free to dance away across the heather and back. 'You saved my life that day...' and her thoughts went back to the way he'd warmed her body with his and led her back to Staddens. She turned away from him, afraid of betraying her feelings, and suddenly he turned her back to face him.

'Why did you come?' he demanded, his face dark with passion, his lips full, his eyes alight. Tansy, so determined always in her actions, so sure in her speech, stuttered and stammered as she tried to explain the compulsion that had led her first to Staddens, then here.

'I missed you at chapel.' She paused. 'I waited at the Oak, you never came' She went on with a rush, 'I thought you might be sick.' Martin turned away from her to start back and she saw that he was smiling.

They retraced their footsteps and as they reached the linhay heard the hiss of milk in pail and found Sarah stripping the last creamy liquid from the cow's udders. She got up, shading her eyes to make them out against the sun streaming in.

'I'm going to start a stew, Martin. It'll take me an hour or so then us must be getting back.' She went into the house, taking Moss with her. Tansy and Martin lingered in the sun-filled court, not touching and yet wanting above all to release the tension which had steadily grown between them.

'So what do you think of Teignhead?' he asked gently. She looked across the valley towards Fernworthy where sun and shadow moved in an ever-changing pattern coloured brown, green and now mauve, where patches of early heather grew.

''Tis wonderful, Martin, 'tis wonderful.' She turned to him and he bent and kissed her, at first gently, then more urgently, until she felt her mouth open to his. Then his hand began to caress her body, following its gentle curves, returning to her breasts which swelled in response to his work-roughened hands.

'Let's go in the linhay,' he begged, and she rose like someone in a dream and let him lead her inside and lay her down on a pile of straw. He removed his jacket and trousers and eased them beneath her, kissing her again. She, knowing she should resist him, undid her blouse and allowed him to take her nipples into his mouth and caress them until her body came alive in a way she had never experienced before. Now he removed her skirt and she threw off her shift and drawers in an ecstasy of anticipation. They rocked back and forth until her pleasure turned to pain. Tansy's eyes flew open.

'Don't,' she gasped. 'You're hurting me,' and instantly he withdrew, laying her back gently. 'I've waited for you so long,' he said. 'I can wait a while longer.' He dressed quickly and helped her to put on her clothes. When they were done she stood up and again he kissed her gently.

'I'll always love you, Tansy Drewe,' he said. 'But don't come here again unless you come to stay.' He left her and, whistling for Moss, set off up the hill away from her. She watched him go till Sarah came to tell her it was time to leave. Still she moved like a sleepwalker, turning once to look back at Martin who stood, Moss at his side, silhouetted against the rise of the moor.

Neither Tansy nor Sarah spoke till they reached Moreton, where she was to catch the train back to Newton. When she turned to thank her for the ride Sarah's face softened and she bent swiftly and placed a kiss on Tansy's surprised cheek.

'One day,' she said, 'you'll come to know your heart, learn as I did what's really for the best.'

She slapped Tom's back and was gone and Tansy wondered if she knew what had taken place in the linhay. Knew perhaps and approved? And as she sat in her corner of the carriage, watching dusk fill fields and valleys, she waited for regret to overtake her. The sudden realisation of what she had done. That was what she had wanted from Geoffrey at Christmas when they'd been alone at The Manse. Her instinct had told her then of her needs, today it had been her body that had issued the commands. How could she have given herself to Martin when it was Geoffrey she loved? Still no regrets came, only an exultant feeling of fulfilment. She left the train, climbed the hill to Courtenay House and went straight to her room instead of visiting the kitchen as was her usual habit.

She filled the china basin with cold water, stripped and began to wash, but she felt again Martin's hands on her breasts and thighs, firm, strong, demanding, and longed that one day it would be Geoffrey who would want her, give her his body and mind in such ecstasy as she had experienced with Martin. Slowly she put on her nightgown and lay for hours, puzzling over what had happened, falling into an uneasy sleep as pink coloured the sky beyond her window.

⚜ Chapter Twenty-Six ⚜

Mafeking

Letters continued to arrive for Tansy from Norah, extolling the beauty of cherry orchards white with blossom, fields full of hops climbing poles and horse bus rides to The Leather Bottle at Cobham where Dickens had drunk with friends. She also wrote of supper parties where she and Geoffrey sang 'Madam will you walk?'

From him came a print of the high altar of Canterbury Cathedral, entitled the 'Death of Thomas Becket', and on the back he'd written 'Keep up the good work. I'll expect results when I get back.'

Tansy snorted as she struggled to keep her mistresses' wardrobes in immaculate condition. She was up just after five in the morning to put away dresses and jewellery from the night before, to clean the hearth, brush the carpet and put aside items for mending. At half past six she would snatch tea and toast with Cook and Blodwen, who were about to begin their day's work. Next she would help Caroline and Emma to dress, then, while they breakfasted, she dusted and polished tables and made lists of potions for Caroline to buy in town.

'Miss Emma's always going to tennis parties now and the Missus to teas and dinner,' she told her mother. 'So how that woman in Chicago that Geoffrey told me about gets her servants to do all that in eight hours a day beats me. Takes me all my time to keep my ladies looking spotless, working till 'tis time to go to bed! How Geoffrey thinks I've time to wage a campaign for shorter hours and work from morn to night... well!' Eva clucked and tried to soothe Tansy as she mended lace for Caroline Vallance and generally helped her daughter keep up with things.

'Just you wait till I sees Geoffrey Llewellyn!' Tansy muttered as she brushed gowns and pressed creases from muslin. The only relief came when Miss Emma set off on her bicycle and Tansy was asked to chaperone her. They would follow the river path through Bradley Woods to the mill and back, or take the lane through Netherton and Stoke to Shaldon. There they removed boots and stockings to paddle in the river or watch Seine fishermen trawling for salmon on the tide. These outings, as well as the joy of having a room of her own, acted as compensation for the long hard hours of work. It was ironic that, now she was free to read all night, she usually fell asleep from exhaustion the moment her head touched the pillow. Although Tansy was forbidden to have visitors in her room, Hetty slipped quietly through her door one evening to tell her Jack's plans for their belated honeymoon.

'We'm going to his Mother's at Torquay so he can try for work there. They Mauser bullets have done so much damage to his leg Army don't want 'un no more. He hopes to get work in the gardens on the sea front. Us'll have to see.' Tansy envied her future, the security of loving and being loved in return. How long, she wondered, would she have to wait before her own path was clear, her heart sure.

She had heard of Geoffrey's return and told Hetty, 'He might as well live on the moon for all I see of him now!' And when Hetty left she fell into a daydream where Geoffrey and Martin fought each other in mountainous seas while she sat on a rock awaiting the outcome.

The next day there came a light tap on her door and Blodwen, looking hot and bothered, called through the door, 'Can I come in, Tansy? Is it all right?' Tansy, knowing it would mean trouble for both of them if they were caught, smiled and gave her a hug, drawing her into the room and placing her in her own chair by the fire.

'I was up home yesterday and Mam says allotments was wrecked last Saturday night!'

Tansy put down her sewing to exclaim, 'Oh no, not after all that hard work! Who did it? Not Jess Hallett again?'

Blodwen, her eyes large with the enormity of it, told her, 'Mam says Ben Brealley went to Farmer Cull to get them turned off and he refused, said Dadda and Tom Moore and the rest of 'em weren't doing any harm. Then they say Ben Brealley paid Jess Hallett to smash marrow plants, rip up beans and peas. Owen found a billycock hat. He's sure 'tis Jess's'.

'Wants locking up, that villain,' Tansy exclaimed, 'along o' that Ben Brealley, and him chairman of the Local Board too!' She thought of the hours spent on clearing the ground, burning weeds, planting seeds and climbing up and down the highest, steepest hill in Newton, and now nothing to show for it. 'What about the police? Didn't anyone go for them?' she asked.

Blodwen shook her head. 'They was all down The Newfoundland sorting out a fight between some sailors and a group of Chudleigh men. Not one of 'em came to help. 'Tis all been hushed up. Dadda says the police say without witnesses they can't bring charges.'

Blodwen opened the door a crack to make sure the coast was clear, then slipped from the room, leaving Tansy fuming with frustration at what had happened. She thought of Geoffrey who'd been away singing with Norah in some sitting-room instead of being here to support Evan Williams. 'Tis all very well preaching sermons, she thought, but words on their own just aren't enough. It was action that was needed. She'd wait and see what he did about it when he found out what had happened.

※※※

'Mafeking's been relieved,' Edward shouted to Eva as theirs and every other telegraph in England jiggled out the long-awaited news relayed by the Reuters news agency. An exhilaration equalling nothing experienced before filled the hearts of every man, woman and child. As the mood of exultation swept through the land people poured out of factories, offices and shops to fill the streets of every town, city and village, intent on celebrating the freeing of a small group of Britons a long way over the sea. The Government dealt with it the best way they knew how by declaring 19 May 1900 a public holiday.

Robert and James rushed home from school, faces flushed with excitement. 'We'm not to go tomorrow!' Robert declared and James chimed in, ''Tis Maffkin Day!' - then paused and a puzzled expression filled his face - 'What's Maffkin, Father?' Edward sighed and did his best to explain. 'There's going to be fireworks in the park,' Robert shouted. 'Please may we go?'

Eva laughed and compromised. 'We'll see. You can go but only if you behave yourselves during the day!'

At Courtenay House, Master Harry, home from school, lined up soldiers and canons in victory order on the morning-room table and extracted a promise from his father that he would take him to Courtenay Park in the Lanchester. 'I wish Mr Llewellyn was here now, he could have helped me fire the salute.'

Charles patted his son on the back and told him, 'The 2nd Devons are due home tomorrow so perhaps you'll see some real soldiers.'

The next day each member of Courtenay House found a reason to visit town, reporting back on the portraits of Redvers Bullers and Robert Baden-Powell, rescuer and rescued, displayed on the outside of the Town Hall. The former's heavy jowls were decorated with a moustache under a plumed helmet, the latter clean-shaven in the uniform of a newly promoted Major General, in acknowledgement of his brilliant defence of the South African outpost.

Factory sirens sounded, steam whistles blew from engines in railway sidings, and by late afternoon crowds gathered at St Leonard's Tower where the Silver Band warmed up instruments for the night ahead. When they struck up 'Rule Britannia' the crowd began to sing and when the music changed to 'Goodbye Dolly Gray' the volume swelled until the sound reached the kitchen at Courtenay House.

Even Cook decided this was an occasion not to be missed and began on her own toilet. She put on a full-length black taffeta gown, which smelt strongly of mothballs. Next she added strings of jet beads which sparkled and swung on her large bosom. She quelled Blodwen's giggles with one look and sent her to fetch her feather boa.

'You may laugh, my maid,' she exploded, 'but 'tis good to have a best black. It do come in so handy for funerals and weddin's. Real handsome, ain't it?' She appealed to Tansy, who watched, fascinated.

'I never knowed you go out of a night afore!' Hetty exclaimed as she prepared to leave on Jack's arm.

'Last time was Jubilee so 'tis time I went out again,' Cook declared stoutly. 'Not going to miss this celebration neither,' and she fastened her hat with two dangerous-looking pins and threw the feather boa around her wrinkled neck with a flourish.

'How're you going to get back, Cook?' Blodwen wanted to know, but Cook just stuck out a stubborn chin.

'I'll face that when the time comes,' she said. 'Now I'm going down to the Railway Arms for a glass of gin while I waits for the band.' Grasping a stick from the hall-stand, she set off out through the garden and down the drive, with Blodwen hopping about her like a tug round an ocean liner.

Upstairs Charles Vallance tried to persuade Beatrice to accompany them in the automobile. 'We're going as far as the Tower, then back to the park for the fireworks. You won't have to get out, just sit and watch what's going on.'

But she shook her head and said, 'One journey a day is quite enough for me at my age, Charles. I shall stay in my room with a book and a pot of tea. It's a lot of fuss and bother over a lot of Dutch settlers and tribes of fuzzy wuzzies.'

But this time her son didn't agree with her. 'You're wrong, Mama,' he objected. 'It's really about land and gold. The war has made many people rich in this country. We've done well at the Mill too.'

Beatrice ignored him and immediately commandeered the Lanchester for the following day in order to visit Biddy Pidsley. This sent Caroline into a rage and she banged brushes so hard onto her dressing-table that perfume bottles rattled and spilt their contents.

'Last year it was the carriage,' she fumed, 'this year it's the Lanchester. I had planned a trip to Williams & Cox,' she snorted – but Charles just shrugged.

'She's only here for two weeks, Caroline. Surely you can make allowances. It will give her such pleasure to ride in the automobile.' He went through to his dressing-room for cuff-links. While Caroline fastened them for him she struggled with her disappointment. She would not have the joy of driving the length of the promenade in Torquay, and not be able to take tea at the Pavilion with Maude. She loved every minute of these outings, from the moment of arrival when Stephen Howell, resplendent in blue, opened the door, assisting her to alight, to the moment of departure when a large crowd would have gathered to admire the elegant machine.

'Come, Caroline, we must say goodnight to Mama before we leave.' They hurried downstairs to find Beatrice asking querulously for Tansy, who came at the run. 'I want to go to Lustleigh tomorrow. Be ready at nine, Drewe!' she commanded, and no amount of protests by Caroline or explanations that Tansy's position had changed and that she was needed at home would prevail. 'We'll call in at Staddens on the way back,' Beatrice added, and Tansy's heart skipped a beat. Since her visit to Teignhead with Sarah she had thought constantly of Martin and the moments in the linhay. She had worried about servants' talk of bodies meeting and producing babies. She had tried to put him from her mind – and failed. What if she had fallen.

'Yes, M'am,' she said, dropping a curtsey. 'I'll be ready.' She watched as the Holy Terror slowly mounted the stairs, holding her skirt with both hands, her back straight as a rod. Tansy turned to Caroline who stood staring after her mother-in-law with loathing, and took the opportunity to plead with her. 'May I go down to the Tower, M'am? We can hear the band playing from the kitchen.'

Caroline nodded, extracting a promise. 'Don't be later than ten and keep an eye on young Blodwen Williams. Oh, and before you go leave out my grey linen for tomorrow.'

She'd hardly finished before Tansy was gone, out through the Servants' Hall, leaping down 148 steps to call for Rosemary and Johnnie. When they reached Courtenay Street people were pouring from public houses and terraces to swell the crowd. Linking arms they swept along towards the station where a platoon of the 2nd Devons had just arrived. The officer in charge, a weather-beaten young man with moustache and cane, marshalled his men behind the band. They marched along the road, turning smartly into the park where, rifles at the slope, they marched and counter-marched across the grass to the strains of 'The Soldiers of the Queen'. Robert and James joined a squad of boys who walked raggedly behind, union jacks against their shoulders.

The band ascended the stand and the platoon of soldiers were dismissed to greet families and friends in a great show of hugging and kissing. Couples walked about and when Tansy saw Miss Emma and Christopher Westaway kissing beneath the cherry tree she felt a pang of such yearning for Geoffrey and hurried about looking for him without success.

The sun went down behind Wolborough Hill in a haze of red and the North Star appeared in the azure of oncoming night. Tansy bought the twins ices from the Hokey Pokey Man and waited for the firework display to begin. At last a knot of men advanced on a roped-off piece of grass and there was a flash of light, a whoosh and crack as the first rocket climbed into the sky. Robert and James suddenly reached for Tansy's comforting hands as red, blue and green lights announced the ignition of Roman Candles, gold and silver showers lighting up the town as the crowd roared its approval. Edward appeared with Evan Williams and held the little ones shoulder-high for a better view while Master Harry jumped up and down on the back seat of the Lanchester and Charles and Caroline held hands under cover of a picnic rug in a rare mood of mutual affection. Cook and Blodwen were nowhere to be seen.

The show ended with a set piece of Queen Victoria, evoking three cheers which grew into applause for the returning soldiers, General Buller, Robert Baden-Powell and, last but by no means least, for the men who had set up the fireworks. Suddenly the park began to empty and Tansy looked for Blodwen, noticing the station clock read eleven thirty. She hurried uphill, hoping against hope that they were already there.

'Come on, my beauty.' Seth stood by the gates, a lamp in his hand. 'You'm the last. I'm just going to close the gates and lock up.' When she asked about Cook and Blodwen he laughed and told her, 'Brought home by the Master, so you don't need to fret. Both the worse for drink too!'

She ran up the drive and into the kitchen where Blodwen, hiccuping and giggling, tried to get Cook out of her best black. Tansy didn't like the look of Cook's high colour and quick breathing and went for the sal volatile. After she'd forced a spoonful down Cook's throat she and Seth made an effort to get her to the door and upstairs to bed, but as fast as they dragged her, so she resisted them.

'Leave me,' she protested. 'Leave me here by the stove in the warm.' She waved Seth away. Tansy shook her head at him.

'She'll be all right, Seth. Off you go. Blodwen and I'll manage somehow.'

After a great struggle, during which they all ended up on the floor, they managed to divest Cook of her dress, undo her corsets and, with the aid of cushions from the morning-room, build a nest where she lay snoring gently until morning.

❧

The next day, when the Lanchester turned into the track at Staddens, Beatrice fixed Tansy with her steely eyes. 'Still seeing that young farmer, Tansy?'

Tansy blushed and protested, 'We'm friends still, Mrs Vallance, M'am.' She wondered if what had happened between them could still be described as friendship. 'He's his own sheep run up above Chagford now. Keeping Dartmoor long wools,' she added, surprised at the sense of pride it gave her to tell Beatrice this piece of news.

'I shall have to have a word with him,' she said. 'Can't let a girl like you slip away.' The noise of the automobile sent hens flying in all directions, bringing Sarah out of the house to see what was to do.

'Why, 'tis Mrs Vallance!' Sarah declared. 'Come you in and have a dish of tay. I've a tipsy cake setting in the larder just beggin' to be eaten!'

When they were seated by the fire the Holy Terror began her usual inquisition. 'Tansy tells me your son Martin has gone away?' She wiped jam and cream from her mouth and waited for Sarah's answer.

'Rented a sheep farm in Teignhead,' she replied. 'Us do miss 'un about the place but 'twas his heart's desire.'

'Has he gone there on his own?' Beatrice enquired. 'Must be too far to travel there and back each day surely?'

Sarah sighed and looked past Beatrice to where Tansy sat fiddling with her skirt and avoiding Sarah's eye.

'That's right, M'am. Waited for a young 'oman to make up her mind to wed 'un,' she paused to wipe her hands on her apron. 'When she wouldn't say a definite yay or nay he went, didn't want to miss his chance. He's been gone these last twelve weeks.'

Beatrice rose and announced, 'Like to see your son's place. Is it far beyond Chagford?'

Tansy felt a rising panic at the thought of what Martin would expect of her should she turn up again. His last words rang in her head. 'Don't come ever again, Tansy. Not unless you come to stay.' But all was well as Sarah extolled the difficulties of getting to Teignhead, ''Tis possible to get to Fernworthy in a trap. Then you'd have to walk.' She looked down at Beatrice's neat black shoes. 'Have to wear boots, the track's a mite too rough for shoes.' She shook her head, then brightened. 'But my Martin'd be most honoured by a visit from 'ee to be sure.'

Beatrice tapped her lorgnette while Tansy held her breath and tried to think of something to say that would dissuade the Holy Terror from embarking on such a journey.

''Tis obvious we can't go today. I must be back to fetch Charles from the Mill. Perhaps next week would be possible, we could go in the gig.' She turned to Tansy. 'Do you know the way?' and Tansy, feeling Sarah's eyes keenly upon her, had no course but to admit that she did.

'I've been there but the once, Ma'm but, yes, I'm sure I could find the way.'

It was with relief that she watched as Sarah invited Beatrice to look at her garden. Tansy slipped away to wander about the rickyard, hoping to see Adam or Fanny Luscombe for news of their courting and perhaps hear something of Martin. But the tumbling ricks and linhays were deserted. The warmth of the spring day settled on her and, with thoughts of Martin so fresh, she waited for Beatrice and wondered, not for the first time, how she could hanker after him while all the time it was really Geoffrey she loved, wasn't it? Even now, thoughts of Martin brought the familiar response from her body, the longing for his touch, the mounting need to feel his hands and mouth caressing her. She got up and walked about. Perhaps she should go away. Find a position as a companion, go off and see the world as she'd threatened to do. Surely Beatrice Vallance would know of some titled lady who could employ an energetic girl, espcially as she was now experienced in lady's maiding. Why was she waiting for Geoffrey? After all, whilst treating her with affection he'd kept their relationship like that of brother and sister. Any past moments of intimacy were usually inspired by a triumph in the parish. Then he'd emerged from their embraces to look at her as if he were seeing someone else. She sat down on a bale, plucked out a straw and sucked it while she struggled with her feelings, trying to resolve the puzzle.

Her ploy of returning to Courtenay House in the hope that Geoffrey would come and rescue her had failed. Now she saw him but briefly, on days off or at chapel. At first she'd rushed to the front door whenever she heard his gig approaching but now, jealous of his visit to Kent with Norah, she stayed in her room, hoping against hope that eventually he'd be driven to come and seek her out.

She became conscious of Sarah and Beatrice approaching, their words coming to her across the clear air. She rose and brushed straw from her skirt.

'I wish that son of yours success in his venture,' Beatrice was saying. 'But tell him to get himself a wife. 'Tis hard enough life for a man up there in the hills, let alone with no woman to care for him.'

She turned to Tansy. 'Come along. Mrs Webber's given me the recipe for her delicious tipsy cake. Cook shall make it for my dinner next week.' She took herbs and flowers from Sarah and thanked her, then strode away along the track to where Stephen waited by the automobile. He stubbed out a cigarette as she approached. Sarah caught hold of Tansy's hand as she made to follow the Holy Terror.

'Have 'ee any message for my Martin when I sees 'un on Sunday?' she asked, and Tansy didn't stop to consider, but, without thinking, invited him to the Parish Outing.

'Tell 'un the boat leaves Town Quay nine o'clock, July 17. He kin come if'n he wants.'

Sarah nodded, then went on, ''Ee's nothing else to tell 'un?', her face expectant, but Tansy shook her head. Whatever should there be, she thought, and hurried away to take her place in the Lanchester beside Beatrice Vallance.

❖ Chapter Twenty-Seven ❖

The Dinner Party – A Year On

Beatrice's visit to Teignhead had to be postponed when Charles departed in the Lanchester for North Devon to buy sheepskins more suitable for the officers' uniforms now under contract at Vallance's Mill. The weather changed to that of sudden storms that built rainbows to span Newton from hill to hill and made riding in the gig unsuitable. The day before the dinner found Beatrice and Caroline bickering about numbers, the latter not pleased when the former told her she had invited Geoffrey Llewellyn, and Alyn and Jenny Jones.

'I believe she's with child and her time near,' Caroline grumbled to Maude Westaway, who pursed her lips and looked disapproving.

'Let's hope she doesn't spoil your mother-in-law's dinner party,' she replied. 'It's been known.'

Caroline retorted. 'She says "There must always be room for the radical thinkers, Caroline, look what they've achieved so far." But I can only see the people they've upset as a result. Ben Brealley's been asked to resign from the Local Board. His tenants are leaving Moon Court I hear and some of the older members of chapel don't like the changes Geoffrey Llewellyn's made. Don't approve of the new form of service or his sermons based on John Ruskin's writings!'

Downstairs, Tansy had given up her half-day off to make the tipsy cake. When Cook had read the recipe Tansy thought she'd explode with fury and Hetty had hurried for the smelling salts, fearful that she'd have one of her turns. 'I'm going out to Staddens one day,' she'd muttered darkly. 'Gonna have a word wi' that Sarah Webber. Ask if'n she'd like to make tipsy cake for fifteen at the same time as she'd have to roast ducks for a Missus what demands crisp breasts and my best orange sauce.'

However, Cook, although accepting Tansy's offer, had seemed unwilling to hand over the whole thing to her, hovering nearby, the reason for this soon apparent. 'Us've got sponges from bakers, haven't us, Blodwen?' she'd said. 'Now make a hole in middles then pour in this 'ere slowly.' And she'd measured sherry and brandy, watched Tansy pour the liquor into the cakes then snatched up the measures and drunk what was left.

''Tis best left a couple of hours, my maid,' she said, wiping her mouth with the back of her hand. 'You kin blanch almonds and cut 'un into strips for decoration if 'ee likes.' She returned to plucking ducks, leaving Tansy to get on with the custard. By the time she'd steeped the milk with laurel leaves and sugar, heated it by the fire, added whisked duck eggs, strained and stirred it – 'Slowly now,' Cook commanded. 'It'll go lumpy else.' – Tansy ended up as hot and bad-tempered as Cook, who for once remained calm.

'That's it, my beauty. 'Tis a'most ready,' and she added yet another measure of brandy to the yellow cream.

'I can see why 'tis called tipsy cake,' Tansy had said tartly as the remaining measure had disappeared once more down Cook's throat!

❖

The next evening found Beatrice, joined by Emma, in the hall to await the guests. 'You're looking particularly pretty tonight, my dear,' Beatrice said. 'I like the way Drewe's done your hair.' Emma whirled around in her new emerald gown for her grandmother's approval.

'She knows how to sweep it up and she's learnt how to curl my fringe since she came back.' Emma came and kissed Beatrice with a new-found confidence and poise.

Meanwhile, down in the kitchen, Tansy, who had been pressed into helping, piled plates and checked dishes and Blodwen hovered in the background not knowing what to do. Cook, her face fiery, checked the oven and peered into the battery of iron pots on the range. 'Three more mouths to feed!' She exploded. 'And all at the last minute too. Let's hope Maister'll get fifteen helpings out of they three ducks!' She wiped sweat from her face and eased her corsets. ''Twas a good thing I made three salmon moulds 'stead of only two!'

Tansy and Blodwen exchanged looks and their apprehension, lest anything should go wrong above or below stairs, expelled in nervous giggles. Now the bells above the door began to jingle and dance. Hetty and Tansy hurried upstairs to take their places in the dining-room – Hetty by the buffet, Tansy by the dumb waiter. This year Stephen took Seth's place and had changed into footman's livery. He stood waiting to pour wine and usher guests to their places.

Tansy felt anxious, knowing Geoffrey was to be one of the party. She prayed he wouldn't introduce the subject of servants' hours or comment on the fact that, although now a lady's maid, she was still having to wait at table.

The door opened and Gertrude and Reuben Widecombe came in with Beatrice.

'Dudd'n seem a year since we come to dinner, Beatty!' Gertrude exclaimed. 'Then us still had the Emporium.' She began to snivel. Reuben produced a handkerchief and handed it to her with an air of one who has heard it all before. 'An Act of God they called 'un, that flood. What did us pay 'un for I'd like to know!' And Reuben retorted, 'That's just it, Gertie. You forgot to pay the premium, didn't 'ee. Nothing to do with God.'

Beatrice patted her arm and made consoling noises. 'Count your blessings, Gertrude. At least you're alive and well. Not like poor Pachell Hood. Took a chill during last winter's snow, turned to pneumonia. Now she lies in Holne churchyard.' And with that she saw them seated and turned to greet Robert Hood and Daniel Gill.

'I do miss my Pachell,' Robert said as Beatrice kissed him on the cheek. She nodded and commiserated with him. 'It's natural when you've spent most of your life with someone. I still look for Absolam each morning when I wake, even after eight years. You must sit by me, Robert, and we'll speak of the times we spent together.' Now Charles Vallance came to speak to Robert and Beatrice turned to Daniel.

'It's a sign of our age, Daniel, when each year sees another dear friend gone.' He nodded and sought to lighten their loss.

'Let me sit beside you, Beatrice. We'll drink to absent friends, make the most of the time we've left.'

Stephen Howell struck the dinner gong and the rest of the guests flooded into the room, where early roses scented the table and candles caused reflections in cut-glass and silver vases and fragrant orange blossom floated in finger bowls.

Geoffrey held a chair back for Jenny, who wore the bloom of coming motherhood. Robert Hood and Jack Avery looked pleased when Emma and Mary Westaway sat down between them, Mary's dark looks and soft pink dress contrasting with Emma's blonde hair and emerald gown. Henry Westaway shot a triumphant look at Maude as he was shown to a place beside Jenny, clearly delighted at exchanging his wife for such an attractive companion. Maude looked annoyed as she was separated from Caroline by Dr Weekes, who she detested.

They wouldn't be able to plot and scheme now, thought Tansy, sensing the influence Maude Westaway had over her mistress.

Tansy tried not to look at Geoffrey, knew she must pretend he wasn't there. That was the only way to control the tell-tale blushes that, even now, she could feel were about to break out in her cheeks. She watched as guests took up napkins and turned to neighbours. She admired the way Beatrice had separated friends and joined enemies, no doubt hoping sparks would fly when appetites were satisfied and thirsts slaked, when conversation began in earnest.

Tansy waited for Hetty to give the signal to begin serving. Hetty's Jack, now discharged from the Army, had been unable to find work and Charles Vallance had given them rooms over the stable block so Hetty could continue as parlour-maid. Tansy and Hetty handed round helpings of salmon and returned to their places, then collected empty plates while Beatrice sent Stephen with compliments to Cook on its excellence.

Geoffrey immediately embarrassed Tansy by jumping to his feet to help her carry heavy vegetable dishes from dumb waiter to table. 'Well, just look at that!' Maude muttered to Caroline behind Alan Weekes' back. Caroline glared at Tansy, then turned to watch anxiously as Charles began to carve the first of the ducks. Stephen passed around the table filling glasses with French wine. Geoffrey covered his glass with his hand as Stephen approached.

'Just water please, Howell' he said, and Henry Westaway enquired, 'Signed the pledge then have we, Llewellyn?' and he turned to Dr Weekes. 'Drop of wine never hurt anyone, isn't that so, Alan?' But before he could reply Geoffrey said in level tones, 'It isn't the wine that does the harm taken in moderation, it's those who drink excessively!' He paused, then went on. 'Have you seen a woman bruised, her spirit broken by a drunken man?' Alyn Jones nodded while Tansy listened. It hadn't taken Geoffrey long to introduce a provocative subject, she thought.

'We see them at the surgery all the time. Of course, they won't admit the cause,' Alyn said, and his senior corroborated his words.

'Yes, Alyn. You and I know only too well the cause. But when they say they fell or bumped into a door, what can we do? Until women forget pride and admit to the real cause there's nothing we can do to help them!'

Tansy began to take round portions of duck until everyone was served except Geoffrey, who held up his hand.

'No duck for me, Charles. Vegetables will suit me very well.'

Charles looked up at him in surprise. 'No wine, now no meat?'

Geoffrey responded, 'I've decided not to eat anything that's been killed solely for the purpose of being fed to man!'

Now a buzz of conversation broke out. 'He's mad!' 'What else can we eat but meat?' 'Why else was animals put on God's earth?' Charles banged his fork on the table for silence. 'Well, Llewellyn, what do you say in answer?'

Geoffrey smiled and said, 'Would you be eating this duck if you'd had to wring its neck?' The response was immediate. All the ladies, except Gertrude, laid down knives and forks, their action a declared intent not to eat the bird on their plates. Tansy held her breath, admiring Geoffrey's stand and the decision of Emma, Mary and the other ladies. Even Beatrice looked uncertain and glanced at Charles for support. But he dismissed Geoffrey's remarks and pushed away the plate bearing Geoffrey's portion of the bird.

'We have a farmer among us. What do you say to such a decision, Robert?' Robert showed the strength of his feelings by rising and turning toward Geoffrey. 'There's many as would be grateful for the food on our plates. Those who cannot afford to buy any sort of meat. Who need the strength of a good dish of beef to keep them healthy. To keep them fit enough to work and support their families.'

He looked around the table as the men, including even the doctors, nodded in agreement, and went on. 'There's no room for sentiment in farming. Animal husbandry's been going on for thousands of years on Dartmoor. You'll have to go a long way to convince country folks we can live without meat'.

Now Daniel Gill sought a way out, a means of bringing back the party mood to Beatrice's dinner. 'Are you behind the creation of allotments on Wolborough Hill?' he asked and Geoffrey shook his head. Murmurs of 'Eat up, doctors say it'll do us good' rose from among the women as Emma and Mary, deeply affected by Geoffrey's words, toyed with their duck.

'I can't take credit for that,' Geoffrey said. 'That was Evan Williams' idea.' Charles Vallance nodded. 'Although he can sing like a lark.'

'And dance like a dervish,' Tansy added, then, realising her words had been heard, covered her mouth with her hand.

Charles gave her a severe look and continued. 'As I was saying, although he can sing like a lark he does seem to have a penchant for attracting trouble.'

'What trouble was that, Charles?' Daniel Gill asked.

Tansy waited to hear what would follow. Would the truth emerge here at this table?

'The allotments were raided, I'm told. Seems hard after all the work the men from Bowden Hill and Moon Court put in.'

Tansy had to bite her tongue to stop herself from interrupting with Blodwen's account. But she might have known they had a champion in Geoffrey, who looked up, grim-faced.

'The allotments had the blessing of Farmer Cull, who told Evan he had no need for such a small area of rough ground. The men who took up the plots didn't deserve the treatment meted out to them by a certain gentleman who has, I'm glad to say, received his just desserts!'

'Were the police called?' Robert Hood wanted to know, and Alyn Jones took up the story.

'They were called but all six were engaged in sorting out a brawl at The Newfoundland that night. Rumour has it that Ben Brealley paid Jess Hallett to wreck the allotments but he gets away scot free.'

Geoffrey came to his support. 'I'm told the Local Board's applying for two extra constables to help keep the unruly element of Newton in order. Perhaps in future the guilty will be caught and made to answer for their actions.'

Tansy thought of the billycock hat found at the allotments, the only piece of evidence that Jess Hallett had been involved. Charles Vallance now took up the cudgels.

'Be careful what you say, Jones. There's such a thing as slander if you can't prove the veracity of what you're saying.'

Tansy made a mental note to look up 'veracity' after dinner and find out what it meant. She helped clear away dinner plates, from which most of the duck had disappeared. She breathed a sigh of relief, imagining Cook's reaction if her food hadn't been eaten. She was glad too that Geoffrey's verbal fireworks hadn't touched on unions and servants, both subjects uppermost in his mind. Only the pudding and dessert to go.

But when the dirty plates were on their way down to the kitchen and the tipsy cake on its way up she was dismayed to hear Daniel Gill ask, 'What's this I hear about Evan Williams trying to start a Union at the Decoy clay pits? Do you know anything about that, Llewellyn?'

This was dangerous ground, Tansy thought as she took a deep breath and picked up the tipsy cake, catching a strong smell of brandy and cream as she did so. She began to advance upon the table. Beatrice's voice came towards her, breaking into the conversation.

'This conversation's much too serious to accompany such a frivolous pudding! Keep it till you're on your own,' she begged, but Geoffrey wouldn't let the opportunity pass and continued. 'You factory and shop owners must face the fact that Unions are here to stay. It's only a matter of time before the workers will call the tune.'

He paused as all eyes turned to Tansy and the tipsy cake. 'How much did Cook get paid to make this magnificent pudding?' he asked, then turned towards Tansy. 'And how many hours a day do you work, Miss Drewe?'

She was taken by surprise by the question and dropped the dish, which fell sideways, spilling its cream and sponge into Caroline's lap. All was pandemonium! Caroline screamed and leapt to her feet, shouting at Tansy who fled to the bathroom for a cloth. How could he have done that to her? Tansy wondered as she hurried back downstairs, dreading the moment when she would have to face Caroline Vallance and the guests. As she hesitated outside the dining-room door, it opened and Hetty came through.

'I'm going for the summer pudding Cook's got in the larder,' she said, and seeing the stricken look on Tansy's face added, ''Tis all right, Daniel Gill's come to the rescue. What a gentleman! Why the Holy Terror wouldn't marry him I'll never know.'

Indeed the conversation had taken a turn for the better and Tansy was able to glide round the outside of the room to scrape the remains of the tipsy cake from her mistress's lap. 'I'll speak to you later,' was all Caroline said, and Tansy wondered how she would ever remove the growing stain which even now was soaking over Caroline's new cream silk gown.

'Yes,' said Beatrice. 'I've heard of Padey Paddington. I believe he was at Exeter last winter.'

Maude spoke up. 'Well, we had him at the Assembly Rooms this spring and he was quite brilliant. He'd a clown for a puppet, moved it this way and that. Even threw his voice till it seemed the puppet was really alive.'

And now Emma added, speaking out for the first time since the meal had begun, 'Yes, and he traced a missing medal for Kezia Chard. Just when she'd given up hope of ever finding it again.'

''Twas her husband's Waterloo medal, belonged to his father avore 'im,' Gertrude interrupted, and Beatrice smiled and nodded approval of this more entertaining conversation. She looked sympathetically at her daughter-in-law, who sat in some discomfort.

'Bring the pudding to me, Westcott,' she commanded, and proceeded to serve the helpings of bread soaked with raspberries, blackcurrants and gooseberries while Tansy handed out dishes of clotted cream and sugar. Tansy watched them mop up their plates, wondering where they put it all and hoping they'd leave something for the servants' supper later on.

Cheese and fruit circulated without further incident until at last Beatrice rose and the ladies followed her to the sitting-room for tea. Tansy breathed a sigh of relief and removed napkins from the table. She found his hand touching hers as she took hold of the linen from Geoffrey's place.

'Norah sends love,' he said, and she felt a sudden pang of jealousy that her sister seemed to spend more time with Geoffrey than she did herself.

Stephen Howell placed the port before Charles Vallance and at last she and Hetty could leave the room and close the door on the men's talk.

❖ Chapter Twenty-Eight ❖

The Chapel Outing

July came at last, bringing with it the day of the chapel outing. Tansy got up even earlier to carry out her duties and at Teignhead Martin penned ewes and lambs and set Moss to guard them. He walked through early mist to Fernworthy where Tom Osborne had promised to overlook his flock later in the day. Tom gave Martin a ride to Moreton Station, where he agreed to meet him at midnight.

When Tansy got to the quay thirty families were gathered, waiting for the boat.

'Here's our Tansy.' Robert and James came running, grasping her hands and swinging her arms back and forth. In their other hands they carried buckets and spades brought from under the stairs, where they'd been put at the end of the previous summer.

'Have you seen Geoffrey?' she asked as she looked for him among the crowd of young men in chapel suits and girls in frilly dresses, with flower- and ribbon-trimmed straw hats. Children rushed between the adults' legs, got in the way and tripped up, then cheered when at last the launch appeared around the bend of the river.

Tansy wondered if Martin would come – such a long way, she thought, then there were the sheep to think of. I don't care she thought, as long as Geoffrey's here.

Robert and James pointed excitedly at the grey flapping wings of a heron as it circled slowly over the marshes. When the boat drew closer they ran to the edge of the jetty and Bessie Brimmacombe shouted, ''Tis the Saucy Sal again! Same as last year, the good old Saucy Sal!'

Swans scattered, swimming swiftly from the wave which broke over the bows. As soon as the boat was moored there was a rush to climb the gangplank. Eva and Edward settled themselves and their picnic basket in the bows, where the twins could kneel on the seats and trail their hands in the water.

Then Geoffrey appeared with Norah at his side, followed by Martin, looking tense and hot in his chapel suit. Not knowing why, Tansy spoke to him crossly as he helped her aboard.

'Thought you weren't coming!' she snapped, and pulled away from his supportive arm. She hurried after Geoffrey to the upper deck and tried to sit beside him. He smiled at her politely, then changed seats so Norah could sit beside him. Tansy glared at Martin, who promptly took Geoffrey's old place. Furious, she got up and stood at the rail, looking down into the water.

'Tide'll turn soon, then there'll not be enough water to float a duck!' she said and Martin, strong practical Martin, looked alarmed.

'Then how will us get back? I've sheep to think of!'

Tansy laughed, pleased to be on home ground, to be in charge for once. 'You and your sheep,' she teased. 'Can't you forget them just for one day?!' And Martin, who had spent the last three hours getting to Newton, looked hurt.

'We'm coming home in wagons from Teignmouth Pier,' she went on. 'You'll see, 'tis fun. Sometimes they stop at the Passage House Inn and we sing songs and stroll about the gardens. There's beer for the men and tea for the women.' At last she stopped looking cross, her face taking on a glow of anticipation at the thought of the day ahead.

'I've bought my bathing suit – I'm going to learn to swim!' she announced, while Martin scoffed at the idea of swimming in the sea.

'Bovey or Teign's best for swimming. Can't beat fresh water at the end of a day haymaking or sheep dipping.' He produced a cigar from his top pocket and made a great show of lighting it. 'But you should learn to swim, Tansy. Do you remember the day you nearly drowned in Quarry Pool?' He slid his arm around her waist as if to reassure himself that she was safe here beside him. But his action only reminded Tansy that it was Geoffrey she wanted to be with and she shrugged away from him, looking round for Geoffrey, who paced the deck with Norah.

As the boat navigated the shallows and deeps, lapwings rose at its coming. They passed Coombe Cellars, where shags dried their wings on sandbanks and a group of cyclists leant their machines on the sea wall and drank from glasses. They exchanged waves and shouts with the party on board while Tansy told Martin how she and Miss Emma had passed the Inn on their way to Shaldon.

'Beatrice Vallance has bought another bicycle so I can go with her, 'tis great fun! Almost as good as riding Norsworthy's pony.'

Martin laughed and admonished her, 'You'd best take care. Make sure 'un has good brakes, you'll fly downhill else and land in the river.'

Now the boat passed through a curtain of mist, coming out into bright sunshine on the other side. Soon they passed under Shaldon Bridge where fishermens' cottages lined the harbour at Teignmouth and boats lay at anchor. Still the *Saucy Sal* chugged on and crossed over to the Shaldon side. Edward pointed to currents which swirled and eddied beneath the harbour lights.

''Tis dangerous here. Don't ever swim in the river mouth. Keep round towards the pier,' he told the twins, his face serious.

Now they gazed up in awe at the cliff, towering red above them. 'Can we climb up there, Father, when we'm big enough?' He smiled and shook his head. 'Climb the Ness? We'll see. Perhaps we'll take the ferry across and explore smugglers' tunnel later on. But he knew all thoughts of leaving the sands would fade when castle building began in earnest. So it proved as he and Eva tried to persuade them to stop and eat their pasties at dinnertime.

Suddenly they passed the harbour light, making for the gap in the sandbank. The boat drove parallel to the beach until they reached a landing-stage close to the pier, then the boat dipped low into the sea as everyone rushed to the landward side to disembark, eager to begin their annual treat.

Bessie Brimmacombe chose a place at the top of the rising beach, spread a rug and anchored it to the red sand with a stone jar of ginger beer. Everyone under eighteen – and quite a few over – tucked skirts into drawers, rolled trousers to knees, removed boots and shoes, and advanced upon the sea. Shrieks rose as hot feet met freezing water. The girls linked arms and strolled the promenade, exchanging glances with young men.

'They look so pale, must be down from London or some such place,' Rosemary giggled in response to a greeting from a bold-eyed man in striped blazer and brown and white Oxfords.

'Hey there, Miss, like your tit-fer-tat!' he called, and Rosemary blushed and looked back at him over her shoulder, retying the pink bow under her chin.

Tansy, however, had eyes for no one but Geoffrey, who seemed to have adopted Norah as his companion for the day. She followed them doggedly and Martin, perspiring in his thick suit, followed Tansy. She trailed after them to the new parish church, the fair on the Den and the Hokey Pokey stand, where Martin bought her an ice-cream which she accepted with such bad grace that he exploded. 'I could do with a swim in the river right now!' He mopped his brow, while Tansy retorted, 'Well, there's the sea, what are you waiting for? You can teach me to swim while you're about it!'

Martin shook his head. 'Got no costume have I?'

'Only sissies wear bathing costumes!'

A sudden sound of screaming came to them from the beach. They hurried along till they came upon a crowd which surrounded Bessie Brimmacombe, who danced about her rug, flapping wildly with her black straw.

"Tis a wopsie! Get her away! After me jam tarts her is!'

Meanwhile, Johnnie sat calmly whittling at a piece of wood and pleading, 'Stay quiet Mam and her'll go away. Her'll not sting if you sit down!'

At last picnics were demolished, sandcastles judged and winners awarded with ice-creams. The tide turned and horses drew bathing huts down the beach into the advancing sea. Tansy and Rosemary changed into long, frilled bathing dresses and lowered themselves into the salty waves where they splashed each other and shrieked, being lifted up by the incoming waves. Evan Williams watched them and, ever ready with a plan to fit the mood of the moment, sensed boredom creep over the men, who were unused to a long day spent in the company of their families. He approached Geoffrey Llewellyn.

'Why not have a swimming race? Tide's turning. Sea's coming in over the sand. Perfect. Some of the lads are keen to take part.' He stood on the sea wall and wound a bull roarer in his hand until its clacking bought the party crowding round.

'Who's for a swimming race? Hundred yards from the pier to Cockle Stall!' After a few minutes' hesitation Geoffrey agreed and remarked in an aside to his friend, 'No bets, Evan, remember today's a chapel outing!' Tom Coish and Harry Brooks, already wearing bathing costumes, immediately volunteered.

'We'm good at swimming, Harry and me. Swift as a salmon I be.' The young lad lay on the sand making rapid swimming movements with his skinny arms. Everyone joined in the laugh and soon eight young men had been persuaded by mothers and sweethearts to take part. Evan urged Martin to join in, nodding in sympathy when he learned of his predicament.

'You could swim in your combinations, under water no one will see!'

Martin, seeing Tansy hovering near Geoffrey yet again, threw down a challenge. Speaking loud enough for them to hear he declared, 'If the minister will swim then so will I!'

Geoffrey now came in for much cajoling from both Norah and Tansy. 'Do take part, Geoffrey. They say there's to be a prize.'

Geoffrey looked embarrassed. 'I've no costume,' he protested and Martin, seeing a chance to outface Geoffrey repeated, 'I'll swim if he will!'

Henry Westaway came forward to announce, 'I will give a ride in the automobile to the Passage House Inn and a free supper to the winner and lady of his choice!'

Now a buzz of conversation began and both Norah and Tansy pressed him again to take part. 'A ride in the auto, how wonderful! You must join in, Geoffrey.' Reluctantly he agreed.

Charles Vallance now intervened. He advanced across the beach from the shade of a large umbrella Caroline was using to protect her complexion from the sun.

'We must have some order here,' he announced, producing his pocket watch. 'Line up all of you who're taking part. Tallest farthest out, shortest close to the shore.'

Then, as Martin and Geoffrey ran past him into the water, he called, 'That's right Llewellyn, Martin. Out you go!' As he realised both were stripped down to their underwear he looked round hastily. 'Hope Caroline and Emma aren't watching,' he muttered to himself as a chorus of oohs and aahs rose from the ladies of the party, who turned away to hide their blushes, then looked back to watch them enter the water. Both men dived beneath the waves while Charles continued his instructions.

'Tom Coish, Harry Brooks. Move forward a bit, that's right. You're younger than the rest. Now I need a flag.'

Tansy, remembering Martin's red handkerchief, fetched it from his pile of clothes on the beach. Charles held the hanky aloft.

'When the minute hand reaches six o'clock I'll drop the flag.'

'My, don't 'ee look handsome, Tansy?!' Rosemary exclaimed.

'Geoffrey always does!' Tansy replied and Rosemary laughed. 'I meant Martin, so broad and strong. I'm sure he's going to be the winner.'

Charles dropped the makeshift flag and the swimmers struck out, Tom and Harry going quickly away from the main body of swimmers, their slight bodies providing no resistance to the water. Half the chapel party moved for a better view to the pier, the other half stood at the cockle stall, awaiting the arrival of the winner. Tansy watched anxiously as within five minutes they'd covered half the distance. Martin swam strongly in the middle of the pack. Geoffrey waited till everyone had begun before making his own effort, swimming lazily at first on his back, then rolling over onto his front.

'What does he think he's doing?' Tansy wrung the muslin tie from her hat. 'He'll come in last at this rate!' But slowly and surely he caught them up, passing all but Martin.

'Come on Martin, you can win sure 'nuff!' Rosemary shouted, while Tansy willed Geoffrey to go ahead. The parish divided, half shouted for Martin, the others for Geoffrey, as yard by painful yard they closed the distance between their cleaving arms and the cockle stall. The keeper stood, striped apron standing out like a beacon, straw hat held aloft, ready to drop it the moment the winner reached him.

Norah came up to Tansy. 'Do you think Geoffrey's going to win?'

Tansy turned away. 'I can't look. It's too much!'

Scornfully, Norah said, ''Tis only a race – who cares which one of them wins?!'

Tansy rounded on her. 'I do. I care who wins. One of them will take me to supper in Westaway's automobile and I want it to be Geoffrey. Of course I care!'

Now Norah's face lost its look of calm acceptance. 'You're very sure of yourself aren't you, Tansy! I should wait till I'm asked before I say something like that!'

Leaving Norah, Tansy ran along the shore, bare feet slapping wet sand, shouting encouragement to Geoffrey. She knew he would win, and he did, his lithe figure carried less weight than that of Martin's sturdy frame, and he reached the goal post half a minute ahead of him. A great cheer greeted Geoffrey as he dragged himself free of the water, then Martin shook him by the hand as they made their way to the bathing huts. The losers splashed each other then advanced on the watching crowd with intent, quickly read by sisters and aunts who ran off to a safe distance.

Tansy stood waiting while Geoffrey and Martin dressed. She smiled to herself, imagining sitting high in the Westaway's Rolls and pouring tea for Geoffrey in the gardens. She shivered as a breeze blew down the river and looked up at a drift of cloud which was hanging above the beach.

Mothers called to children. 'Pack up your spades, my dears. 'Tis time to go home.' And there was much carrying about the beach, washing sand from feet and packing of belongings. Seagulls descended to forage on the beach and little ones were lifted up and carried to the promenade.

Charles Vallance turned to Geoffrey and invited him to choose his companion for the ride to the Inn. Geoffrey stood beside him, his hair sleek and wet, looked across the happy crowd and announced in ringing tones, 'I choose,' – Tansy stood happily waiting – 'Miss Norah Drewe. Will you accompany me home?'

Tansy darted forward, fearing she had misheard. 'There must be some mistake,' she said, while Norah walked past her to accept Geoffrey's proffered arm. Tansy watched in disbelief while they walked across the prom and climbed into the automobile which stood, red and gleaming on the carriageway. Everyone clapped and cheered.

Edward Drewe stepped forward and said, 'You won the race fair and square, Geoffrey, and we all wish you an enjoyable ride. Now,' he added, 'who would like to make the swimming race an annual event?' As hats flew high in the air, all shouted 'Aye'. Everyone began to pile into the wagons drawn up behind the Rolls. Tansy turned away, her face burning with embarrassment and anger. Yet again Norah had taken her place. It was she, Tansy, who should be sitting there with Geoffrey.

She felt a hand touch her arm, a familiar voice address her. 'I would be honoured if you'd accompany me to the gardens.' She turned and Martin held out his arm to her, his face full of compassion. 'Everybody's watching,' he muttered under his breath. She struggled with her anger and hurt pride, took his arm and walked bravely to the first wagon. The horses stood waiting, their head collars dressed with coloured ribbons, their coats polished like conkers. She climbed up, trying her best to look as if she didn't care. Didn't care that Norah had once again usurped her from the place she thought to be hers.

'Tidd'n fair,' she muttered as the motor disappeared up the road. 'First to be given the chance of going to college while I'm skivvying at Courtenay House, now she takes my place in the motor. She knew it was me that wanted to go. She,' and she spat out the word, 'didn't even care who won.'

Martin tried to cover his smiles, relieved that Geoffrey had chosen Norah, and bit his tongue, holding back the thought that if Geoffrey Llewellyn was fool enough to prefer Norah, dark, quiet Norah, to his Tansy with her flame-coloured hair and temperament to match, then he deserved all he got. He tried to distract Tansy from the sight of the two backs riding high in the dickey seat of the red automobile.

'Look, 'ee can see Hey Tor, Tansy. Looks grand with the sun high above it!' Tansy was so busy trying to control her temper that she didn't notice when Martin slid his arm round her waist. When they reached the gardens she was so determined not to show Norah how much she minded that she let Martin fetch her tea and a plate of cockles. When Rosemary sat down at the piano and played a polka she danced with such verve and energy that heads began to nod and more than one voice was heard to murmur, 'There's a handsome couple, my dar. Shouldn't be surprised if'n there wasn't wedding bells avore long.'

But when the wagons arrived at the station and Martin left her to catch his train, she climbed the hill to Courtenay House, threw herself on the bed and cried as if her heart would break.

❖ Chapter Twenty-Nine ❖

The Trial

Two months after Ben Brealley's attack on the allotments, Tom Moore moved his family to a house in Bradley Terrace, right opposite Vallance's Mill.

'Us'll have nothing more to do with that varmint!' Tom said, and when Tansy heard she made up her mind to visit Avril.

'I've bought 'ee some fresh cabbage from Courtenay House.' She placed the crisp, white hearts down on the scrubbed table.

Avril smiled her thanks and invited Tansy in. 'You'll stay, won't 'ee? 'Tis so good to see you.' She hugged Tansy and went on, 'I'll never forget what you did. How you helped me over Eleanor.' They sat silent for a moment, remembering the dreadful night of the flood. 'If only I'd taken her with me,' she burst out, 'she'd be here now growing fat and rosy in my arms.'

'You mustn't blame yourself, Avril. You weren't to know water'd rise so fast. Weren't to know someone'd shut the street door! There's hardly a family in town as hasn't lost little 'uns one way or another. You've four fine healthy sons, Avril. What do they think of school?'

Avril brightened, sorrow giving way to pride. 'William and young George are that proud of their new boots. Charlie'll be going in September, and 'tis all due to you and Mr Llewellyn. And we've our own plot out back. Come and see!' As she got up, Tansy noticed the loose smock, half-concealing the swollen body. Immediately she felt concern for her friend.

'I see you'm in the family way again?' Avril nodded and smiled, obviously pleased. She smoothed down her smock to show Tansy.

'Please God let it be a little maid.'

But Tansy chided her. 'I thought Alyn Jones said you should wait before having another!'

Avril blushed like a young girl and rushed on. 'I did so want a girl. When Eleanor was born it was such a comfort after all they boys. She was to be my helper. Keep me company when the boys grew up and left home.' She cradled her stomach with her hands. 'This 'un'll take her place.' As they walked through the neat kitchen Tansy sent up a prayer that the newcomer would indeed be the girl Avril so desperately wanted, and that both would survive the birth.

Tansy admired the freshly dug plot and sat down on a bench in the sun. 'I can't stay long. I've a pile of ironing waiting for me up the hill.' She sighed and added, ''Tis never ending!'

Avril nodded in sympathy. 'You know you'm always welcome to come and stay as long as you can. 'Tis good to have another woman to talk to. I never thought I'd miss the women at Moon Court but they were good to me after the flood. Now,' she lowered her voice, 'there's only Maudie Pengilly next door poking her nose in where 'tisn't wanted.'

Now at last there was a pause in their conversation. Tansy knew she should leave but, taking the chance now it had presented itself, she asked ,'How do it begin?'

'How do what begin?' Avril looked puzzled, noting Tansy's blushing face.

'You know, the baby? How do 'ee know it's started?'

Immediately Avril knew why Tansy had come, knew the reason for the tenseness she'd felt when they'd embraced.

'Well,' she said, watching Tansy's reactions, 'first 'tis missing the monthly time. 'Tis best to wait till you'm gone past two of they avore tellin' anyone.' She paused, a look of proud knowledge on her face. 'Then there's the tightening here,' she placed hands on breasts. 'A course there's the sickness in the mornings and sometimes night times as well. Mind,' she added, 'not all gets it, though that's the worst part of it. The sickness,' she concluded with great feeling. Now she looked at Tansy with concern. 'Why do 'ee want to know?' she pressed.

'I thought it was something like that,' Tansy stuttered. 'Mother never speaks of it and...' her voice trailed off.

"Ee's not fallen have 'ee, Tansy?' Avril was determined to establish whether her friend needed help. 'Have 'ee been with anyone?'

Tansy began to explain her situation in short bursts of speech. 'No, no,' and she twisted her hands together in her skirt. 'I don't know!' She turned to Avril, her face worried. 'Could it happen the first time?'

Avril sought to comfort her in the only way she knew how. 'Only you can tell me that. 'Tis unusual to be caught first time. Then there's medicine you can take avore 'tis too late! Mind you, that doesn't always work.' She took Tansy's hand in hers. 'You'll come and see me if ever you'm in trouble, won't 'ee?' She said no more, sensing Tansy needed to digest all she had told her.

Tansy hurried through the front door, almost bumping into Maudie Pengilly who stood at her own door, a piece of crochet in her hand. She stared at Tansy and then nodded briefly, without smiling. Tansy hurried along the leat into Steppes Meadow, making for the spring where she scooped up water and, as she drank, she reached a decision.

Tansy found Geoffrey working at papers in his study. He got up at once, pleased to see her, went to the kitchen and asked Aurelia to make tea.

'How are you, Tansy? I've not seen you since the outing.' He motioned her to a chair opposite him. 'How's the campaign going up at Courtenay?' he asked. When she said nothing he went on, 'I feel you could have an ally in Beatrice Vallance. She came from humble beginnings, after all. Just a dairymaid on a farm, wasn't she?'

Tansy shook her head, remained standing. 'That might well be but she only comes once a year and then she'm busy visiting and giving dinner parties.' She stopped, looking at him accusingly, remembering the disaster of the tipsy cake. 'Always driving about the Moor.'

Geoffrey looked at her keenly and noticed the new bloom about her. A bloom that suited her. Was it his imagination, he wondered, or had she filled out since she'd left his employ? It seemed perhaps she was leaving the days of her girlhood behind.

He went on, 'I seem to remember you usually accompany Beatrice Vallance on these excursions?' When Tansy nodded he continued. 'Then wouldn't that be the ideal time to broach the subject?' She felt she had let him down. For, yes, she could have spoken to the Holy Terror, hadn't the fear of losing her new position loomed over her. She drew in a sharp breath and came to the purpose of her visit.

'Do you remember when I left here?' she asked, then rushed on. 'You gave me a box?' She blushed as she remembered the force with which she'd flung it in his face. 'I wondered,' and now she stammered as an amused smile began to play around Geoffrey's mouth. 'Have you still got it?'

He answered slowly, spinning out the words, 'And what if I have? Why do you want to know?' Now he teased her but, determined to get what she'd come for, she went on. 'If you still have it... and still want me to have it... then, please give it to me.'

He laughed. 'What if I've given it to someone else, what then?' She felt her face grow hot with disbelief that he could have done such a thing. Suddenly he took pity on her, reached for the drawer by his side, took out the box and came round the table towards her. He came towards her just as he'd done on the first occasion when he'd tried to give her the gift. Now he smiled at her, placed the box in her hands and she opened it, making sure the St Christopher was indeed inside, then looked up at him. He watched her quizzically.

'What made you come for it after all this time?' he asked, but she would only shake her head. Quickly she went toward the door, turning to face him.

'I just wanted what was rightfully mine! After all,' she said, holding her head high, defiant, 'as you so rightly said, I did earn it!' Then she hurried from the study, almost knocking over Aurelia, who stood listening at the door.

Later that day she pressed the pendant close to her lips. No harm she thought, could surely come to her all the time she wore Geoffrey's gift.

❦

Storm clouds which had begun to gather the night of the outing hung over Newton, bringing humidity which made the slightest effort exhausting. Eva sorted coins into three bowls – sovereigns, silver and copper. A week's sales of postal orders, telegrams and stamps. She looked up as Edward came back from a meeting of the Chapel Elders. He looked grave.

'What's wrong?' she asked, surprised at the furtive way he looked over his shoulder.

'Seems there's been a complaint lodged with the Chapel Administrators.'

She looked puzzled. 'What sort of complaint?'

He sighed and lowered his voice. 'Levelled at Geoffrey.'

Eva looked shocked. 'Surely not!' she exclaimed. 'We've never had a minister who worked harder, was more caring.'

Edward nodded and leant against the counter. 'It's serious, Eva, very serious...' He paused. 'It's one of conduct unbecoming a member of the cloth!'

'I don't believe it!' Eva struggled to assimilate Edward's news. 'It must be a mistake.'

'Of course it is.' Edward straightened. 'Popularity always gives rise to jealousy,' he added. 'Of course there's been talk from time to time.' He hesitated. 'You must prepare yourself for a shock, Eva.' He walked around the counter to her and put his arm around her shoulders. 'There's to be an enquiry and Tansy's been called to act as a witness.'

'Tansy! What can our Tansy possibly have to do with it?' Eva demanded and Edward shook his head.

'Seems as if the complaints are about events alleged to have taken place during and after the time she worked with Geoffrey. Charles Vallance has the full list.'

Eva's face paled, her pulse quickened. When Tansy had first gone to work for Geoffrey at The Manse, Edward had said no good would come of it. She had laughed away his fears but this, this was worse than anything she could have imagined.

'Does she know?'

Edward patted his pocket. 'I've a letter for her. The hearing's Wednesday. If she's to get time off I must get it to her quickly.' He left immediately for Courtenay House.

When she answered the door of her room to his knock, Tansy was surprised to see her father standing there. 'Tidd'n bad news?' she demanded, alarmed at this unexpected visit, 'The twins?' She relaxed as he shook his head and pushed past her into the room.

'No,' he said. ''Tis to do with Geoffrey,' which startled her even more. 'He's to appear before the Chapel Council to answer certain accusations.' He handed her the letter. 'You'd best read this.' Bemused, she opened the envelope, taking out a thin sheet of paper. Quickly her eyes scanned the contents.

''Tis very formal. They want me to attend at the Public Rooms Wednesday. What's it all about, Father?' She looked up at him, full of concern, this time for Geoffrey. 'Why do they want me?'

He tried to allay her fears. 'I believe it's to do with Geoffrey's activities during the time you were working for him. Just come along and answer the questions truthfully, there's a good girl, like you've been brought up to do. I'll be there with the Elders.' He looked round the neat room, the kettle simmering on the hob, the pile of books by her bed.

'You've done well,' he said, then hesitated. 'Don't do anything to spoil it.' He hugged her to him, then looked at her and said gravely, 'Remember, the truth never hurt anyone,' and was gone, leaving her to puzzle over the nature of the enquiry. She wondered what Geoffrey could possibly have done to make him the subject of such a happening. She hoped Caroline Vallance wouldn't make a fuss about giving her the afternoon off. She returned to mending Emma's skirt.

❧

The day of the enquiry brought with it a deepening of clouds into black, threatening shapes which hung low over Newton as Tansy, dressed in her best, ran down 148 steps to call for Edward. When they arrived at the Public Rooms, Geoffrey was already there in the foyer. He stepped forward and took her hands in his.

'I'm sorry you've been brought into this,' he said. 'Don't think of me, just answer the questions whatever they are.' They parted when an usher came to show them to their places.

The seating was arranged in a rectangle. Edward sat among the Chapel Elders at a long table and opposite them were three men Tansy had never seen before. At the lower end of the rectangle were two rows of seats and at the back was Ben Brealley, between Maudie Pengilly and Aurelia Brown. In front of them Evan Williams sat beside Avril Moore and Tansy took the remaining seat. Completing the rectangle were two seats. Geoffrey took one, to be joined by a short, slim man wearing a monocle in his left eye, his neck framed by a high wing-collar.

When everyone had been seated, murmuring among the participants stopped and all eyes turned to the clock as it ticked away the minutes till the hour hand reached two o'clock. The chimes when they came acted like a starting pistol. The central member of the three unknown men rose and addressed them. His hooded eyes and aquiline nose reminded her of a bird of prey, his thick hair and beard of feathers. He looked about him and began.

'I have been appointed by the Chapel Council to carry out this enquiry into certain allegations which have been made about our minister here in Newton.' He paused, looking to see that he had everyone's attention, and continued. 'Geoffrey Llewellyn's background is well known to us. My two associates were members of the appointing body when he came to the town last year. Came, I might add, with the highest of recommendations. It has come as a great shock to us that he should be the subject of such complaints. In view of the serious nature of such complaints, we have therefore allowed him the assistance of a lawyer, Henry Watson-Bates. He is the independent voice, connected with neither Chapel nor the Parish of Newton Abbot in any way.'

There was a great deal of murmuring now and Aurelia Brown, looking pleased, turned to Ben Brealley with a congratulatory look. Tansy felt a chill strike into her being and an uneasy feeling churned in her stomach. Avril turned to her. 'Sounds serious, don't it?'

Now the man on the right of the first speaker rose to his feet. He settled a pair of spectacles on his nose and began. 'My name is Gregson. You have heard my senior, Mr Cuthbert Whyte, announce the allegations made against Geoffrey Llewellyn. I act as

Secretary to this Enquiry. The witnesses will be called to answer any points which we feel may throw light on these complaints. At the end of each witness's evidence Henry Watson-Bates will be given the opportunity to question him or her on behalf of the accused. Mr Cuthbert Whyte will act as Chairman.' He paused to polish his glasses with a large, red hanky, then continued. 'I will now read the letter of complaint received by the Chapel Council and then we will proceed with the questions.

"To the Chairman
Council of Chapels
  Dear Sir
  It has come to my notice that Geoffrey Llewellyn, minister of the Wolborough Chapel, has behaved in a manner unbecoming one of his adopted profession, in that:-
  1 He has incited citizens of the town on occasion to act in an illegal manner by seizing land for their own use, such land belonging to others.
  2 He has dismissed his housekeeper, Miss Aurelia Brown, without just cause, causing her to become homeless.
  3 He was seen to have behaved in an unseemly manner in public on the occasion of the Chapel Outing on 17 July this year.
  4 That on various occasions at The Manse, his official residence, he has been alone in the company of a young unmarried woman while purporting to be engaged in Parish affairs but, in fact, to have been involved in immoral activities.
  I await to hear what action your Council is prepared to take in dealing with these complaints.
  Yours faithfully

Signed: Benjamin Brealley
Ex-Chairman, Local Board of Wolborough."'

When the last complaint was read Tansy gasped and tried to catch Geoffrey's gaze to express her sympathy over this libel. She understood now why she had been called to the Enquiry. Recognised in the accusations the hand of Aurelia Brown.

Gregson continued. 'Copies of this letter have been given to the Chapel Elders and the Reverend Llewellyn.' He sat down and the chairman rose, accompanied by a long rumble of thunder. A sudden gust of wind tore open the entrance door and Edward rose swiftly to refasten it.

'I call on Benjamin Brealley to substantiate the first complaint. Please step forward.'

Tansy felt like hissing as he passed on his way to the witness-box in front of her row. His bulk blotted out the vision of Geoffrey who sat, pale but composed, beneath a skylight which admitted a shaft of sun to light his flame-coloured hair.

'As Landlord of Moon Court I suffered damage to my property the night of the February flood.' He paused and looked round the room. 'As if this wasn't enough the Preacher encouraged the tenants to knock down the end wall, laying my property open to East Street.' Cries of 'Shame' and 'Disgusting' arose from the rows behind Tansy. Ben Brealley continued. 'On another occasion he,' and he pointed at Geoffrey, 'incited the tenants of Bowden Hill and Moon Court to seize farmland for their own purposes.'

Gregson now invited Henry Watson-Bates to question Brealley. The advocate dealt with him swiftly and thoroughly. 'I have here in my hand,' he announced, waving a blue paper aloft, 'a signed affidavit from your own agent purporting that he himself approached you for permission for the tenants to break down the wall at Moon Court. That, in fact, the tenants carried out the work themselves rather than having to pay the cost of labour as suggested by Councillor Brealley himself.'

Evan and Avril now added their voices to the scene. 'That's right that is. Absolutely right.' 'Fancy charging his tenants for that!'

After a word or two with Geoffrey, Henry Watson-Bates concluded. 'The reason for the dismantling of this wall was that, as a result of the Court being flooded, a life was lost.'

Avril, at this sad reminder, took out her hanky and wiped her eyes, while Tansy sat back, relieved that at least the first of the complaints had been successfully dealt with.

Next Evan Williams was called. He confessed, 'It was my idea entirely to seize the rough ground at the top of Wolborough Hill for allotments. When Ben Brealley approached him Farmer Cull refused to turn us off. Said he had no use for it.' Now Evan looked across at Geoffrey. 'Perhaps the inspiration to form allotments did come from Geoffrey Llewellyn's sermon in the Pit. But that sermon was based on the writings of John Ruskin.'

Henry Watson-Bates exclaimed, 'Perhaps we should have called on John Ruskin to come here today as witness!' and there was a general laugh among the chapel men.

The chairman held up his hand for silence. 'I believe him to be very ill at his home in the Lake District. In any case,' he added, 'who are we to question beliefs and ideas which have helped to improve life for so many of the citizens of this country.' He waved his hand towards Gregson, who proceeded with the second complaint.

'Will Miss Aurelia Brown step forward and tell us why she believes she has been wrongfully dismissed as Housekeeper to the minister.'

Tansy turned to watch the thin figure of Aurelia, dressed in black chapel coat and hat, scuttle sideways to take the stand, a look of excitement on her sallow face.

'He,' she said, pointing a long bony finger at Geoffrey, 'wanted me gone soon as Tansy Drewe come on the scene. Suggested I get another position first time he met her.' She turned and glared at Tansy, took a deep breath and went on. 'Took away my duties as Clerk which I'd carried out for twenty five years without complaint for the Reverend Havelock Childers and give them her.'

Here Maudie Pengilly shouted 'For shame, treating someone like that!'

Aurelia continued. 'Then after the last visit of Tansy Drewe to The Manse he sacked me!'

'And when was that?' Gregson asked.

'Week avore the Chapel Outing.'

Now Henry Watson-Bates asked if he might question Miss Brown. 'Was one of the reasons Reverend Llewellyn suggested you look for another job that of lack of loyalty on your part? That you had been found carrying gossip of a scurrilous nature about Miss Drewe?'

Aurelia stood, her colour heightened, and blustered, 'I don't know why he should have thought that. I do everything for him, don't I? Cook, clean, wash his clothes?'

The barrister turned towards Geoffrey. 'Will you please tell us why you gave Miss Brown notice.'

Geoffrey stood up and faced Aurelia from the opposite end of the room. A flash of lightning burst into the gloom of the room, heightening the drama of the moment.

'After repeated warnings I caught her eavesdropping yet again. I felt I could no longer tolerate such behaviour. I had lost confidence in her loyalty. Felt Chapel affairs were not safe from discussion outside my study all the time she was employed at The Manse.'

The chairman nodded, paused, wrote on a piece of paper then motioned Gregson to proceed to the third complaint, that of unseemly behaviour. He looked along the row of witnesses.

'Were any of you present on the day of the Chapel Outing?' All nodded except Ben Brealley. Gregson looked at him questioningly.

'On what grounds are you lodging this complaint if you weren't there?' Ben Brealley rose and alleged with a sneer. 'You have only to ask anyone. 'Tis common knowledge all over town that Llewellyn took part in a swimming race dressed only in his combinations.'

Gregson turned to Geoffrey and asked, 'Is this true?'

The minister laughed and confessed. 'I have no apology to make. I entered into the race as a gesture of good sportsmanship. All I can say in my defence is that there were several men in the party without swimming costumes. However, if I've given offence to any of the ladies who were present, then I offer my sincere apologies. If a letter in the local newspaper is deemed necessary, then I will be only too happy to oblige.'

Evan Williams leapt to his feet once more in Geoffrey's defence. 'I instigated the swimming race as a means of passing the time between the end of the afternoon's pleasures and the departure of the wagons from the beach.' He added, 'May I say that the event proved so popular 'tis hoped to hold it again next year. Sixteen men and boys took part and the minister himself, after a close contest with Martin Webber, did in fact win the prize.'

Gregson thanked Evan for his assistance and turned an enquiring eye to Henry Watson-Bates who shook his head, adding, 'It seems we must leave this in the hands of the Council to decide whether this complaint is justified or not.'

The chairman rose, adjusted his spectacles, stroked his beard and waited for the laughter caused by the preceding complaint to die down. 'We come to the last and perhaps most serious of the complaints levelled at the Reverend Geoffrey Llewellyn. Perhaps to refresh our memories you will read again the charge against him.'

As Gregson repeated the charge Tansy looked at Geoffrey and was transported back to his study on Christmas Day. Was he recalling at this moment how she had kissed him, asked him to take her? Was he remembering the night of the flood when she had helped him take off wet clothes? Could he still feel her arms around him as she had tried to bring warmth into his chilled body? She knew their actions had had no consequences of an immoral nature, but how would she convince this self-appointed jury that their motives had been innocent even though she, not Geoffrey, had wished it otherwise? Her attention was brought back to the present as Gregson invited Aurelia to take the stand once again.

'Perhaps it would be best if we were to ask the chief witness to tell us why she thinks anything untoward ever took place between Geoffrey Llewellyn and Tansy Drewe.'

Aurelia, full of importance, hurried to the table, eager to give her damning testimony. 'The first time 'twas at Bradley Mill when they were crossing the ford, arms around one another.'

Tansy realised now how it was that her mother had known all about the incident by the time she and Geoffrey reached home from that first parish walk. It had been Aurelia who had carried the news back to town. She looked up as Aurelia continued. 'Then they spent hours together in his study after she'd been dismissed for stealing from Emma Vallance.'

Geoffrey leapt to his feet, speaking out in Tansy's defence. 'That was slander! If you recall Miss Brown, as I'm sure you will, the real culprit was Janet Luscombe who also had set out to blacken Miss Drewe's name.'

Tansy felt grateful to him for coming at once to her defence. Now a look of such venom filled her assailant's face that Tansy felt alarmed for Geoffrey. How could Aurelia so twist and turn innocent happenings to make them seem that what she'd told Benjamin Brealley was actually true?

'They spent a night in the study after the flood,' Aurelia continued, ignoring Geoffrey's interruption. 'Next morning when I went to open the shutters I found them together on the Chesterfield. He was wearing nothing but a blanket!' she ended triumphantly exchanging looks with Ben Brealley.

'And then there was Christmas Day, when the two of they shared a meal alone.'

Now Geoffrey was on his feet, his face furious. He ran his hands distractedly through his hair and bent to speak to Henry Watson-Bates who questioned Aurelia. 'Were you a witness to the alleged incidents?'

She blushed and stammered, 'I was going home past Bradley Mill on the first occasion.'

'And were you in the house on Christmas Day?'

She hesitated, sensing a trap. 'Of course. I cooked his meal, didn't I, which is more than she ever did.'

'So did you lie in your note to the minister in which you said you were going to lunch with your friend Maudie Pengilly?'

Aurelia replied immediately, 'I did go to Maudie's like I said.'

'At what time did your friend arrive at your house, Miss Pengilly?' – the question followed on smoothly.

Now, in spite of Aurelia's signals to her, Maudie spoke up briskly. ''Twas three o'clock by the clock in my best room!'

There was a murmur in the room as the implications became apparent to all.

'So, Miss Brown, you were in fact in the house on Christmas Day while Geoffrey Llewellyn and Tansy Drewe shared the meal you yourself had prepared for them?' She hesitated, caught in her own web. 'Yes or no?' he pressed, and her answer came in a whisper, 'Yes.'

Tansy remembered the feeling of a presence in The Manse after Geoffrey had left to visit Evan Williams and she had felt the strong compulsion to go and look in his room. Aurelia had been there in the house all the time, trying to catch them out. An audible gasp of astonishment hung on the air.

'So you set out deliberately to trap the Minister and Miss Drewe, by pretending to be absent when you were not? For shame, Miss Brown! Had anything untoward happened you would yourself have been partially responsible, would you not?'

For a long moment Aurelia looked close to defeat, then she threw back her head and shouted. 'Then if they'm so innocent, why did he give her a present?'

Without thinking, Tansy's hand flew to the St Christopher which hung around her neck.

''Tis because she'm carrying his child, that's why!' Maudie Pengilly's voice came loud and clear.

Edward jumped to his feet in astonishment and shock. 'That can't be so!' he exclaimed, looking at Tansy for confirmation.

The chairman motioned him to be quiet. 'I must have quiet if we are to resolve this issue,' he said. 'Now is your name Maudie Pengilly?' And when she nodded, full of self-importance, he continued. 'Will you come to the stand and tell us on what grounds you base your accusation that Miss Drewe is carrying Geoffrey Llewellyn's child.'

Tansy was on her feet, waiting to hear what she would say. Geoffrey too had risen and stood, looking extremely agitated.

'I was sitting outside my front door on 30th August and overheard her asking Avril Moore,' here she broke off to explain to the room at large. 'She's my next door neighbour – asking Avril Moore what the signs were that would tell 'ee she was expecting!' Pleased with herself, she folded her arms across her chest and looked across at Aurelia Brown, smiling triumphantly.

Henry Watson-Bates spoke again, his voice icy. 'So your accusation is based entirely on overheard remarks?'

'If'n you don't believe me,' she said, looking around the room wildly, 'then ask her.' She pointed a finger at Avril Moore who sat, tense and worried, twisting her hands in her scarf. The chairman asked Avril to step forward and answer the question. 'Tell us, Mrs..., it is Mrs...? What was the purpose of Miss Drewe's visit to you on August 30th?'

Avril looked at Tansy who sat, hands wet with perspiration, remembering only too well what she had gone for, and spoke nervously but quickly. 'She came as a friend with vegetables to make up for all we lost when the allotments was ruined by Ben Brealley's men.'

'Was that the only reason?' the chairman's voice persisted. Avril's face took on a desperate look. Beseechingly she looked at Tansy.

'If there was another reason then you must tell us, Mrs Moore,' he pressed, and now her voice came low, too low to be heard above the clap of thunder which heralded a sudden squall of rain which hammered on the roof. Gregson now asked, 'Please repeat your answer, Mrs Moore.'

Avril was forced into repeating. 'She asked how you knew.'

Again he pressed her. 'Knew what?'

With a hopeless look at Tansy, Avril said, 'She wanted to know how you knew when you were carrying a child.'

Leaving the stand, Avril returned to her place beside Tansy, took her hand and said, 'I'm sorry, Tansy, but he made me tell.'

Tansy comforted her friend while Geoffrey whispered urgently to Henry Watson-Bates, who stood up to face the Council. 'My client says that the St Christopher he gave Miss Drewe was in recognition of work done for him on Bell's School. He gave it her on the occasion of her giving up work in the parish to return to work at Courtenay House.'

Tansy felt the silver pendant burning into her neck. The chairman was looking at her.

'Were you happy to leave Geoffrey Llewellyn's employment, Miss Drewe?' She knew if she said 'Yes' she would be lying and yet if she said 'No' it would look bad for Geoffrey. She hesitated, trying to decide.

Ben Brealley was on his feet again. He shouted across the room, 'There's still no answer to the accusation. Is she carrying a child or isn't she?'

All eyes turned to Tansy, who looked at her father, longing for the protection he had always given her. She wished with all her heart she knew if she was carrying a child or not. She gathered her courage and rose to answer both questions.

'I was sad to leave the minister's employment because I enjoyed working for him. He taught me a great deal about the running of parish affairs. Taught me how to research and report findings. Also I had become fond of him.' A fresh murmur arose from her audience, who now hung on her every word. 'But I am not expecting his child.' She sat down, sought her father's face and prayed her answers would satisfy the Council, stop Ben Brealley from probing further.

Geoffrey looked relieved and spoke to Henry Watson-Bates. Pieces of paper passed between them. The chairman called Gregson to the table. 'Please ask what Mr Llewellyn has handed to his advocate.' Gregson crossed the room and took papers from him, which he in turn gave to the chairman, who now spoke to Tansy.

'Will you take the stand just for a few moments more? As she stood, legs shaking, full of dread, wondering what more they could want of her, he asked, 'We have heard accusations from various people, now we wish to hear from your own lips the answers to three questions.'

He referred to the paper in his hands, looked at her searchingly. 'Did Mr Llewellyn ever give you reason to believe he cared for you?'

Geoffrey's eyes held an appeal that she should deny the assumptions she had made that he loved her. She realised that all her expectations were foundering here in this room. 'No,' she answered steadily.

'Did anything improper ever take place between you?'

'No,' she said firmly.

Again Ben Brealley was on his feet. 'We have no evidence that the minister and the girl are not lying!'

Now Henry Watson-Bates looked at Geoffrey, who nodded. He cleared his throat, shuffling the two pieces of paper in his hands. 'I believe these documents will prove that the minister had no intentions of any kind towards Miss Drewe. May I proceed?' The chairman waved his hands as a gesture of encouragement. 'My client has handed me two letters which he would have preferred to have kept private but there now seems no choice but to disclose part of their contents. The first is from Miss Norah Drewe, sister of Tansy Drewe and resident at Goldsmith's College, London. It is dated the 13th March 1900 and I will read the pertinent extract.

"Dear Geoffrey

I'm so grateful to you for the support and friendship you've given to Tansy over the Emma Vallance affair. Let's hope life will run smoothly for her from now on. She's young and impressionable but very dear to my heart.

I understand how long it must take to banish the hurts of a past love and pray that by the time I have finished at college you will have reached a state of mind and heart when you can claim mine, which are already yours.

Best love, Norah."'

Tansy felt as though a black chasm had opened up in front of her as the full meaning of her sister's letter began to make itself clear. She clenched the edge of the stand and listened as Henry Watson-Bates began to read from the second letter.

"Dearest Norah

You have given me hope that I may one day be free of the past, free to follow the dictates of my own heart. But, dearest Norah, you must give me the time to forget the one who has held my bruised heart for so long. Your letters continue to act as a lifeline and my instincts tell me that one day soon I shall be able to come to you. To come and ask you to be my wife.

Best ever, Geoffrey."'

Now Tansy knew without doubt that she had lost Geoffrey. Knew that she had never at any time held his heart. She felt she would suffocate, her heart beat in a slow pounding rhythm in her throat, waves of faintness attacked her temples and threatened to overwhelm her and when she heard the chairman ask Geoffrey, 'Do you confirm that the contents of these letters represent the state of affairs that exist between you and Miss Norah Drewe?' and his answer just the one word, 'Yes,' her hands slipped from the stand and her father's arms closed round her as she fell.

Tansy regained consciousness in Edward's arms. She saw the look of shock on his face, a mirror of her own.

'I didn't know!' he said as he helped her to her feet. 'Neither I nor your Mother. She would have told us.'

Geoffrey waited for them but Tansy drew back, couldn't look at him. 'I must get out,' she said, and Edward guided her past the crowd which hovered there, awaiting the verdict. She turned to him, a question in her eyes.

He nodded. 'He's been cleared of all charges except conduct unbecoming...'

She turned to Edward. 'I must be alone for a while.'

He looked at her with concern. 'Did you love him very much?' he asked, but a numbness took possession of her and she stood silent, the wound deep. 'You'll get over it,' he said. She broke free, turning away from him. 'I'll be all right,' she agreed, and began to run towards the market.

'Where are you going?' His words came after her but now she could brook no further restraint. Crossing the square she passed under the Drum Clock, fought against the storm along Queen Street till she reached the station. There a train stood at the platform, steam up, the guard holding a green flag at the ready.

'Come along, maid, if you wants Lustleigh!'

She didn't hesitate but ran to the office, bought a ticket and scrambled on board just as the whistle blew. She chose a seat by the window, looked through her reflection as houses gave way to marsh, field to halt, and all the while rain beat against the window and she struggled to overcome a sense of loss too great for tears.

When the train stopped at Lustleigh, she walked quickly away, her feet taking her in the direction of Staddens. How long, she thought, since the farm had become her refuge? How long since she'd met him? Her thought went back to the first glimpse of him, struggling with Thirza Hill's May Day bower, his face hot as he struggled uphill to the crowning stone. She hurried on, intent on finding Martin. He would understand how she felt, he always did. Her boots splashed through puddles, formed long since in every rut and pothole. She felt comforted by the thought that now she had a purpose. It was only when she arrived at the end of the track to the farm that she remembered Martin wasn't there. She stood, bereft, forlorn, lost, clothes clinging to her body, not knowing what to do. She leant on the gate, an emptiness taking possession of her being.

Close by came the sound of whinnying. She heard but didn't react until this sound was followed by that of hooves advancing towards her, thudding softly on wet grass. She looked up and ran away from the track, along the hedge in the direction from which the sounds came. At the gate stood a pony, white blaze on its forehead, flanks shining with rain, wickering with pleasure at the sight of her.

'Fairy!' she exclaimed. 'How good it is to see you. We're old friends, you and I!' And on impulse she looked round and found what she sought in the hedge, a length of worn rope. Quickly she tied each end to the head collar, tucked her skirt into the legs of her drawers, climbed back on to the gate and slid across onto Fairy's back. She took her scarf and tied her straw boater securely against the gusting wind which blew along the valley. Then she walked the pony from the field and into lane, closed the gate and set off.

'You and me,' she murmured. 'We're going to Teignhead,' and, squeezing her legs into the mare's sides and talking all the while, urged her into a trot.

Her mind wandered back one year, to when they had lost the carriage wheel and all the events which followed. Geoffrey. With the memory of the loss of his love came sudden anger. Anger so hot and bitter that she slapped Fairy with the rope. Startled, the pony broke into a gallop while Tansy clung to her mane. They got to the crossroads and almost knocked down a black figure emerging from the White Hart straight into their path.

'Whoa! Whoa!' it shouted, catching the rope and hanging on with all its might. The face that looked up at her wore an iron mask, eyes gleaming from holes. 'Where be going in such a hurry and without a saddle?' it demanded and she gazed down in terror, fearing it could only be the Devil.

'Let me pass!' she shouted, trying to pull the reins from the wrinkled hands. Still he held her till, in desperation, she said, 'We're going to Teignhead to see my cousin.'

The voice behind the mask came again. 'Don't be frightened, my beauty! 'Tis only old Josh and his shot-away face. 'Tis best if 'ee goes straight on. Don't turn off however much the road twists and turns. When 'ee gits to Warrren House ask agin.'

He let go the rope and slapped the pony on its rump. Fairy snorted in terror, as frightened by the masked man as Tansy herself, and set off again till houses were replaced by scattered farms, fields of battered corn. The wind blew cold and shook rain from overhanging trees. Ahead sombre clouds formed and reformed against an angry yellow sky. The sound of thunder came nearer, and she could almost hear their voices – 'Is she carrying Llewellyn's child?'

Tansy leant into the wind, 'If only that had been true, Fairy, what then? Would he have left Norah for me?' She patted Fairy gently to make up for the earlier slap and settled her down into a slow walk as the road began to climb towards the moor. She hadn't seen blood since her visit to Teignhead. Any child she carried must be Martin's. Was this why she was going to him? she asked herself. Now the road steepened and she dismounted, leading Fairy between stones, washed proud of the surface by continual rain. They gained the summit, where heather and gorse replaced verge and hedge, and shadows appeared for a brief moment as an angry sun slid below the hills behind her.

'How could she have taken the only thing I ever wanted?' she complained bitterly. 'Even from as far away as London she still managed to steal away the man I loved.'

She clambered onto the nearest bank, climbed onto Fairy's back again, clicked her tongue and set her face into the wind, matching the rhythm of the mare's stride to the tumult of her mind. The words of the letters that had passed between Geoffrey and Norah rang in her head. 'Banish hurts. Friendship for Tansy. Love dictates. Dearest Norah. Dearest Norah.'

Tom Moore, returning from the Warren House to the Vitifer Mine, carrying more ale in him than was good, almost cannoned into the wild pair as they careered towards him.

'What the devil!' he exclaimed, but something about the slight figure astride the steaming pony jarred a memory so strong that recognition came. 'Tansy, is it really you?' She hauled on the rope, squeezed legs sore from contact with the pony's sides and brought them to a standstill.

'Tom?' and now his face filled with anxiety. 'Is it me you've come for?' he asked, remembering the last time he'd had a message from Newton, the night of the flood. Tansy immediately set his mind at rest.

'No, no, Tom. 'Tisn't you we've come for. 'Tis Martin. How do we get to Teignhead?'

Tom turned about, took hold the rope reins. 'Tidd'n but a mile or two from the Inn. I'll set 'ee right.' He looked at the clouds hanging low above them. 'We'm in for another storm. You'd best make haste if you'm to get there avore 'un.' And he pointed across undulating ground to a dark shape in the distance, a shape which appeared then disappeared among swirling cloud.

'Make for they stones. Teignhead's beyond.' As she urged Fairy off the road onto soft turf he called after them. 'Keep to high ground.'

They were traversing a long ridge when a clap of thunder overhead frightened Fairy, who changed her canter to a gallop which Tansy sought to restrain as she saw the ground begin to drop away in front of them. Her eyes strained for the black outline of stones. There they were, away to the left. She guided the pony between scattered rocks and reached the track when jagged lightning lit the path before them, setting Fairy to dance across cotton grass to crash into black bog. Tansy hauled at the rope with no response, and slid from the mare's back to find herself sinking to the knees, caught in the morass. She grasped the nearest tussock of cotton grass and hauled until her legs came free, then lay flat across the quaking ground, gasping for breath.

The clouds opened and with a final roll of thunder rain came, lashing them both. It turned into hail which bit into flesh like stinging darts. Tansy began to shout. 'Help! Help us! Lord help us in our hour of need!' She lay, believing this to be the end for them both. Who would be out on the open moor on such a night? She thought of home, saw Eva, Edward and the twins gathered round the fire, safe. She thought of Martin and the stone house beyond the tor. He'd be inside by the fire. She thought of stories of men disappearing without trace – Seth Howell's favourite one of a coach and horses disappearing in Foxworthy mire, never to be seen again. Tears of self-pity welled in her eyes.

'Don't be silly, Tansy,' she told herself, ''tis no good crying!' And she was in the hall at Courtenay House, Geoffrey by her side. 'Come on, my soldier,' he had urged, 'fly the flag!' She raised her head and spoke to the exhausted pony.

'We're going to sing, my beauty!' She began, her voice wavering at first then growing stronger as she warmed to her task. 'God rest ye merry gentlemen, Let nothing you dismay, Remember Christ...'

She stopped, her body numb from shock and cold, what came next? At that moment she heard distant barking.

'Fairy, did you hear that?' she listened. Was it her imagination or was the barking coming nearer? She began to shout.

'We're here. Over here.' And as the sound grew ever closer, she called, 'Moss, Moss!' Moss had come to look for them. Now she heard the voice of a man, scolding. 'Come here boy! Moss! Heel, I tell you.' Now she was conscious of the glow from a lantern falling across the bog, heard the sharp intake of breath followed by an oath.

'By all that's holy! What a sight!' he addressed the pony who neighed in recognition of Martin, for indeed it was he. 'You're in a proper pickle, my beauty!' he exclaimed. 'We've gotta git 'ee out of there.'

Martin seized the rope and began to pull, then, when this made no impression, he got out a knife, cut a branch of heather and set about the pony. He beat him again and again till the animal, urged on by pain, made a tremendous effort and sprang from the mire back across the cotton grass, back onto firm ground.

'Martin!' Tansy shouted in desperation, terrified he was going to leave her. He stopped soothing the pony to gaze into the stormy black night, holding aloft the lantern till it reached her prone figure, half drowned in a mess of reeking peat.

'Tansy? Is it you? Can't be!'

She shouted, impatient to be rescued. 'Don't stand there gawping! Get me out!' Martin began to laugh. ''Tisn't funny,' she protested. 'I can't bear it much longer.' Now his voice changed. He gave short words of command to Moss.

'Stay, boy. Watch. Stay.' He called to Tansy. 'I'm going for planks. If I try to cross we'll both be stuck. Moss is here. He'll not leave 'ee. I'll be back soon...'

✣ Chapter Thirty ✣

Return to Teignhead

An hour later Tansy, half conscious, felt warm hands drag her from the stench and slime, wrapping her in rough blankets. She felt herself carried over rough ground and heard the rattle of runners as Martin and Fairy hauled the sled over the clapper bridge into Teignhead Farm.

She drank hot sweet tea from the cup her shaking hands refused to hold, and was grateful to Martin for holding back questions. He held them back until the extent of her suffering became apparent as he bathed her frozen feet and rubbed life back into her rope-burned hands, which made her cry out in pain. He peeled filthy sodden clothes from her shivering body and felt her wince as he pulled clinging drawers from sore legs. No longer able to contain his anger he gave vent at last to his feelings.

'Whatever possessed you?' he demanded. 'Coming across the Moor in a thunderstorm? And after dark! Why, 'tis dangerous for a woman alone daytimes let alone after sun's gone down.' 'You'm lucky I went to Staddens from market today – lucky I'm so late coming back!' He was appalled to see tears slide unbidden down her face. He had never seen Tansy cry, strong in every crisis, and this only served to fuel his anger.

'Did you ask if you could borrow Moses Norsworthy's pony?' When she shook her head his anger spilled over. 'I thought not! Riding without a saddle. You could have been thrown. And who's going to take her back? Can't be tomorrow. She'll need to rest. Let's hope she'll not take a chill. I've known horses die from trapping a leg in a gate!' Then he bit his lips and the question as to how she was going to get back to Newton hung unspoken between them.

She slipped in and out of troubled dreams where Ben Brealley strode toward her holding a bundle in his arms. When she pulled back the wrappings Josh's masked face shone up at her. For two days she tossed in a delirium, emerging from time to time to find Martin standing over her, a look of concern on his face.

'You've had bad dreams,' he said, as he fetched soup from a pot on the fire, but she was still too exhausted to eat. 'I'm going to Fernworthy, see if Tom Osborne'll take a message to Bowden Hill on his way to market. Sleep now,' he said. 'Perhaps you'll be ready to eat when I get back.'

Now the fever passed and she slept, awoken by the roar of storm winds rattling doors and window frames, draughts sending lamplit shadows to leap on rough stone walls. She slept again, this time free from nightmares, slept the deep healing sleep of recovery. On the third day a weak sun filled the tiny windows, sending a sliver of light onto the hearth, where Martin had spent his nights on a straw pallet. Tansy felt cool and rested. She looked for Martin, missed him. She looked for her clothes, but couldn't find them. She peered through the window and saw her skirt, blouse, drawers and chemise all blowing straight into the wind. She fetched water from the pot well, washed all over, then, finding nothing else, dressed in Martin's chapel suit, turning up sleeves and trouser legs. Next she washed her hair with a block of soap, went out into the court and let it dry in the warm breeze. She breathed in, filling her lungs and listened to lark song, looking for the black speck of the bird soaring high in the blue sky.

At last the storm passed, taking with it her feelings of dread. Nothing, she knew, could bring Geoffrey back, now she must face whatever lay ahead. A sudden movement brought her attention to a figure coming towards her, crook under arm, dog at heel. A feeling of apprehension came with the recognition that it was Martin and Moss. If only he would accept that she was here, not look for explanations. Now, always ahead of his master, Moss came to her knees, his pleasure expressed in his greeting whines. Martin arrived a few moments later and laughed out loud at the sight of her.

'I see you'm ready for chapel!' he said ironically, 'but you'll have to wait a day or two.' She felt a rush of tenderness for him sweep over her, an overwhelming gratitude fill her heart, too strong for expression.

'I'll get you some food,' she said abruptly. She turned and went back into the house, found eggs and bacon and cooked them quickly, cutting thick slices of coarse bread, and laying the table, conscious all the while of Martin watching her as he had the Sunday she'd come here with Sarah. They ate, neither speaking, as if to do so would break the spell.

'I see you've got your appetite back,' Martin said at last, then sat looking at her across the table and she knew from the even tenor of his voice that the moment of reckoning had come at last.

'Why did you come?' he asked.

She drew a deep breath and began. 'I needed to see you.'

When he said, 'But you've not needed to come before so why now?' she realised this was going to be more difficult than she'd expected. How could she have been such a fool to think she'd be welcomed without question? She bit her lips, wondered how she could tell him she'd simply obeyed her instincts. Tell him she had come because Geoffrey had rejected her. Tell him she might be carrying his, Martin's, child?

He moved restlessly, repeated his question. 'Well, is it so hard to tell me why you came?'

She plunged on. 'When I came here with Sarah that Sunday you said "Don't come again unless you mean to stay".' She paused, looking at him searchingly.

'Did I?' he asked, his face controlled, not giving his thoughts away. He wasn't going to make it easy for her, Tansy thought. Surely he'd remembered the fateful words. She grew hot. Would he say he didn't want her after all?

'If you don't remember what you said, then those words can't have meant much to you when you said them!' She spoke sharply and suddenly he reached across the table, taking her hands in his, his face alight, eyes smiling.

'That's more like my Tansy!' he exclaimed. 'Of course I remember.'

'And did you really mean them?' she persisted, needing to hear his confirmation. It came quickly, his voice rising now on a note of hope.

'Do you mean you have come to stay? This is why you're here?'

When she nodded, adding hesitantly, 'If you'll have me,' he bent forward to kiss her, then drew back, unable to speak for a moment, overwhelmed by her sudden capitulation. Then, face serious, he said, 'I'll have you on one condition, Tansy Drewe. That you're sure it's what you really want. No going off to see the world after the first bad storm finds the leak in the roof and the peat's too wet to burn.'

When she laughed in delight he rose, came to her, drawing her into his arms where they kissed, pulling apart to gaze into each other's eyes. He held her away from him.

'I'll have you,' he repeated, 'even if it means rescuing you from quarry pools and bogs for the rest of my life!' He laughed, dropping gentle kisses on her head. 'But now I want you to stay a little longer before you finally decide.' He put her away from him when she would have melted in his arms. 'I have to go to the horse sales at Chagford. I'll be back on Sunday.' And he left, leaving her Moss for company.

❦

Angry at first that he'd left her she ran from the house and climbed the nearest hill, Moss at her heels. She gazed about her, shouting into the wind, 'If he thinks I can't stick it out here on my own... well, he's mistaken!' She could see the cluster of grey buildings across the moor. 'I could walk back there easily.' The sky was so clear she felt she could reach out and touch the gathering clouds. She ran back down the hill and set to work. As she scrubbed stone and wood, and polished glass, she thought of life at Courtenay House, confined to her room or at the beck and call of the Vallances. Thought of the long hours using up her resources until there was nothing left for herself. And as she worked she purged herself of the past until all was finished. Then she opened the door to the sweet summer breeze and, taking a hook down from the wall, went out to hack at heather and gorse until she had enough blossom to fill a stone crock. This she placed in the centre of the table then, exhausted, went to bed, Moss lying at her feet.

Again she slept, deeply, completely, all night, waking to the steady drip of rain where it spread a dark stain by the chimney breast. It was cold and she got up, dressed quickly, fed Moss, put more peat on the fire and began to collect oats and eggs to make a meal for Martin when he returned.

As she bent she felt a sharp pain low down, a sudden flood of moisture between her legs. Her spirits lifted as she searched for a cloth to absorb the flow. She felt strong. The need to tell Martin she carried his child suddenly gone, gone with the worry that had nagged at her since they had lain together in the linhay at Teignhead. And with the flow of blood came the realisation that she was free. Free to leave. Free to travel the world as she'd constantly threatened whenever Martin had tried to pin her down. Was this freedom really what she wanted? Until a few days ago all she had wanted was Geoffrey Llewellyn. Would it be fair to marry Martin knowing that her heart belonged to someone else even though this goal was unobtainable?

Something pulled her towards the door. She opened it to a sheet of water, rain blowing sideways along the valley, water rushing downhill, filling the pot well and spilling over into the porch. She peered through the rain, saw a huddle of grey moving along the newtake wall, a dark figure which detached itself from the sheep. A man on a horse began his struggle up the track towards her and, recognising Martin, Tansy released Moss who ran, body low through the westerly, barking his welcome.

Tansy watched man, horse and dog approach and knew that the three days Martin had given her to make up her mind hadn't been enough – it would take more than three days to banish Geoffrey completely from her heart and mind. To stay here with Martin at Teignhead would be cheating but what else was she to do? She had no money for travel took resources and she was loath to leave this place which had been her sanctuary, its owner her saviour on more than one occasion. The man who had taught her to ride, to learn about the moor, to offer his strength. Tansy knew that the next few hours would decide the future for them both.